After an eventful career as a spin doctor to the powerful, rich and notorious, Quintin Jardine fou... hat his talents were equa... ime fiction. Now he i... e mysteries as well a...

His int... g football, talking ab... le lives, as quietly as ... nd in Spain.

Praise for Quintin Jardine's novels:

'Perfect plotting and convincing characterisation . . . Jardine manages to combine the picturesque with the thrilling and the dream-like with the coldly rational' *The Times*

'Deplorably readable' *Guardian*

'Jardine's plot is very cleverly constructed, every incident and every character has a justified place in the labyrinth of motives, and the final series of revelations follows logically from a surreptitious but well-placed series of clues' Gerald Kaufman, *Scotsman*

'If Ian Rankin is the Robert Carlyle of Scottish crime writers, then Jardine is surely its Sean Connery' *Glasgow Herald*

'It moves at a cracking pace, and with a crisp dialogue that is vastly superior to that of many of his jargon-loving rivals . . . It encompasses a wonderfully neat structural twist, a few taut, well-weighted action sequences and emotionally charged exchanges that steer well clear of melodrama' *Sunday Herald*

'Remarkably assured . . . a *tour de force*' *New York Times*

'Engrossing, believable characters . . . captures Edinburgh beautifully . . . It all adds up to a very good read' *Edinburgh Evening News*

'Robustly entertaining' *Irish Times*

Also by Quintin Jardine

Bob Skinner series:
Skinner's Rules
Skinner's Festival
Skinner's Trail
Skinner's Round
Skinner's Ordeal
Skinner's Mission
Skinner's Ghosts
Murmuring the Judges
Gallery Whispers
Thursday Legends
Autographs in the Rain
Head Shot
Fallen Gods

Oz Blackstone series:
Wearing Purple
Screen Savers
On Honeymoon with Death
Poisoned Cherries
Unnatural Justice

Blackstone's Pursuits

and

A Coffin For Two

Quintin Jardine

headline

BLACKSTONE'S PURSUITS first published in Great Britain in 1996
by HEADLINE BOOK PUBLISHING

A COFFIN FOR TWO first published in Great Britain in 1997
by HEADLINE BOOK PUBLISHING

First published in this omnibus edition in 2004
by HEADLINE BOOK PUBLISHING

A HEADLINE paperback

10 9 8 7 6 5 4 3 2 1

ISBN 0 7553 2253 3

Typeset in Times by Avon DataSet Ltd,
Bidford on Avon, Warwickshire

Printed and bound in Great Britain by
Mackays of Chatham plc, Chatham, Kent

Papers and cover board used by Headline are natural,
recyclable products made from wood grown in sustainable
forests. The manufacturing processes conform to the
environmental regulations of the country of origin.

HEADLINE BOOK PUBLISHING
A division of Hodder Headline
338 Euston Road
London NW1 3BH

www.headline.co.uk
www.hodderheadline.com

Blackstone's Pursuits

This book is dedicated to the City of Edinburgh.
(Sorry)

In which I stare death in the face, Uncle Hughie swamps the Yellow Peril, and McArse and I meet our match

Being a Private Enquiry Agent isn't all it's cracked up to be. In fact, there are some days when it cracks *me* up. And this was going to be one of those days, all right.

Quite a few of the people I'm sent to interview start out by being difficult. Many of them have a two-word vocabulary . . . if you know what I mean. It's as if they blame *me* for their wives having found out about them shagging that nice brunette person, or for their having been caught nicking a few quid from the partnership account.

This guy had done both, and I could tell at once that he was just not going to be the co-operative sort. It wasn't only that I'd walked in on him and caught him stark naked. My main problem was that the poor, sad bugger was stone dead.

Looking at him, stretched out on his back on the crumpled bed, I could tell that he had been a wee man, a bit closer to five feet than six. But equally, I could guess at once what the nice brunette had seen in him. People are always going on to me about my favourite adjectives. They say I use them for effect, but that's not true. It's more that I take pleasure in words which strike me as particularly descriptive. At that moment, looking at him, stretched out on his back on the crumpled bed, '*disproportionate*' thrust itself to the front of my mind and lodged there.

The knife was impressive too. At least its big hilt was. The rest of it, the blade, was rammed up under the wee man's chin, nailing his mouth tight shut, away up behind his bulging eyes, all the way up, I guessed, into his brain.

Standing there, with the newly opened curtain still swinging behind me, I must have looked about as daft as he did. I stared at him, my eyes bulging out like organ-stops, just like his. He was ludicrous, lying there staring at the ceiling, so ludicrous that an idiot grin flickered around the corners of my mouth. Oddly, I felt myself feeling self-conscious, although why, God above knew. The wee man wasn't aware of anyone's presence, not any more, and his erstwhile companion was long gone.

It was the stench that drove home the enormity of it all. During my short, unhappy service as a probationer constable in Lothian and Borders Police I was called to the scene of precisely one death; yet another stupid kid found up a close in West Granton with a needle hanging out of her arm. My job had been to stand guard at the close-mouth, to keep a respectable distance between the wee girl – fifteen, she was, I remember – and the gawpers, oh yes, and between two bored, disinterested reporters who'd seen the same thing a few dozen times and who were pissed off because, but for this dead nuisance, they'd both have been freeloading at a civic lunch. The close-mouth was as close as I got to the victim, and until I walked into that room, that poor lassie was the only certifiably deceased person I'd ever seen.

At first, the shock shut out everything but the sight of him, but after a few seconds the hum forced its way up my nose. By and large, sphincters are a closed book to me, but not to the wee man on the bed. His had opened all of a sudden.

I turned back to the window, my stomach churning. The frames were the old wooden sash-cord type, the kind that usually you'd find stuck tight with paint. Thank Christ, though, once I'd freed the catch this one slid up nice and easy. I stuck my head out and took a deep breath, but it was no use. Normally, old Uncle Hughie eases up on you, giving you a couple of nudges so that you can be in the right place when finally he puts in an appearance. Not this time. The old familiar fist gripped my belly and squeezed as hard as it could, forcing up everything in there in a single violent shout, and firing it on to the pavement fifteen feet below. Well, almost on to the pavement. Instead of a splash, there was a yell.

'Whit the . . . Away, ya dirty bastard!'

My eyes were still shut tight from the effort of my mighty boak. I opened one of them, fearfully, and looked down into Ebeneezer Street. The flat top of the traffic warden's cap, and the shoulders of his tunic had caught most of it, but I was pleased to see – it's funny, the details the mind registers in times of crisis – that some of Uncle Hughie's output had landed on the page of his notebook on which the Yellow Peril was noting down the details of my out-of-date tax disc.

I opened the other eye and looked at him, pleading. 'Aw come on, man! It only expired last week.'

He stared up at me, sending the mess on his hat cascading down the back of his heavy, porous uniform. 'Yellow Peril' had never been a more fitting nickname.

'Whit's the game, Jimmy?' He didn't have the wit to be astonished, only angry.

'Lamb Rogan Josh,' I muttered. 'From the takeaway in Caroline Street. Sorry!' I decided that I preferred the sight on the bed. Besides, the traffic warden probably smelled even worse than him. I pulled my head back into the room. As I did, I felt a current of cool air on my face and realised that I must have left the front door open. I walked out of the room and into the hall to close it.

I almost felt offended when she didn't scream. I mean, isn't that what women are supposed to do when they step into their flat and find a six-foot stranger standing in the lobby, even if he is wearing a Savoy Tailors' Guild suit and holding a Motorola cell-phone in his hand?

When I got round to asking her, she really did offend me. 'You just looked terrified,' she said. 'I felt sorry for you.' I could have handled it if she'd said that fear had struck her dumb, or even just plain surprise. I could even have lived with revulsion. But being told I was pitiful was as hurtful as a smart kick on the kneecap, and the effect lasted longer.

In the there and then of it, she just stood and looked at me, her big brown eyes not startled, not even slightly wide, just questioning. She wore faded jeans, a crumpled tee-shirt and trainers with more than a few miles on the odometer. The bag slung over her shoulder looked bigger than she was. She let it slip to the floor as she shut the door behind her. In her right hand she held a bunch of keys big enough to choke a horse.

'Well?' she said, and I could have sworn she was smiling. 'Are you him, then?'

I looked back at her: blankly, I think. 'Eh?' Right at that moment that was all the articulacy I could manage.

'The mystery man. Dawn's wee bit of illicit rough.'

The hair at the back of my neck prickled. This was like stepping into the middle of someone else's movie. I decided that I'd better get a grip on reality, double-quick.

'Look, I'm sorry. My name's Oz Blackstone. I'm a private enquiry agent. I work for lawyers, insurance companies and the like.

'I had an appointment to meet someone here this morning, at ten o'clock. When I got here, the door was unlocked. I knocked, and it just swung open. I shouted, but there was no answer. I thought that was odd, so I stepped inside and took a look around.' I pulled a card from the stash in the breast pocket of my jacket. 'Here.'

She looked at it. 'Oz, eh. You don't sound like an Australian.'

I scowled at her. Always, the same wisecrack. I sighed, and gave her the stock answer. 'I'm not. It's just that Osbert doesn't cut the mustard down Pilton way.'

She gave me an odd smile, with a *touché* look about it. 'I know what you mean. My name's Prim Phillips. It's short for "Primavera". In English that means "Springtime". I was conceived in May, on a holiday in a tent in the Costa Bráva, and my Maw's a terrible romantic. I decided early on that there was no bloody way I was going through life answering to "Vera", therefore . . . You and I are kindred spirits in the daft name stakes.' She shook her tousled sun-bleached head and smiled, and flashed me the sort of look that doesn't stop at your eyes, but drills right into your head. 'Imagine,' she said, 'giving a wee girl a four-syllable name!'

She picked up the huge bag. 'Hold on till I stick this in the bedroom. Then you can tell me the rest of your story.'

I stepped between her and the door. She frowned, and for the first time, looked just a touch apprehensive. I tried to sound cool and reassuring, but it came out flustered and panicky. 'Don't go in there, Miss Phillips. I said there was no reply; I didn't say that there wasn't anyone here.'

She was afraid now. 'Dawn . . .' she began. She tried to push past me, but I gripped her arms and held her. It wasn't easy. She's a strong wee package.

'No, it isn't Dawn . . . unless she's balding and helluva well hung.' See me, see gallows humour! She looked at me, twisting against my grip and wincing. I realised that the Motorola was digging into her arm, and let her go. 'Sorry!'

'That's my bedroom. I want to see what's in there,' she said. 'However bad it is, I've seen worse. Come on.' There was something in her voice which told me that 'Don't,' would always be the wrong thing to say to this woman. I tried, 'Are you sure?' instead, but that didn't work either.

'Okay,' I said finally. 'But don't get the wrong idea about me when you see in there.' She looked at me, incredulously.

When I got round to asking her whether, finding two strangers in her flat, one with a head like a kebab and the other heading for the door, it hadn't occurred to her for a second that the live one might have had something to do with the dead one being dead, she offended me again. 'Don't be daft, Oz. I've met people who could do that sort of thing. You couldn't, not in a month of Sundays, not if your life depended on it.' It can do something to your manhood when a slip of a woman looks you in the eye and tells you that you don't have the stuff to be a cold-blooded killer.

Back in the there and then of it, she stood beside the bed, looking down at the wee man. 'That's got to be him, all right. Dawn's bit of illicit. She said in her last letter that he was built like a cross between Danny deVito and Nijinsky. I thought she meant the dancer, not the horse!'

His hands were by his sides. She leaned over and lifted one up. 'Been dead for a while,' she said. 'He's cold, and the rigor's beginning to wear off. When did you find him?'

I glanced at my watch, embarrassed by the tremble of my hand. It was almost ten-thirty. 'About half an hour ago.'

All of a sudden I couldn't take it, all that coolness in the face of crisis. 'Look, Miss Phillips, Prim, whatever: what is it with you? You walk into your flat and you find a strange guy knifed to death in your bed, and you're standing here as if it's just something that the cleaner's missed. What sort of a world do you live in?' My voice rose as I spoke, and suddenly there was a crack in it that I'd thought I lost in my teens.

She took me by the arm and led me out of the room, through the hall and into a narrow kitchen. 'Sit down, Oz.' There were two chairs, one on either side of a gate-leg table. She picked up a white plastic kettle and filled it from the mixer tap over the sink, then switched it on. She lifted a jar marked 'Tea' and shook it. Turning, she bent her back against the work-surface and looked down at me, as the kettle began to hiss and bubble behind her.

'I'm a nurse. I've just spent a year in a refugee camp in Central Africa, in the middle of a tribal war zone. When I say I've seen worse than that in there, I'm not kidding.

'On top of that, I've just spent the last umpteen hours wide awake in aeroplanes. All I wanted, when I came in here was a shower, a vodka and tonic, and a sleep. Instead, I've got a slightly hysterical private eye in my kitchen and a corpse in my bed. If my reaction seems odd to you, it's because all this is a dream; because none of it's happening.

'It's also because I'm trying not to imagine where my sister is, or how she's involved with what's through next door.

'That's me. Now, before we do anything else, what's your story?' She turned her back on me as the kettle boiled and set about the business of making tea. I sat there, bewildered and dumb.

She looked over her shoulder. 'Well?'

I stood up, in a feeble attempt to assert myself. I searched for something smart to say, but all I could manage was a shrug of the shoulders. She handed me a mug of tea. It reminded me of the dark, hot, sweet char that was my Granny Blackstone's standard remedy for shock, exposure, skinned knees, a wee touch of the flu and a host of other conditions up to and including mild coronary incidents. My Granny's tea was a wonderful brew. Apart from its therapeutic value, she used it to dye Easter Eggs, and swore by it as a tanning agent. She used to keep it cold in a jar, and slabber it on herself every time the sun poked its nose into the back court. She was found one day, dead in her deckchair. My Dad reckoned that she'd finally pickled herself.

I took a sip of Prim's version. It was sweet, as I'd expected, yet different. I took a deeper swallow, and felt it go to work, stilling the trembling in my arms and legs. 'Nice,' I said. 'What's in it?'

'A spoonful of honey. Better for you than sugar. Now, come on. Let's hear it.'

'Okay.' I took a deep breath. 'Like I said, I work for lawyers and insurers in the main. Taking statements from witnesses in court cases and so on. This commission was a wee bit different. A few days ago I was called in by the senior partner of a firm of stockbrokers called Black and Muirton. I'd heard of them, but I tend to do my investing through bookmakers. The guy, Archer, he's called, said to me that they had a problem with one of their partners.

'It seems that their practice accountant found some heavy irregularities in the books. The firm keeps an offshore bank account in Jersey for holding clients' money on a short-term basis, when it buys and sells for them. Cash goes flying through it all the time, very serious cash sometimes, because it's a big firm with some high-roller clients, plus, they handle business for banks and fund managers. What the audit found was that the account didn't balance. In fact it was off balance by nine hundred thousand squigglies.

'It took them a while but eventually they tracked it down. The cash had come from the sale of some loan stock held by one of their multi-millionaire clients. It had been transferred, electronically, to a numbered bank account in Switzerland. The sale had been authorised, and the transfer made, by one of the partners, a Mr William Kane. The trouble was, there was nothing on Black and Muirton's records to show that the client had instructed it, and nothing to show that the bank account was his.

'Archer pulled some strings in Switzerland. He found out that the account was opened by a Scots woman called Dawn Phillips. It was a real cloak and dagger job. When she set it up she showed the Swiss people half of a Bank of Scotland fiver, serial number AF 426469. Her instructions were that access was to be given to any two people who showed up with both halves of that same note.'

Prim nodded. 'That sounds right up my sister's street. She was the only wee girl I've ever known to ask for an Action Man for Christmas. She was reading James Bond by the time she was ten. There was no way she was ever going to grow up to be anything but an actress.'

Quite a family, I thought, Mother Teresa and Madonna in the same brood. 'Some part she's playing this time, then,' I said. 'Guess what happened next? While Archer was trying to figure out what to do, Mrs Kane dropped in on Mrs Archer and poured her heart out. She said that William had been keeping some odd hours. They've been married for twelve years, and she could set her watch by him. But all of a sudden he started working late at the office on pretty much a nightly basis, and having to go off and see clients at the weekend.

'Like any sensible wife she started to go through his pockets on the quiet, and found the usual. Ticket stubs for two at UCI, credit-card slips for hotel bills in Inverness when he was meant to be in London and so on. She fronted him up but he just told her she was being silly. Then one day she got home from the shops and there was a "Dear Joan" note on the kitchen table, telling her that he had met this wonderful girl called Dawn, and sorry as he was, that was it.

'To cut it short, Mrs Archer told Mr Archer and he had Kane into his office. He confronted him with the sale order and told him the story about the Swiss account. Kane admitted the lot. He told him that he had fallen truly, madly, deeply in love with your sister, and that he had come up with this daft scheme because he knew his wife would cut the nuts off him financially. His idea was to leave her to it and to shoot the craw with Dawn and the nine hundred thou.

'Archer reckoned that he was completely off his trolley. He told him to bail out while he thought up Plan A, but to leave an address where he could be contacted, and a telephone number. He did. Yours.'

Prim puffed up with indignation. 'The cow! I let her use this place while I was away on the basis that I didn't want any bloke's shaving tackle in my bathroom.'

'That's the least of your worries. Those sheets of yours are definitely a goner, and I don't think the mattress'll be too clever either.'

She wrinkled her nose. 'Ugh! Thanks, Oz. I was trying not to think about that.' Wrinkled or not, as noses go it was a right wee cracker. It set her brown eyes off a treat, and didn't bully her perfect mouth either. I realised that I was beginning to feel myself again.

'So what happened next?' she asked. 'What brought you here?'

'Archer sent me. He called me as soon as Kane was out of the office. By that time he was shitting himself about the good name of the firm. You know what a village Edinburgh is. One whiff of the unsavoury and his client list would disappear like snow off a dyke in August. He'd decided that the only thing for it was to get that nearly million back into the client's account and to spin him a line about crystallising capital gains for him, or some such stuff like that.

'He told me to go and see Kane, to get both halves of the fiver from him, then to get my arse over to Switzerland with some close-mouthed helper, and bring back the lolly. He promised me a five per cent success fee. To spare you the mental arithmetic, that's forty-five grand. For me, more than a year's wages in one hit.

'I phoned your number last night. A woman answered; I guessed it must have been Dawn. She put me on to Kane, I told him what the score was and he said "Yes sir, very good, sir. Come here at ten tomorrow morning, and I'll give you the bank-note." That's us up to date.

'I've never seen Kane, not even a photograph, but I'm assuming that's him through there on your bed. Unless your sister's lying under it in the same condition, then it looks as if you're in for a family scandal.' Her face twisted in pain, and I bit my tongue, to punish it for running away with itself, like always.

'That's your theory, Mr Detective, is it?'

'Prim,' I said, 'I'm a private enquiry agent, not a detective. I interview witnesses in court cases for lawyers, and that sort of stuff. I was a policeman for six months, once upon a time, and I turned it in because I couldn't stand the Clever Bastards in the CID, and the bullying sergeants in uniform who'd spent the best part of their service sitting on their brains.

'But what I said there, I'm sorry, but it's the first thing they'll think. No, it's the *only* thing they'll think. If these blokes see any easy answer, they don't spend a hell of a lot of time looking for a difficult option. They're not trained to be clever, they're trained to be logical.'

The old tongue was really running away with itself now. I suppose I could have stopped it, but I wasn't prepared to bite it that hard.

'Look Prim, I find it difficult to believe that anyone could do something like that next door, especially someone with a sister as . . .' I gulped, but I had run straight off the cliff, like Wiley E. Coyote, and all I could do was keep on running and hope that I didn't hit the ground. '. . . as downright tasty as you, but the boys and girls from the Leith Polithe won't dithmith the idea. And like it or not, we're going to have to call them.'

She nodded. Her blonde hair was cut fairly short, and more than a bit untidy after her journey. Suddenly I found myself wanting to smooth it.

'I know we are,' she said, 'but how about if we have a shooftie round to see if we can find that fiver before we do? Your clients would like that, wouldn't they.' Until that moment, I'd never grasped what 'askance' meant, but when I looked at Prim, I knew for sure. 'Well,' she said, picking up my expression. 'If it's there, all of it, it'll mean that Dawn . . . and we don't know for sure she was here . . . didn't kill him for the money. Won't it?'

I saw the sense in that. But I saw even more in the forty-five thousand good reasons I had for wanting to find the fiver too. 'Aye, okay. Let's look, at least.'

Policemen are like buses. When you need one, they're nowhere to be found. But when you don't . . .

I'll never know why anyone could call a game 'Postman's Knock'. I mean, when it comes to knocking there's no-one in the same league as a polisman. We had just stepped out of the kitchen when the thump on the door echoed around the hall. Prim's flat was on the first floor of the tenement. I'll swear that I heard at least three doors open as the sound swept through the building. She stepped up to the door and peered through the spy-hole.

'It looks like a traffic warden,' she said. 'But his uniform . . . !' The second knock sent her reeling backwards. 'Okay,' she shouted. 'Keep your hair on.' She swung the door open. The be-fouled traffic warden was there, all right, flanked on either side by two of Edinburgh's finest. One of them, I recognised. When I did my probationer spell at Oxgangs he had been the senior constable and chief barrack-room lawyer at the station. He was one of those guys who was determined to see it out to pension time and sod all the rest. Wherever they go they infect the whole station, whingeing and bitching until they've pulled morale down to rock bottom. Eventually they're rotated to start all over somewhere else. This one's name was McArthur, but at Oxgangs everyone, from the Chief Inspector down, had called him McArse.

His sidekick could have been me seven years earlier. He was a fuzz-cheeked probationer, so spick that I guessed his Maw still did his laundry, and so span that I guessed she pressed his uniform for him as well. I shook my head at the thought of what could happen to the poor wee bugger on the beat in Leith.

McArse stared right over Prim's head, straight at me. I could see something stirring behind his eyes, but his sort have trouble putting a name to their chief constable, let alone a short-serving wet-ear from almost a decade earlier. He gave up as soon as he started and went straight into Chapter One of the training manual, 'The Policeman as a Public Servant'.

'Hey, youse. Mister. What the fuck about this then?' He thrust Exhibit A into the hall, with the evidence of the outrage drying on his cap and shoulders. '*Another fine mess you've got yourself into, Oz*,' I thought.

When you're as thick as McArse very few things will stem the tide of your aggression, far less rock you back on your heels. The only one I know that works every time is a counterblast from a small, furious woman. When the woman in question has just stepped off a transcontinental flight minus a night's sleep, after twelve months in the middle of a genocidal African war, well it really is no contest.

From behind I could see her shoulders quiver as she surveyed the soiled public official before her. The warden stood there, wishing suddenly that, rather than stopping the first idiot he had encountered with flat feet and a black and white check band round his cap, he had made his way quietly back to his depot, to blame the incident on a large family of incontinent seagulls, attracted by the shine of a car he was booking.

'Constable!' hissed Prim. A good hiss is far more effective than a bellow, any time. 'Get this apparition out of my flat, at once, and take a grip on your manners.' McArse looked at her, noticing her for the first time. The ponderous wheels of his brain weighed up the situation for a few seconds, until without a word, he took the quailing warden by the collar and drew him backwards out on to the stairhead.

'That's better,' she said.

When I was a kid, if I was ever bullied, I used to get my big sister to sort it out. Standing there behind Prim, I felt a wave of *déjà vu* sweeping over me. 'Look pal,' I said to the warden, more from a need to assert my independence as a man – or even my presence – than from any wish to appease the thing, 'accidents will happen, okay. Sorry and all that.'

Prim looked at me over her shoulder, incredulous again. I made a face that was intended to say, 'Look I don't normally throw up at crime scenes, and even less frequently over traffic wardens, but the smell in there just got to me all of a sudden. Okay?' That's what it was meant to say, but it didn't work. Incredulity stayed in place, until it was replaced by one of my big sister's playground looks, the one she would throw me just before she put the boot into the Primary Three class bully. It said very clearly, 'You can explain yourself later!' Oddly, I felt a surge of delight when I caught the 'later'.

She turned back to the odd trio in the doorway and pulled off a masterful role switch. 'Yes Constable, we're sorry, but you see, the most terrible thing's happened. We were just about to call the police.

'I'm just back from abroad. My boyfriend picked me up from the airport. When we got in he went into the bedroom and he found . . .' From somewhere, she conjured up a sob. 'You'd better look for yourselves.' She pointed behind her to the door.

McArse was no better with a tearful woman than with an angry one. He nudged the probationer. 'Gaun, Jason . . .' '*Bugger me*,' I thought. *'He's called Jason!'* '. . . away and take a look.' He glowered at the traffic warden who had led him into this pit of torment. 'You! You can go. Ye're stinkin' the place oot onywey.' The Yellow, Orange and Slightly Pink Peril slunk off, out of the picture forever. McArse gave the reluctant boy Jason a shove towards the bedroom.

I *know*. I should have said something. I'd been in the boy's shoes once, yet I let him walk unwarned into that bedroom. Rotten bastard, eh? 'Fraid so.

Unlike me, Jason didn't throw up. Mind you, I'd take throwing up every time rather than what he did. A low, keening sound came from the room. A wailing 'Oooowwhhh,' which grew in intensity and distress, the sound of knees and thighs being squeezed tight together in a fruitless effort to prevent the inevitable.

'Ooohh!'

In the doorway the old soldier pretended not to hear. He stood there like Pharaoh trying, in the midst of the Red Sea, to ignore the fact that something very significant was happening to the water table – an apt comparison in the circumstances.

'Hector.' The call came from the room. If you've ever wondered about 'tremulous', that was it. The veteran looked at the ceiling.

'Hector!' Slightly more urgent this time. 'And whereabouts were you abroad, Miss?' the reluctant visitor asked Prim.

'McArse!' It was a howl from Hell. 'Get fuckin' in here!' Shocked into movement, the constable lumbered through the hall and into the bedroom. Five seconds later, he backed out white-faced.

'Oh my God, Miss. Was he like that when you found him?'

I almost said, 'No, you stupid bastard, he was alive!' but decided that silence was a better option. Prim had figured that one out too; she nodded meekly.

The probationer Jason eased himself awkwardly out of the bedroom, trying desperately not to look at anyone. I didn't have the heart to ask if he was all right, because I could see that he wasn't. I could recognise a career cut short when I saw one. I let him go as he shuffled along the hall and out to the stairhead.

At last, McArse, from somewhere, dredged up the memory of what it was like to be a policeman. 'Where's your phone, Miss?' he asked, quietly. The one thing that keeps guys like him alive in the force is their knack of knowing when to delegate, upwards or downwards, and that is just as often as they can.

Prim and I retreated silently to the flat's small living room as he went into the kitchen to phone.

'Why did you say that about getting back from the airport?' I asked her.

She looked at me. Shyness sat oddly on her. 'I don't know. It just came out. I suppose I thought it would be awkward for you if I told them what really happened. I mean your client's secret would be out and everything.'

'Aye, and I'd be in the frame as Obvious Culprit Number One.' She smiled. She didn't say 'Hardly.' She didn't need to.

Instead, she said, 'What happens now?'

I shrugged. 'The serious boys arrive. The CID. The Clever Bastards with absolutely no sense of humour. Not a bit like those two out there. Look, Prim, we're going to have to be straight with them. Nothing held back. What I mean is you're going to have to tell them that Dawn was living here.'

'We'll see.' Somehow, that didn't reassure me.

In which Dylan gets the blues, we get lucky and I seize my chance

The Clever Bastards who turned up were from Leith CID. Ebeneezer Street was only a short hop from their station and so we heard rubber burning on the road outside less than five minutes after McArse's call.

The officer who burst into the living room might as well have had 'High Flyer' stamped on his forehead. He radiated ambition as he looked down at us, sat together on the couch facing the window. Guys like him can be very dangerous. Turn them loose on a criminal investigation, especially one that's heading for the High Court and the tabloids, and they don't see people, they see rungs on the ladder of success.

I knew his face from the wine bars and fancy pubs around Charlotte Square, but not his name. He filled in the blank in my knowledge at once. 'I'm DI Michael Dylan. The plate on the door says Phillips. Is that both of you?'

Prim shook her head. 'No, it's my place. We don't live together.' '*You're telling the truth, Prim,*' I thought. '*Careful, that could be dangerous.*'

She squeezed my arm. I don't know whether she meant to dig her thumbnail into my wrist, but if she did, it was unnecessary. I'd learned enough about Primavera Phillips in our short acquaintance to be happy to let her lead the dance. I sat there dumb. 'This is Oz Blackstone, my boyfriend,' she said. I did my best to look gormless. From Dylan's expression, I succeeded.

For a DI he looked pretty young. Early thirties, I guessed, not much older than me. He was a real designer polisman, dressed in an olive-green suit that looked like Armani, and with his feet encased in tan leather shoes that definitely were not made for pounding the beat. Someone once said to me that Dylan saw himself as a bit of a cult, and that most of his colleagues agreed . . . only they spelled it differently.

Everything about him said that he was aiming for the Command Suite, and the predatory look in his eye told me that he could see Prim and me helping him on his way.

He didn't disappoint me. 'How about making it easy for me?' he said. 'The way I see it, honey, you set the wee chap up. You lure him to this place with promises of unbridled passion. You've got him gasping for it and helpless, then Oz here comes in and knifes him.

'All you really need to tell me is what you were after. Was it money, or is this a contract job? The rest is pretty obvious.'

'Mmm,' said Prim. 'Indeed.' There was a long, dangerous silence. Dylan looked down, all smugness and expectancy. 'And having done that,' she went on, softly, but with an edge to her voice that made me think of a demolition ball swinging unstoppably towards its target, 'the cold-eyed hitman here went and barfed out the window all over a traffic warden? Yes?

'Then, after that mishap, the death squad hung about the

scene until PC Murdoch and Oor Wullie arrived.'

She stood up and squared up to the Armani suit and its contents, which suddenly seemed a touch less sure of themselves. 'Let me tell you a few things, Mr Dylan. First, this is my flat, that ruined bed next door is mine, and I'm not happy about it. Second, no way would I let a thing like that through there anywhere near me.' I wasn't quite sure which thing she meant, the whole or the part. I guessed, she meant the latter, and felt a lot better about life, manhood, and associated issues. 'Third, if you care to repeat that allegation before independent witnesses, Oz and I will sue you right out of that suit.'

I sat there on the couch, staring at Prim's bum in her tight, faded jeans. It was a nice, round bum, generously fleshed but firm. I tried to imagine her committing acts of unbridled passion upon the person of the late William Kane, but somehow I wound up taking his place, with a bridle figuring somewhere in the scene, too. Eventually I forced myself to look up at Clever Bastard Dylan. He stood there, his face working itself into a cheesy grin as he fought to protect his dignity. 'Okay,' he said, finally. 'Just testing. Have you any idea who that is, through there?'

She looked him dead in the eye. 'Neither Oz or I have ever seen that man before in our lives.'

He missed the fact that she hadn't answered his question. 'Okay. The constable said you got back from the airport and found the body?'

'Yes,' said Prim. She dug into her vast bag and produced a boarding card. 'There.' She thrust it at Dylan. 'That's the flight I was on. Eight o'clock shuttle. It was a bit late so Oz and I didn't get back here till after ten.' He bought the lie without question.

'The guy in there's been dead since last night.'

'Oh, you know a lot about bodies do you?' Dylan was the sort of prat who patronises women automatically. This time he didn't even realise he was doing it until the axe of Prim's sarcasm fell on his neck.

'I'm afraid I do. I've seen all sorts over the last twelve months. A few days ago, in fact, we went into a village and found a policeman with his testicles in his mouth. Just as well for his sake that *he* was dead. I mean what good's a policeman without . . .'

Quite suddenly, she began to sob. '*Thank Christ,*' I thought, relieved that she wasn't *that* tough. I stood up and turned her towards me, holding her like the concerned partner I was supposed to be. 'There, love,' I said, warming to the part. 'You had a hell of a time out in Africa. A dead stranger in your bed's the last thing you needed to come home to.'

I glared at Dylan. He was completely conquered now. 'Look, Mr . . . eh Blackstone, was it? Why don't you look after Miss Phillips. My people will just have a look round . . . if that's all right, that is?'

'Aye, sure. You get on with it.'

I expected Prim to break the clinch when the door closed behind him, but she hung on in there. Her sobs were subsiding, but every so often a fresh outbreak would set her generous chest rubbing against my belly. Remembering that she had been a stranger an hour before, I racked my brains for images which would distract me and kill the reflex which Prim's bra-less nipples were triggering in me. I thought of Hibernian defending a one-goal lead on a wet Saturday in January. I thought of an evening at the ballet with a woman I didn't like. I thought of the bit in *Pulp Fiction* where John Travolta shoots Marvin in the face by accident. I thought of

Van Morrison. I thought of a bottle of duty-free Grolsch after midnight on a cross-channel ferry.

None of it worked. Before she could get the wrong idea, which would have been right all along, I held her away from me at arm's length. 'Come on Prim. There'll be time for that later.' She looked back at me tear-stained, and nodded. It's funny how there are people you can know for an hour and it seems like a lifetime.

'Yes, you're right. That prick'll be back.' ('*You never know,*' I thought mischievously to myself.) 'I'll need to work out a story that'll protect Dawn, as far as I can.'

Dylan must have had a pressing lunch date, because the prick was back within fifteen minutes. 'The Doc's arrived,' he said. 'Her first estimate is that he was killed between ten and midnight last night by a right-handed man. If you're up to it now, Miss Phillips, perhaps you could clear up just one or two things.'

Prim nodded.

'How long have you been in Africa?'

'A year.'

'And you don't have a key, Mr Blackstone?'

'No, he doesn't. Nor do I to Oz's place. That implies a permanent commitment, and we're not ready for that.' '*Speak for yourself,*' I thought, falling deeper in love by the minute.

'So who's been using your flat while you've been away.'

'I have a sister,' said Prim. She sounded casual, but I knew she was measuring every word. 'She's an actress. She never knows where her next job'll be, so she doesn't have a place of her own. She sleeps on my couch or rooms with other performers when she's in town. Sometimes her friends crash down here too. When I left I gave her a key and said that she could let her crowd use it as long as they kept it clean and didn't smoke dope.

'You could say that this flat's been a sort of doss-house for luvvies for the last twelve months. I've got no idea who might have been here last night. And as for the bloke next door, I told you I've never seen him before.'

'How about you, Mr Blackstone?' said Dylan quickly, with a failed attempt at slyness.

I was ready for him. 'As Prim said, me neither.' I chanced my arm. 'Do you know who he is?'

Dylan shook his head. 'His wallet seems to have been taken. There's nothing there to identify him.' He looked down again at Prim. 'We've found some keys in the kitchen, Miss. Could you have a look at them to see if the one you gave your sister's among them?'

He led us back across the hall. In the kitchen, a leaf of the table had been raised, and various objects were spread on it. Half a dozen keys of various sorts. An empty pill bottle. A five pound note, serial number AF 426469, cut into two halves.

She didn't break stride, catch her breath or anything else. She looked at the keys carefully. 'These two are for the coalshed down in the back yard. These two are for my parents' place. That one's for the Yale in the front door. The other fitted a lock I had changed when I moved in here.' She picked up the pill bottle. I leaned over and sneaked a quick look. The label read 'Prozac: Miss D. Phillips.' She picked up the two halves of the fiver and looked round at Dylan. 'You found my secret stash, then. Very thorough!'

Dylan looked embarrassed and nodded at a pile of muesli heaped on the floor, surrounded by the shattered pieces of a ceramic container. 'Sorry about that, Miss. One of these clumsy sods knocked it off the counter. We can replace it if you like.'

'That's all right,' said Prim. 'I never liked it anyway. I'll use this to buy another, one that doesn't break this time.' Casually, she slipped the two halves of the note into the pocket of her jeans.

'Why did you cut it?' asked Dylan.

'Added security,' she replied, mysteriously.

'What else can we do, Inspector,' she asked, ingenuously.

Dylan shrugged his shoulders. 'I'd like you both to call into the Police Station in Queen Charlotte Street to give us formal statements, but tomorrow'll be fine for that. Make it around midday.'

We each nodded. 'So when,' asked Prim, 'will you be finished here?'

The Inspector sucked his teeth. 'Hard to say, Miss. Depends on the technicians. They'll want to pick up every hair and every piece of fluff from that bedroom, so we can match it to a suspect, sooner or later. Don't you worry about that, we'll get him.

'I shouldn't reckon they'll be any more than a couple of days.'

'Two days!' She puffed up like a pigeon in her indignation. 'What the hell am I going to . . .'

I seized her hand, and my chance. 'What the hell else are you going to do? Let's take your kit round to my place and leave these guys to it.'

In which Jan gets a shock, Primavera meets Wallace, and I gain a sleeping partner.

Out in the street, I was delighted to see that the Traffic Warden from the Other Side had been so disconcerted that he had neglected to paste me up for my out-of-date disc. The blue Nissan wore no adornment other than bird-shit, and a few specks that weren't.

I opened the tailgate door and slung Prim's kitbag first into the boot, and then the smaller one which she had packed with a few 'sensible clothes' from her wardrobe and cupboard, under the supervision of a young woman detective, who, she told me, had kept sneaking astounded glances at the tiny colossus on the bed.

Neither of us spoke as I coaxed the engine into life and reversed out of my parking space. I weaved my way through the police cars which were thronging the street like ants round a peach-stone. We were heading up Leith Walk, when Prim said: 'So where is it then? This refuge I'm bound for, this pad of yours.'

I grinned, thinking it would put her at ease. From her

expression, my grin must have been more of a leer. 'Not that far. It's in the Old Town, down one of the closes off the High Street.'

'And will Mrs Blackstone be gone for long?'

'My mother is dead,' I said solemnly.

Prim frowned. 'Don't be cheap. You know what I mean, Mrs as in spouse, or even Ms Something Else as in live-in partner.'

I shook my head. 'I don't have any of those. My last live-in girlfriend was two years ago. She died of "dish-pan hands, Mummy", or so she said. Since then I've preferred my independence. There are some bloody good takeaways around the centre of town, you know.' I let the silence fill the car as she weighed up Oz in a new environment, and pondered the prospect of Oz on Oz's turf.

'Mind you,' I said, after a suitable interval, looking sheepishly at the dashboard as we turned into Leith Walk. 'I don't know how you'll take to Wallace.'

She gasped. 'Wallace! You're not . . .'

I relished the sight of Prim on the back foot. 'What about it if I am?' She looked at me, uncertain for the first time in our short acquaintance.

'Actually, if there was anything between Wallace and me they'd have to invent a new name for it. Wallace is an Iguana. He's the last of the dinosaurs. I named him after a wizened old fisherman uncle of my Mum's.'

Her jaw dropped. 'Let me get this right. You're taking me to a flat that you share with a lizard?'

'Wallace would be hurt by the description, but yes, that just about sums it up.'

She threw back her head and laughed. 'The first time I saw you, Oz Blackstone, I thought there might be some mileage in you. Could be I was right.'

'I'm touched, my dear.'

'Yes, that was what I thought.'

'Thank you again, on behalf of loonies everywhere. But seriously for once, we're clear of that lot back there. Is there anywhere else you want me to take you? How about your parents?'

'God no, Oz. For a start they're in Auchterarder; and for seconds, sooner or later Mum would ask me about Dawn, and I've never been able to lie to her.'

'But Prim, you're going to need to talk to her. The murder might be reported on telly tonight. She could see your flat on the news.'

She shook her head slowly. 'No, I think not. My parents cling to this planet by their fingertips. Mother's hobby is Romantic Novels and Dad devotes his life to making model soldiers. He sells them to collectors through magazines. Anything from one-off Kilties to whole battle scenes, to order. They're just not interested in what's on the telly, unless it's by Barbara Taylor Bradford or Kate Adie.'

'Is there anyone else, then?' Suddenly I was seized by the thought that taking this woman under my roof would be the biggest step into the unknown that I'd ever made. 'Do you have any friends in Edinburgh?'

She turned in her seat and looked at me. 'Do I feel the chill of cold feet? Do you want to be shot of me?'

'Absolutely not,' I shot back at her, too fast in the circumstances. 'I just don't want you to feel that you're being . . .'

'Spirited away to your lair, were you going to say?' Her smile was delicious. 'Don't worry, Oz, we fell into this thing together, and I reckon we should see it through together. More than that, you're my best bet for a shower and a sleep. Shower first, though. Do I need one!'

I creased my nose and looked sideways at her. 'Funny that. I was just thinking that it's been a long time since I had a really ripe woman in this car!' She slapped my arm, hard enough for me to feel her strength, not hard enough to hurt. I saw her tanned nurse's bicep bunch.

We made our way up the Walk, pausing occasionally for red lights. It was a beautiful warm day in early May, and the trees in the central reservation were in blossom.

'You know, Mr Oz Blackstone,' said Prim, 'this may sound like the wrong thing to say in the circumstances, but I'm glad to be home. Even Florence Nightingale must have become de-humanised after a while. If you need an example, just think back to how I reacted to finding a corpse in my bed!'

'Hey,' I said as gently as I could. 'You *are* home. Just hang on to that. You're in Edinburgh and it's beautiful. Look around you.' The car swept round the Elm Row island, and up towards Picardy Place. She laughed. 'Come on Oz. That's the St James Centre up ahead. Not even a homeboy could call that beautiful.'

'Okay, well just hang on a minute. We'll get to some nice bits!'

My house is in one of the nicer bits. Less than half a mile from the Palace of Holyroodhouse, so for a week every year I can say that I have the Queen for a neighbour.

'What's this?' said Prim, as I slid the Nissan into my parking space.

'My house. Where I live. It's a conversion. It used to be a grain store or something, until a developer got hold of it. I live in that pointy bit up there. It's more of a loft than a flat. See the bit right at the top? According to the estate agent who sold me the place, that's called a belvedere. There's a ladder up to it. Quite often Wallace climbs up it to sun himself. Yes, there he is, look.' As if wakened by the sound of our arrival, the iguana peered down at us solemnly.

'Jesus,' said Prim, shaking her head. 'I find a dead dwarf in my bed, and now I'm going home with a guy who has an iguana as a flatmate.'

'A loft, not a flat,' Must get the terminology right.

'Loft, flat,' she said. 'What's the difference?'

'About five grand in a good market, I reckon.' That got her attention.

We made our way up the narrow, twisty stairway to my pad, and stepped into the tiny square area which passed for my entrance hall. Two doors and a staircase led from it. 'Kitchen to the left, bathroom door to the right,' I said. I opened each door to demonstrate. When I opened the door on the right, a red-faced woman screamed. She was sat on the toilet, so it was understandable.

'The rest of it's up there.' I said hurriedly. Weighed down by bags, I led the way up the staircase to the heart of my stronghold. Prim stepped up behind me and tapped me on the shoulder. 'Er, Oz. About Mrs Blackstone?'

I frowned. 'I told you, my mother's dead. Anyway, she always bolted the door when she went to the toilet. That was Jan. She does my books, but she sets her own hours.'

Well, it was true. Jan and I were at school together. She did my books. Occasionally she ironed a shirt if she felt sorry for me. On even rarer occasions, when something was troubling her or she just felt like my company, she gave me a cuddle in the night.

Downstairs we heard the toilet flush. I looked across the room. Fortunately my ledgers were spread out on my desk. Prim followed my eyes, then looked around the rest of the place.

'You never said it was open plan!'

'You never asked. Anyway, it isn't. The living area's down here. The sleeping area's that raised part, up that wee ladder. When you're in bed, you can't be seen from down here. Well, hardly.'

'Very comforting!' She's good at irony, is Prim.

'Remember the pointy bit I showed you? Well, you get to that through the sleeping area. You see the foot of the second ladder there?'

'It looks sort of like a square funnel from the inside, doesn't it,' she said. At that moment Wallace, the curious iguana, eased his cumbersome frame down the ladder, and swung across to walk along the railing which enclosed the raised area, and against which my bed was pressed.

She shook her head, and then did something which turned my knees to jelly. She stood on her tiptoes and kissed me. Not on the cheek, on the lips. Chastely, you understand. Hands by her side and everything. But still, not on the cheek, on the lips.

'Osbert, you may be a fruitcake, and you may live in a fucking mad-house, but you are my saviour and protector, my knight in shining armour. You're here when I need you, and I thank you.'

The gallows answer stuck in my throat. It was the nicest thing anyone had ever said to me, and I was unspeakably touched.

Jan wasn't. She smiled at Prim as she appeared at the top of the stairs, and she smiled at me. I could grade the warmth of Jan's smiles pretty well, and the one she threw at me was straight from the fridge. She's a tall girl, with looks and dark hair that fell off a Jane Russell poster, and a chest to match.

'Hi,' I said. I was about to add, 'Sorry about surprising you on the bog,' but I thought that I'd better not. 'Jan, this is Prim

Phillips. Prim, Jan More. Prim's got a problem, she needs somewhere to crash for a couple of days.'

Jan smiled again, with a glint in her eye, but there was nothing malicious in it. 'Must be a big problem, for you to wind up here. Watch out for Wallace, darlin'. That bloody iguana was right up my kilt this morning.'

She turned back to me. 'Oz, your books are done. Your VAT slip's ready to go. I've written cheques for that and all your other bills, and I've written one for me too.'

'Fine,' I said. I picked up my chequebook, signed the second cheque, tore it out and handed it to her. I didn't even check the amount. Jan hadn't given herself a rise in four years. Mind you, she'd given me a few.

'Thanks. Right, I'm off. See you next month, or whenever.'

I saw her to the door. 'Look, Jan, you'd never believe . . .'

She turned in the doorway, but she was smiling. 'Don't "look" me, Oz. I'd believe anything about you. Our rule is ask no questions, and I'm not going to break it now. Good luck.' She gave my balls a friendly squeeze and closed the door behind her.

I went back upstairs to Prim. She had carried her smaller bag up to the raised area, but had left the monster for me. I looked up and saw her feet disappearing up the ladder to Wallace's sun-room. 'Hey, this is terrific,' her voice echoed down. 'You can see a lot from up here.'

'That's why Wallace likes it,' I shouted back. 'Incidentally, Jan was only kidding about him being up her skirt.' I grabbed the sullen iguana and shoved him into the cage which was his bedchamber, hoping that I was right. The eaves space in the loft was lined with cupboards, where most of my possessions were stored. I dived into one and pulled out a towel. As Prim climbed down the ladder, I threw it to her. 'There. The shower's electric. Instant hot water. You'll find my dressing gown behind the door. Fancy something to eat?'

She thought about it for a few seconds. 'Which takeaway is it at lunchtime? McDonalds?'

I put on a hurt look. 'I do cook sometimes. For example, I do an ace tuna sandwich.'

'That'd be great.' She invaded the vast bag once more and emerged with a bottle of shampoo, and some other stuff. 'Meantime, I have earned this shower. I've come a long way for it. I'm going to enjoy it. Hope your lecky bill can stand it. I may be some time!'

Leaving her to undress, I jumped down to the kitchen. A quick glance at the green things in the bread basket persuaded me that I should take her at her word about lunch. As soon as I heard the bathroom door close, I slipped out of the flat, sprinted down the stairs, out of the building and along the narrow wynd which led to the High Street.

Fortunately there hadn't been a run on Ali's ace tuna, sweetcorn and mayonnaise rolls. I grabbed a handful, added a couple of yoghurts for luck and a quart of milk to replace the yellow stuff in the fridge, and paid my be-turbanned pal. Ali shot me a questioning look, one that said '*Surely not at lunchtime?*' but said nothing. I gave him the expected knowing wink and bolted back the way I had come.

By the time Prim emerged from her shower, I was in my chef's apron, with the woman's naked body turned to the inside and chaste blue stripes on show. Lunch was laid out neatly on plates – the paper bag and wrappers out of sight in the wastebin – and the cafetière was full and steaming. I depressed its plunger with a flourish, and offered her a stool at the breakfast bar, facing mine.

'I'm impressed,' she said. My dressing gown, rarely worn

in any event, had never looked better. It clung to her body, doing things for her that Marks & Spencer could use to great effect in their advertising. My towel looked pretty cool too, wound round her head like an outsize version of my pal Ali's turban. She suited it better than he did.

'Thank you ma'am,' I said. Score a point for the boy.

'I didn't think you were that quick on your feet. I forgot my toothbrush, so I had to run back upstairs. Either you were up in the belvedere or the place was empty.'

'Milk,' I said, assertively. 'Needed some more.'

She bit a huge chunk from a tuna roll. 'Mmm,' she said, as she chewed. 'Pity you didn't get some fresh rolls as well. These are a day or so older than they should be.'

I tried one for myself. 'Nonsense,' I said eventually, relieved to discover that she had been pulling my chain. 'They were fresh this morning.'

We demolished our rolls, slurped our yoghurt and drank our coffee with the enthusiasm of the newly reprieved. Prim held her mug in both hands, leaning forward with her elbows on the bar, holding them carefully so that the dressing gown didn't flop open. I offered her a top-up, but she said, 'No thanks. I really would like an hour or two's kip. I'm not jet-lagged or anything. I was in more or less the same time zone. I'm just knackered.'

'Okay, come on and I'll change the bed for you.'

'Er. Oz . . . ?' she said.

'Don't worry about it. The sofa folds down. That's where I sleep when my Dad's here.'

'I'll have that, then.'

'No, because that'll mean I can't work at my desk. I've got a couple of witnesses to interview this afternoon, and I should go back to see Archer.'

The deal was struck. She helped me change the sheets – I'll swear I heard them sigh with relief – making no comment on the stains which were a relic of Jan's last stopover three weeks earlier. As I shook out the Downie, she asked me quietly. 'What are you going to say to Archer?'

I looked at her. 'I could tell him about Kane. If I did that he might decide he had to go to the police. They'd find out what I was really doing there, and that we told them porkies. Then we'd both be in the shit. Your sister would be too, right up to her nose. Alternatively, I could tell him that when I turned up the street was crawling with polis, so I did a runner. That's safer but it leaves us with the problem of what to do about the fiver.'

'Yes,' she said, softly. 'What about the fiver?'

I looked down at her, flexing my sincerity muscles. 'Well,' I said, 'if I hadn't been there you wouldn't have known what the fiver was all about. You might not even have picked it up.'

She shook her head. 'My flat, my fiver. I'd have had it all right.'

'On the other hand, if you hadn't been there to pull that stunt, I'd never have laid a finger on that note. Archer would have had to go public to get it back. So the way I look at it, Miss Primavera Phillips, we're partners.'

She looked at me across the bed. The afternoon sunshine spilled down in a column from the belvedere enveloping her in its light. Slowly, she unwound the towel turban and let it fall to the floor. 'Partners, eh?' she said. Then she reached across the bed and stretched out her hand. It was a chubby wee hand, but her grip was strong. 'Okay, Oz, it's a deal. You know, I didn't come out of the bathroom to get my toothbrush. I came upstairs to fetch the fiver from my jeans pocket. When I found that you were gone but that it was still there, I felt really guilty. You'll do, partner.'

She glanced up; the beam of reflected sunlight glinted off her damp hair and shone in her eyes. 'Let me close the trap door if you're going to sleep,' I said.

'No, leave it. It won't bother me.

'So: will you tell Archer that we've got the note?' she asked.

'I don't know. My gut tells me that the fewer people who know we've got it, the better it'll be for us. You and I have got to face up to some nasty truths about this situation, not least about your sister's part in it. But not now, eh. I've got these people to see, and you've got some kipping to do.'

'Okay.' She was beginning to sound fuzzy. 'One thing though, Oz, partner.'

'What's that?'

'Figure out the best way to tell Archer, but five per cent isn't enough.'

I held up my hands. 'One step at a time. Let's just concentrate on getting through today in one piece. Now sleep!'

I turned and jumped down from the sleeping area. I couldn't help looking back as I hit the lower level, and caught a back view of Prim dropping the dressing gown on the floor and slipping naked into my bed. A quick shudder ran through me from top to toe. I pinched myself hard, but I didn't waken up. If I went back up those steps she'd still be there.

Instead I went across to my desk and began to prepare for my two interviews. Ten minutes later, as I set the telefax to auto answer and picked up my case, soft sleeping sounds floated down from the upper level. She didn't snore; she simply breathed and it was like music whispering its way around the room. I thought of other people who had slept in that bed. My Dad, with his stertorous snores; Jan, with her snorts, snuffles and occasional gentle farts.

Suddenly I had a strange feeling that my loft had been invaded by a haunting spirit, and that life there was never going to be the same again.

In which the Daft Laddie does a deal.

My two witnesses, coming after my adventures of the morning, were almost refreshingly normal. One was an air steward, who was taking his former employer to an industrial tribunal to contest his dismissal on grounds of sexual misconduct. His defence was that as an adult male over twenty-one he was entitled to have private relations with another man.

The airline's case was that the male staff shower room at Heathrow could not be construed as a private place. I could see that the publicity accruing to my lawyer client would be worth far more than his fee.

My second witness was a punter whose claim for fire damage had been knocked back by his insurance company, and who was suing as a result. The fire had been caused by a faulty gas heater. Neutral though I was, even I could see that his lawyers would have trouble coming up with an answer to the key question. Why had the heater been lit on the afternoon of the hottest day of the year? If the punter's story, 'because my greyhound was sick,' couldn't convince gullible Oz Blackstone, then I could only guess at the likely reaction of the Court of Session.

Archer was waiting for me in his office when I arrived at 4.20 p.m., twenty minutes late. He was almost on tiptoes with tension as he paced around the room.

'Did you see him?'

I still didn't have a clue about what I was going to say to him, so I decided to use the Daft Laddie Gambit as a stalling device. 'See him?' I said, wearing what Granny Blackstone used to call my 'Gowk' expression.

'Willie Kane. Kane and his bird. Did you see them, and have you got the two halves of the fiver?'

Maybe the morning had made me paranoid, but there was something about him, an edge of tension that made me afraid to trust the man. After all, someone had rammed that big knife up under Kane's chin. Someone had searched Prim's flat, and had failed to find the divided banknote. Someone had taken Kane's wallet to hold up the identification of the body.

Suddenly I realised that, if I was to draw up a list of suspects, Mr Raymond Archer would be quite near the top. Nine hundred thousand was a strong lure even to a senior partner, especially if the theft could be blamed on the wee man, and the loss to the firm could be recovered from his assets. Support I had been sent along there just to discover the body, and to fill the time-honoured role of fall guy?

I tried to stop my eyes from narrowing as I looked at him. Playing safe, I decided on Plan B: when cornered, lie with total conviction. I shook my head. 'No. I never got that close. All hell was breaking loose on down there. When I got to Ebeneezer Street, the place was full of blue uniforms, and the entry to the close was guarded. I decided not to announce myself. I didn't even get out the car, just turned it around and drove off.

'I picked up a *News* this afternoon.' I threw the tabloid down on his desk. 'They found a man's body at that address. There's no way of telling which flat it was, but you never know.'

He picked up the paper and scanned the front-page story, which was accompanied by a mugshot of DI Mike Dylan. Either Archer couldn't conceive of Kane being the victim, or he was a bloody good actor.

'What do we do now?' he asked.

'Wait till they identify the body.'

Archer looked at me. 'Surely it couldn't be Willie?'

'Is he immune to knives, then?' I bit my tongue for a second until I remembered that the *News* story, quoting Dylan, had referred to stab wounds.

'But if it is him?'

'Then we have to wait until the police are well clear of the place, then find an excuse to go back in there to try to find the fiver. Unless that's what he was killed for.' That's it Oz boy, plant as many thoughts in his mind as you can, to steer him away from the thought that you might have it. 'Even if it isn't him, we have to let the police get clear before we make contact again.'

Archer thought for a moment. 'Okay. Play it that way. You still happy to work on a contingency basis?' It didn't take me a second to shake my head. 'Not now. It's a new game. I need a fee to cover my time, fifty an hour, plus expenses to Switzerland if we do find the fiver. I want a bigger cut too. Ten per cent's not unreasonable, given the down-side to you if you don't get that money back.'

Archer took even less time to think than I had. 'You're a

hard man, Blackstone, but okay. If you pull it off it'll be worth it.' He ushered me to the door. 'Keep in touch.' I was outside in George Street almost before I knew it.

In which secrets are revealed, there is a chance meeting, and deeply held principles are discussed.

Back at the loft, Prim's soft sleeping sounds sounded as if they might go on for a while, but they had been joined by the scrabbling of an irritated iguana. Wallace had his own version of 'Don't fence me in'. He looked at me with a cold imperious eye as I released him.

There were no phone messages, but two faxes from solicitors giving me interview commissions on a non-urgent basis. I switched on my Performa and sat down to type up my notes of the afternoon's interviews. I had almost finished the second, when there was a shout behind me, choked off, followed a few seconds later by a long exhalation.

'Christ, Oz, I was having a dream there about waking up in bed beside that wee man, then I did wake up, beside a bloody lizard!'

'Dinosaur!' I said sternly. I stood up and jumped up on to the sleeping area. Prim was propped up on her right elbow. Her left breast had rolled out over the edge of the Downie, but she hadn't noticed, or didn't care. I sneaked the briefest of glances.

It fulfilled earlier promise, bigger than a handful, but not so large that it was heading rapidly south. I perched myself on the edge of the bed as she sat up, pulling the Downie right under her chin and in the process dislodging Wallace. He shot her a look filled with bale, and reached for the first wooden rung of the ladder to the belvedere.

'Feel better for that?' I asked. I reached out and touched her hand, tentatively. She took mine and gave it a quick squeeze. 'Yes and no,' she said. 'The "yes" part is that you're still the guy I thought you were before I went to sleep, if you know what I mean.' I thought I did, and the hamster who lives in my stomach at such moments did another quick lap of the track. 'What's the "no" bit?' I asked.

'That what happened this morning isn't a movie any more. I have to start treating it as real, and I can't go on blanking Dawn from my mind.'

'Yeah,' I said. 'I know.' I looked at my watch. 'Prim, it's after six. I've got some work to finish off, then I have to get it on the fax. While I do that, why don't you get dressed, then we'll go out somewhere. A drink and a pizza maybe. In the process, partner, we can talk about Dawn, I'll tell you about Archer, and we can decide what we're going to do next.'

She dragged herself along the bed on her bum, until she was right alongside me, the Downie still up to her chin. Then she leaned over and kissed me, on the lips again, and not quite so chastely this time. 'You've just said the magic words, Osbert. I have spent most of the last twelve months dreaming about a drink and a pizza. Now here I am, back home, about to make it all come true, and with a bloke I quite fancy at that.

'I warn you now though: never on the first date, and I mean *never*!'

I didn't know what to say, so she said it for me. 'Sometimes you meet someone and you're attracted right away,' She grinned. 'Like you're attracted to me. So far you're winning: it cuts both ways. Just remember! First date? *Never*!'

I took a hell of a chance. I kissed *her*, on the lips. 'You know the trouble with women?'

'Whssat?'

'You just assume that all us guys are easy lays! I have to go out at least *twice* with a girl before I decide whether she's worthy of my body!'

She dipped her shoulder and shoved me off the bed. 'Go!' she demanded. 'Finish your work, while I turn myself into a human being again.' I did as I was told. Behind me I heard the riffling sound of the Downie being shaken up and spread over the bed. Then Prim's feet sounded lightly on the staircase.

I refocused myself on my reports and finished them off, neat and tidy, set out in question and answer form, with a summary attached. I fed each into the fax then slipped confirmatory copies into envelopes. Quick, experienced and thorough, that's Oz Blackstone, Prince among Private Enquiry Agents, the man most wanted by Edinburgh's legal community, even if much of his work does bore him out of his scone.

I pride myself that on each day of my life I try to learn something new. '*So what's today's lesson, Blackstone?*' I asked myself, out loud, as I stamped the two envelopes.

'Stick to the boring stuff,' I answered, **'and forget the Philip Marlowe dreams. Dead people don't look attractive close up, even if the money is good, and the work's exciting.'**

'*That's good, Oz; now what's the bonus lesson?*'

'That's easy. Don't give up believing in miracles. Most people find at least one in a lifetime.'

I turned around, and there she was, Primavera, Springtime in Spanish, standing beside the bed, fastening a single string of pearls around her neck. The jeans and tee-shirt had gone, to be replaced by a close-fitting grey skirt and a sleeveless white blouse. Her sun-bleached hair had been teased into order, carefully but casually, and she was made up with blue eye shadow, a touch of blusher and a vivid red lipstick which sat on her perfect mouth like country wine on a summer evening. She was so beautiful that she made me breathless.

I stood there, dumbstruck for a while, until the inevitable nonsense sprang to my tongue. 'Springtime,' I said, holding out a hand in invitation, 'would you care to join me in my garden?'

My loft opens out on to a tiny terrace, on which a few geraniums and a woebegone palm struggle for survival in the heart of my Scottish city. I threw open the double doors, and held out my hand for her as she approached across the big room, passing through a beam of light from one of the four Vellux windows set on each side of the sloping ceiling.

If I was an aesthete I would say that sunlit May evenings are my favourite time of the year in Edinburgh. Those few days, as the year shakes off the dying grip of winter, can be sublime. They are moments not to be missed, yet all too fleeting, before the Scottish summer asserts itself in all its wet, windy drabness.

As Prim stepped out on to my south-facing terrace, I felt suddenly full up, and it came to me that this was one of those times in my life that I'll remember on my dying day.

My fifth birthday, when my Mum baked a cake, I had a party, and my Dad gave me my first set of real football boots. My first day at primary school. My first Hearts–Hibs game. My first day at secondary school. Sneaking in among my sister's crowd one night to watch a bootleg video of *The Exorcist*, and being chucked out for laughing at the bit where Linda Blair's head spins all the way round. My first, and last, cigarette. My first fumbling, incompetent but affectionate shag with Jan at a party in her house while her folks were away. My Mother's death. A weekend my Dad and I spent walking in Derbyshire, eating wholesome food and drinking a different beer every night, as part of his emergence from our bereavement.

Seminal moments all of them; now here she was, this woman I had met in the most bizarre circumstances a few hours earlier, taking her place, perhaps at the head of them all.

She looked out across the southern aspect of Edinburgh, across Arthur's Seat, up the ragged line of the Old Town's rooftops, up to the craggy Castle on its flat-topped hill. She breathed deeply of the evening air. She took my arm, and squeezing it, leaned against me, laying her head on my shoulder. 'It's good to be back, partner,' she said, softly and musically. 'If only for now.'

There was nothing I could say to add to the moment, and so, for once in my life, I said nothing. Instead, I eased her gently into one of the two green wooden folding chairs on the balcony. I stepped back into the house and trotted down to the kitchen, re-emerging from the loft a couple of minutes later with two glasses and my prize bottle of reasonably good champagne. It had been a present from a lawyer client, and had been languishing in my fridge since Christmas, awaiting an appropriate moment. I balanced the glass on the balcony's broad wooden rail and filled them carefully. Handing one to Prim I raised the other in a toast. 'You're back; so welcome,' I said. 'I hope that it's for good.'

She looked at me for a long time, the glass pressed to her

lips. 'We'll see,' she said at last. 'When I left a year ago, it was because I didn't have anything to stay for. For now though, as I say, I'm glad I'm back.' She sipped the champagne and nodded in polite approval. We drank in silence, looking out over the park, watching the joggers on the Radical Road, until the sun slipped round the corner of the loft, and the balcony, and my shivering palm tree, fell into shade.

'Come on,' I said. 'Let's go on a pizza hunt. D'you fancy a walk first? Along Princes Street?' She nodded. I left her outside for a minute or two while I changed into my pub-going gear, then, locking up everything but Wallace's cage, we headed out and up towards the old High Street. 'You got that fiver?' I asked as we left.

'Too damn right!'

'Well look after it. Don't spend it, or anything daft like that.'

She gave me a woman's smile which made it clear that there was no chance of that happening.

It was Thursday, and so, although it was evening, the city was bustling with shoppers. We walked arm-in-arm, up towards St Giles, turning on to the Mound and down the long flight of steps which led down to the National Gallery and to Princes Street beyond. The pavement outside the record shops and bookstores towards the West End was thick with people and so we turned up Castle Street and along Rose Street, until it opened out into Charlotte Square.

'Drink first?'

She nodded. 'I could slaughter a pint.' '*Oh Jesus*,' I thought, '*this woman gets better and better*!'

We walked along the square's south side and down the few steps to Whigham's. As usual it was thronged. I excused my way up to the high counter and ordered a pint of lager for the lady, bartender if you please, and the same of the day's guest beer, Old Throgmorton's Embalming Fluid or something similar, for me. We found elbow space at a shelf beside the bar. Prim closed her eyes and took a deep swallow. 'Not the same as champagne, but not too damn bad either,' she said. 'Okay, Osbert. Out with it. Tell me about your life.'

I jammed my knuckles against my forehead. 'Where shall I begin?

'It's pretty dull really. I'm twenty-nine years old, staring the big Three-Oh in the face. I was born in Cupar. My Dad's a dentist and my Mum was a teacher, so I'm a real middle-class boy. When I was four, we moved to Anstruther, and my Dad lives there still. I meant it about my Mother being dead. That happened nine years ago. Dad was doing her teeth one Saturday morning, and he took an X-ray. He found a shadow on her jawbone. From being perfectly well that day, she was gone in seven months.' I tried to tell her that part of the story as casually as I could, but that's a trick I've never mastered. I tried to hide it with a swallow of Old Throgmorton's, but Prim saw through me. She touched my cheek, lightly. 'Poor thing,' she said.

'Who? Me or my Mum?'

'All of you. It must have been dreadful for your Dad.'

'Yeah, it was. He was chewed up with guilt. He saw her through to the end, and then he started on a course of serious therapeutic drinking. He'd always liked a bevvy – as I said, he's a dentist – but this was something he was doing as a punishment. Ellen was at home at the time, I was at university. Eventually she called me about it.

'I went up to Anstruther for a weekend, and watched him at it. He did his regular Saturday morning surgery, as usual, then started into the Bacardi and Coke for lunch. After a while I sat him down at the table and I said, 'For fuck's sake, Dad, this has got to stop. That Coke is *murder* on the teeth.' He looked at me and he laughed. Then he began to cry. He cried all day, and all through Sunday. Monday was a holiday, so he and I played golf. Then we went to the cemetery and said hello to Mum. We both sensed the same thing, that she was pleased to see us. He was all right after that. We visit each other a lot now. He comes down here, I go up to Anstruther. He sees a bit of Jan's mother. She teaches in the same school my Mum did. She's divorced and they live near each other.

'Ellen's my sister, by the way. She's three years older than me. She's nice, our Ellen, but she's married to a real chuckie. He's in Marketing with an oil company. They moved out to France last year. He works in Lyon, and they live a bit outside it, quite close to the Swiss border. It's funny, when we were kids I thought Ellen was a real tough cookie. No, scratch that, Ellen *was* a real tough cookie. Now she's a housewife, with a teaching qualification and no job, waiting on her man and, as far as I can gather being ignored by him most of the time.'

I looked at her. 'Bored?'

'No, fascinated. Go on.'

I sloshed some more of the old T down my neck. 'Where was I? Grew up in Anstruther, played for the school team, kept myself physically intact by being the fastest thing on two feet in the whole school. Buggery was a playground sport in our place, but none of the guys with low foreheads and trailing knuckles could catch me!

'I left school at eighteen and came to Edinburgh to do an Arts degree. I've been here ever since. I came out with a two–two in Philosophy, Politics and Economics. I had dreams of getting a job as a researcher for the Labour Party, but I discovered that those jobs were filled by firsts or two–ones, and more often than not by Americans. I also discovered that my Mum's death had left me feeling that politics isn't worth a monkey's anyway. So I joined the police.

'I hated it from Day One, but after I'd been in a few months, I met a pal from university. He was working for an Investigation Agency, and he said that they'd a vacancy. So I hung up my truncheon and went to work for them.'

'I thought you were self-employed?'

I tilted my head back and sent the last of the Old Throggies on the start of the long journey to the sea. 'I am. The guys we worked for were a pair of real rat bastards. They were ex-RAF Military Policemen, and they'd taken their talents for persecution into the private sector. They came from the time when there were big bucks to be made from matrimonial work, and they were never happier than when they were photographing a misbehaving couple on the job, or pounding on hotel room doors, shouting "Come out, come out, the game's a bogey!" I could see that these plonkers were living in the past, and I couldn't see why they should be doing so on the strength of our honest toil.

'So I hung in there for a year, until the clients got to know me. Then my pal Jimmy and I went round them all, offered them the same service for less money than Fagin and Bill Sykes were charging, and signed the lot up. We ran it as a partnership until three years ago, when Jimmy's Dad retired and he went off to run his pub. Since then I've been on my own, although Jimmy still helps me out when I'm on holiday, or over-booked.

'When I'm not working, I play golf with my Dad, go to the movies, listen to an eclectic collection of music, and pursue women.'

'You mean they don't pursue you?'

She finished her lager. 'Two for the road?' she asked, gladdening my heart still more. A woman who buys her round! I nodded, and she eased her way through to the bar, fishing a tenner from her purse as she went. I watched, anxiously, to make sure that not even one half of the fiver slipped out.

She was back in a couple of minutes, carrying a pint in each hand. 'On the subject of women . . .' she began. I guessed what was coming. '. . . what about Jan? If your Dad and her Mum are friends, how about you two?'

'Jan's great. We grew up together. Same class at school and all that. She's someone's dream woman, no doubt about it, but not mine. We tried the getting serious bit, went on holiday together a couple of times, but we agreed early on it wouldn't work long-term. We know that we're best off being pals. I haven't had a real steady since Thingummy left a few years back. Jan, on the other hand, if she felt like it, could pull blokes as easy as picking her nose. She's just got her own tastes, that's all.'

She looked at me over the top of her glass, teasing. 'And you haven't?'

For once I was ready. 'Oh contrayre, Madame. Fussiest of the fussy, that's Oz Blackstone. Look at the company I keep.'

She smiled, and I wasn't sure that under the blusher, she wasn't blushing. I slipped my arms around her waist and drew her against me. We smiled at each other, saying nothing, but exchanging secrets and making promises for the not-too-distant future. Yet I could tell that underneath it all her sexual self-confidence was something of an act. Every so often she would break off eye contact, only to look up again into my face, with a half-grin that said, 'Be kind to me, that's all I ask.'

'Of course I will,' I said, and she understood. I felt the air begin to sizzle between us. '*It's kissing time in Whighams*,' I thought. We leaned closer to each other.

'Hey there, you two!' The voice was unmistakable. We separated and looked across the crowded bar, guiltily I expect, at the gallus figure of Mike Dylan. As he pushed his way over to us, another man followed behind him. Dylan's introduction was unnecessary; I knew this one well enough. He even knew me. 'This is my boss,' said Dylan, 'Detective Superintendent Richard Ross, area head of CID. I was just filling him in on this morning's events.

'These are the poor people who found the body. Miss Phillips and Mr Blackstone.' He looked at me, with just a trace of truculence. I could read his mind. '*Tough shit, Dylan*,' I wanted to say, '*she's taken*.'

Ricky Ross was a different sort of copper to the DI. For a start he really *was* a Clever Bastard. He was a big, athletic bloke, good-looking, his dark hair flecked with grey; a man of substance in every way, unlike his sidekick, who had nothing behind the Armani suit but brass neck and ambition. In his younger days, he'd been quite a sportsman, with about a dozen rugby caps for Scotland as a flank forward. 'I remember you,' he said. 'Oxgangs, a few years back. You were a probationer, but you took our training into the PI line. I forgave you, though, when you stitched up those two bastards Banks and McHugh. They needed taking care of. So how's business?'

I gave him the obligatory shrug. 'I'm doing all right. Not as well as you, though. You seem never to be out of the bloody papers.'

It was his turn to shrug. 'People keep committing crimes, we keep clearing them up. It's the law of supply and demand in reverse. The public demands action, my lot supply it, and I take the credit.'

He glanced at me with a grin I didn't like. 'You must have

had a scare this morning. Christ, I remember you on a turn-out once. It was a drugs overdose, but CID got involved. You were the greenest probationer I'd ever seen, greener even than Michael here at his first murder.'

He looked down at Prim. 'And how about you, Miss Phillips? Are you okay now?'

'Fine thanks,' said Prim. 'I'm just glad that Oz was with me, otherwise I'd have been scared to death.'

'Mmm,' said Ross, with a half-smile. 'Just as well. Tell me, have you made contact with your sister yet?'

She looked up at him, sharply. 'I haven't a clue where my sister is, any more than I know which of her friends had the key to my flat. Believe me, when I find out . . .'

Ross nodded. 'Aye, sure. Just let us know when you do.'

I decided to chance my arm. 'Have you identified the body yet?'

'Naw,' said Ross. 'Not a notion. We were thinking about circulating a description of his cock. That's probably our best chance of a response.'

Prim frowned at him. She has a rare talent for making men feel ill at ease, but Ricky Ross was beyond her reach. He simply ignored her, continuing to smile at me. 'Nae use to him now though, Blackstone, is it? Wonder if he's left it to anyone in his will?'

'Aye,' I agreed, 'and even if it was shared out, I can think of a couple of polismen who'd find just half of it an improvement! Present company excepted, of course,' I added, after a pause. 'Can I get you a drink?' I asked, as Prim spluttered beside me.

The phrase 'Can I get you a drink?' is a device which is, as far as I know, peculiar to Edinburgh. Its meaning depends entirely on the company in which the enquirer finds himself, and, with the finest inflection, shifts from a wholly sincere, 'Can I get you a drink?' to an equally sincere, 'If that's all you've got to say, why don't you fuck off and leave us alone?'

Ross read my meaning correctly. 'No thanks, we're meeting someone. He's over there, in fact.' I turned to follow his gaze and caught the eye of a thin, sallow man, who I seemed to remember was a car dealer with a reputation for supplying MOT's to fit all price ranges.

'Oh. Okay, then. We'll look in tomorrow to give you those statements, Inspector.'

The men in suits made their way round the bar, the pack opening up to let them pass at my deliberately loud mention of Dylan's rank. As they reached the other side, Ricky Ross shot a look towards us, back across the crowded room, which made me feel suddenly that I might just have taken too big a liberty.

'I didn't like him at all!' said Prim, as they were out of earshot.

'No,' I said. 'Welcome to the club. It's difficult to underestimate a bloke like Dylan, but Ross is in a different league. He operates at a much higher level of nastiness.'

I reached for my glass, but found that during our conversation with the forces of the law an over-zealous bar steward, or an out and out thief, had removed it, and Prim's lager, although each had been at least half-full. I started towards the bar, but she tugged my arm. 'Come on. Forget those, it's time for that pizza.'

I should have known. It was Thursday and so the Bar Roma was heaving, without a table in sight. Prim looked at me, frustrated beyond belief, until I put yet another Plan B into operation. We commandeered a taxi from the rank outside Fraser's and headed for the Pizzarama, halfway up Leith Walk, purveyors of the biggest pizza in town. We bought two monsters to go, then grabbed another taxi and went back to the loft and my extensive, if inexpensive, wine cellar.

A great takeaway pizza is always slightly underdone. The Pizzarama giants, covered in tomato, pepperoni, ham, artichokes and God knew what else, fitted into my oven at a squeeze, and by the time we had finished the champagne – if you leave a teaspoon in the neck of an opened bottle of fizz, it keeps its fizziness; not many people know that – and opened a bottle of Safeway Chianti, they were ready.

Watching Prim eat her first pizza for a year was another of those seminal whatnots. She cut the huge thing into segments which she attacked with her fingers, savouring each ripped-off mouthful, smiling all the time, even as she chewed. When she finished, I still had a third of mine to go. She looked across the breakfast bar at me, her eyes huge and appealing. 'Okay,' I said. 'I give in. Would you like some more, my dear?'

The Chianti was new and strong. As we reached the end of the bottle, I felt relaxed, uninhibited and very, very . . .

Prim licked the last of the pizza from her fingers and gazed across at me. 'Remember that poor young policeman today?'

'Who could forget the poor wee bugger? And that effing troll stood in the doorway trying not to hear him? Why d'you ask?'

'It's just that tonight, when you said what you said to Ross, I thought for a second, I was going to do the same thing as the boy did.'

'I'm almost sorry you didn't. There have been many firsts in my life today. That would have been yet another.'

She drained her glass, and reached for another bottle from the rack, but I reached out a hand and stopped her.

'Prim,' I said, doing my level best to make my eyes outshine anything in the night sky, framed in the kitchen window. 'I've been thinking. How would it be – and this has to be a mutually agreed thing, you understand – if we decided, first of all that our deeply held principles and rules must remain unbroken, but that in all the circumstances, you should regard lunch today as having been our first date, and by the same token, that should regard myself as having been out with you at least twice?'

Our elbows were on the breakfast bar. I slipped my right hand into hers, as if we were about to arm-wrestle, and pulled her gently towards me. I kissed her, on the lips again, on her full red lips, not at all chastely this time. Her mouth opened, and I felt her tongue flick against my teeth.

She tasted of the finest sweet wine, delicious, refreshing, making me long for more.

'In all the circumstances,' she whispered, our foreheads touching lightly, 'and given the duration of our acquaintance I would say that such an agreement is, at this moment in time, absolutely . . .'

In which the Earth moves.

'Primavera, Primavera . . .' I moaned her name in the moonlight which flooded down upon us from the belvedere. She leaned over me, kissing my chest, gently biting my nipples, responding to my touch and moving her self against my hands.

'Where have you come from?' I asked, drawing her down upon me, and throwing the quilt to one side so that I could wallow again in the perfection of her body, in her firm, full, big-nippled breasts, in the amazing narrowness of her waist, in the round curve of her hips, in the flatness of her belly, in the thick nest of wiry blonde hair at her centre, shining and sparkling as she moved in the moonbeam.

'I've always been here,' she said, and she kissed me with her lips of velvet, as I had never been kissed before. 'I think we've both been moving towards each other, all our lives. I believe in destiny. You're part of mine, I'm part of yours. We were set on a course towards each other.'

'And will we go on together, Springtime and Oz?'

'Who knows? That's the thing about destiny; you believe in it and let it take you where it will. *Right now* we're together, and it's always the now that counts.'

I rolled over with Springtime in my arms, burying my face in her. As I flicked my tongue in and out of her navel, she gasped and arched her back. 'I want you now. I need you now. Come into me now.'

I placed a finger across her lips. 'Time enough,' I said, although she could see that I was more than ready. I bent and kissed the inside of her thighs as she spread them wide, licking my way towards her. She moaned again. 'Now, Oz, now.'

'Yes, Primavera, yes!' I covered her and she took me into herself with a supple movement, the sweetest embrace I had ever known. We lay entwined, barely moving. Her tongue was in my mouth again, her fingers wound through my crinkly hair. She pulled my head back and looked at me with smouldering eyes. 'This is right!' she hissed. Then her eyelids flickered and she began to shudder, gripping me tight, inside, tighter than I had ever imagined. Her fingers dug into my back, and she cried out, once, twice, again, again. And then I realised that two voices were calling out and that one of them was mine. I was lost. As I thrust into her and held myself there, we were washed by wave upon wave of sensation, by a feeling that every nerve-ending in our bodies was being bathed in soothing oil. It went on and on until I thought it would never stop, but finally the crest was reached and we started back down the slope towards the world, a world which I knew now, for certain, would never be the same again.

She lay there, eyes closed, with a sheen of sweat on her face. I licked it off; she tasted salty and sublime on my tongue. I felt myself start to subside, but she held me inside her. 'No, don't go,' she sighed. 'I want to keep you there for ever.'

'That's all right with me,' I said. 'I can't think of a better place to be. Primavera . . . stop me if you think I'm being daft, but . . . Primavera Phillips, you are the most beautiful, wonderful woman I have ever met, and I love you. You're the dream I've had all my life, and now you're here.

'I know we've still to see our first sun come up together, but say you'll stay with me.'

She touched my cheek with her soft, strong hand. 'I'll stay with you for now, Osbert Blackstone. But you're crazy; you don't know me. You never really know another person. Some people, many people, maybe most people don't even know themselves.'

I smiled, filled up to the brim with more happiness than I had ever imagined I could hold. '*I* know myself, lover. And whatever you say I know you too. I want you now, and for all the tomorrows I've got coming.'

We lay there, in each other's arms, together. I closed my eyes, as she began to move over my body, sliding, animalistic. Suddenly I felt her nails dig deep into my chest. I don't mind being submissive on the odd occasion, but I've never been too good at masochism.

'Oww!' I yelled with the pain . . .

. . . and suddenly I was wide awake, staring into Wallace's accusatory reptilian eye. His claws were digging sharply into my pecs as he balanced himself upon me.

'Get off me, you green bastard,' I hissed, picking him up, carefully to avoid ripping more flesh, and placing him gently on the floor. I had forgotten that the settee was one of Wallace's favourite night-spots. I lay there, under my lonely blanket, in my bulging boxers, and tried to go back to my dream. But it was no use. Instead, I lay there, listening to the sleep sounds of Primavera Phillips, comparing them with those of Jan, my other night visitor. I decided that they were much the same, except that I hadn't noticed Prim farting yet.

'Two people are truly together,' my Dad told me once, when he was giving me my degree course in the meaning of life, 'only when they can fart freely and as loud as they please in each other's company.' I remember looking at him, appalled, quite certain that my Mother had never farted in her life.

I chuckled in the dark, quietly, lest I disturb Prim's melodious sleep.

'. . . at this moment in time, absolutely out of the question.' She had said, but with a delicious smile that told me she was in no way offended that I had put the proposition to her. And so we had retired, she to the bed, and me to the instrument called my sofa-bed. I can never decide whether it is an instrument of torture or of music. Some nights it's both as your toes and knuckles hit the sharp-cornered metal frame or as the springs dig into you, singing out tunelessly as you twist and turn, trying to negotiate the pathway to sleep's dark gate.

I rolled over on to my side and the full spring orchestra played. The twang even startled Wallace. I heard Prim start from her sleep, and saw her silhouette as she sat up.

'Sorry,' I said. 'This thing can be bloody noisy.' I bounced on the machine to show what had wakened her. 'I'll try to lie still.'

'No, it's okay. I had a good kip during the day, remember. What time is it?'

'Around five, I think.'

'Ow. D'you want to swop over? You take the bed and I'll have the sofa?'

'Thanks, but it's okay,' I said to her. I paused. 'Hey, now we're awake how about you telling me your life story. Let me into all your secrets. After that, how would it be if we get up and go for a walk up Arthur's Seat, to watch the sun come up behind Berwick Law?'

There was silence as she weighed my latest proposition. 'Yes,' she said at last. 'You know, Oz, my love . . .' Her tone may have been bantering, but my heart jumped as she said the word. '. . . I reckon that if I stripped everything away from you, right at your core I'd find a hopeless romantic . . . just like me. Yes, let's go for that walk.

'But first, the unexpurgated adventures of Primavera Phillips. If you think you're ready.'

Twenty minutes later, there was nothing I didn't know about her. She had been born in Auchterarder to her oddball parents thirty years before. Her mother – when she wasn't reading Barbara Taylor Bradford – had been a social worker, but was now a moderately successful writer of children's books. Her father's modelmaking had evolved from a cabinetmaking and furniture design business. She and her sister Dawn, who was five years younger, had been educated solidly at local authority schools, until they had been old enough to escape from their home village.

Prim had trained as a nurse in Glasgow, and had worked in Edinburgh Royal, before joining the dedicated staff of St Columba's Hospice. 'If you'd been there a few years earlier, you'd have nursed my Mum,' I said, when she told me. 'That's a vocation, and no mistake.'

'Yes, I thought it was, but it wore off after four years. I found that was I drinking too much; worse than that, I was drinking too much on my own, at home. I was narky, too, all the time. I wasn't me, any more.' I sensed her looking at me in the dark, suddenly, strangely intense. 'Never forget that, Oz. I always have to be me!'

In the gloom, I could see her scratching her nose. 'I don't

know why, but while I was working there, gradually I gave up men. Not that I was promiscuous, mind you. Up until now, I've had six lovers, but hospice work turned me into a celibate.'

I propped myself upon an elbow. 'What are the chances of a miracle cure?'

'Let's just put it this way,' she said, with a laugh in her husky voice. 'A vacancy may arise in the future. Your application for the post has been noted, and is under consideration. You will be advised of the outcome in due course. For now, that's all I'm saying.'

I tried to look solemn. 'Thank you for that information. You may keep my application and my CV on your files until further notice.' I've never been much good at solemnity. I grinned in the dark. 'So when did you notice the first signs of a thaw?'

'This afternoon. When I woke up in your bed with that weird bloody iguana alongside me! I looked across at you, and saw you at work, and I thought "*Look at that daft bugger there! What's he like?*" And all of a sudden I felt that, yes, it might be possible to get some fun out of life again.'

I almost said, 'Oh it is! Let me show you!' Instead, trying to convince her that I really am responsible and self-disciplined, I steered the conversation back on course.

'Why did you leave the hospice? Had you just had enough?'

'Yeah; as much as I could take. One thing more than any other finished me, though; I had this pal on the staff. She hit the compassion wall, and left. A year later, she was back as a patient. We couldn't tell her anything about what was happening, of course. She knew it all. The day she died, I resigned, to give myself a chance to forget. I never will though. I'll never go far enough to forget that.'

'Is that why you went to Africa? To forget?'

'No. I had reasons, two of them. First, I was overcome by a sudden inability to sit still. It didn't matter where I was, I felt shut in. Second, I wanted to help people live, not die. I got very grand, and decided to go on a personal crusade. So I answered an ad, and went to work for a UN-sponsored agency in Central Africa. I thought I'd be teaching nutrition, working with babies, that sort of thing. So I was, for two months. Then a Civil War started, and the casualties started to arrive.

'I had no idea what modern armaments can do to the human body. Now I have. I've patched them up, and helped cut bits off. But there's worse; you have no idea what people can do to other people. That wee man yesterday, he had a quick finish, believe me. The story I told Dylan was true, but . . .' Even in the night, I could see her shudder, suddenly, '. . . what they did to the women!'

'Was it like that for a whole year?'

'No, I couldn't have taken that. We were rotated. Most of the time we were in a hospital in a safe zone, but every so often we were asked to go up front with the troops.'

Now it was my turn to shudder. 'Weren't you in danger?'

'I don't think so. We had UN soldiers as our escort. They taught us to shoot, too, and gave us handguns.'

'Christ, I must remember that!'

'You do that! I'm a crack shot.'

'Me too,' I murmured, too quietly for her to hear.

In which the Earth moves . . . again.

Back to back like old school chums, we dressed ourselves in heavy sweaters, jeans and boots . . . Primavera seemed to have everything in that vast holdall.

I drove us down Holyrood Road and into the Queen's Park, up the hill to the wee loch, where, thanks to the trippers, no ducks ever had it so good. The moon was long gone, but there was a hint of daybreak in the east as we set off up the steep slopes of Arthur's seat, so that we could see the path well enough. Prim took the lead; gallantly, I thought, I allowed her to go ahead. It took me around three minutes to realise that she had mountain goat in her ancestry. Our conversation dried up as I saved my breath to keep up with her brisk pace. Up and up we climbed, scrambling hand and foot up the final stretch, until we came to the summit of the old volcano, to stand beside the Solstice cairn.

At our backs, the street lights of the Old Town shone softly, and the floodlit buildings stood out on the hill, with the Castle at its summit. Before us, as we looked east, recovering our breath, the day was beginning to assert itself. Around twenty miles away, we could see the outline of North Berwick Law, a slightly scaled-down version of the hill on which we stood. All down the Forth, in the mouth of the estuary, lighthouses still sent out their signature beams; on the great seagull's head that was the Bass Rock, away across at Barns Ness in Fife and most distant of all on the Island of May.

I took out two Mars bars which I had secreted about my person, and handed one to my lady. 'There y'are, Springtime. Our first breakfast together!'

She looked and laughed, 'Did you make these at the same time you made those tuna rolls yesterday?'

'Aye. I'm a dab hand. They're not a patch on my Curlywurly though!' See me, see sexual innuendo!

We looked eastward again and saw the line of light along the horizon deepen, and eat its way upward into the sky, diluting and beating back the darkness. Patches of morning mist lay in gullies along the plain between the Lammermuir Hills and the sea, moving and shifting very slowly, as they began to yield to the rising temperature.

'It's like being in an aeroplane, above the clouds,' said Prim. 'Do you do this often?'

I looked down at her, held in the circle of my arm, and I smiled. 'Never done it in my life before. It's been one of those things you think of doing, but never quite get round to. Tonight, this morning, whatever, I realise that I've been saving it to share with the right person.'

'That's very profound, for you, Osbert.'

'Aye, but don't worry, I'll be back to normal soon.'

Around the Law, in the distance, the light began to intensify. We watched as it strengthened; we watched the rotation of the planet at the horizon dipped, revealing the great golden ball, and the day began. 'D'you realise what's happening, Primavera? The Earth's moving for us!'

She squeezed me tight, almost crushing my ribs. 'I was right, Blackstone. You're a romantic to the core.' She stood up on tiptoe and she kissed me, softly, her arms round my neck, my arms encircling her narrow waist. 'D'you still fancy me, then, even in this gear?' she asked.

'Dressed from head to toe in a black bin-liner, I'd still fancy you,' I said in a sudden outburst of total candour. Something welled up in my throat, and I realised it was a lump.

Suddenly there was a noise below us, a panting, scrambling noise. We looked down in surprise, to see the first of the morning joggers cresting the summit. She pulled herself on to the small flat peak and fell face-first against the cairn, gasping.

'Morning,' said I.

The woman looked round. 'Christ, you're early,' she spluttered.

'Oh, I'm sorry to disappoint you, Miss,' I said. 'I'm not him. He's got a beard, and he wears a dress. You never know though, if you wait long enough, this is the sort of place where he might turn up. More likely it'll be in Glasgow, though. He's more needed there.

'Come Magdalene,' I said, tugging Prim's waist, and wincing as she nipped my bum to shut me up. 'We'd best get back down.

'So long,' I said to the speechless, knackered jogger. 'Enjoy the morning, it's worth the effort.'

We picked our way down the almost sheer path from the summit, on to the gentler, but still steep descent. Two more runners were starting out from the road below. As we walked hand in hand, more relaxed than on the ascent, a flight of swans made their way slowly and clumsily across the sky, on their way to St Margaret's Loch and another hard day's work, posing for tourist photographers and gobbling stale breadcrumbs.

'They're not very good at flying, are they,' said Prim.

'Thank the Lord for that. They're good in the water and aggressive on land. If they were air aces as well the CIA would be training them as operatives!'

As we walked on down the path, a piece of the day before came back into my mind. 'Prim, that bottle in the kitchen. Prozac. Why should Dawn be on the happy pills?'

She looked up at me anxiously. 'I don't know. It came as a shock to me. Dawn's always been moody, very up one minute, very down the next. Maybe, with me being away, there's been no-one to help her through the down bits.'

'Not even Willie Kane?'

'Seems not.'

There were three more parked cars when we reached the roadway, one per jogger, I assumed. We drove around the south side of the great hill, until the Old Town stretched before us again, blinking itself awake. I parked and we walked up to the High Street, to pick up the makings of a real breakfast from Ali's.

The turbanned one was on duty early as always. If there are people there and pennies to be taken in, Ali will take them. 'Hullaw ther, Ozzie,' he bellowed. I've never been quite sure whether Ali accentuates his Scots accent. 'Hullaw tae you, hen,' he added, catching sight of Prim.

'Ali, this is Miss Phillips. Remember her and don't give her any of your past sell-by stuff.

'See him, love,' I said, pointing to the grinning Asiatic. 'This one is Edinburgh's cheekiest grocer. Ali thinks customer relations means . . . No. On second thoughts I don't think I'll tell you that!'

Ali's one of my best pals. He and I, and eight other nutters, play five-a-side football together at Meadowbank Stadium, every Tuesday evening in life. We arrange our lives around our weekly session, which, like most informal football clubs, is simply on excuse for a few bevvies.

Ali's at his best as a defender. Me, I see myself as a cultured midfielder, in the Jim Baxter mould. The truth is, the Great Jim and I have one thing in common. We're both Fifers; that's it. Where he could have opened a combination lock with his left foot, mine is purely for standing on. The other one isn't up to much either, except that in our team, I am the acknowledged master of the toe-poke, a distinctive way of shooting, stiff-ankled, with great power and accuracy. The toe-poke is derided by all serious footballers, and brings me much scorn, but usually from opponents, as they pick the ball out of their net.

That morning, instead of a neat through ball, Ali passed me bacon, eggs, rolls, bread, orange juice, honey, milk and, on a 'Please,' from Primavera, square, spicy, sliced Lorne sausage. Continentals look down on the British as sausage-makers. Their idea of sausage is something to be sliced razor thin, something that looks as if it came out of an animal, rather than being made from it. Give me German, French, Italian or Spaniard, and let me confront any one with a square slice of Ali's Scottish sausage, grilled, in a white crusty roll. That would put the buggers in their place.

We ate ours with HP sauce for extra body, washing them down with orange juice. Then we showered and dressed for the day. I suggested showering together to save energy, but Prim offered me a pound coin for the meter.

Afterwards, we sat upstairs on the sofa in the loft, Primavera in my dressing gown and me in a sort of towelling kilt thing with a Velcro fastening that an ex had given me one Christmas and which I found buried in a heap at the foot of the wardrobe. The doors were open, and Wallace lay somnolent on the terrace, looking back at us, occasionally and disdainfully. Wallace lives for three things, sunshine, sleep and sustenance. The last of these takes many forms, most of them crunchy.

On our first morning together we drank honey-sweetened tea, settling into our new situation. I punched her shoulder lightly. 'Hey, Springtime. If I get that job we were talking about how about bringing the rest of your stuff down here?'

She looked at me, seriously for once, just a bit guarded. My stomach twitched.

'It's fine where it is just now. First things first. I've been putting off the evil hour, but I've got to find out what's happened to my sister.

'I don't believe for a second that Dawn killed that poor wee man; but she *has* disappeared. Before we think about what we do with that fiver, I've got to know where Dawn is, and to be sure she's all right. Oz, you're the detective. I need your help.'

I squeezed her hand. 'I told you love, I'm an enquiry agent, not a private eye. Different jobs, different people. But for you and Dawn, I'll help all I can.'

I sat silent for a while, trying to think not just about facts, but about the conclusions which they suggest. All my working life, I've trained myself not to use my imagination, or to encourage in any way embroidery by witnesses. All of a sudden I found that putting my mind to work, as well as my listening, interviewing and literacy skills, was a stimulating prospect.

'Okay then. What we have to do is to think of the options, and discount them if we can.

'One, and let me finish. Are you wrong, and *did* Dawn bump off Mighty Mouse? Did she encourage him to embezzle the money, and set up the bank account, with the intention of killing him when the time came?' Prim frowned at me, and shook her head.

'Think of how we found Kane. He died having sex, or at the very least in an aroused state. The police lab will know by now which it was. Whichever, he was Dawn's lover, so that seems to put her at the scene. Did she get him excited, get on top of him and at the right moment produce that knife from under the bedclothes and summon up the strength to shove it up under his chin? That's Option One.'

'And I don't believe it, not for one bloody minute!' said Prim, vehemently.

I shrugged my shoulders. 'I don't either, but it's the easy option, and that's the one the police will go for, unless we can show them different.

'Option Two. Dawn has another man, an accomplice. They found Kane, set him up by the oldest means known to mankind, then the other bloke killed him. That paints a nasty picture, and I don't buy that either, but again, when they know the whole story, the police would. They could even find a second suspect without too much trouble.'

She looked at me, puzzled. 'Who?'

'Raymond Archer. He knew everything about that firm. He could have done everything that he told me Kane did, if he'd had Dawn to help him. Sending me along to find the body could just have been part of it.'

'Okay,' said Primavera. 'So what's Option Three?'

'Someone else knows about the fraud, and about the bank account. He breaks into the flat, and kills Kane. He tried to make Dawn give him the fiver, but she persuades him she doesn't know where it is. He leaves and takes her with him.

'Again, that someone else could just be Archer.'

I squeezed her hand again and turned her face towards me. 'Those are all the possibilities I can see. I prefer the third one, for a very good reason. If either one or two was right, the banknote wouldn't still have been there for the police to find and you to pick up. My best guess is that Dawn's been taken, and that she's safe. Without her, the guy has a slim chance of getting his hands on that fiver.'

She looked me in the eye, earnestly. 'Thanks Oz, but there is a fourth choice. Maybe Dawn wasn't there at all. Maybe the story I spun the police was true. Maybe it was someone else.'

'*Yes, Prim, and maybe Willie Kane, the poor, innocent, browbeaten, middle-aged, infatuated stockbroker with the wee body and the huge cock, wasn't just two-timing his wife, but your sister as well, in your flat. Because he sure was diddling her. She wrote and told you all about him. Nijinsky, remember?*' That was what I thought. But what I said was, 'Okay love, let's check that out. She was with a theatre company, yes?'

She looked at me gratefully. 'Yes, the Lyceum, usually.'

'Right, we'll go there this morning. I've got a couple of quick interviews. I can do them both by ten-thirty, and type them up later, after we've been to the theatre and after we give our statements to Dylan.

'Meantime, let's see what the papers say.' We had picked up a *Scotsman* and a *Daily Record* at Ali's. With little to go on, each paper gave the story inside-page treatment, reporting that the police were still trying to identify a man found stabbed to death in a flat in Ebeneezer Street. He was described as around forty, portly, and around five feet four inches in height.

It struck me, idly, that if we handed the fiver to Archer, and sold our story to the *Record*, we would make more than the ten per cent cut on offer. It came to me also, forcefully, through the enshrouding mist of love, that as well we would stand to do at least six months each for wasting police time, withholding information, stealing evidence, and anything else the Clever Bastards chose to chuck at us.

I gulped, and looked down at Prim, her head resting happily against my chest, her hand lying innocently on the outside of my thigh. I decided that I would keep the dangers of our tightrope walk across the chasm of uncertainty strictly to myself.

'The things you do for love, Oz,' I whispered. She heard me and smiled up, quizzically. As she did, her hand moved fractionally on my thigh. I stood up quickly, before she found out, before she was ready, that it's true what they say about us Scots guys, even when our kilts are made of towelling.

In which we meet a camp follower and learn of Dawn's big break.

I'm not exactly a regular theatregoer. Every so often I've been persuaded by a lady to take her to one of the big musicals they put on for long runs at the Playhouse, but live events are not really my thing. That said, on the few occasions when I have been lured along there, the Lyceum has always struck me as a nice wee hall. It's got a friendly feel about it; it isn't grandiose like the Festival Theatre, or such a big barn of a place that the sound bends into funny shapes if you're sat up in the Gods.

When we parked in Grindlay Street, I jumped out of the car and headed off towards the glazed foyer. I thought that Prim had fallen in behind me, but she stopped me with a whistle. '*Wow, she can even whistle*,' I thought.

'Not there,' she said, 'the offices are across the street.' So instead, I followed her, watching her skirt swish from side to side with the delicious movement of her explosive hips.

The administration and rehearsal rooms of the Lyceum were up a close, and behind an anonymous door. There was no obvious reception area and so we wandered along a corridor, looking for signs of life. The corridor ended in a double door. I looked at Prim, shrugged my shoulders and opened it, gently and slowly.

We stepped into a big room with a few chairs and other odds and ends of furniture scattered haphazardly around. In its centre, a man sat, with his back to us. He hadn't heard us come in and stayed in his seat, bent over as if reading something in his lap.

I felt that a theatrical cough was appropriate. The bloke straightened up with a start, then twisted in his chair to peer over his shoulder at us. He wore glasses and had a long nose. The way he stared, I formed the distinct impression that he was looking down it at us. And I didn't like that much. 'Yeasss?' he said, in a voice that rang with luvvieness. 'Are we lost, little people?'

I don't like being patronised at the best of times, and especially not by a tall, disjointed pillock with limp wrists, long, highlighted hair, a shirt with a frayed collar and a sweater that looked like an insect colony. 'No, chum,' I said, trying my best to sound like a private eye, 'we're not. But we're looking for someone who could be.'

He stood up. His jeans were even scruffier than his shirt and sweater. 'Indeed. And who might that be?'

Prim stepped forward, smiling her sweetest. 'My sister actually, Dawn Phillips. I'm Primavera. I've just got back from Africa and I've no idea where she is.' She waved a hand vaguely at me. 'This is Oz Blackstone, my boyfriend.' My heart swelled with pride, knowing that today it was pretty close to the truth.

'Ah,' said the thespian, 'once more, the fragile Dawn. I don't know if I'll be of much help to you, but I'll do my best.'

His tone was different. It's funny, but Prim is one of those people that it's just impossible to patronise, as Dylan had discovered, the hard way.

'I am Rawdon Brooks,' he said, with the briefest of courtly bows. '*What a prat!*' I thought. 'I am the Artistic Director of this humble repertory. Normally, Primavera – what a wonderful name – you would find Dawn here or close by, but not today, I'm afraid.

'We have a visiting company in the Lyceum at the moment. We don't go into rehearsal for another ten days. During that time, your sister should be making her big breakthrough into moviedom. Far from being lost, you could say she's been discovered.

'There are some Americans around, making one of these awful kilt and claymore things. *Son of Rob Roy* or some such nonsense. Dawn has a small part in it, but she'll get billing for it. She's playing a camp follower . . .' '*A bit like you then*,' I almost said. '. . . or something, dressed up in a scanty plaid, I should imagine, and being ravished by the fearful Redcoats.'

'Billy Butlin's got a lot to answer for,' I muttered, but Brooks was in full declaiming mode.

'The trouble with these operations is that they shoot to a tight schedule, moving around all over the place. One day here, next day there, the day after, God knows where. So, while I am sure that she will be somewhere north of Perth – if she has scenes today, that is – I have no idea exactly where that would be.'

As you may have gathered, I'm the sort of guy who's big on first impressions, and this man had triggered off a creeping dislike in me. I did my best to suppress it. 'When did this gig begin? How long has she been away?'

'Since the beginning of last week.'

'So she's been out of town for the last ten days or so?' said Prim, questioning.

'That's possible, my dear, but she could have been back, then off again. As I said she has but a small part. It's unlikely she'd be shooting every day, and in Scotland – fearful place that it is – the wilderness is only a couple of hours away.'

I'm no rabid nationalist, but that was too much for me. 'Come on, pal. Wilderness! Ever heard of Moss Side?'

He looked at me, down that long nose again. 'Mmm. A touchy Jock, is he? Your wilderness is earning your country millions of dollars, my dear boy. You shouldn't be ashamed of it.'

'I'm not. But this "fearful" place is feeding you right now, so maybe you should show it more respect. And I warn you, if you say anything smart about pearls and swine, I shall kick you sharply in the balls . . . my dear.'

Brooks laughed and threw up his long flapping hands. 'Pax! Pax! I must stop provoking you chaps, or I really will get into trouble. The fellow yesterday was just as upset as you, but he was a policeman, so I got away with it.'

'I wouldn't bet on it. You'd better be careful where you park your car. What policeman was this, then?'

'He called here yesterday. He said he was CID, and he was asking questions about Dawn, too. I hope the child is all right. She's your sister,' he said to Prim, 'so you'll know how sensitive she can be. Just lately she's been very emotional. Every so often a spontaneous weep, other times unnaturally cheerful. I asked her if she had something on her mind, but she wouldn't say.'

'This copper,' I asked. 'Was he alone?'

'Yes, quite.'

'What time did he call?'

Brooks scratched the stubble on his chin. 'Just after I got in. Must have been around ten-fifteen.'
'What was his name?'
'You know, he didn't say.'
'Did he show you ID?'
'I didn't think to ask. It upsets them, you know. One doesn't like to provoke.'
'Can you describe him then?'
The actor laughed again. 'My dear boy, I have always assumed that policemen are called pigs because they all look exactly alike. He was just another aggressive chap in a raincoat, that's all.
'But tell me, why do you ask?'
Before I could conjure up a half-decent lie, Prim jumped in. 'Dawn was involved with a policeman for a while. He didn't like it when she chucked him, and he gave her a hard time.'
'Then she should complain to his superiors, surely.'
'That could be asking for even more trouble,' she said. 'You can't think of any quick way for us to trace Dawn, then, other than driving around the Highlands looking for movie lights?'
Brooks paused for a second or two. 'There's a company called Celtic Scenery, based down in Leith somewhere. They maintain a database of potential film sites. Visiting companies use them for advance work, choosing locations to suit story-lines, making sure that there are no electricity pylons in the background of the highland heroes, that sort of thing.' I smiled briefly to myself, remembering jet trails in the sky in a B-movie Western that I'd seen on TV as a kid. 'If they've been involved, they might have a copy of the shooting schedule.
'That's as much help as I can give you. Now I must return to my script.' He turned his back on us abruptly and rearranged himself, artistically, on his chair.

'Thank you very much, Mr Brooks,' said Prim. Without turning, he waved a hand, feebly. We made our way back into the corridor and out of the building.

The morning sunshine was refreshing after the gloom of the rehearsal room. 'What an arsehole that guy is!' I spluttered as we emerged.

'Ah, my darling,' said Prim. 'That's your inherent Scottish homophobia coming out.'

I looked at her in surprise. 'Homoph . . . So you reckon he is too?'

'As queer as a nineteen pound note, so Dawn said in one of her letters. It used to be a three pound note: that's inflation for you, eh?'

I thought about it. 'No, I won't have the term homophobia used about me. I've never been afraid of a homosexual in my life. I'm a liberal in that respect. A couple of my best friends are gay. That bloke in there could be as straight as an arrow and he'd still be an arsehole.'

'I agree,' she said, 'but he was useful though. Celtic Scenery can be our next stop, after we see Dylan. Could he have been the policeman who visited Brooks, d'you think?'

'Not unless he was hell of a quick on his feet. Mike Dylan was at Leith to respond to Constable McArse's call only a few minutes after Brooks had his visit. And why would he have been asking questions about Dawn *before* Kane's body was found?

'There's no saying it was a policeman anyway. He was on his own, which isn't right. Brooks didn't see a warrant card, or even ask to see one.'

Prim smiled, mischievously. 'He was probably too busy having fantasies about truncheons.'

'Unworthy! No, that could have been anyone. It could even

have been the real killer.' A shudder swept through me. 'In fact, it probably was!'

Her eyes lit up. 'And if that's the case, it means that Dawn must have got away from him.'

'Aye, but it also means that he's looking for her. We'd better get a move on. Let's go back to the loft and see if we can find an address for Celtic Scenery in Good Old *Yellow Pages*.'

In which Prim says 'Hello Mum', and the quest goes on.

GOYP let us down for once, but the good old Royal Mail Postal Address book turned up trumps. Celtic Scenery was listed at a quayside address in Leith Docks, less than a mile from the police station in Queen Charlotte Street, where we were to meet Dylan.

We sat on the sofa, clothed this time. At our feet, Wallace's endless pursuit of the sun had taken him to a square in the middle of the varnished wooden floor where he sprawled contentedly, crunching away at a bowl of Wonder Weinie Iguana Superfood.

I put the Royal Mail book back in a drawer in my desk. 'Ready to go?' I asked Primavera.

She stood up. 'Yes, but can I make a quick call first, to my Mum. I should have called yesterday, but with one thing and another . . .'

'Sure, you do that, I'll leave you to it.'

'No, you wait right here.'

She picked up the black handset and punched a telephone

number into the dialling panel, fidgeting nervously as it rang out.

'Mum?' Her face lit up with a huge smile. 'It's me. I'm back home. Yes, I'm safe, and I'm well. In fact, I'm better than I've been in years.' She paused. 'Why should you leap to that conclusion? Yes, I am; but we're friends that's all. Yes, he's here. I'm at his place in fact . . . Don't "Oh yes" me, Mother!'

She glanced up at me. 'His name's Oz Blackstone and he's daft. Here Oz, say hello to Mum.' She thrust the phone at me.

'Hello Mrs Phillips,' I said to British Telecom, 'how are you?'

'Very well, thank you Oz.' Her voice sounded hearty, in a country sort of way. 'So you're daft, are you. In that case you and Primavera should get on very well together. She sounds very happy.'

I tried to think of an appropriate answer. 'I think she is, Mrs Phillips. There's no accounting for taste. Here she is again.' I returned the phone to Prim.

'Mum, we've got to go out right now, but we'll come up to see you as soon as we can. Let's see how the weekend goes. Yes, he is. 'Bye.'

She hung up. 'Mum said you sound charming.' She kissed me, quickly. I kissed her in return, more slowly.

For a second or two her body moulded itself against mine, until she pulled herself away and held me at arm's length. 'Oz, I told you, first things first. My sister's in trouble, and it's up to you and I to find her.'

In which we tell porkies for the record, pick up Dawn's trail, and discover that the law isn't as big an ass as it looks.

Prim's phone call had made it impossible for us to fit in Celtic Scenery before the police, and so we headed directly for the Leith Station, a drab Victorian building in Queen Charlotte Street.

I went up to the bar of the general office and introduced myself, and Prim, to the constable on duty. 'DI Dylan's expecting us,' I told her. She looked at me in what I took for slight surprise. 'Take a seat over there,' she ordered, pointing. I looked at the uncomfortable wooden bench and decided to disobey.

A few minutes later a businesslike young man in his mid-twenties appeared through a half-glazed door labelled 'Private'.

'Good morning,' he said, although incorrect by a few minutes. 'I'm Detective Constable Morrow. Mr Dylan's apologies, but he had to go out on enquiries. He's asked me to take your statements. He said it was just a formality.'

He led us through to a small, windowless, airless interview room. It smelled of earlier occupants, and I guessed it was that special kind of room you hear about in police stations, with walls which move about on occasions; such as when a suspect proves difficult, or provocative.

Morrow was a nice lad, and actually meant it when he apologised for the conditions. 'We have all this high-tech stuff now,' he said, 'yet we still have to interview ordinary decent folk like you in smelly wee rooms like this.'

He asked us only the most basic questions, allowing us to tell our stories unprompted to the tape recorder. We were lying for the record this time, and that worried me, more than slightly. But with Archer's secret, my doubts about him, and Dawn's predicament whirling about in my mind, I plunged on, comforting myself with the hope that one part of our story might well become true, even if retrospectively.

It didn't take long. When I was a trainee copper, I'd had to take my statements down in longhand in a daft wee notebook, in the knowledge that I might have to read them aloud in court. I had heard tales of what could happen to policemen in the witness box, and afterwards in the Chief Constable's office if their jotters had been doctored in any way. 'Let me see your notebook, officer,' is the last thing any Plod wants to hear the judge say when he's up there, in the box, under oath. My book was always impeccable, but for all that I was still a pretty awful copper.

'Thank you very much,' said young Morrow, when we had finished talking to the tape. 'I'll have these transcribed, then I'll ask you to sign them. It'll take about twenty minutes, half an hour at most. You can either wait, or look in again later. It's up to you.'

'We'll come back in,' I said, taking an executive decision. 'Will you be ready by one?'

He nodded, and showed us out through the front office and

into the street, where yet another traffic warden was prowling around my car. We jumped in quick and drove off, leaving her scowling in frustration.

It took us a while to find Celtic Scenery. You don't expect to find business offices right on a dockside, but that's where it was, tucked in behind the Malmaison Hotel, not far from the radio station.

The entire resources of the company turned out to be two networked computers, and two bright, energetic young women. This time, I left the talking to Prim.

The ladies looked at us in surprise as we entered. I guessed that theirs was a business which attracted few customers to the door. There was no counter and only one spare chair. We stood there awkwardly for a few seconds, until they stood up and came round from behind their desks.

'Hi,' said Prim. 'I hope you can help us.' She fished in her handbag and produced a driving licence. 'I'm looking for my sister, on a very urgent family matter. She's an actress; her name's Dawn Phillips. And here's mine, look.' She held out the driving licence for the women to inspect. They looked at it, but the suspicion on their faces was unwavering.

Prim ploughed on, using everything she had to establish her credibility. 'Rawdon Brooks, at the Lyceum, sent us down to see you. He told us that Dawn has a part in an American movie that's being shot on location over here. He couldn't remember the name, but he said it was a Highland epic, and he thought that you might have been involved with them.'

The women looked at each other, then at Prim, then at me, then at each other again. Finally one of them nodded, and went back to her work-station, leaving the other to deal with us. She was stocky and confident, dressed in jeans, a tee-shirt and sandals.

'It sounds like the remake of *Kidnapped*,' she said. 'It's Miles Grayson's new project. He's playing the lead and directing as usual. It's the second time he's used us to do set-ups for him.' Her face shone with professional pride. I wasn't surprised. Apart, maybe, from the President of the United States, the Pope and the Queen, Miles Grayson is the most famous human on the planet.

'We don't see the cast list,' the woman went on, 'so I can't tell you if your sister's there or not, but yes, we do know where they'll be today.' She paused. 'Look, it would be more than my life was worth to send you to the set, but I'll take a chance and tell you that they're booked into the Falls of Lora Hotel, in Connell Ferry, tonight and tomorrow.'

'Could we phone the hotel and check whether Dawn's there?' asked Prim.

The woman shook her head. 'No. We made a block booking for them, and they won't have checked in yet. If it's as urgent as all that you'll just have to go up there to look for her. It's not that long a drive, actually. Go via Bridge of Earn and you'll do it in about three hours.'

We thanked the girls and went back out to the dock. There was a breeze coming in off the sea. We stood there and looked around, across the grey-blue river mouth to the Waterfront Bistro, and beyond, to the new Government office building, in all its white awfulness. We grabbed a coke and a quick sandwich in the Malmaison Bar, then drove back up to the police station, parking this time outside the bakery in Elbe Street, seeking sanctuary from the wardens.

Young Morrow was in the front office as we entered the old building, at about twenty past one. 'Sorry,' I said, 'did we keep you from your lunch?' He smiled and shook his head, giving me the impression that lunch was for wimps.

'Here you are; they're all typed up and ready. There's no need to go through to the Black Hole again. If you'll just read them and sign them, that'll be it.'

We did as we were told. I gulped inwardly as I put my pen to our economies with the truth. 'How's the investigation going?' I asked, by way of conversation.

Morrow looked at me, unsmiling for the first time. He leaned towards me and whispered, so that only I could hear. 'The boss said to me that you used to be one of us, so I'll tell you. We identified the guy an hour ago. His name's William Kane. He's a stockbroker. He left his wife a wee while back, for another woman. The wife says she doesn't know who it was, but Dylan's going on the assumption that it was your girlfriend's sister. So if she shows up, we're going to want to speak to her.'

I winced with a show of concern. 'Shit!' I said quietly. 'Thanks for that. I can't believe that Dawn would get herself involved in that kind of situation, but don't worry, if she shows up in town I'll bring her to see you myself.'

We turned to leave. My hand was on the doorknob when he called after us. 'Oh! Miss Phillips, I almost forgot. Mr Dylan told me to ask you about that torn fiver you picked up yesterday. He said that technically he shouldn't have let you take anything from the house, so he asks, could he have it back for now?'

Prim looked at the young detective, all sweetness and blushing innocence. 'I'm really sorry,' she said, 'but I taped the two halves together and spent it. On groceries, I think. Inspector Dylan won't get into trouble, will he?' Morrow smiled grimly, as if trouble for Mike Dylan wouldn't bother him too much.

'Let's hope not,' he said, untruthfully.

In which we have a visitor, and Ali does too.

Heavy clouds covered the sun when we stepped out into Queen Charlotte Street. It looked as though the weather was about to break. As I drove back up Leith Walk towards the Old Town, we talked tactics, and agreed that we would head straight for the Falls of Lora Hotel. By the reckoning of the girl in Celtic Scenery, and it was her business to know these things, we would be there by five-thirty.

I looked up at the belvedere as I drew up to my parking space. 'That's funny. Old Wallace must think the sun's still shining.' Prim followed my gaze. Our loftmate was sprawled out along the window ledge, pressed to the glass as if he was trying to reach some sunshine just outside.

'You going to like living with an iguana?' I asked my new flatmate, as I parked.

'Oz my dear, if I can cope with you, I could cope with a tyrannosaurus.' She smiled. There's something about Prim's smile that goes straight to my knees. You can see right through it into her heart, and know that she's happy. It's the sort of smile that made it seem right then as if the sun was still shining inside my old Nissan, for me alone. She kissed me quickly on the cheek and jumped out of the car.

We knew that something was wrong as soon as we stepped through the front door, and saw the kitchen. All of the contents of the cupboards were laid out along the breakfast bar, every last tin of beans, every last jar of herbs.

'Bloody hell,' I said. 'Those mice are getting too bloody cheeky for their own good!'

Prim beat me up the stairs, but only just. Her cry of alarm was still hanging in the air as I reached the living area. 'Ransacked' is a word I'd never used in my life until then. There's nothing else in the *OED* quite like it, and when you think of it, it's as descriptive as you can get. Everything I, everything we, had was laid out in neat piles. Prim's bag was empty, on the floor. Her clothes had all been turned inside out. A dozen tampons in their paper casing were lined up neatly beside their box. I think that, more than anything else, was what made her cry.

All of the cupboard doors lay open. The drawers of my desk were stacked upon its surface, one on another. Even the lining of Wallace's cage had been disturbed.

Ever seen an outraged iguana? That's the only way I can describe the look on his face as my dinosaur appeared down the ladder from the belvedere. He glared around the room in human indignation, then at us, as if to say, 'What the hell's this then?'

Prim saw him and all at once her tears, which had been making my shirt decidedly damp, turned into laughter.

'Poor old chap,' she said, jumping on to the sleeping level, and for the first time in either of their lives, picking him up. The old bugger swelled with pride. I'll swear that he nuzzled his head against her breast. Imagine, for a fleeting second I was jealous of an iguana. She carried him down, and separated some food from the pile on the floor, putting the rest back into its box. As she did, she looked up at me.

'Who did it, Oz, do you think? Were they looking for . . .' My nod cut off her sentence unfinished.

'What else? Or did you smuggle some uncut diamonds back from Africa? As far as "who's" concerned, who knows about the fiver? Mike Dylan asked about it, but that doesn't prove that he understands what it's about. It's quite possible young Morrow's story was straight up, and that Dylan was just trying to cover up a mistake.

'No, the only people we know of who understand what that fiver's really worth are Ray Archer and your sister, although it's possible that Dawn only opened the account, and doesn't know what's in it.'

Prim shook her head and stood up, leaving Wallace munching on the floor. 'There could be another.'

'Who's that?'

'The mystery man who was looking for Dawn before we found Kane's body.'

'True, unless that was Ray Archer – and it could have been. Whoever it was, he still doesn't have the fiver, does he. And with the sort of dough it unlocks at stake, somehow I don't think he's going to give up looking.

'The safest thing we can do, love, is go to see Mike Dylan, give him the fiver and tell him the whole story. If we were lucky he'd only charge us with wasting police time.'

She squeezed my arm. 'I know that, but . . .'

I cut her off again. It's a bad habit of mine. 'Yes, I know. That would land Dawn right in it. Even if she could prove she was out of town when Kane was killed, she could still be charged as a party to theft, for opening that bank account. The police, and nine juries out of ten, would assume that she knew what Kane was going to do.

'There's also the small matter,' I added, 'of our cut from Ray Archer for picking up the money.'

'Except that if you're right and if Archer is involved in Kane's death, that cut might be our throats.' Primavera has a wonderful knack of getting to the nub of a situation. 'So what are we going to do, Oz?'

'The same thing we set out to do this morning. Find your sister, before someone else does. Leave this place exactly as it is just now. Let's stuff that bag of yours with enough clothes for a few days, arrange an iguana sitter, and head on up to Connell Ferry.'

She nodded and began to pack. Five minutes later, we closed the door behind us. This time, I locked the mortice as well as the Yale. We looked around as we stepped into the street, as ready as we could be for anything, but no-one was watching us that we could see. I threw our bag in the boot of the car and turned the key in the lock, then taking Prim by the hand, I led the way up to the High Street.

As I looked down the street before crossing, I thought I saw a familiar Armani suit in the distance.

'Hullaw ther youse two. Enjoy the breakfast then? Mair sausage for lunch, or is it back tae the tuna rolls?' I shook my head and explained to Ali that we had decided to go away for a couple of days. Some people think that I take a hell of a chance asking Ali to look after Wallace, but that's a racist slur. I happen to know that he's very particular about what he puts into his curries.

I handed him my spare key, then took a flyer. 'You just had the police in here?'

'Aye. Did you see the bastard? It was that flash boy Dylan, him that's in the papers a' the time. He came marchin' in saying something about fake banknotes, and wantin' tae check the cash in the till. Cheeky sod. Accusin' me of handling bent money! He had a look through it, but he didnae find anything. 'S as well he didnae come yesterday. Ma lunchtime relief took a tenner that was practically still wet. Ah wis dead lucky. Got rid of it in change tae a whisky salesman!'

Smiling at Ali's good fortune, and mulling over all the possible connections between Dylan's official search, Prim's off-the-cuff fabrication to young Morrow, and our visitor with the ability to open Yale locks without a key we jumped into the Nissan as fast as we could and put the old grey streets of Edinburgh behind us.

'Why would Dylan lie to Ali?' Prim murmured, eventually, as we passed the towering bowl of Murrayfield on our way out of the City. 'Why would he spin him a line about fake money, when all the time he knows that he's looking for just one particular note? All he had to say was that the note was evidence in a case.'

Smart girl, my Primavera, isn't she. I glanced at my watch, which told me that I had known her now for over twenty-eight hours. A day and a bit. The longest day and a bit of my life, the most memorable, and even if we didn't come through this whole business intact, the greatest. We were flying, Primavera Phillips and I, high on adrenalin, high on the thrill of the chase. And we were flying too, from a city where danger lived. More than likely we were quarry ourselves, in the eye of someone with the ruthlessness and the physical strength to ram that knife all the way up into wee Willie (or big Willie, if you want to look at it that way) Kane's head. Now, I guessed, we had what that someone wanted, the key to a bank vault containing a serious amount of hot, and once it was moved on, untraceable money.

'Why's Dylan after the fiver in the first place?' I said. 'The boy Morrow was right. Technically he shouldn't have let us take anything out of that house, in case it had an essential print on it or a piece of DNA. Maybe he's embarrassed by that. But if he is, why stir the thing up? The best way for him to cover his tracks is just to forget about it.

'Instead, he has Morrow ask us about the fiver. Yet he's so keen to get it back that at the same time he takes the chance of breaking into the loft and turning it inside out.'

She looked at me in astonishment. 'You think Dylan did that?'

'Aye, of course he did. Policemen know a thousand ways of opening lockfast places as quick as you like without making a mess. And whoever did the loft went through two locked doors, the one to the street and m . . .' I caught myself. '. . . ours,' She smiled and squeezed my hand at the plural, 'without leaving a mark. Point one, a real housebreaker would have gone straight through the door with a crowbar, point two, would not have been daft enough to try the street door in the daylight, and point three, would have had no way of knowing that the loft was empty. Last and finally, point four, straight after the break-in Dylan walks into Ali's, just round the corner, and talks his way through the till. What's the betting he'd just phoned young Morrow?'

'Aghast' is another of my favourite words, but I'd never seen anyone looking that way until Prim looked at me in the car. 'But that's desperate!' she gasped. 'Why would he do all that?'

'Either because someone's cut him in on the deal, or because someone's put the fear of God into him over his career prospects if he doesn't get the fiver back, having broken procedure by letting you take it from the flat.'

'But who could do that?'

I opened my mouth, the usual smart-arsed 'Ah, my dear, that is the sixty-four dollar question!' hanging on the edge of my tongue. And all at once I knew. I saw for certain who could put the fear of God in Mike Dylan. I saw too, that he was not a man to concern himself unduly with a trivial oversight. He didn't want that fiver back as a point of principle. He wanted it for what it was. Oh no: whatever the incentive, it came to me that the threat that had shaken the creases out of Dylan's Armani suit had issued straight from the mouth of the man who had killed Willie Kane. '*Smart bastard, that Blackstone!*' you may be thinking, but I knew him all right, in that very moment, and for the first time since I had walked into Prim's flat and discovered the befouled corpse on her bed, I was scared. Really scared for me, but absolutely terrified for Prim. Dylan I could cope with. Dylan was a clown, a slightly bent and mentally limited copper, but no threat. But this guy . . .

Prim was looking at me. Her aghastness had changed to expectation. My hands gripping the wheel as I turned towards the M8 junction, I smiled, sideways, the first and last insincere smile I've ever given her.

'Ah, my dear,' I said, 'that is the sixty-four dollar question!'

She laughed and punched my arm. 'Oz, that's my first disappointment. I thought you had an answer for everything!'

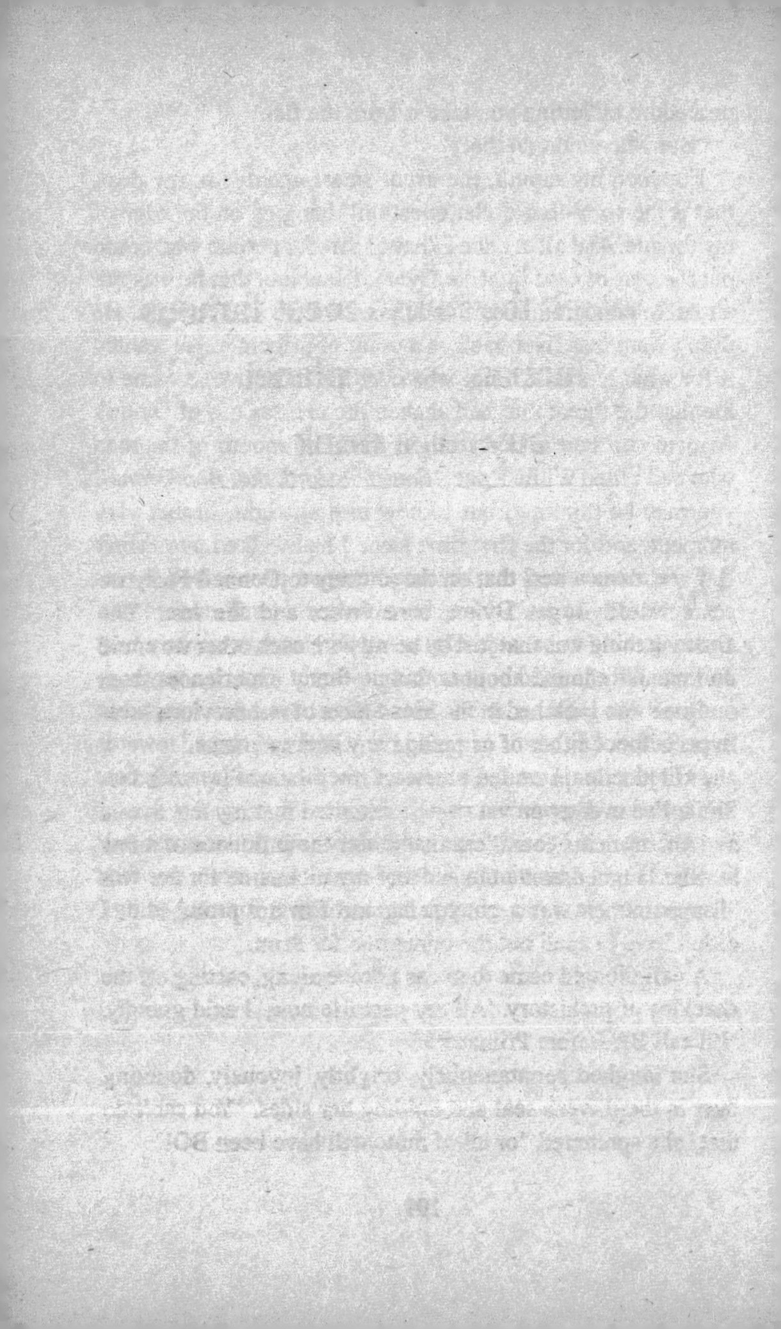

In which the fourth most famous human on the planet buys us a drink.

We made a deal that on the journey to Connell Ferry we would forget Dylan, torn fivers and the rest. The amazing thing was that just by being with each other we could do that. We chatted about nothings, funny experiences from our lives. We sketched in the broad facts of our previous love-lives, without either of us feeling any strange pangs.

I filled Prim in on the basics of my relationship with Jan. She tutted in disapproval when I admitted that my last live-in had left after she found out that under the influence of a few bevvies, I had admitted to Ali that my nickname for her was 'Tomorrow'. It was a cruel thing and I'm not proud of it. I didn't have to spell out the punchline for Prim.

A daft thought came to me as I drove along, casting off the shackles of prehistory. 'All my past life now,' I said grandly, 'I'll call BP, Before Primavera.'

She laughed spontaneously, brightly, joyously, doubling over in the driver's seat and holding her sides. 'You can't do that,' she spluttered, 'or all of mine will have been BO!'

It wasn't that funny, but tension made us laugh so hard, that I had to pull the car into a parking place. We sat there, our chests heaving from our mirth . . . heaving very provocatively in Prim's case, I have to say. Occasionally one of us would look at the other, and we would break out again. Eventually, I reached across and held her shoulders, and as I did a feeling came over me, as yet another emotional height was scaled. 'In that case, my love, since acronyms are out, all my life till now has been Winter. I've spent it waiting for my Springtime, and now she's here.' I was only slightly surprised when I realised that Mr Lump was back in my throat.

She looked at me and smiled. 'You're really laying it on the line, aren't you,' she whispered. 'Just give me time. That's all I ask.'

After a while we drove on, heading towards the West, watching as the leafy countryside gave way to moorland, and as the surrounding hills grew into mountains. Eventually a salty tang came into the air and flooded the car through Prim's open window.

'God, but you don't know how good the taste of this is, my dear, daft Oz, after twelve months of Africa. The heat, the poverty, the cruelty, the blood. I never ever want to go back to that place again.'

'What, not even to minister to the sick?' The old Oz was disappearing. There wasn't a trace of irony in my question.

I glanced across at her. She was sitting with her legs pulled up on the squab, grasping her neat ankles. She shook her head slowly and deliberately. 'No way on Earth. I've hit the compassion wall too, just like my late pal. I left the hospice for a different world, and what I found was far, far worse. I can't take it any more. Sister Phillips has hung up her starched bunnet for good and all.

'Although I haven't a clue what I'm going to do next!'

'Don't do anything, then. I can look after us both.'

She flashed me a glance, suddenly sharp and serious. 'Don't even think that, far less say it. I'll consider living with the right man, although that's something I've never done before. But I'll always want my identity, and working is part of it. What if you and I got together, and it wore off, or something? Where would I be?'

'Primavera,' I said, 'when it wears off for me it'll be because your zimmer keeps on blocking the stair up to the loft; and even then I'll just rig up a pulley and haul you straight up to the balcony.'

She took a hand from her ankles and rubbed it, gentle as silk over the back of my hand on the steering wheel. We drove on for a while, safe in our island away from the action, and the danger.

'Where are we going to stay tonight?' asked Prim.

'That kind of depends on whether or not we find your sister, doesn't it. Let's play it by ear.'

Connell Ferry's a bit of a misnomer, because there's a bridge there, a big iron single-track thing that was built in the days when, even north of Oban, the prospect of today's traffic volumes would have looked like visions from one of H. G. Wells' wilder efforts. We saw it well before we reached the village, and slowed up, looking for the Falls of Lora Hotel.

It wasn't hard to find. It's a big building on the left, as you come into the village; once it was someone's grand house, no doubt, but extended now, in a totally uncomplementary style. The car park looked as if it might have been a cowshed once, but now it was empty, save for a Land Rover with the Falls of Lora logo on its spare-wheel cover.

I parked the Nissan under the curving roof, and jumped out.

Prim took my arm, as we crunched along the gravel towards the entrance.

The reception area was small, and empty. There was nothing fancy about it, just a dark-varnished counter in the shadow of the staircase, with a doorway leading off. Prim pushed the service bell, and after a few minutes a girl appeared, fresh-faced and not far out of her teens, wearing what looked like a waitress's uniform.

'Yes?' she said, in a lovely island lilt. 'Can I help you?'

All at once my mind swam back to a night in the cocktail bar of another hotel, in St Andrews, with my Dad and his sailor pal Archie. The girl there was as fresh-faced as this one, with an accent as soft as mist, and as wild as heather. Archie said to her, 'Where are you from, then?'

'Tiree,' the lass replied.

'Ah,' said the old salt. 'They'll have had to lasso you to get you over here, then!'

Back in the present, Prim said, 'I hope so. I'm looking for my sister. She's with the film party, and I understand they're booked in here. Have they arrived yet?'

'Not yet,' said the girl. 'We're expecting them any time now, though. Why don't you wait in the bar. It's just through there.' She pointed along a narrow hallway to her left.

'Okay.' Prim took my hand and started off along the corridor, but I held her back, gently. 'Suppose we wanted to stay tonight,' I asked, 'have you any room left?'

The girl shook her head. 'Sorry. The film party have booked the whole place.

'But there are plenty of hotels down in Oban,' she added, doing her best to please. 'You'll get booked in there all right.'

We made our way through to the bar. It was a big room, square but for an alley off one corner, where a dartboard hung on the wall. A big open fireplace was set in its centre, topped by a copper flue which disappeared up into the roof. Prim took a seat in the corner, near the window. 'What would you like to drink, love?' I asked her.

'Just a lime and soda. If they have any sandwiches, I wouldn't mind one. It seems forever since lunch.'

I pressed the service bell; after only a second or two, a door opened behind the bar, and the young receptionist appeared. 'Jesus,' I said, 'they work you hard.'

She shrugged her shoulders. 'Och, I like it. You get to meet all sorts of interesting people.'

'Aye, I can imagine,' I said. 'A right wee metropolis Connell Ferry must be.'

Prim and I sat together in the bar, munching thick crab sandwiches and looking northward out of the window, across the narrow mouth of Loch Etive, with the great Bens rising in the distance. 'It's amazing how insular people can be.' She was speaking a thought aloud. 'I've been to five European countries. I've straddled the equator. Yet here I am in Scotland in a place I've never seen before, in a different country to the one I thought I knew.'

'You and me both,' I said, slipping an arm around her waist. 'You and me and thousands of our country-folk. Most central-belt Jocks get panic attacks as soon as they leave a built-up area. All this "Flower of Scotland" stuff is so much crap, you know. Our nation is like everywhere else in the world, a collection of tribes and villages, each one holding on to its own and living in suspicion and fear of its neighbours.'

'That's very profound, Osbert.'

I sipped my Coke and smiled, a touch self-consciously. 'The mask slips occasionally. Just don't tell anyone.'

She smiled and kissed my cheek. 'I promise. The serious

Oz is someone I'll keep to myself.'

As she spoke, the door from the corridor creaked open, and in the same moment, the receptionist-barmaid-waitress appeared behind the beer-taps without being summoned by bell.

We recognised him at once, as soon as he stepped into the room. Miles Grayson was an impressive guy on screen. But I knew he had to be forty-something, and I had a cynical view of what he would look like close-up, once the make-up was stripped away. Come to think of it, I have the same cynical view of all actors and politicians. I was wrong about this bloke.

My Dad has a great saying, applied most often to our current Head of Government, 'He seems to make a room bigger just by being in it.' Miles Grayson was the opposite. He was one of those rare human beings who shrink the space around them. Even as he was then, tired after a long day, the vitality came from him in waves. He wasn't very tall, around five ten, I guessed, but he carried himself like someone six inches taller. He was wearing black denim and black hiking boots, every inch the New Age Cowboy. He looked across and smiled at us, and automatically Prim and I nodded back, mouths hanging slightly open.

He turned to the barmaid and melted her with The Smile. 'Is that Fosters cold, honey?' She nodded vigorously, speechless. 'I mean like really cold?' I thought the lassie's neck would snap. 'Okay, then I'll have a pint, in a straight glass please.'

Prim tugged my arm and whispered in my ear. 'What do we do now?'

'Seems like a good idea to let the man get outside his pint, then we'll see.'

Grayson solved our problem. 'What can I get you?' he called across the bar.

'I'll have one of them, thanks.' I pointed at the Fosters. 'How about you, love?'

'Lime and soda, thanks,' said Prim.

The movie star turned barman, bringing the drinks across on a metal tray. 'Do you two live here?' he asked, as he sat down beside us. His accent was strange, a blend of Aussie, American and received pronunciation from drama school.

'No,' I said. 'Edinburgh. How about you?' Cheeky bastard, Blackstone, but I couldn't resist it. Grayson's right eyebrow twitched, and he smiled, not taken aback in the slightest. 'Sorry,' I said. 'Cheers.' I took a swallow of the Fosters. The girl was right. It was icy.

I put the glass down and held out my hand. 'My name's Oz Blackstone, and this is Prim Phillips.

'You finished work for the day?'

Grayson ignored my question. Like many celebrities, he had perfected the royal art of acknowledging hundreds, even thousands of people simultaneously, putting out his own presence but absorbing none of theirs. Now it was as if he was looking at Prim for the first time. 'Phillips,' he repeated.

'Yes,' said Prim. 'You might know my sister, Dawn. I think she's working on your film.'

He looked at her, and a smile lit up his face. 'Yeah, I know Dawn. In fact only three days ago I made wild, abandoned love to her . . . but only for the cameras, worse luck. She's a tough nut to crack, is Dawn.

'So you're her sister. The one with the great name. She told me about you, but she said you were in Africa.'

'So I was, until Wednesday. I thought it'd be a nice idea for us to surprise Dawn. Is she here?'

Grayson looked at her, curiously, for a while, as if he was considering his answer. At last he shook his head. 'No, she isn't. She has a few days between scenes, and she asked me on Wednesday if she could take some time away. She left that same morning.' His eyebrows rose, as if in anticipation. 'She is due back on Monday, though.'

'Dammit,' said Prim, frowning. 'She didn't say where she was going, did she?'

'No. She only said that she had some things to sort out, and needed a few days. I was disappointed, because I thought we'd been getting on pretty well together, but I said okay, because I could tell that she meant it.

'I rate your sister in every respect, Miss Phillips. Quite apart from turning me on every time she walks on set, she's a damn fine actress. In fact, I've told her writers to expand her part. This movie will make her a star. Then maybe she'll have time for me. Like I said, she's a hard nut to crack.'

He caught something in Prim's eye. 'Hey, I'm legit, honest. I came out of a relationship about a year back.'

A thought struck me. 'I thought you were doing a remake of *Kidnapped*.'

'Yeah, that's right,' said Grayson. 'Great story, ain't it.'

'So who are you playing? With respect, you're a bit mature for young David Balfour.'

'Just a bit, yeah. No, I'm playing Allan Breck. He's the real hero, after all. Why d'you ask?'

'No reason, really. It's just that when I read *Kidnapped* at school, I don't remember Allan Breck getting his leg over. I don't remember there being any sort of a part for an actress, either, far less one that could be expanded.'

Miles Grayson spread his arms wide, with a grin that was as honest and disarming as the midsummer day was long. 'Come on, guy, this is Hollywood. We're out to entertain. The reason *Kidnapped* hasn't been a hit before is that it's been made like the story, a Buddy movie. You want to put bums on seats, like you say over here, you need some love interest.'

I shook my head. 'Aye, man, fair enough. But next time you're in Samoa, make sure you visit Robert Louis Stevenson's grave. If you put your ear to the ground I'm sure you'll hear him spinning round in his coffin.

'What's next? Long John Silver with two legs, so you can work in a tap-dance routine.'

The actor laughed. 'Hey, Oz! How did you know I used to be a dancer?'

We were still laughing when the door behind us creaked once more. A harassed, bald, fat man heaved his bulk into the barroom. 'Miles,' he called. 'There you are! Thanks for commandeering the limo! I had to come back in the bus with the technicians and the rest of the cast.'

Grayson waved a hand at him, dismissively. 'Don't give me that crap, Charlie. A good assistant director is a team member, not the team leader. Anyway, I had a call coming in from my agent, and I had to be back here to take it.'

The fat man ambled over to our table. 'Too bad. You missed the excitement.'

'Excitement! Up here?'

'Yes. We had a visit from the law. The local crimebusters.'

'What, looking for work as extras?'

'No. Looking for that young lady you're sweet on.'

Beside me, Prim sat bolt upright. Grayson glanced round at her, briefly. 'Did they say what they wanted?' he asked.

The director shook his head. 'They muttered something about her being a witness in a court case. Nothing serious, they said. I told them, "In that case, come back on Monday." That seemed to satisfy them.

'Look, old boy. I'm off for a bath. I'll see you down here

for a drink before dinner. Seven-thirty okay?'

'Yes, fine,' Grayson muttered, absently. The fat man nodded, a farewell and slouched out of the room.

'A court case,' said the actor, looking curiously at Prim. 'What d'you think that's about?'

'I told you,' she said, batting not an eyelid. 'I'm just back from Africa. How would I know?'

'Mm. Yeah, of course. Funny, I had this feeling there was something troubling her, something she wasn't telling me, but I didn't press her. Look, if you do find Dawn over the weekend, tell her that if she does have a problem, old Miles'll fix it for her.'

Prim nodded. 'I'll tell her that. I'm sure it'll be nothing, though. Dawn's one of nature's worriers, even when there's absolutely nothing to worry about.' She took my hand again. 'Oz, if Dawn's away till Monday there's no point in hanging about here. If we leave now we can get back home tonight.'

I followed her lead and stood up. 'Okay, let's hit the trail. It's been a pleasure to meet you, Miles. We'll make sure that Dawn's back on Monday, raring to go.'

We started to leave, but I couldn't resist. I'm just a punter at heart, after all. 'I don't suppose you'd autograph a beer mat, would you?' I asked. 'For my Dad, like.'

Grayson laughed, as if reassured that life really did hold no surprises. He took a pen from his breast pocket and scrawled a signature on a Foster's mat. 'Cheers,' I said. 'I'll buy the beer next time.'

'Hold you to that. So long.'

We waved him goodbye and made our way out of the bar, leaving him draining his Fosters.

'What a nice guy,' said Prim.

'Aye, and he fancies your sister too. She could be all right there, if we can just keep her out of the slammer.'

She flashed me a worried smile.

'Are we really going back to Edinburgh?' she asked.

'No thank you very much. I don't think we want to do that right now. Eventually Mike Dylan will have been through every grocer's till in town, and he'll realise we told young Morrow a porky about the fiver. I think we should body-swerve him for now, till we find Dawn. And to be on the safe side we should get out of here too, in case the plods come back looking for *us*.

'Tell you what, it's been a few weeks since I've seen my Dad. We can make it to Anstruther as easily as Edinburgh. Let's head for there, unless you want to go to Auchterarder.'

She shook her head. 'No, I need more time to think up a cover story about Dawn. Let's go to Fife: I fancy meeting the old man who could spawn a son like you!'

In which we dine in style and Mac the Dentist is caught *in flagrante*.

I have this thing about drinking and driving, so I let Prim drive us eastward, retracing our route as far as Lochearnhead, where we followed the Perth road, along the lochside, rather than heading for Stirling. The sun was low in the sky as we left the M90 at Milnathort and cruised around Loch Leven, into Fife.

It's a funny place, the old Kingdom, my birthplace; a real amalgam of cultures, with its agriculture in the north, its Black Country to the west, and away on its tip, jutting into the sea, its East Neuk.

'I suppose that the place where you grow up always seems different from anywhere else,' I said to Prim as she drove, quickly but with assurance, 'but every time I go back to the East Neuk now, to Anstruther, I feel like I'm stepping into fairyland. Life has a different pace there, as if time passes more slowly. I don't know another place like it.'

'I know what you mean. When I was wee, and when Dawn was a baby, we went to Elie for our holidays. We took a house for a month. I remember days on the beach, whatever the weather, and scones and Coca Cola in the tennis pavilion. My Granny came with us; she used to sit all afternoon by the bowling green, watching the play. She didn't understand what was going on, but that didn't matter. It was her thing, and she did it.

'I have this secret dream that one day I'll live in Elie.'

I frowned and tutted. 'Us East Neukers don't really approve of Elie. "Elie for the elite", we say. Too many of the houses belong to weekenders. My Dad says that when he was a kid, Elie was a working village. It had fishermen, golf-club makers, market gardeners and so on, and everyone let rooms in their houses to holidaymakers. But then more and more of the houses were bought up by folk from Glasgow and Edinburgh, lawyers and doctors and the like. All of a sudden the place was a ghost town in the winter, and there were fewer holidaymakers in the summer too, as those houses weren't let out any more.

'Now the second and third generations of weekenders are there. Yuppies, most of them are.'

Prim laughed as my mouth curled with distaste. 'Intolerant bugger, aren't you. I'll bet that in Anstruther, they think you're a Yuppie too!' I looked at her in mock horror. 'No. I'm Mac the Dentist's son, him that works in Edinburgh. Jan More, she's the teachers' lassie, her that used tae hang about wi' Mac the Dentist's son. In Enster, there's no way any of us can get too big for our Wellies.'

'No,' she said, almost involuntarily. 'Otherwise there wouldn't be room for the sheep.' I looked at her astonished, but she stayed poker-faced and went on. 'Do Jan's parents still live there?'

'Her Mother does. Her Father, fool that he was, traded her

in for a younger model years ago. Lives in the West somewhere. Jan never sees him.'

Prim glanced at me, as she took a corner. 'You and Jan. It is "used to", isn't it?'

'It is now. Jan and I have known each other since we were in our prams. We were best pals when we were kids. As we grew up, things happened between us almost automatically. Everybody in Enster – that's Fifer-speak for Anstruther by the way – everyone assumed we'd get married, and I supposed that we did too for a while. But eventually, once we hit our twenties, we realised that we weren't meant for that. We weren't on fire for each other. So ever since then we've settled for being the best of pals, and occasional lovers. We'll go on being the best of pals.'

Prim nodded. 'Good. I like her. Is there anyone else in her life?'

'There sure is, as you'll find out in time.'

'Oooh. Mysterious, is he. I'll look forward to meeting him.'

The cloak of night was sweeping across the fields as we drove the last few miles, through Colinsburgh, and into Pittenweem. We were both starving, and since Pittenweem's fish and chip shop is legendary far beyond Fife, we stopped there to pick up supper, and extra chips for my Dad.

The lumpy brown paper parcel was hot in my lap as we swung into Anstruther and pulled into the drive. Dad's house faces out to sea, and his surgery is built on to the back, so that the patients don't have to trail through the hall spitting blood on the lino, or worse, on the carpet. Once upon a time that's how it was, until my Mum put her foot down, and made him move his business out back.

We parked at the side of the house and walked round to the front. The moon was up, turning the cold, blue river mouth to silver. We stopped and looked across Dad's immaculate garden, and out to sea. 'This is lovely, Oz,' said Prim. 'And you grew up here.'

'Yup. My Dad would say I'm still growing up.'

I looked up at the big bay window of my Dad's living room. The curtains hadn't been pulled – they never were – and the blueish glow of the television shone in the dark. In the window above, my Dad's bedroom, a light shone.

I have my own key, but when I turned it in the Yale and pushed the front door, it was stopped by a chain. 'Dad,' I shouted. 'It's me. Come and undo this thing. The fish suppers are getting cold.' There was no immediate response, and so I rang the bell. Eventually, a muffled cursing sounded from behind the door and the hall light was switched on.

'For fuck's sake Oz, you might have let me know!' My Father's voice came from behind the door as he fiddled with the chain. After a few seconds, the door swung open wide, and my Dad, Mac the Dentist, stood there, in his big, old dressing gown. His jaw dropped as he saw us, me holding the fish suppers and Prim lugging our travel bag.

'Sorry, Dad,' I said. 'I never thought. Anyway, you know me, I like surprises. And this one's a cracker. Dad, this is my new friend, Primavera Phillips. Prim, this is the man you wanted to meet, Macintosh Blackstone, LDS, the bugger who christened me Osbert!'

My Dad shook his head. 'Jesus, I don't know. Come in and welcome, lassie. I don't know what you've done to deserve this guy for company, but I'll do my best to see that he behaves himself.

'As far as surprises go, Oz my boy, two of us can play that game.'

In all my life, I've never managed to put one over on my

Father. He is absolutely the most resourceful, wise, devious, cunning and artful old bastard that I know.

We stepped into the hall and it was my turn for the dropping jaw. I saw her feet first as she came down the stairs, then black slacks, then a colourful blouse, and finally . . . 'Auntie Mary!'

Mary More, Jan's Mother, has been an honorary aunt all my days, except at primary school when I had to call her 'Miss' like all the rest of the teachers. For all that she is fifty-three, she is still a slim, handsome woman, and, according to her daughter, a walking testimonial to the benefits of hormone replacement therapy.

She smiled, and tossed her carefully maintained auburn chest. 'Hello Oz. Are you still playing detectives or is this a pure accident?'

'Accident, Mary, honest. If I'd known, I'd have . . .'

'What,' said my Dad, 'stayed away? Don't be daft. Drop that bag and get through to the kitchen. There'll be no fish suppers in my living room. Hope you've got some chips for us. Primavera . . . lovely name . . . would you like tea or coffee, or something else?'

Auntie Mary took charge. 'Mac. Upstairs and get yourself dressed. I'll take care of the tea or whatever. What will it be, my dear?'

She looked at Prim with a friendly, enquiring smile, but hidden in there I caught a line of communication, an inflection in her gaze. I know that she wouldn't have meant to let it show, but I caught it clearly. It told me that I had just snapped the last faint thread between Mary and an unspoken wish, one that I never dreamt was there, that eventually Jan and I *would* be a couple, that we would toe the line and become a conventional pair of thirty-somethings, with a house in an acceptable suburb, a decent car in the garage and two point four cats or whatever. Poor Mary; if I'd only known, I could have told her long ago. Jan did tell her, but now it was clear that she never quite believed it.

But the look passed. Prim glanced across at me, and I rescued her. 'I think what we really need is to raid the fridge, Mary. Unless that old bugger's finished the Becks' I left here last time.'

She laughed. 'No chance of that. You know how your Dad feels about beer that doesn't come in pints.' She turned again to Prim. 'We haven't been introduced, dear. I'm Mary More. Don't let the "Auntie" stuff give you awful ideas about Mac and me. "Friend of the family" is how I am best described.

'How long have you known young Osbert here?'

I held my breath. Prim grinned and shrugged her shoulders. 'Who knows? The moment I met him it was as if he'd always been there.'

'That's it then,' said Mary. 'Just make sure you always are, Oz.' She led the way into the kitchen, and reached into the cupboard above one of the kitchen worksurfaces, to produce two white dinner plates. I noticed that she knew exactly where to look.

Prim unwrapped the fish suppers and loaded one on to each plate, while I knocked the tops off of two cold Becks'. I held one out to Mary, but she shook her head. 'No thanks Oz, I must be off home.'

'Don't be daft, Mary. Just because we're here . . .'

Her eyebrows arched, in much the same way they had when someone spoke in class. 'As if I would bother about that! Oh no, you don't think I stay over do you? Remember where you are. This is Anstruther. The first time my bedroom light doesn't go on after *News At Ten* the jungle drums will be sounding all over town.' My Dad appeared, as she spoke, in the kitchen doorway, looking reasonably tidy in a crew-neck sweater and grey trousers. Too bad about the trainers, though. 'Isn't that right, Mac?'

'Oh aye. Ps and Qs must be watched. I think they're on to us though. We went along to Elie for a meal in the Ship a few weeks back. One of my patients was in. Ever since then I've been getting funny looks in the paper shop.' He took Mary's hand. 'Come on, hen. Let's be daring. I'll walk you home.'

'Indeed you will not! Besides, you've got your chips to finish. Goodnight both.' A wave and she was gone. Dad was allowed to see her to the back door, her shortcut home, and then he was back, plopping himself beside us at the big, pine kitchen table and wolfing his chips straight from the paper.

'Well,' he said, between mouthfuls, as we tore into the Pittenweem haddock, 'what brought you two up here unannounced, interrupting my Friday night tryst?'

I swallowed some of my Becks', from the bottle. I'm not a poser, honest. It really is the best way to drink it. 'Spur of the moment, really, Dad. We just decided it was time for you to meet Prim.'

'Mmm. And delighted I am too. You've been sharing your life with a fucking lizard for far too long!'

He looked across at Primavera. 'Pardon the barrackroom talk, my dear. It's the way we are, Osbert and I. We used the word to give emphasis to a point.'

Prim, resting from her attack on the fish and chips, propped both elbows on the table and took her beer in both hands. 'That's all right, Mr Blackstone. I've been in barrackrooms, in Africa. You should hear, and see, how those boys emphasise their points.'

Dad smiled. 'I can see you're going to fit in around here. There's one thing though. To everyone but that insolent bugger there, my name is Mac. Fair enough?'

She nodded. 'Fair enough.'

We went back to our fish suppers, but before the end, I realised that I was flagging. I looked across at Prim, and I could see that she was drooping too. I glanced at my watch. It was 10.30 p.m. We had been flying, with precious little sleep, for thirty-six hours. Now the tanks were empty and we were both ready to crash.

She caught my glance, and looked at Dad. 'Mac, would you mind if I had a bath and went to bed?'

'Not at all, the pair of you look as if you've got a fair few miles on your clocks. Oz, show the lady where we keep the zinc bath.'

My room looks out across the Firth too. It used to be Ellen's, by right of primogeniture (there's a big word for a simple boy), but as soon as she left home for good I moved myself in there. I held Prim, in the dark, and we looked out of the window across the river. Night had fallen completely now and we could see the lights on May Island, closest to us this time, across on the Bass Rock and further along on Fidra, as each lanced its different signal into the night.

'D'you want to watch the sun come up again?'

She turned and kissed me, her lips tasting richly of salt and vinegar. 'No, my dear, I want to sleep till around midday, if that's all right with you.'

'Sleep as long as you like, as long as you don't waken me.'

'There's no danger of that,' she whispered, kissing me again, and smiling. 'Because you'll be next door.'

I put yet another gallant proposition to her, but she silenced me with a finger on my lips. 'Oz, you're too knackered to do me justice.' I had to admit it: she was right.

I checked to make sure that there was a sheet on the bed

under the duvet. There was, and the pillow slips were crisp and fresh. 'You sleep here, then,' I said. 'Have your bath, and I'll go down and crack another beer with the old man. He's dreaming if he thinks he's going to get away without being interrogated about Auntie Mary!'

I produced a couple of big, fluffy towels and my spare dressing gown from the hall cupboard, and showed her where the bathroom was, at the end of the landing. The bath was huge and deep and had been there since the house was built. When I was really wee, I could swim in it. There was even some scented stuff, for making bubbles. I leaned over to twist on the brass taps. By the time I straightened up and turned around Prim was half undressed. Her shirt was on the floor, her skirt was unfastened, and her bra hung from her shoulders, loose and unclipped.

Her erect nipples, showing clearly through the lace fabric, tilted slightly upwards; they caught and held me like a burglar in a searchlight. I reached for her. She smiled, and put her hands on my chest. 'I know bravado when I see it, my man. Go and have that beer. I'll leave the water in the bath. From the size of this thing, even half-full it'll drain the tank.'

I nodded, kissed her, said farewell to her glorious headlamps and went back downstairs. My Dad was still in the kitchen, finishing the chips that we had left. I uncapped another bottle and we went through to the living room, where he poured himself a whisky. A very small whisky, I was pleased to see.

He slumped into his chair, facing the window, and I sprawled on the couch. There were no lamps on, and since it was early summer, the fire was unlit. Dad and I like to sit in the moonlight. A pair of lunatics, he says.

He sipped his malt. 'I like your lady, Oz. She's for you. How long have you known her?'

I smiled in the shadows. 'If I tell you, you'll really think I'm daft.'

'Always have, always will. Come on.'

'Okay then. I met her yesterday morning. Go on then, laugh.'

But he didn't. His domed grey head slumped, and his wise eyes stared into the hearth, at the fire screen that my Mum embroidered the year before she died, as if he was looking into the past . . . as he was.

'Son,' . . . he only ever calls me that when he's being deadly serious . . . 'the day I met your mother, I said to myself, "I'm going to marry her." The next day, I said it to her. She said, "All right, now that's sorted out let's take some time to get to know each other." I'm not going to laugh at you, boy, because I've been there. Good luck to you both.'

He looked across at me and I saw his eyes glisten.

'Thanks, Dad.' I didn't have anything more to say.

He did. 'One thing, though. Your moments haven't had spurs on them since you were about fourteen. What's brought you tearing up here when by rights you should still be shacked up in that loft of yours?'

I shook my head. 'Tomorrow, Dad, tomorrow.

'Anyway, enough about me. What's with you and Auntie Mary then? I knew you'd been seeing a bit of each other, but I didn't realise how much. How long's this been going on?'

'About a year.'

'Is it serious?'

'What's serious when you're fifty-eight? Sure, the old loins still catch fire from time to time, but the difference is that you're less likely to go hunting for the matches. No, pal, by that time your preoccupation is with the prospect of going into old age alone.

'Mary and I have known each other for donkey's years. Truth be told, I've cast an eye over her for most of that time, but while your mother was alive, and Alex More was around there was never any thought, on either side, of any . . . any, misbehaving.

'Things have changed now. We're both single, for different reasons. After a while, well, it just happened. Now, I think Mary's happy enough, and she sure keeps me on the straight and narrow. Her basket would be full if Jan . . . but I suppose not.'

I shook my head. 'Not much chance of that, Dad, I don't think.'

'No? Ach well . . .'

'Does Jan know about . . . ?' I asked, hesitantly.

'No. If she did, d'you think she'd have said nothing to you?'

I shook my head. 'D'you think you'll get married?'

He looked at me, frankly. 'If we do, you'll be the first to know. But come on, boy, don't sit here any longer. Get away upstairs before that lass forgets what you look like.'

'Come on, Dad. We're not at that stage yet.' I pushed myself out of my chair. 'I am off to bed, though. See you after your surgery. Maybe we'll hit a few balls, eh. I'll see what Prim says.' A wonderful thought struck me. 'Hey, maybe she plays golf!'

I saw the light still shining under the bathroom door as I reached the top of the stairs. I tapped the door and Prim opened it, swathed in one of the towels. Her hair was hand-dried and stood up in spikes. Her face was scrubbed shiny; without a trace of make-up her eyes seemed even bigger, her lips fuller. I thought she was the loveliest thing I'd ever seen in my life. Come to think of it, I still do.

She smiled at me and pulled me into the bathroom. She'd

been as good as her word. The bubbles were clearing, but the bath was still steaming gently. 'In you go, if you want. I'll still be awake, if you want to say goodnight.' She stood in the doorway, smiling.

'The water's okay, is it?' I said. 'You didn't pee in it or anything?'

She giggled. 'Of course I did! But you love me, don't you?' She pulled the door closed behind her.

Her body was still hot from the tub, like mine, when I slipped into my room and sat on the edge of the bed. I stroked her cheek as she lay on the pillow. 'Do you want me to pull the curtains?' I asked her.

'No,' she said, drowsily. I kissed her forehead, and as I did I looked into her heavy eyes, and felt sleep begin to take me too. 'Goodnight, then,' I whispered in her ear. 'Oh yes. I almost forgot to ask. Do you play golf?'

In which we play seventeen holes and the Jag stays on the road.

She does, of course. Pretty well too. We were lucky to get a threesome off at Elie on a Saturday afternoon, but my Dad's been a member there since God was a boy.

Elie Golf House Club has to be the only course in the world with a submarine periscope built into its starter's hut. No. I'm not joking. A submarine periscope.

We were waved off, and my Dad clumped an awkward drive halfway up the face of the hill, 100 yards in front of the first tee, which makes the contraption necessary. Prim and I, sharing my clubs – the Nissan's boot serves as a locker for all my sports gear – clipped our shots safely over the direction post, and we were off.

The quirky old course, spread out on its three fields, unfolded itself for us in the afternoon sun. Our golf was pure mince but we didn't care. It was a nice afternoon, if a bit windy, and Prim and my Dad got on like a house on fire. Eventually, like many an Elie golfer, we decided to skip the eighteenth hole and go straight to the nineteenth. The old Golf

Tavern has changed less, probably than any pub I know. My Dad still calls it 'Elrick's', although that licensee has been gone from it since I was a child.

I got them in, and we sat at a table in the window, crunching crisps and playing dominoes.

'So what's this story,' said my Dad, slamming down the double five, 'that you were going to tell me? What brought you up here?'

I looked at Prim. She nodded.

'Okay, but we better finish the dominoes, 'cause it'll put you right off your game.'

'Nonsense. You could poke me in both eyes with a sharp stick and you still couldn't beat me at Doms. Come on, tell me your story.'

'If you insist. After you've got them in.'

He shook his head. 'My God! Does everything have a price?' He stood up and took the single step across to the high bar counter. He was no sooner back with two pints of Deuchars and a small whisky for him than the door creaked open. The Golf Tavern is a great place for old bodgers. This one had a dog, a great, fat, slavering labrador. It was the sort of dog you find at one time or another in every country pub, its function being to see its master home in time for supper.

The old bodger turned out to be a patient. 'Hello Mac,' he hailed, the red capillaries standing out on his nose. 'Don't see you along here very often. Glad I bumped into you. Had this terrible bloody ache for a week now.' He hauled his loose lips wide apart to reveal a yellow canine of which the lab would have been ashamed. Half an hour and two more dog walkers later, we made it back to Dad's elderly Jag, parked outside the clubhouse. 'Jesus!' he spluttered, as he eased himself behind the big dish of the steering wheel. 'No wonder I don't come along here too often. One of them in there actually asked me to look at his fucking dog! Did you hear him?'

He shoved the lever into Drive and eased smoothly out of the car park, up through Elie, past the grey church, and out of the village. 'Right,' he said as Prim, in the back seat, pointed to the jagged shape of the Lady's Tower, 'let's have your story.'

And so I told him. Everything. From the moment when I found the late Willie Kane, to the time when we interrupted his coitus. The only part that I left out was my flash of insight about the identity of the killer. I didn't think Prim was ready for that.

I was about eight when I found out what 'phlegmatic' meant. 'It's what your father is,' said my Mum, and I understood. The Jag only looked like swerving off the road once, when I told him about meeting Miles Grayson in the Falls of Lora. 'Did you get his autograph?' asked the old movie buff.

'As a matter of fact I did.' I smiled at Prim. 'Bet you thought I was kidding when I said it was for my Dad.'

He was silent for the rest of the drive home. I knew better than to interrupt him. Mac the Dentist is a great ponderer. When he's come to a view he'll share it with the world, but while it's hatching in his brain, best to leave him alone.

We didn't go back into the house at once. Instead Dad motioned us over to his long green garden seat, positioned at the top of the lawn. We sat down, Prim between us. There was a big black tanker making its way out to sea, riding low in the water with its cargo of oil. He pointed to it. 'See that thing? When I was a young man, if anyone had told me that one day we'd be exporting oil from this river, I'd have told him he was off his fucking head. Now we take it for granted. But when it's all gone, we'll miss it.' He sat silent for a minute or so longer, then dug Prim in the ribs. 'You still got that fiver then?'

'Yes.'

'And you, boy. You don't trust this man Archer, do you?' I hadn't told him that.

'If I were you, I'd go back to see him one more time. Tell him you think Prim's sister has the fiver, and that you're looking for her. See how he reacts, then decide what to do.'

'What are my choices?'

He raised an eyebrow. 'Say "Bugger it", give up on the reward, go to the police, tell them the whole story and give them the fiver. That's what a sensible man would have done by now. Or, come clean with Archer, go and collect his dough, and take your cut. Or, and daftest of all, keep it to yourself, and once you've found Prim's sister and covered her backside, go to Switzerland, pick up the money and then make up your mind what to do with it.'

'And what would you do?'

'I, oh Mighty Oz? What would I do?' His face creased into a sly grin. 'I've never been accused of being too sensible, have I!'

He jumped to his feet. 'Come on, you two. The day presses on, and we have a date. Mary phoned this morning while you were still out of it, and bade us all to dinner at her place.'

In which Mac the Dentist gives us some good advice, and I become a lighthouse keeper.

It had been years since I'd dined at Auntie Mary's, and then I'd been too much of an airhead to appreciate what a wonderful cook she is. We ate salmon terrine that she'd made herself, braised venison from an estate a few miles away, garnished with peas straight from the pod, carrots and new potatoes, all home-grown, and a huge pineapple, quartered and soaked in Benedictine. Fortunately we'd taken a couple of decent bottles of wine with us, not Dad's usual supermarket crap. That would have tasted like vinegar alongside Mary's gourmet meal.

The table talk avoided relationships. Instead Prim told us tales of Africa, I told us tales of accidental comedy among my witness interviews, and Dad told us tales of dental dereliction. I watched him as the evening went on. The old bugger had his feet under the table, no doubt about that.

Auntie Mary brought out the port with the coffee and truffles. Damn good stuff it was too. Dad took to it, for sure. After his second glass he was clearly on his way. I wasn't worried about a slide back to the bottle. Before Mum died, he had always enjoyed a good bevvy as a form of fellowship. He had been a happy drunk, one who used alcohol to enhance enjoyment rather than drive away worries. It was funny, but looking at him across the table, I was actually pleased to see him getting pleasantly pissed. It was just like old times. Mary might as well have been my Mum, except, although I feel disloyal in admitting this, she's a better cook.

At last the port bottle was down to only the dregs. Dad toyed with the idea of finishing it, but thought better of it. He muttered something about the eye of a needle at thirty paces and put the bottle down. Suddenly he leaned across the table and took Prim's hand. 'Tell me, my dear,' he said, heavy-lidded. 'What are you going to do t'morrow?'

Prim looked at him, smiling lightly, her cheeks slightly red from the port. 'What do you think I should do, Mac?'

'I think you should go and see your Mum.'

The smile left her lips. She frowned uncertainly.

'Listen, love,' said my wise old father. 'You owe it to her. It's her right to worry about her daughter; goes with the position of parent. If there's cause for her to be anxious, she won't thank you for keeping it from her. Most of us old yins are capable of facing up to life, you know, whatever it throws at us.'

She looked at him for a while, and the smile came back. 'You're right, aren't you. I was treating her as if she was in her dotage. Okay, tomorrow we're off to Auchterarder. Apart from anything else, it's time she found out what her older daughter's up to!'

Dad nodded, and rattled the port bottle again. I took my cue, and stood up. 'Mary, that was wonderful, but it's time we were off.' Prim stood up and took my hand as I stepped round the table.

'Coming, Dad?' I said.

'No, no. Think I'll hang on here for a wee while.' He glanced across at Auntie Mary. She answered his slightly raised eyebrow with a nod.

The door was almost closed when he called after me. 'Tell you what, Oz. Be a good lad and put my bedroom light on for a wee while. Just to keep the neighbours happy, you understand.'

It might have been no more than the creaking of a chair, but as I closed the door, I was sure that I heard him fart.

In which we find she who wasn't lost at all, in which I experience the full glory of a Scottish Sabbath, from which we make an escape, and in which something very unpleasant happens.

To me, Auchterarder isn't a place at all. It's a stagecoach halt that's managed somehow to carry itself over into the twentieth century. It's something of a dormitory town, I suppose, but its main purpose today seems to be to meet the needs of Gleneagles Hotel, the fat cat up the road; to keep its kitchens filled; to make sure that its golf courses are all in the mint condition that its American and Japanese patrons have been told to expect; to ensure that there's always a taxi available to run same to and from Glasgow and Edinburgh Airports. Other than that, there isn't a logical reason for its existence.

Except of course that it's where Primavera Phillips was raised to womanhood. That makes it special.

We drove up the motorway in midmorning – having left a 'Thanks and see you later,' note on the kitchen table for my still-absent Dad – and took the fast road down from Perth.

'Our house is on the edge of the town,' said Prim as we took the turnoff from the A9. 'It's a big barn of a place up on the right.'

That was far short of a reasonable description. It struck me at first when I saw it that if it had had the Bates Motel at the foot of the garden, it could have been lifted straight out of *Psycho*. Closer to, I realised that I should have been thinking of the Addams Family. The Phillips homestead is a big spacious villa, with two high storeys and an attic, and a steep roof that must have been a slater's nightmare when it was built.

'There you are. Semple House. What d'you think?' said Prim, smiling, biting her lip, as the Nissan's tyres scrunched up the red gravel path.

'You don't have a butler called Lurch, do you?'

'Swine!' she shouted, laughing, and punched my arm. We eased ourselves out of the car and trotted up the six steps to the front door. Prim fumbled in her handbag for her keys. Eventually she found the bunch and fiddled through it for the right one.

She needn't have bothered. The door swung open . . . with an authentic Addams Mansion creak, I was glad to note. Prim looked up, and gasped.

They aren't instantly alike. They're both gorgeous, but in very different ways. Dawn Phillips is dark, while Prim is authentically blonde, even when her hair isn't bleached by the sun. Dawn's natural expression, the one with which right there and then I guessed she opens every door, is one of apprehension, while Prim's is one of total confidence, welcoming whatever challenge the world has to offer. But there is something about their eyes, about the tilt of the nose, which marks them out as sisters, beyond a shadow of doubt.

They stood there like statues, on their parents' doorstep, staring at each other, their mouths hanging open. It struck me that it was like watching someone looking in a distorted mirror.

Dawn cracked first. Her eyes filled with tears. 'Prim! Oh God, you're safe. We've been so worried about you, out there with all that trouble going on. When did you get back?' She stepped out from the doorway and hugged her sister.

'Hey, girl,' said Prim, disengaging and holding her at arm's length. 'Didn't I write? Didn't I phone when I could? Didn't I call Mum on Friday to say I was home?'

Dawn shook her head. 'I didn't know. I went up to Perth on Friday to chill out with Jenny Brown and get pissed. I've been so screwed up lately. I only got back half an hour ago.'

'Before Friday, how long had you been here?'

Dawn jumped when I spoke. She was edgy, and no mistake. Prim smiled, and took my arm. 'Sorry, I should have done the introductions first. This is Oz; Oz Blackstone, my new friend.'

The young Miss Phillips looked me up and down. My jeans had seen better days, but haven't everyone's, and at least my white tee-shirt was clean and my trainers didn't smell. Eventually she held out a hand. 'Pleased to meet you, Oz. Did she bring you back from Africa?'

I shook my head, and her hand. 'No. Anstruther, in fact. And before that, from Connell. We've been looking all around Scotland for you.'

She frowned, looking genuinely puzzled. 'But . . .'

Prim cut her off, shooeing her inside the house and pulling me in after her. 'We'll get to that in a minute, Dawn,' she said, carefully. 'First of all let's get the kettle on. Where are Mum and Dad?'

'It's Sunday. They've gone to church.' '*Mmm*,' I thought. '*People still do that, do they*!'

It was a nice old house on the inside. Full of character. It seemed that the Phillips family hadn't thrown anything away for about three generations. As I looked around the hall, I had a funny feeling that I couldn't pin down for a moment or two. Eventually it came to me. 'It's like stepping back into my Granny Blackstone's house.' I spoke the thought aloud.

'Yes, sort of old-fashioned comfy, isn't it,' said Prim. 'My Dad likes old things.' She pointed me into a big living room, off the hall, and disappeared with Dawn in another direction. I looked around the room. It was dominated by a huge brown three-piece suite in leather and velvet, and the pleasant smell of the hide hung in the air. Everything else – curtains, rugs, furniture, huge wooden-framed radio – was of the same 1930s vintage. A telly would have seemed obscene in there.

'It's a museum, isn't it,' said Prim, from the doorway, behind me. 'Lovely to visit, but not to live in. Not for me, anyway.

'Sit down,' she ordered. 'Dawn's making the tea.' She flopped on to the big sofa, pulling me down beside her. The big velvet cushions whooshed up around me with my weight. I've never laid on a feather-bed, but when I do, I imagine it'll feel like the Phillips family settee. Prim curled up on her cushion, sitting with her legs pulled up like she does in the car. She was wearing a white sleeveless wool top and pale blue shorts. The way she was sitting I could see her knickers. Suddenly my jeans felt tighter as old Mr Stiffy began to make his presence felt. I reached out for her, but she jumped up, a smile on her delicious lips. 'Oz! It's Sunday. My folks are Sabbatarians. No radio on Sunday, no playing cards, and absolutely no nooky on the living-room carpet!

'Besides, this is serious. What are we going to tell Dawn?'

Dragged back to reality, I shook my head. 'We're going to ask her a few things first. She . . .'

'Ask me?' Dawn was in the doorway carrying teapot, cups and saucers on a big tray with folding legs. 'Ask me what?'

'How you came to be in a movie, for a start,' said Prim, quickly.

'Oh,' said Dawn. 'All that hasn't really sunk in yet. It was pure luck. There was a part for an actress and Miles wanted someone Scottish. He came to the Lyceum one night when I was on and saw me. Next day, I had a note from the director asking me to come for a test.'

'That's great. How's it going?'

'Terrific, so far. I was supposed to be ravished and killed by the Redcoats quite early on, but Miles has given me a reprieve. They've written some more scenes for me and I'm getting supporting billing. A bit more money too.'

'You seem to be doing all right in other ways,' I chipped in. 'We met Miles. He fancies you, and no mistake.'

Dawn glanced at me as she poured the tea and smiled self-consciously, nervily. I could see that, temperamentally, she was her sister's opposite.

'So,' said Prim, 'with all that's going for you, how come you're screwed up. What's with the Prozac?'

'Oh it's lots of things, but mostly, as usual, it's men. I've got myself trapped in a sort of, situation, and I was having trouble finding a way out.' '*Christ*,' I thought, '*if that was her solution I found in Prim's flat it was a bit drastic*.'

'I was having stage fright, quite badly. The Prozac sorted it out, but it didn't do anything for the root cause of the trouble.' '*No?*' I thought again. '*Maybe it took the kitchen knife to sort that out*.'

'Remember the guy I told you about in a letter?'

'Danny deVito meets Nijinski?' said Prim.

'Yes, that's right. His name's William Kane. He's a regular at the theatre. His firm are corporate sponsors. I met him at our theatre club one night. We got talking, and I thought he was sort of funny, but sad at the same time. He was carrying a burden, I could tell.'

Prim sighed. 'Aah. Another bloody bird with a broken wing! I thought you'd grown out of that.'

'You don't though, do you. At least I don't. Anyway Willie isn't like that. He isn't helpless or anything. He phoned me a couple of days after the reception and asked me out. He came to the play, then took me to dinner, and it was fun. We did it again, and soon it was a regular thing.'

'He's married of course, Dawn, isn't he?' There was an edge of disapproval in Prim's voice. Her sister's cheeks flushed, quickly. She nodded.

'Yes,' she said quietly. 'Look, I know this'll sound awful, but his marriage is a sham. He and his wife are around forty; they've been married unhappily for years. She's unfaithful to him, and she doesn't hide it. In fact she rubs Willie's nose in it. She has a relationship with someone she was at school with.' Prim shot me a raised-eyebrow glance. 'They were boy and girl school captains at the same time, but afterwards they went their separate ways, until they met up again a couple of years ago.

'The way things were, I didn't feel uncomfortable about sleeping with Willie.' She grinned, suddenly with a strange, mischievous look in her eyes. 'Except . . .' She flushed again and glanced at me.

'Yes?' said Prim.

'Tell you later,' she said, looking meaningfully in my direction once more. '*You nearly let on about Willie's big Willy, didn't you.*' I was bursting to say it, but I resisted. 'Let's just say there was a physical problem,' she added. I coughed on a sip of tea. Prim shot me a '*Shurrup*' look.

'It was fun at first,' Dawn went on. 'But Willie's obsessive.

Pretty soon he was telling me he loved me and everything. That made me nervous, but I thought it'd wear off. It didn't though. One day he turned up on the doorstep of your flat with a suitcase. He said he'd left Linda and was moving in with me. I didn't know what to do. I mean if I'd chucked him out he'd have had nowhere else to go, but . . . well, to tell you the truth, nice as he is, when we got down to it I found out pretty soon that physically, I don't really fancy him.'

'Bloody great,' said Prim. 'The guy turned you off, but you let him shack up with you. And in my flat. A bit of a bloody nerve that, wasn't it? Having it off with another woman's husband in my flat. Private eyes at the door and all that.'

'Oh come on,' said Dawn, defensively. 'His wife wouldn't do that.'

Prim shot me another '*Shurrup*,' look, but I decided that it was time to get into the discussion. 'When was the last time you saw him?' I asked, as casually as I could.

She looked blankly at me. 'A couple of weeks ago,' she said. 'I left him in Ebeneezer Street when I went off filming. I told him he'd have to find somewhere permanent to live. I didn't *say* I wouldn't be coming with him, but I tried not to make him think that I would.

'He just said not to worry, that everything would be sorted out soon.'

'You didn't go back to Edinburgh on Wednesday?'

'No. I came here, to see Mum and Dad. The thing is, I really fancy Miles too, and I want to clear the decks. I thought I'd ask Dad to go to see Willie, to say I want out, and to ask him to be sure to move out of the flat before I got back.'

Prim snorted. 'That'd be really nice of Dad. Have you asked him yet?'

'No, I haven't plucked up the courage. I don't suppose

you'd . . .' And then something struck her, something very obvious.

'But hold on. You're back, Prim. So you must have been to the flat. Wasn't Willie there? Have you chucked him out already?'

Primavera shook her head. 'Sit down, Dawn,' she said quietly. Her sister obeyed. 'Yes, I've been to the flat, and yes, I've seen Willie. So has Oz. But he was dead. He was murdered. On Wednesday night, the police say.'

The girl's face went ashen. She hid it with her hands and slumped backwards, collapsing into the soft cushions of the big armchair. I thought that she was crying, but she wasn't. She was too shocked for that. It was Prim who was suddenly in tears. She rushed across the room, and threw her arms round her sister. 'Oh Dawn, I'm sorry, but I'm so relieved. We didn't want to think it, but we were afraid that you might have had something to do with it, or that you might be in danger too. That's why we've been looking for you.'

I felt helpless, so I got up and put my arms around them both. 'It's okay,' I said. 'It's okay, Prim. We've found her now, and she's going to be all right.' I drew her to her feet and held her against me. In the armchair, Dawn took her hands from her ghost's face and looked up at us.

'Do the police know who did it?' she said, huskily.

I shook my head. 'No. The guy in charge is going to want to talk to you. Was Willie in touch with anyone? His wife, for example?'

'Not as far as I know? But I haven't seen him for two weeks, remember.'

'Did he tell you about the money?'

'What money?' Prim and I looked hard at her. She was an actress, but I couldn't imagine that anyone could fake that sort of astonishment.

'Did Willie send you to Switzerland to open a bank account for him?'

She gave a soft gasp. 'Oh, that. Yes. He said he wanted to hide as much of his money from his wife as he could. He said she'd be suspicious if she found out that he'd gone to Switzerland, so he asked me to do it. I flew to Geneva and opened the account, then flew back on the same day.

'The account's in a bank called Berners: it's one of these cloak and dagger things. Withdrawals can only be made by two people, each carrying half of a fiver. The account number is the same as the number on the banknote. The bank took a photo of it. When I got back I gave the two halves to Willie.' She pulled herself up in the chair.

'But why did you ask about money? Did Willie use the account? Did he transfer his cash out there?'

I smiled. 'I don't know about *his* cash, but he transferred nine hundred thousand of his firm's money out there. I was hired by the senior partner to recover it. I went to see him on Thursday, to get the fiver back. He was dead when I got there, and when Prim arrived. That's when we met.

'We've been a bit busy since then,' I added.

Dawn sat there staring up at us as she fitted the pieces of the story together. By now I was quite certain that Prim's sister was just a touch slow on the uptake, but eventually she got there. 'Do the police think I killed Willie for the money?'

'The guy who's leading the investigation, Mike Dylan, he doesn't know about the money. And that's the way I want it to stay. Black and Muirton want to keep that part of it quiet. But if Dylan ever does find out about it, and about you opening that bank account, then yes, he'd fancy you for it right away. So let's hope you can prove where you were when Kane was killed.' Dawn gulped. Her mouth dropped open slightly. Prim looked at her anxiously.

'So,' she said, 'when did you get here on Wednesday?'

'About two-thirty in the afternoon.'

'And were you with Mum and Dad all day after that?'

'Yes. Dad had an order to dispatch that day for a customer in London. I helped him box it, then we went to the station in Perth and put it on a train. That would have been around nine in the evening.' She paused. 'Hey, I signed the dispatch slip, and it has the time on it!' Her face lit up with relief.

'After that we came back home and had supper with Mum. I told them all about the film. We sat up until about one in the morning.'

It was my turn to grin with relief. I mean, you don't fancy even the outside possibility that your girlfriend's sister might be a knife-wielding maniac, do you? 'Dawn, that's brilliant,' I said. 'Dylan won't be able to lay a glove on you.'

'Should I go to the police?'

'I don't know. Let's think about that one for a while.

'One thing though. Just remember, if and when you do see Mike Dylan, don't mention a word to him about the bank account. If he should ask you about it, look blank, then tell us.'

She nodded. 'Okay. What about the fiver? Who's got that?'

I looked at Prim. Prim looked at me, and shook her head, imperceptibly. 'The important thing, Dawn,' I said, 'is that whoever killed Willie *doesn't* have it. They couldn't find it at the time, but they sure as hell want it now.' I thought some more, and as I did, there was a loud creak from the hallway. Prim drew a finger across her throat in a 'Keep your mouth shut!' sign, then rubbed her face quickly with her hands to clear away the traces of her earlier tears.

Looking at Mum and Dad Phillips in their churchgoing

clothes, I had a sudden strange feeling that Prim, Dawn and I, the three of us, were time travellers, who had taken a flip back sixty years. Mum was dressed in a long brown velvet dress with a fur stole and a funny, shapeless wee hat that sat on top of her head like a cowpat. Dad wore a heavy black suit, with a jacket so long that it was almost a frock coat. He wore, big round glasses, and a gold watch chain hung across his waistcoat. His high shirt collar was starched stiff, and secured by a brass stud which showed just above the knot of his striped tie. I guessed that he was in his early sixties, his wife maybe five years or so younger. Each was probably around the same age as their clothes.

'Primavera! When we saw the car, we hoped it was you!' Mrs Phillips had a voice like a bell. It rang grandly around the room, and I thought for a second I could hear the glassware tremble. But it had a kind tone, and I knew at once that I was going to like her. Prim rushed across to the doorway and hugged her mother. Behind them, her Dad smiled awkwardly, as if taken aback by such a show of emotion. Then she turned to him, and pulled him to her also, kissing his cheek. I was surprised when his eyes glistened, and so, I think was he. I thought about shedding the odd tear myself, to spare the poor bloke's embarrassment.

Eventually, they noticed that I was there. They couldn't help it. I stood there in my jeans and tee-shirt, fidgeting and feeling as awkward as I ever had in my life. They didn't stare at me, they just looked, as they'd probably look at a deer that wandered into their garden. '*Nice, isn't it?*' '*Yes, as long as it doesn't eat the tulips!*' Prim took pity on the alien life-form whom she'd brought into the house. She came across and wrapped herself around me, holding me like a drunk holds a bus-stop, as if he's taking it home to the wife.

'Mum, Dad. This is Oz Blackstone. He's crackers, but I think you'll like him. I do.'

How do you respond to an introduction like that? I came out with, 'Pleased to meet you, after all this time.' The words sort of fell out of my mouth. It was as if they'd been generated by something other than my brain. Without breaking Prim's bearhug, I reached out and shook hands with them both.

Mrs Phillips looked me up and down one more time. 'Well, Oz,' she said, slowly, weightily. 'I've waited a long time to hear my older daughter say something like that, so I'm pleased to meet you too.' She flicked a finger towards Dawn and added, archly. 'That one, of course, says something like that every three months or so, and from the way she was talking on Wednesday, I think we're about to hear it again.'

'That's not all we're going to hear, I hope,' said Mr Phillips, eyeballing his wife meaningfully. He's a dry sort, Prim's father. He looks as if he was made from the wood he carves himself, and he tends to say not much more than one of his toy soldiers. But when he does contribute, it hits the spot.

'All in good time, David,' said Mrs Phillips, 'but first, lunch. Come on, girls.'

'I'll help too,' I said at once, faced with the possibility of being left alone with the totem pole. But it wasn't that easy. 'Not at all, Oz,' said Mother. 'You sit down.' Prim looked back at me, smiling, as she followed her towards the kitchen.

Dad Phillips and I stood there for a few moments, in an awkward silence. And then he coughed, and I realised that he was even less at ease than I was. 'This must be very, er, sudden, for you,' I ventured. 'Both daughters at home more or less out of the blue, and one of them with a bloke in tow.'

He eyed me, checking for any sign that I was humouring

him. Then, all at once, he nodded and the ice was broken. 'Yes, you're right. I haven't had much practice at small talk in recent years, not since I sold my factory. Elanore and I each have our own interests, and they tend to be solitary. She writes, I carve wood into interesting shapes and paint it. We don't have many visitors, apart from the occasional girl chums our daughters bring with them. As a matter of fact, you're the first man friend that Primavera's brought here since she was at college.'

I beamed, bursting with pride, until very gently, he pricked my balloon. 'She's always been an individual, has Primavera. Odd tastes in most things.

'What's Oz short for?'

I told him. He nodded, in sympathy, I thought.

'What do you do?'

I told him. 'No divorce work,' I added hastily.

He shrugged. 'No matter. Someone's got to do it. Does it pay well?'

'I'm self-employed. I expect thirty grand net in a reasonable year. Forty in a good one.'

'Mmmm.' There was something in his 'Mmmm' that told me I'd passed my first test.

'D'you play chess?' said Mr Phillips, suddenly.

'I know how the men move,' I said guardedly. One thing more do I know. If anyone over sixty ever offers to take you on at dominoes, darts, chess or squash, be careful: especially if it's squash. There's nothing worse than being humbled at a young person's game by someone who puts his bus pass at the front of the court and adjusts his knee bandages before you begin. I know this from experience.

'That's enough,' he said, a decision made. He walked over to a side window and returned carrying, carefully, a chessboard on a stand. The pieces were set up, ready for battle.

They were unlike any I had ever seen. The kings, queens and their courts were all hand-carved, in forms dredged from a clearly remarkable imagination. They were delicately painted and sealed in hard varnish, but there was no doubt as to which side was which.

The black pawns were twisted, leering goblins; the castles were tall forbidding tower; the knights were dragon heads; the bishops were horned, hunched things; the royal pieces were cloaked, and oozed menace from under their twisted crowns. The whites, on the other hand were smooth wee beauties. The pawns were beautifully armoured; the castles were straight and topped with tiny, carved, hand-coloured banners; the knights were plumed; the bishops carried crooks, and had long beards; the Queen was a perfect, narrow-waisted lady, with a wimple, rather than a crown; the white King had long, flowing hair, wore a simple, gold-painted circlet and leaned on a great broadsword.

I picked up the menacing black King. It was surprisingly heavy, and I realised that there was a weight set in its base. I held it up, and gasped at the way its pinprick eyes seemed to follow me, glowering.

'Did you make these?' I asked. 'They're brilliant.'

He smiled, and I could see that he was the sort of bloke who's embarrassed by his talent. 'Thank you. They're just a one-off, though. I couldn't do them commercially. Take too much time. My model soldiers are easier.

'Right, Oz, you're black.' The game didn't last long. He marched his soldiers out methodically, as I pursued my usual tactic of going for a quick kill, crashing my main attacking pieces all around the board, looking for an opening. He took my offensive apart, pawn by pawn, knight after knight, until all but nine of the men were on his side of the board. Finally he zapped me with a Queen–rook move that I saw only when I was beyond redemption.

He nodded as I tipped over my King. 'Excellent. You'll do for my daughter all right. People approach chess in the same way they approach their lives. You, Oz, play with your heart, rather than your head. Exactly like Primavera; you couldn't be better matched.'

Right on cue, my beloved appeared in the doorway. 'Come on you two. Lunch.' She led us through to a long dining room at the rear of the house, where a long table – more Corleone Family than Addams this time – was set for five.

'It's as if we were expected,' I said to Prim; quietly, I thought, but her mother can hear a mouse break wind at the foot of the garden.

'Sunday, Oz,' she boomed. 'We always cook a big bird on Sunday. It does us for a couple of days.' The big bird turned out to have been a goose, but before we got that far we were faced with the sort of thick soup that my Granny Blackstone used to make. You know the kind; you can draw your initials in the middle and they won't go away till you spoon them up. As I tackled and conquered the strong-flavoured goose, I looked out of the window. The Phillips' back garden was of the market variety. On one side vegetables were set out in rows; potatoes, carrots, leeks, pea stalks, runner beans. On the other, there were lines of raspberry canes, with strawberry patches next to the house and rhubarb under the boundary wall.

'What do you do with all that?' I asked Dad Phillips. 'You can't handle it all, surely?'

'Of course we can,' he said. 'We're not completely Norman Rockwell, you know. We do have a freezer. Everything we can't eat fresh goes in there, potatoes included, either cut into chips or sautéed.'

Naturally, there were raspberries for desert.

As we sat over our coffee, Mr Phillips looked across the table at Dawn over the top of his big glasses. Suddenly he was stern. 'Now, young lady. Perhaps you'll tell us why we had the police at our door yesterday, looking for you.'

Dawn went white for a second, then flushed bright scarlet.

'Didn't they tell you?' said Prim, with a combative edge to her voice.

At once, Dad Phillips abandoned his attempt to be the heavy father. It isn't a role that suits him, anyway. 'No, they didn't. They said something about wanting her to assist with an enquiry in Edinburgh.'

'Yes, that's right. But it's got nothing to do with Dawn really. A man was found dead in a flat in Ebeneezer Street, on my stair. The police want to talk to all the neighbours, to find out if they saw anything. But Dawn was here when it happened, so she can't tell them anything. End of story.'

I could tell that he didn't believe her. But I could tell also whose word is law in the Phillips family, when push comes to shove, and that, whatever was happening, he trusted her to handle it. Dad and Mum don't really want to play in the Nineties, and sometimes the world frightens Dawn just a bit. If Semple House, Auchterarder, was an independent state, Prim would be Foreign Secretary.

'Poor chap,' he said. 'Yet it was a bit much of the police to come chasing Dawn up here, in the circumstances. Could you two talk to them when you go back to Edinburgh?' He glanced at me.

'Sure,' I said. 'That'll probably keep them happy.'

'What did you tell them?' Prim asked.

'They asked me a straight question, so I gave them a straight answer. I said that Dawn had been here, but that she was away for a day or two with a friend in Perth. I said that she'd be back on Sunday, and we'd ask her to contact them as soon as possible. They seemed happy enough with that.'

'When *are* you two going back?' said Mrs Phillips.

'We thought we'd stay overnight,' said Prim, 'if that's all right?'

'All right! Of course it is. Your bed's made up, Primavera. I put sheets on it after you phoned. Thee's fresh linen under the stair for the fourth bedroom.' My heart sank, and I think my face must have gone down with it, for Prim kicked me under the table. I supped my coffee to cover my tracks.

There's not a lot you can do to escape a Scottish Sabbath, but eventually, after the girls had washed the dishes, Dad had massacred my goblin army on the chess-board a few more times, and we'd had totally unnecessary tea, scones and jam, Prim came up with a cover story. 'Mum, I think I'll take Oz to meet Julia.' It was around 6.30 p.m.

'Who's Julia?' I asked.

'My best pal from school. I visit her every time I'm here. She lives at the other end of town. We'll walk. Dawn, you come too.

'Oz, go and get our stuff out of the car, there's a love.'

Mrs Phillips was crossing the hall when I came back inside. When she noticed that I was carrying just one bag, she glanced at me and I'll swear a tiny smile flickered around the corners of her mouth. I guessed that there was something left of the woman who had christened her daughter after the time of her conception. She's a great believer is Prim's Mum. She believes in God, in her family and in all of life's certainties; the return of the seasons, and all that.

Of course, Julia wasn't in. We could have telephoned first, but we didn't. Instead we walked all the length of

Auchterarder's Main Street to find out, then made a detour up to the Gleneagles Hotel, which turned out to have been our real objective after all.

I thought we'd be lucky to be served in denims, but the Phillips sisters are well known there. We sat in the big bar sipping half-pints of Pimms, which Dawn insisted on buying with her movie money. Eventually I asked her how much she was being paid. When she told me I think she heard me grind my teeth. Sometimes it takes me more than six months to make the dough that Dawn was earning for a couple of weeks' work.

'Don't think it's all like that. Once this gig is over, chances are I'll be back in Edinburgh, doing stock plays at the Lyceum and being paid sweeties for it. That's if I've got a job at all.

'I won't complain if that's how it turns out. I like the Lyceum. You feel really close to your audience there, and the regulars feel close to us. Our Chairman came up with a really good idea last year. He started a theatre club for us performers and for our season ticket holders and regulars. We've got our own bar, and we can go in there after rehearsal – anytime really – and mix with the punters, making them feel part of the theatre family. We get some odd sorts turning out.' Her expression darkened all of a sudden. 'That's where I met Willie.' She sat there for almost a minute, in silence. Prim and I said nothing, letting her come through it in her own time. At last a faint smile returned to her lips. 'Willie. A bird with a broken wing all right.

'But he was just one among many. We've got a real cross-section of members. We've got civil servants, lawyers, a couple of hairdressers, housewives, flash young guys out to pull an actress. We've even got a member who's a prostitute. She offered Rawdon a freebie one night! I doubt if he took her up on it though! Oh yes, and we've got one policeman. A real Mr Plod, but he's dead keen. Surprising: you'd never guess it to look at him. McArthur, his name is.'

My eyebrows rose. 'What! A big beefy bloke with a red face?'

'Yes, that's him. He comes to every play, and he's in the bar about every second night.'

'My God,' I said, shaking my head in disbelief. 'McArse the theatregoer. You never know the hidden depths of people.'

It was just after nine-thirty when we finished our third round of Pimms and decided that it was time to call it quits. Night was still a way off as we strolled up the Gleneagles driveway and out towards the road, but the sun had gone and there were patches of darkness under the trees. If Auchterarder is famous for anything other than Gleneagles, it's because it lays claim to the longest Main Street of any Scottish town. All of it lay between us and Semple House as we turned into it and set off three abreast, with me in the middle and Dawn on the outside.

A pint and a half of Pimms seemed to have relaxed Dawn. As we walked she asked us how we had traced her, and laughed as Prim described our encounter with Rawdon Brooks. 'Poor old Rawdon,' she laughed. 'You shouldn't be hard on him. I know he's outrageous, he's a bit of a junkie, and he could seduce the College of Cardinals, but he's really nice. Gay men can be the kindest people, you know. There's no-one better when it comes to sharing your troubles. No offence, Prim, but they're even better than sisters.

'You can tell them anything you like, and they won't hold it against you, or tell a soul. So many people have cried on Rawdon's shoulders, they must be mildewed. He helped me a lot when I was going through agonies with Willie. He did his best to help Willie too, being a friend, and making him ask himself whether he was certain about what he was doing.'

'A real heart of gold,' I said, and she dug me in the ribs with her elbow.

'So tell me, you two. What d'you think I should do, then?' she asked, lisping slightly.

'No doubt about that,' I said. 'First thing tomorrow you should get your shapely arse back up to Connell or wherever the next stop is, and cuddle up to the leading man. "Tell her if she's got a problem, Old Miles'll sort it out." That's what he said. I'll tell you, I reckon he could, too. When you've got as much clout as Miles Grayson, you can sort out most things.

'Yes, Dawn. You head back to the Highlands and cuddle up to Miles.'

She looked up at me, then across at her sister. 'Hey, Prim,' she called. 'Where did you find this guy? I like the way he thinks!'

We were laughing so loud we might have not heard the car, but there was something about the engine tone that broke through to me, something about the way it kept on revving when the driver should have been changing gear. I looked up, just in time to see a black shape, travelling flat-out, swerve and head towards us, at racing speed, climbing on to the pavement.

If there had been a high wall on the other side of us we'd have been dead. All of us. But, thank God, there was only a low stone thing, with a sickly privet hedge behind it. The car was almost on us as I grabbed each sister around the waist and jerked them off their feet – diving, plunging over the wall and through the hedge. In mid-air, I felt something catch the outside of my left foot, twisting it, but somehow we made it, all three of us, to the other side.

Behind us we heard a crunch, the sound of breaking glass

and the scream of metal as the speeding car crashed into the wall. We lay there breathless waiting for it to stop, but it went roaring on, on down the longest Main Street in any Scottish town, and away into the gathering night.

I helped the girls to their feet and looked around. We were in a long garden. It stretched for at least a hundred yards, up to a big detached villa. We waited for lights to come on but none did. Amazingly, no lights came on in the surrounding houses either. Auchterarder's a bit like that. Plenty of Levites, but not too many Samaritans.

Eventually, I took a chance and stuck my head out of the garden, checking to see if the black car had come back, if it was lying out there, waiting for another shot. I felt like a character in a Stephen King novel.

'Who was it?' said Prim behind me. 'Did you see?' It was remarkable that not one of us thought for a second that it might have been a drunk driver.

'No,' I said. 'Och it was probably a drunk driver.' Even through the gloom, I felt the eyes of the Phillips sisters boring into me.

'Did you get the number?' asked Dawn.

'Do us a favour. I was too busy saving your life.' I shuddered and tried to replay the scene in my mind's eye. Again, I saw the car screaming towards us. I tried to freeze the picture. Suddenly, unexpectedly fragments of detail came back. 'A Mondeo, I think. Navy or black. "N" registered.' I tried to push everything else from my mind. 'The last two registration letters could have been "BL". But I couldn't swear to it.'

' "BL"?' said Dawn. 'Then it could have been hired.'

'How do you work that out?' asked Prim.

'The film unit have hired minibuses. And Miles has a big

stretched Ford thing. They all have "BL" registrations. But what does that tell us?'

'It could tell us that whoever did that didn't want to be putting their own car in for repair. Or it could tell us that it was a visiting Yank, driving, pissed, away from Gleneagles.'

We stood there for another five minutes, waiting, listening, watching every passing car, before we braved the road again. My jarred foot pained me with every step I took. We had been walking, or in my case limping, for less than a minute, when a taxi drove by, I hailed it and it stopped. The driver was a guy in his late twenties. He knew Prim and Dawn from school.

As we drove towards Semple House, I squeezed Dawn's hand. 'Hey. Remember what I was saying about cuddling up to Miles.' She nodded. 'I don't think you should wait till morning. I think you should go tonight.'

'Why? You don't think that was meant for me, do you?'

'No, of course not. I can't think why it should be meant for any of us. But whoever that was, it wasn't an autograph hunter. The best place for you is back with the crew.

'Tell your Mum and Dad you have to be back early. Then get on your way. Tonight.'

In which Mother offers black pudding, and we take a decision.

I don't know how long she'd been knocking. The sound started as part of a dream, a nice dream of domesticity, in which Prim and I were, I think, in the process of living happily ever after. I tried to dismiss it, but it was persistent, forcing its way from the back of my mind right up to the front.

Eventually it carried me back to the world of the wide-awake. I propped myself up on an elbow, taking care not to disturb the dozing blonde bundle lying beside me, on top of the quilt. One of Africa's gifts to Primavera is the ability, when she feels secure, to sleep through virtually anything.

'Morning,' I called drowsily to the door.

'Wakey, wakey Oz.' Mum Phillips sounded bright and breezy. 'Breakfast in twenty minutes. D'you like black pudding?' I squeezed my eyes tight to clear them, and looked at my watch on the bedside table. It was ten past eight.

'Thanks,' I called. 'See you there. And, yes, I love black pudding!'

'Good.' There was a pause. 'By the way, you haven't seen my daughter, have you?'

'I'll look under the bed.'

Beside me, Prim was beginning to stir, uncoiling, like a cat, sighing, murmuring, stretching. Eventually she shook her head and looked up at me, puzzled at first, then remembering. She pulled herself up and leaned against the heavy walnut headboard, flinching slightly from the coolness of the wood on her back, even through her nightshirt.

'What are you doing here?' I asked her. 'Have I got that job?'

She smiled, rubbing her eyes. 'I don't think that this is quite the place for the audition!

'Sorry to disappoint you, but I couldn't sleep for thinking about what happened last night. So I came in here, thinking you'd be in the same state. You were out like a light.'

'No imagination,' I said. 'That's my trouble.'

Her right breast hung a few inches away from me. Automatically, as if I had done it a hundred times before, I rubbed my forehead against it, and flicked my tongue across the protuberance of her nipple, through the cotton of her shirt. She shivered, then slid, supply, down the covers once again to lie beside me. I could feel her warm breath on my face as we kissed. Her nightdress, which was no more than a long tee-shirt, had ridden up around her waist. I laid my hand on her naked hip and pulled her closer to me as I kissed her again. Her tongue sought out mine, and her fingers wound through my hair. Suddenly she rolled over on top of me, moving her body against me. I could feel the heat of her through the covers, and her eyes burned into mine.

I smiled, 'What's it to be?' I said. 'Me, or your Mum's black pudding?'

She laughed. 'You lose,' she said, biting the end of my nose, gently. 'For now.' She pushed herself back and sat upright, straddling me. I gasped, and her eyes widened, as her weight bore down on my most critical region. 'It's nice to know I can command your attention when I want to,' she murmured.

'Darling,' I said, 'right now you're commanding a hell of a lot more than my attention!'

Gymnastically, she raised herself up again and swung her legs around to sit on the edge of the bed. When she turned and looked at me again, the tease was gone from her eyes.

'Who, Oz?' she pondered. I had fallen asleep asking myself the same question.

'I don't know,' I said.

'Unless . . .' she said.

'What?'

'No, forget it.'

'Come on!' I grunted. I hate it when someone sets me up and then says, 'No, forget it.'

'Well, *why* would anybody want to kill *us*?'

'What d'you mean?'

'Well, why *would* anyone? Not because of what we know. The only person who knows that *we* know about the money is Ray Archer, and right now we're his only chance of getting it back. And not because of what we've got. This gets complicated, but whoever is after the fiver doesn't necessarily know that *we* know what it's for. And they wouldn't want to kill us, would they, at least until they'd got it?'

'So?'

'So could the driver have been after Dawn?'

'Aw, come on. Who'd want to kill Dawn?' as I said it a thought nagged at my brain.

I looked sideways at Prim and shuddered. 'Ugh! Stop.

You're doing my head in. The main thing is we're all alive, and Dawn's safely off to her movie. Now, if you're still turning down the best offer you've had all day, concentrate on breakfast, and on getting your brain into gear. We've got some decisions to make.'

The tease was back in her eyes. I pushed myself upright and drew her backwards, pulling her down until her head rested on the pillow. Her nightshirt was drawn up higher this time, and the lower swell of her breasts was in view. She looked up at me: all at once, her right hand was under the covers, feeling, seeking, finding. The smile faded to be replaced by something else. I bent over her and kissed her navel, then flicked my tongue into its cavity, then out, then in then out, then . . .

'Ahhh!' she gasped, holding my head with her free hand, rotating her hips beneath me. I slid the nightshirt up, feeling her lift her arms and raise her head and shoulders to assist me. 'Oz!' She hissed, with an edge of hesitancy in her voice, but with overpowering urgency, and without a shred of teasing. The nightshirt stretched taut as it cleared her shoulder, but in a moment her arm was free. I eased myself upright and began to pull back the barrier of linen and blankets which kept us apart. All the while she held on to me, stroking, kneading, until I thought I would burst.

The knock on the door was as vigorous as before. 'Oz! Five minutes.'

'Bugger!' said Primavera and I, in unison.

Prim shook her head in despair. 'Make it fifteen,' she called out to the door. 'Oz has to shave.' She let me go, then sat up and thrust her arm back into her nightshirt.

'Told you this was no place for an audition,' she said, smiling. 'We found out one thing, though.'

'What's that?' I asked. I felt myself subside, experiencing

also the onset of a condition known and dreaded by all men in such a situation.

'You can command my attention as well!'

Semple House has basins in every bedroom. As soon as I felt confident that my boxers had resumed a normal shape, I vaulted out of bed and turned on the hot tap. The water reached near-boiling point, almost instantly.

She sat on the bed, watching me as I lathered my chin. 'Before we got distracted, you were talking about decisions,' she said. 'What sort d'you mean?'

'The sort we've been avoiding until now. Like, where are we going next? Should we tell Archer we've got the fiver? Should we tell the police everything?'

I drew my razor down my cheek, cutting a clean, shiny swathe through the foam.

'What d'you think?'

I could see her in the mirror, holding her chin as she pondered over my questions. 'I don't know. I do know what common sense says. Until now, we've put everything to one side to find Dawn. Now we've done that, and we know that she's safe, and didn't have anything to do with Willie Kane's murder, then as good honest citizens we should say "Sod the reward, sod Archer and his sordid cover-up", and tell the whole story to Mike Dylan.

'And yet . . .' Her reflection swung her legs off the bed and stood up, stretching her arms high above her head, clasping her hands together and pulling them backwards, thrusting out her breasts and tensing the muscles of her groin. 'I don't know, I've got a bad feeling about something.' As I scraped the last of the lather from my top lip, I saw her cross the room. She stood behind me and wrapped her arms around my waist. 'What d'*you* think?'

I disengaged her and turned round, holding her at arm's length. 'I think we should be very careful. We've found Dawn, she's all right, she's got an alibi, and that's good. But it doesn't take away the memory of wee Kane dead in your bed, and it doesn't tell us who killed him. And it doesn't take away what happened last night.

'I've got a bad feeling too. It comes from Dylan suddenly wanting to know about the fiver, and about the fact that he was so keen to find it that he actually broke into my place to search for it.'

She looked up at me. 'So, should we give it to *him*?'

I shook my head. 'No, that's the last thing we should do. Dylan didn't have a clue about it on Thursday morning, yet on Friday he's turning over Edinburgh, trying to find it. So who told him what it was worth? It's a cert. that Kane was killed for that note, only whoever did it couldn't find it. We only have it now because clumsy Mr Plod knocked over your muesli jar. So who knew about it? One, I did; two, Raymond Archer did.

'So is there a link between him and Dylan, or someone else? God knows, but I think we should try to find out too.'

'You don't think Archer could have killed Kane himself?'

'Nah. I really don't see that. Why should he involve me if he was going to kill the wee fella?'

She looked at me doubtfully. 'In that case, who?'

'Let's wait and see. Dawn said something yesterday that could give us a clue.'

'What was that?'

'All in good time, my dear.'

'Oz, don't be mysterious!' She stepped close against me once more and kissed my chest. Down in the jungle, a natural force began to stir once more. With a huge effort of will, I steered her towards the door.

'Go, woman,' I declaimed, 'and stop trying to seduce me. After breakfast, we'll work out a game plan. Meantime, I can smell that black pudding.'

Dad and Mum Phillips are creatures of habit. Their days seem to be more organised than anyone's I've ever met. Breakfast is one of their rituals, and that morning, they clearly enjoyed sharing it with their older child, and with the big, tousle-headed cuckoo who sat beside her at the dining table.

The black pudding tasted as good as it smelled. Mrs Phillips dished it up together with scrambled eggs and mushrooms, and thick slices of toast. We made small talk as we ate. Dad asked me some more about my work, my family, where I lived, gently filling in the gaps in his knowledge. He looked impressed when I said my father was a dentist.

Mum muttered that it was a pity that Dawn had rushed off. 'That's her all over. Impetuous. One minute she's going back on Monday morning, next she has to be there for early-morning run-through.'

At five to nine, it was suddenly all over. 'Right,' said Mum, standing up abruptly. 'Dad and I are off to work. The washing up's all yours. Come, David. We'll be in the studio; let us know when you're ready for the road.'

I washed, I dried, and Prim supervised, eventually condescending to stack the plates in the kitchen cupboard. 'Right,' she said, when she was finished. 'Decision time. What do we do now, Oz?'

I reached out a hand for her. You may have noticed that I'm very tactile, as far as Prim is concerned at least. I'm never happier than when I'm touching her.

'I've been thinking about that,' I said. 'I reckon it's time for me to treat Ray Archer to another performance of my Daft

Laddie act. There are some things we need to know, and I reckon he might be able to help us . . . as long as he doesn't know he's doing it!'

In which Ray Archer is immersed in his own Genius.

We said our farewells to Mum and Dad Phillips, in the spacious attic studio which they shared. His bench and lathe was on one side, her Apple Mac computer on the other.

'You'll take care of the police business for Dawn, will you, Primavera?' Mr Phillips asked, still a touch anxiously.

'No, Dad,' she said. 'Dawn's going to phone them this morning. We agreed that was the best way to handle it.'

'And you, Primavera,' said her mother. 'What will you do when you get back to Edinburgh? Start looking for a hospital job?'

'Give me a break, Mum. I think I've earned a holiday over the last year.'

'Yes, I suppose you have. Don't let it last too long, though. You know what they say about the Devil and idle hands.'

Prim laughed, and dug me in the ribs with an elbow. 'Hear that, Devil?' she murmured.

Rather than retrace our route to Perth, we took the twisty road down from Auchterarder through the hills, and picked up the motorway just south of Kinross. I tried to call Archer on the mobile, but the cloud was low, and we were in a dead zone for transmission until we were in sight of the Forth Bridge.

Eventually, I got through. When he came on the line, he spoke quietly, as if he had company. 'I need to see you,' I said. 'I've found Kane's girlfriend. She was out of town when he was killed, and she doesn't have the fiver. I have to meet you today, to talk about what we do next.'

'Okay,' Archer whispered. 'But not in the office. Meet me at midday, in the Abbotsford.'

I hate going into pubs at lunchtime. Nearly always, I feel guilty, and wonder about everyone else who's in there taking in alcohol in the middle of what should be a working day. (Oz Blackstone, closet prude!) The Abbotsford's an exception though. It's a real characterful place, still in its original wood panelling, with a big oval bar, and a few booths with benches for those who prefer to drink sitting down.

Prim and I agreed that there were no plus points to be gained from introducing her to Archer at that stage, so when we reached Rose Street, she ducked into Marks & Spencer to replenish her knicker stock while I shouldered my way through the brass-handled double doors of the old pub.

The Abbotsford was still relatively quiet; the place smelled of mutton pies heating in the oven and beans on the hob, being made ready to be hoovered up by the lunchtime rush. There was no sign of Archer in the bar, but when I looked into the back room, I found him there, sat, alone, at a table, nursing a half-pint of Guinness.

He offered me a drink, but I said a quick 'No thanks' and sat down facing him. As usual there were no preliminaries. 'Where did you find the girl?' he asked at once.

I treated myself to the luxury of telling him the truth. 'She was up in Perthshire, with her parents. She was there at the time Kane was killed, and she can prove it.'

He looked at me over his Guinness. 'D'you think she was in the know about it, though?'

'No chance. She wanted shot of the wee man all right, but not that way.'

'She said she doesn't have the fiver?'

'That's right.'

'And you believed her?' There was more than an edge of doubt in his tone.

'Yes. Kane spun her a story about wanting to squirrel his money away from his wife, before he left her. He told her she'd have every penny, otherwise. Dawn's an actress. She's got an active imagination, so it wasn't difficult for her to take his story at face value. She was sorry for him so she agreed to help him set up the account. When she got back, she gave him the fiver, and that's the last she saw of it.'

'Are you trying to tell me she doesn't know about the missing money?'

'That's what she said, and from the way she looked at me when I asked her about it, I believe her.'

His look was one of pure scorn. I was annoyed even before he opened his mouth. Afterwards, I was downright angry. 'Come on Blackstone!' He spat it out, his eyes narrowing. 'Who are you trying to kid? Know what, I reckon you're shagging this tart now. I reckon you and she have done a deal about the money!'

Temper and Oz are not normally associated, one with the other. I've never taken a pop at anyone in my life, but I've never come closer to it than I did with Ray Archer right then. Instead, and it was as if my hand made its own decision, independent of my brain, I picked up his Guinness and threw it in his face.

He started off his bench. I thought he was going to take a swing at me, and so, before he was even halfway upright, I shoved him back on to his pin-striped arse.

Now it was me spitting out the words. I don't know whose voice I was using, but it didn't sound like mine. 'You say that just once more, pal, and I'm going to make a phone call to a guy I know on *Scotland on Sunday*. Then I'm going to see my lawyer. After that, he and I are going to see Inspector Dylan.

'If you want to end up twisting in the wind, with all your partners beside you, then just keep it up.'

His head went down; he took his hankie from his breast pocket and mopped his dripping face. 'I'm sorry, Oz,' he said softly, gazing at the table, not at me. In those seconds his tone changed from aggressive to wheedling. I disliked that just as much. 'I shouldn't have said that. My firm has ten partners and forty employees. The career of every one of them is riding on my shoulders, and it's getting to me. You're the last person I should be upsetting. Please forgive me.'

His protestations of concern for his workforce were lost on me. He was only thinking about money . . . his money. 'Level with me, Mr Archer,' I said, recovering the normal Oz tone, 'how long do I have to get your funds back?'

'A week at the outside. Our client's abroad just now. He'll be back in Edinburgh in ten days.'

'And if we don't get it back, what's the down-side? Do you really go bust?'

He shrugged his shoulders. 'If you can't get that money back by next Monday, my partners and I, and that means mostly me, will have to cover the loss and probably pay a premium to buy back the stock that Kane sold. With luck, we'll keep the firm afloat, but . . .' He gazed up at me, with what he hoped would look like desperation.

'At the moment, only you, my financial controller and I know about this thing. If I have to tell my partners, that makes it all the more dangerous for us. After that, just one tongue loosened in the Drum and Monkey by one pint too many and it could be all up for Black and Muirton.'

A sudden thought ran down my spine, like a mouse with very cold feet.

'Tell me about your financial controller.'

Archer smiled, wanly. 'Jerry? No, Oz. Forget it. Jerry Hannah's sixty-nine years old, and he has a bad heart. Apart from all that, he's the tightest-mouthed old bastard I know. If you told Jerry a secret he wouldn't even repeat it back to you.'

'And you've told no-one else?'

He shook his head, but there was a hesitation there. 'No. Only my wife. I told her the whole story last Monday, as soon as I'd pieced it all together, about the theft, about Berners and the bank account, and how Kane and the girl had set it up. I told her I was going to hire you to get the money back.' He gave me one of those man to man glances. 'I had to confide in someone. Anyway, Marian and I make a point of having no secrets.'

I gave him the nod he expected.

'I don't suppose Willie Kane would have told anyone about his scam. I mean he and Mrs Kane weren't exactly on pillow-talk terms any more, were they?'

He gave a short, choked off laugh. 'No indeed. God, when I think about it, poor Marian. Getting my worries and Linda's at the same time. I told you, she's Linda Kane's best friend. We're near neighbours, so they see each other every day. Linda used to work for Black and Muirton, you know. That's how she and Willie met. She was his secretary. The odd couple, and no mistake.'

'Mrs Kane must have been pretty upset when he walked out on her. Then with him being killed, your wife must have had a hard time with her.'

Archer snorted. 'From what Marian says, "grief-stricken" isn't quite the term for her. She was absolutely furious when he left. But "incandescent", was how Marian described her after the murder. I suppose we all build walls against bereavement in different ways.'

Suddenly he snapped back into his businesslike mode. 'So what are you going to do next, Oz? The trail of that banknote must be pretty cold, if Willie's girl doesn't have it.'

So far, I had gone through our conversation without telling Archer a single porky-pie; now I was struggling to keep up my run. I could have said, 'Look Ray, it's all right, I've got the fiver,' but something held me back. Probably it was the fact that somewhere in the city, outside the Abbotsford, was the guy who had killed Kane to get that banknote. That and the thought that, one way or another, unwittingly or wittingly, Archer must have put him on the trail. I thought about Kane, and that knife, and all of a sudden my tongue stuck to the roof of my mouth. The less Archer knew, the safer it would be for Prim and me.

I gazed at him with an expression that was meant to be contemplative, but which really hid the fact that I hadn't a clue what to do next. But at last, it came to me. 'I think it's time I paid a call on a lady,' I said, in Private Eye-speak, turned on my heel and walked out of the pub, leaving him to the impossible task of wiping drying Guinness stains off a pale blue shirt.

In which we meet the Widow Kane and find her wanting in the grief department.

'Oz, I know you're daft; you don't have to go proving it all the time.' From the moment of our meeting, Prim's faith in my judgement has been touching. 'What will we say to the woman?'

'I don't know for sure. I just think we should go along to offer our sympathies. Remember what Dawn said about her. She was two-timing Willie, according to him at least.'

Primavera looks wonderful when her smile is just about to erupt into laughter. When she throws her head back and laughs it sounds like the pealing of a chime of bells. Right at that moment, the ringers had a good grip on the ropes.

'So we just walk in there, and ask her about it, do we?'

'Not quite, but there's one thing we might learn, if we play our cards right. Just think back to what Dawn said about her.' She thought for only a few seconds, then caught on. Much quicker than her sister, is Prim. When it comes to it, she's much quicker than me. 'I remember now. And you think . . .'

When you're really in love, telepathy is a perfectly feasible proposition.

We found the address with no difficulty at all. In the back of the car, we still had a copy of the *Evening News* which carried the report of his identification, complete with a photo of *Chez* Kane. Even for a stockbroker, it looked quite a place. It was a big villa along Ravelston Dykes, one of those streets in Edinburgh where the poor folk aren't encouraged to get out of their cars.

As I parked the Nissan, defiantly, Prim gazed at the house through the wrought-iron railings which topped the small garden wall. She whistled softly. 'Poor Willie must really have been stuck on our Dawn to walk out of this pile,' she whispered.

'Or he must really have hated his wife,' I said.

The only downmarket thing about the house was the car in the driveway. It was a silver Calibra, where you'd have expected a Five-series Beamer at the very least. But, still, it was top-of-the-range, with a personalised 'LBK' number plate.

I took a quick peek through the living-room window as we approached the front door, hustling along in the light rain, which had been threatening all day. Where Semple House was genuine Charles Addams, 'Achnasheen', for thus it had been named by a fanciful builder, was genuine *Vogue*. The furniture was modern but nondescript, white leather settees, a dull high-board, a hi-fi rack and speakers against the far wall. Prim tugged me towards the front door and rang the bell.

It took a second ring before the door was opened, by a reddish-haired woman. She leaned against the jamb, perspiring and breathing heavily. She looked well on the fleshy side in her leotard and tights, ankle-warmers and trainers, her bosom jiggling formidably as it rose and fell. In the background, an aerobics tape pounded on loudly.

She looked at us as she recovered her wind. For the faintest moment I thought I saw alarm in her eyes; but probably I imagined it. This was a woman who would not be alarmed by heavy machine gun fire. 'Yes?' she gasped, eventually.

'Mrs Kane?' I asked. She nodded, and I ploughed on as wide-eyed and friendly as could be. 'Sorry if it's an inconvenient time, but we wondered if we might have a word with you?'

She was breathing normally now, and looked formidably hostile. 'You're not more bloody press, are you?' I noticed that her voice was harder than the norm among Ravelston matrons.

'Heavens no,' I said airily.

'Oh Christ, not the fucking Witnesses, surely! Sunday was yesterday, chum.'

I smiled, trying to appease her. 'No, Mrs Kane, we're not witnesses. Not that sort, anyway. We, I, wanted to talk to you about your husband. My name's Oz Blackstone. I don't know if the police told you, but it was us who found Mr Kane.'

The hostility lessened a bit, but she was still a long way from offering an embrace. 'I see. So? Do you expect a fucking reward?'

I took a deep breath. 'Well, my girlfriend and I thought we should maybe come along to see you, just to, well comfort you if we could.'

'Do I look as if I need comforting?'

I almost told her she looked as if she needed a couple of weeks on Slimfast, and a compassion transplant, but I held back. We hadn't come just to be slung off her doorstep. Eventually she gave in. 'Oh, come on in, if you must. The Cindy Crawford workout's left me shagged out anyway.' She turned in the doorway and pressed a TV remote. In the background, Cindy was cut off in her splendid prime.

She led us into the 'no imagination' living room. A packet of Benson and Hedges lay on the mantelpiece. She took out a fag and lit it with a big Ronson table model, offering the pack to us as she inhaled.

'So,' she said, as the blue smoke gave the room its only real colour. 'What did you want to tell me about the dear departed?'

'Well, we thought you might like to know that it seemed as if he didn't suffer, that it was pretty quick.'

She took another drag, and looked at me as if I was an idiot. Right then, that was how I felt; if you called Linda Kane a hard cow, you'd be insulting bovines everywhere. 'I'd worked that one out, son. Who d'you think identified the little shit? I imagine that if someone skewers your top-piece you go straight to the Pearly Gates, no stopping.

'More's the pity,' she added with venom.

'Oh, come on Mrs Kane,' surprising myself by coming to the adulterous embezzler's defence.

'Come on nothing. The little bastard left me. He walked out on me for some fucking tart . . . on me! After all I've done for him. I *made* him at Black and Muirton, you know. The number of times I covered up for him. To look at him you'd never have thought he'd the brains to . . .' She stumbled, very slightly, then caught herself, '. . . put his hat on the right way round.

'Nearly said something rude there.' She added, with a coyness that sat on her as easily as a nun on a rodeo bull.

'So you found him, did you?' She looked at Prim. 'That means you, dear, must be that little tart's sister. Little bastard or not he was *my* little bastard; And anyone who takes what's mine . . . Fucking little tart!'

I held my breath and waited for Prim to drive the woman's nose up into her brain. But Linda Kane saved the situation, and herself. 'Look, I'm sorry to be so blunt, talking about her like that, but woman to woman, you must know how I feel. And I know you can't pick your relatives.'

Somehow, Prim managed to look at the floor and say nothing. Then she turned away, and walked a few paces across the room, to the tasteless high-board. There were several silver-framed photographs on a shelf in the middle. She picked one up, and looked at it, then held it up so that Linda Kane and I could both see it. It showed a girl, a mature schoolgirl, in a blazer shirt and tie. 'Is this your daughter?'

Linda smiled. 'Do I look old enough? Yes, well I suppose I am. No, dear, that's me, when I was head girl at Mary Erskine. Let's see. That'll have been taken in 1975.'

I whistled. 'You've worn well then.'

She looked at me with the nearest thing I've seen to a leer on a woman. 'Flattery, son, will get you most places. But not here; not here. I like my men a bit older than you, and a bit bulkier too.'

She took the photo from Prim. 'Now, if that's all you've got to tell me, thank you for coming, but I'm due for a cut at Charlie Kivlin's in an hour.' She ushered us smoothly back to the door.

'Must look my best for the funeral, after all. It's at Mortonhall, on Friday. I've got a fair idea what I'm going to do with the ashes afterwards.' She made an unmistakable flushing movement with her right hand.

'Cheerio, then. If you want to come to the funeral you'll be welcome. The senior partner's talking about having a reception afterwards in the office. That's a bloody sight more than *I'd* do for him.'

She closed the door on us with something grotesque, that we took for a smile.

We hustled down the path to the garden gate as fast as we could and dived into the Nissan, which sat self-consciously under the trees. As soon as we were inside, I looked across at Prim, straight-faced. 'Widow of the Year, eh?' That was enough; we erupted in hoots of laughter.

'God,' she gasped at last, still convulsing, 'I actually feel happy for Willie Kane. Imagine, if Dawn had chucked him out before she left and he'd been forced to go back to that! Whoever killed him did him a favour.'

'Aye, but he did one for her too. With him dead, she'll have the house, free and clear.'

'And what more could she be after?' muttered Prim, ominously.

'Ah, hold on though,' I said, trying to keep her enthusiasm in check. 'She said nothing at all to show that she knows about the theft, or the fiver. She connected you to me, remember, and that's the story the police will have told her, about you and I finding him when we got back from the airport.'

'So what? No, Oz. I'd put nothing past that woman. If Mrs Archer told her about the theft, the bank account and everything, she could have been signing Kane's death warrant. Wish we knew a bit more about the boyfriend though. That's another thing we didn't find out.'

I looked at her, happy in the knowledge that I was about to score a point. 'Remember what Dawn said about him, though. Head boy and head girl at the same time.'

'Yes, I remember; but you remember, Mr Clever Dick. Mary Erskine's an all-girl school. My dumb sister must have got it wrong.'

'Ah Miss Clever . . . eh, Clever whatever. Mary Erskine's

run by the Merchant Company, and there's a partner boys' school less than a mile away. Stewart's-Melville; it's right at the end of this road, in fact. So . . .'

She was like a kid on a treasure hunt. 'So why don't we just head along there now and see what we can find out?'

In which the Old School Archives gives us an answer we don't fancy . . . not one bit.

Daniel Stewart's and Melville College, to give it its full, lengthy title, was formed by the amalgamation of two smaller Merchant Company schools, when economies of scale began to mean something even in the select world of Edinburgh private education.

It's housed in a fine old building on the Queensferry Road, a rectangle with copper-domed towers on each corner. As we reached it, the mothers of its primary school children were just beginning to gather in their second-hand Volvo estates. For some of them, picking up Junior and chewing the fat with the other Mums was probably the highlight of the day. There were so many of them gathered there that we had to park illicitly in the Tourist Board Headquarters and walk back.

The School Office was a slightly chaotic room. That meant that it was like all the school offices I've ever seen, only the accents were more refined, and the weans were better dressed . . . more uniformly, you might say.

The junior secretary was a friendly girl. 'How can I help

you?' she said, and we both knew that she meant it, relieved to be dealing with people from the outside world.

Prim looked at me. I looked at Prim. In the same instant we realised we'd gone barrelling in there without a cover story. 'No, you go on,' said my partner, dropping me in it. Fortunately, my natural glibness, formed out of years spent trying to chat girls just like this one out of their knickers, came surging to the surface. I gave her my best pre-coital smile, the one that says, '*Would you be interested in what I've got here!*'

'My friend and I are researching for a magazine article,' I said, inspirationally. 'We have a commission from the *Sunday Times* supplement for a piece which takes the attitudes of senior-school pupils from the mid-70s and compares them with today's generation.

'We're asking a few schools if they can put us in touch with their head boys and head girls from those times, so that we can set up interviews. We've just seen the head girl of 1975 at Mary Erskine, and she suggested that we should look up her opposite number here.

'Is there any possibility that you could give us his name?'

The girl smiled at me. I could tell that I'd have been in with a chance there.

She put a hand to her chin, as if she was thinking about it, but I knew the answer already. 'I'm sure that I can lay hands on the School Yearbook for 1975,' she said. 'Wait a minute.' She hurried off.

'Smooth-talking bastard,' Prim muttered under her breath as the girl disappeared.

It was only a minute, too. She came rushing back, pink-cheeked and triumphant. 'I knew we had one left. It is only one, though. I can't let you take it away, but I can photocopy pages if you'd like.'

She handed it across the wooden counter. I took it, and noticed that my hand was shaking, very slightly. I held it out so that Prim could see and flicked through the pages until I found the index. 'Captains Courageous' began on page twenty, after the Rector's report on the year.

Naturally, the Head Boy was the first entry. The outstanding chap of the year, beyond a doubt. Captain of Rugby, Captain of Cricket, Captain of Squash, School Athletics Champion, Leader of the Debating team, an all-rounder of the sort in which schools like Stewart's-Melville rejoice. A veritable hero, in fact.

There was a photograph too. He stood there in blazer, decorated with his many sporting colours, slim, squared-jawed, clear-eyed, a man-boy on the verge of a career of leadership in whatever profession he chose. And below the photograph, in rich italics, a caption.

'Head of School, 1974–75. Richard Ross.'

Prim gasped and looked up at me. 'That's Superintendent . . .'

I closed the book. 'Yes, partner. I was afraid it would be him. That's who's got Mike Dylan shitting himself trying to find that fiver. And that's who's been crumpling the sheets with Linda Kane, just like they did twenty years ago.'

We had our backs to the girl, so she couldn't hear us. 'Our FP club keeps very good records,' she said. 'I'm sure they could help you find him.' Helpful to the end.

I handed her back the yearbook. 'That's all right, dear,' I gave her a '*goodnight*' smile. 'Right now, I'm more worried about this chap finding us.' I could feel her eyes in my back, wrinkling with bewilderment, as Prim and I hurried away.

In which plans are made for flight.

'D'you think Linda'll tell him we've been to see her?'

'Abso-bloody-lutely, my darling.' I checked my watch. 'About half an hour ago, I reckon.'

She looked at me; not scared, but anxious. 'We're in trouble, Oz, aren't we?'

'Right up to our pretty little chins, Primavera. You get the picture, yes?'

I didn't need to spell out anything. 'Oh yes, I get it. Mr Archer pours out all his troubles to Mrs Archer. Mrs Archer tells her outraged friend Linda, all about the theft, the account and the banknote. *And* she tells her that Oz Blackstone, PI, is hot on the trail. Linda tells her boyfriend, Superintendent Ross.

'I imagine that gave them a wonderful idea: that they should beat you to it, get rid of the wee chap for good and pick up his money at the same time. Is that how you see it?'

'Sure is. How do you think they went about it.'

'I'd guess that she phoned Willie, and told him she wanted

to see him, alone. Lucky Linda: Dawn was away, so Willie said, "Okay, come to the flat on Wednesday." You said that when you phoned in the evening a woman answered the phone. That must have been her. Think back,' she said. 'Was it?'

I thought back. 'I couldn't swear to it,' I said, honestly. 'It was a funny voice.'

But Prim was in full flow. 'I guess she must have turned on her fading charms for her husband. Something like, "Please come home, Willikins! Let me show you how sorry I am." From the way it looked, Willie fell for it, and . . .' She grimaced, and faltered. I picked up the story.

'The wee man's crowning glory is in the ascendant, when . . . Linda's left the front door on the latch. Ricky Ross slips into the house, and into the bedroom. Poor wee Willie has the orgasm of his life . . . probably Linda does too, for that matter.'

Prim looked up at me. The windows of the Nissan were misting up. I was glad that no-one could see in, otherwise they'd have thought we were having a serious argument. 'There's no other explanation is there?'

'No. None at all. After they killed him, they'd have searched for the fiver. I bet they looked everywhere but in that muesli jar. I suppose Ross asked Dylan next day to report on every single thing his people had found, and Dylan must have mentioned the torn banknote. Hence his sudden interest in getting it back.

'High-flying DIs can be brought down fast if they upset the wrong superintendent. I imagine they can be scared right out of their Loake moccasins too, if they upset Ricky Ross.'

'Can we prove any of this?'

'Not a cat's chance in hell, my dear. We're the ones holding the hot fiver, remember.'

I must have sounded more than a bit frantic, because she took my hand, and wound her fingers through mine, rubbing, soothing. 'So what do we do now, Maestro?'

'We get the hell out of town, chum, that's what we do. Just two calls, and then we're away. Off to do the only thing we can; off to Switzerland to get that money. Agreed?'

She seemed to think about it, for about two seconds. 'Agreed. I guess it's gone too far for us just to give Archer back the fiver.'

'Yes. Ross would probably arrest all of us for being parties to a theft, just for spite. Alternatively he might just kill us. We've got to get the money out of his reach. That's the only answer.'

She nodded. 'Okay. You said we're going to make two calls before we go? Where?'

'I'm going to phone Ali and get him to pick up our passports from the loft. Then we're off to see a laundry lady I know. It's one thing being fugitives, but it's something else wearing last weekend's clothes!'

In which Jan's open secret is revealed to Prim, and in which we find that the heavy has picked up our trail.

After the break-in there was no way we were going back to the loft. We reckoned that there was too big a risk of Ross having it watched.

Rather than use my mobile – that's how paranoid I was – I phoned Ali from a public call-box near Haymarket.

'What's going on, Oz?' My pal was concerned. 'What sort of bother are you and the bird in?'

'Nae bother, Ali, nae bother at all. The flat's such a mess just now that we couldn't face it. We're heading off for a holiday. You'll keep on looking after the green one for us, will you?'

'Aye, of course I will. Ah don't believe a fuckin' word you're telling me, but then you always were a hare-brained bugger, Blackstone. Ah like this "us" stuff, though. It's about time you had somebody holdin' your joystick, permanent-like. She's the real thing, this lassie, is she?'

'She sure is, pal. I'm glad you approve. It's been worrying me all weekend.'

'Sarky bastard! Here, she hasna' got a sister has she?' If only you knew, my dusky China.

'Was he there?' Prim asked as I got back into the Nissan.

'Ali's like the Windmill, love; never closed. He's a good lad, for a grocer. I'd have asked him to bring us some fresh clothes, but if anyone is watching the loft it'd give the game away.'

She nodded, surprised by my unaccustomed thoroughness. There's nothing like a good dose of fear for sharpening the mind . . . and loosening the bowels. 'Where does Jan live?' she asked, as I pulled away from the kerb. 'I take it Jan is your laundry lady.'

'Who else? Her place is in Castle Terrace.'

'It isn't five o'clock yet. Will she be home?'

'With a bit of luck. Jan's a jobbing accountant. She does my tax work as well as my books. Apart from me, she's got a nice wee client list. She does quite a bit of her work at home, so she might well be there. If she isn't we'll go for a walk in Princes Street Gardens.'

She laid a hand, gently on my thigh, as I drove. 'Oz, how will Jan be about me? She was nice enough when we met, but turning up on her doorstep with one bag between us and our dirty laundry, that's something different. I mean you and she have done some heavy breathing together in the past. Are you sure she doesn't still hope you might wind up together. I know her Mum does . . . or did, anyway.'

I smiled at her. 'Don't worry about it. Jan and I are a sister and brother act; okay, we've been incestuous now and again, but that's in the past. Anyway, her heart belongs to another.'

Her eyebrows arched, perfectly. 'What d'you mean?'

'You'll find out.'

There was an empty bay across the street from Jan's place. I put a parking ticket in my windscreen and kept my fingers crossed that my tax disc would attract no fresh attention. Just as I was about to lock up a heavy shower of rain came out of nowhere. I grabbed my anorak and Prim's jacket from the back seat and hustled us both across the street.

Jan's flat is on the second floor. The label beside the entryphone button read 'Turkel/More'. Prim looked at it in surprise as I pushed the plastic stud. 'You mean she lives with someone?'

'That's right. She has done for the last four years. It's a bit turbulent from time to time, but overall they're pretty happy.'

Jan's voice sounded like everyone else's on the wrong end of an entryphone: a bit like a polite Dalek. 'Yes?'

'Hi Jan, it's me and one other. Can we come up?'

There was no answer, only the buzz of the release button being pressed, and a click as the door catch sprung. Jan's stairway is a lot nicer than mine. It's carpeted and there's a chair and cut flowers on each landing. She was waiting for us in the doorway as we reached the second floor, dressed in a white blouse and tight fawn skirt, which showed off her long legs. Jan's legs are her best point, and the rest of her is pretty near to competition class too. 'Hi pal. Hi Prim.' She nodded towards the bag. 'Planning a long stay?'

I was going to spin her a yarn about my Bendix being knackered, but the truth slipped out when I wasn't looking. 'We need some help. Can we run this lot through your washing machine?'

'Sure,' she said, ushering us into the narrow hall. I led the way straight through to the kitchen. 'What's the problem? Mum said you two showed up out of the blue on Friday night.

'Here, that reminds me. What's the score with your Dad and my Mother? I'm beginning to wonder about them.'

'Work it out, Janet. Pre-crumblies can get up to the

naughtiness too. When's she going to make an honest man of him? That's what I want to know.'

She threw her hands up to her face in a comic gesture and dropped into broad Fife. 'My Goad! Can you imagine fit they'll say in Enster, like!'

'You know what they're like. They have to have someone to talk about.' I emptied the bag into the washing machine, loaded Ariel into the sachet thingy, and dialled up a quick wash–dry programme.

Jan gave each of us a beer from the fridge, then pointed us towards the living room, while she went into the bathroom. 'Lock the door this time!' I called after her.

I watched Prim as she looked around Jan's sitting room. You couldn't imagine a bigger contrast to Linda Kane's severe salon. Everything about it fits everything else, and everything in it was chosen for pleasure not appearance. There's a small sofa and two recliner armchairs, all in soft grey fabric, and set around a low coffee table. The floor's varnished but mostly covered by a huge Indian carpet. Over the fireplace, there's an original oil of a beach scene, and a few very tasty watercolours are hung around the walls. The inlaid sideboard was hand-made by a guy in Musselburgh. I'll never forget Jan telling me how much it had cost.

'This is lovely,' said Prim. 'It's saying something to me, but I'm not sure what it is.'

'You'll find out soon enough,' I said. She took hold of my shirt front, and would have had more out of me, if Jan hadn't come in just then.

She looked at us thoughtfully, for a few seconds. 'Yes, Mum was right. About you two, I mean. She phoned me to tell me that Oz had met his match at last. She approves. So, by the way, do I,' she added, in a very matter-of-fact tone. 'Not least because, hopefully, it'll let Mother get me sorted out in her head.' Before Prim could follow up the begged question she changed the subject.

'Right, fugitives. What's the story?'

I know three people in the world who could have handled the truth about our predicament. Happily Jan's one of them. So I pulled Prim on to the sofa beside me and we told her; just like we'd told my Dad, only this time there was an important fact to add which two days earlier had been simply a hunch, plus the part about our narrow escape in Auchterarder.

When we had finished, Jan spread herself in her recliner, her skirt riding away up over her thighs, and looked at us. 'Astounded', just about covered her expression. Her eyes narrowed as she focused on me. 'You know, Oz, I was starting to think that you were turning into a young fogey. A BYF; know what I mean . . . Boring Young Fart. Now here you are, trippin' over corpses, boakin' on traffic wardens, accessory after God knows how many facts, and on the run from a renegade copper.

'Sunshine, you don't just turn over a new leaf. You turn over the whole fuckin' tree!'

She stood up, smoothing down her skirt. 'So what can I do to help?'

'You're doing it. We've decided to head south as fast as we can, with the clothes we've got in that bag. As soon as they're dry, we'll be off.'

'How are you for cash?'

'No problem there. I've got my chargecard, and my PIN number'll work in Europe. Coffee and a sandwich would go down well though.'

She shook her head. 'I can do better than that. I was making a stir fry tonight; I can stretch it to do four. Come on.' She led us back through to the kitchen and busied herself washing and slicing vegetables. Jan's as good a cook as her Mum, but from a different era. Where Auntie Mary works miracles with baking tins and saucepans, Jan tends to use a Wok.

We did our best to help. Prim skinned and boned the monkfish, while I tackled the tough job, cooking the rice. I was watching it intently, and so I didn't see the figure when first she appeared in the doorway.

'Hello Oz. I thought that was your limo outside.'

Anoushka Turkel and I had a difficult relationship until Prim came along. Where Jan's Mum probably saw me as a figure of hope, I'm sure that to Anoushka, I was something of a threat. The old boyfriend, the ever open door when things erupted between them as sometimes they have done, or when Jan's bisexuality caught up with her and she needed a man.

There's nothing bi- about Anoushka. She's a lesbian, and not in the least uncertain, or self-conscious about it. She's a very serious person – a smile from Anoushka's like a rainstorm in the Sahara – but she's kind and she loves Jan to bits. And Jan loves her too. Early on, when first they met, she and I discussed how she felt.

How could I forget! We were in bed together at the time.

As a lover, Jan was one of those people who put everything into it, without ever really getting there herself. I never made the Earth move for her as memorably as she did for me. It was the same that night, only this time I sensed that Jan wasn't putting quite as much into it as usual. So I asked her what was wrong and, being Jan, she told me: how she'd met this corporate lawyer in the office where she was working at the time, and how they'd gone for a few drinks, and how one thing had led to another, and how she'd had the first real, full-blown, screaming orgasm of her life.

I don't think I handled it too well – well, I mean, what bloke would? – until she told me that the corporate lawyer was a woman. Somehow – and I've never figured out how or why – that made it tolerable in a way. With macho rivalries out of the way, I understood what she was saying, and I did my best to help her. I didn't exactly encourage her to set up home with Anoushka, but I said that if she loved her, it was okay with me. When Auntie Mary found out, and it all blew up at home, I stood up for her, and that helped her. Anoushka's never been to Anstruther, but at least after a sticky spell, things are all right between Jan and her Mum.

Of course, the fact that I wasn't in love with Jan helped me be the Boy Scout through it all. Yet I can't deny that on the odd occasion during the year when my doorbell rang late of an evening, and she was there, wearing a look that told me she had a change of knickers and tights in her handbag, well, it didn't half pump up the male ego. Anoushka must have suspected that we had the odd encounter, but, whether out of fear or consideration I don't know, she never raised the subject.

Now she stood there in the kitchen doorway, giving me her odd sizing-up look once again, trying to gauge the significance of Oz Blackstone in her kitchen, helping her girlfriend prepare supper. And then Prim, seeing my gaze, stepped out from behind the door.

A bad analogy, I know, but I took the bull by the horns. I stepped forward and kissed her on her high Slavic cheekbone. 'Hi, Noosh,' I said, as warmly as I could. Then I took my new lady's hand and drew her to me. 'This is Primavera. We're in lurv. Prim, this is Anoushka, Jan's partner.'

Noosh looked at us, stood there together, in total surprise. And then she smiled. It was raining in the Sahara again. 'Well goot for you,' she said, in her funny accent, with its hint of her

Eastern European origins. I reckon that was the most sincere thing she's ever said to me.

'Jan never said about you,' she added, as if to explain her surprise. 'So what brought you to see us. Your good news?'

'That and a knackered washing machine,' said Prim.

'Ah! But you stay to supper?' We both nodded. 'Good. Excuse me, I must change. Back in a minute, Jan darling.' She patted her grey suit, which matched the streaks in her hair, and walked through to their bedroom.

'Oz,' she called through. 'I hope you have that car MOT-d.'

'Yeah. I'm still waiting for my tax disc, but it's okay. Why d'you ask?'

She stepped back into the kitchen, wearing a light dress. ''Cause when I got home there was a policeman in uniform giving it a funny look. I don't think that he was looking at the tax disk, more the number. You don't report it stolen to claim the insurance, no?'

I didn't say a word. Instead I strode back through to the living room and peered out into Castle Terrace from behind the curtain. The line of parked cars had thinned out as the office building next door had emptied, and there were only three to be seen on the far side of the street, mine and two others, a battered old Mini and a Citroen with French plates. There was no sign of a policeman.

Jan and Prim looked at me anxiously as I came back into the kitchen. I answered them with a quick smile and a shake of the head. 'Whatever it was, he's buggered off.'

'That's good,' said Jan, 'because your rice must be nearly ready!'

We ate in the small back room which Noosh and Jan use as a dining room. The stir fry was one of Jan's best ever, full of chunky monkfish, mushrooms, yellow peppers and lemon grass, but it was wasted on me. I kept thinking about that copper, and his unhealthy interest in my car. I excused myself as soon as I had finished, and went back through to the living room, back to my stance behind the curtains.

The battered Mini was gone, but the Citroen was still there. Beyond it, there was a third car, a black Vauxhall Cavalier, with a mobile telephone antenna sticking out of its roof. There was a man in the driver's seat, a big man. It was still raining quite hard, and from that distance I couldn't quite make out his face, but I was in no doubt who it was.

I went back through to the dining room, where the girls were having coffee. 'Jan, have you still got that telescope?' I gave Jan a spyglass one Christmas, basically because I'd run out of ideas.

She looked puzzled for a second, than caught on. 'Yes. Come on.'

She led me through to the bedroom. The telescope was on her bedside table. In normal circumstances I'd have taken longer to wonder what they used it for, but my mind was on other things. Prim and Noosh were waiting for us in the living room. I motioned them to stay back from the window and slid in behind the curtain, taking care not to disturb it. Carefully I focused the telescope on the Cavalier. Just as I did so, the man in the driver's seat leaned forward, and I had a clear view of his face.

I swore softly.

'What is it?' asked Prim.

'It's Ricky Ross. That copper must have called in my number.'

Anoushka stood there looking bewildered. 'I'll tell you later,' Jan said to her.

'What are you going to do?' she asked.

'Good question. Is the washing machine finished drying out gear yet?'

'Should be.'

'Okay,' said Prim. 'I'll pack the bag.'

Jan stood in the centre of the room, mulling something over. At last she nodded, decisively. Then she kicked off her shoes, and ran back through to the bedroom, beckoning me to follow. By the time I got there she had stepped out of her skirt and was unbuttoning her blouse. 'What is this,' I said. 'One last time for luck?' I was comforted by the knowledge that even in times of crisis, the daft side of me could still come to the surface.

She shot me a quick, 'You should be so lucky!' and began to step into a pair of jeans which had been lying across the dressing-table stool. 'Get me your anorak,' she ordered. I began to see what she had in mind. I did as I was told and fetched the horrible, hooded green garment from the hall. She fastened her jeans and pulled on a sweatshirt, then tried the anorak for size. As I've said, she's a tall girl, so it wasn't a bad fit. She pulled on a pair of old trainers, looked at herself in a full-length mirror and nodded her satisfaction, then turned and pushed me out of the room, back into the kitchen. There, Prim was packing the final items into our bag, folding them as best she could. Noosh stood with her back to the sink, still looking bewildered.

'Right,' said Jan. 'This is your best chance. I'll wear this gear. I'll run out, jump into Oz's car and drive it away. I'll tie the hood tight, and with any luck, the guy out there will think it's Oz and follow.

'Oz, my Fiesta's parked in the back yard. Once you see him move off, the pair of you get downstairs and get as far away from here as you can. The car's not long after a service, so it should get you to Switzerland all right.'

All of a sudden I was emotionally full up. I'd never felt closer to the girl; never in all of our lives had I realised how strong was the bond between us. 'Hold on a minute, Jan. This is a dangerous guy. He'll catch up with you.'

'But he won't stop me, not even if he lies down in the road. If I have to I'll just drive to the nearest police station and run in screaming that there's a man following me. Now no more arguments, unless you've got a better idea.'

I hadn't, and I didn't know what to ay, so I just kissed her. For a moment I thought Prim might be mad, but she kissed her too. Just to be on the safe side, I kissed Noosh as well. Prim drew the line at that.

Jan and I exchanged car keys, and we all went back through to the living room. We stood there in a circle, smiling nervously at each other. I tied the cords of the anorak hood tight under Jan's chin, pulling it down to cover her face. We shared a last long look that neither Noosh nor Prim could see, a look that said a hundred things, from 'Thanks' to 'Remember that time in the dunes in the East Bay at Elie, when there was no-one else around . . .' Probably, it was as well that neither Noosh nor Prim could see our eyes.

And then Jan was gone. The front door closed and she was off down the stairs. I went back to my spy-hole and looked down into the street. Every Tuesday at Meadowbank, Ali tells me I run like a girl, so she was a pretty good imitation. I didn't realise she could move that fast . . . well, she's never run away from me. She was across the street in a flash. Unlocking the door, she jumped into the car. Just then I panicked, thinking she'd flood the carburettor, but Jan knows the old Nissan pretty well, and it started first time.

As soon as I heard the engine's cough, I looked back at the

Cavalier. Ross was sitting bolt upright in his seat, fiddling with his key. I heard his ignition snarl, but soon it fired up. Jan had barely swung the Nissan away from the kerb and round into Johnstone Terrace, before he was after her. 'Clever girl,' I said. 'She'll lead him where there are no traffic lights.

'Right, let's do what she says, and make ourselves scarce. Thanks, Noosh, see you soon . . . we hope.'

I grabbed the bag with one hand and Prim with the other, and together we legged it down the stairs, past the front door and down to the basement level. Jan's red Fiesta Sport was next to the exit. It burst throatily into life at the first turn of the key. With barely a backward look we were off, out into Castle Terrace then away down to the Grassmarket, in the opposite direction to that in which Jan had headed.

Ali was waiting in the shop with our passports. Prim stayed in the car as I rushed in. 'Thanks mate,' I said. 'Do one thing more for me, will you. Get my diary and check my faxes and messages. Then call Jimmy and ask him to handle my work till I get back, same as usual.'

My chum nodded his turban. 'Fair enough. That still leaves one problem, though.'

'Eh?

'It means we'll be one short at the fitba' tomorrow night!'

In which we begin a circuitous journey South, and have a surprise phone call.

'So that's Jan's secret, is it?' Prim mused, as we headed down the A1, bypassing Haddington.

'No secret, except from the good burghers of Enster.'

'How long have they been . . .'

'I told you, around four years.'

'You should have said something to warn me, you sod. Mind you, when I saw that living room, I began to get the idea. It's a couple's room, but there's nothing masculine about it.' She thought about it some more. 'There's nothing stereotyped about them, is there?'

'No, they're not your average person's idea of a gay couple. But there's shades of everything you know.'

'They look happy enough. Are they, d'you think?'

'Most of the time. There are tensions, though.'

'Do you think it'll last?'

'I don't know. Look at the number of heterosexual relationships that break up. Why should gay couples be different? They have another complication too. Jan's AC/DC. Could be she'll meet a man who can give her more than Noosh can. I hate to think how Anoushka'd cope with that.'

'Well, I think they're nice, and I hope she doesn't have to.'

'Okay, love, but just don't let Auntie Mary hear you say that.'

I drove on down the road towards the darkening South, taking care not to trip any of the speed cameras. I was still worried about Jan, being pursued by Ricky Ross, and I reckoned that the last thing she would want after that would be a fixed penalty speeding ticket, when she hadn't even been driving.

One of the good things about driving at night is the lack of heavy traffic. With nothing to hold us back, we made Newcastle in Jan's nippy wee motor in just under two hours.

'Oz,' said Prim, as the ring road round the city merged with the A1M, 'where exactly are we going? And do we have to get there in one go?'

She was right. I was just driving, with no clear game plan. 'I guess we're heading for Dover,' I said. 'I just want to get out of this country. Ross must have worked out what we've done by this time. Even if he didn't hassle Jan, by this time he'll know who she is. We've got to assume he's traced her car number through the police computer.'

'What if he has? What can he do about it? Will he have us stopped at the ferry?'

'Hardly. He can't involve anyone else in this or he's in trouble. I guess he'll come after us.'

'And when he finds us?' I wouldn't say that she sounded apprehensive, she never does. But the question was tentative, no doubt about it.

'Remember Willie Kane?' She nodded, getting my drift.

'Could he get ahead of us? Could he beat us to Dover?'

I thought about it. We'd wasted some time at Ali's, and if Ross had been able to do a quick PNC check, then . . . My musing was interrupted by the warbling of my mobile on the back seat. Even though I was driving, I jumped. Prim looked at me. I nodded to her. 'Answer it.'

She reached round, picking up the phone and pressed the receive button. 'Yes?' she said gruffly, disguising her voice, rather pointlessly I thought. Then her face lit up with relief. 'It's you, Jan! Are you okay?' She paused, listening. Suddenly she laughed. 'Serves him right. It was good of you to think of calling.

'Where are we?' She looked out of the window. 'Just passing Durham, I think. On our way to Dover, Oz says.

'Yes, of course. We'll try to keep in touch.' She pressed the cut-off button and put the phone on her lap.

'She's okay,' she said, sounding as relieved as I was. 'Apparently he didn't get alongside her until red traffic lights at Meadowbank. When he looked across, she just pulled the hood down and glared at him. She said she thought he would burst.

'He signalled her to pull over and she did, because there were plenty of people around. He asked her who she was and she told him. Then she asked him what he meant by this. He spun her a story about you being under police observation on suspicion of theft. She said that was rubbish. She said your father was a dentist, as if that would help!

'She told him that you were out of town and that you'd lent her your car since hers was being repaired. Then she got stroppy with him and asked to see his warrant card. That was enough. He said, "Sorry to have troubled you, Miss," and buggered off.'

I winced. 'Thank Christ she's okay. I doubt if Ross'll give

her any more trouble. Still, he has her name. That means he'll have all the rest of it by now.'

I looked at the clock on the dashboard. If it was accurate, it was twenty to ten.

'Tell you what,' I said. 'Why don't we stop for the night? Ross might not be able to catch us before we reach Dover, but he could get there before the ferry sailed.'

'Couldn't we take the Chunnel?'

I made a face. 'I hate Chunnels. Anyway, the same thing could happen there. No, here's my suggestion. We stop now for the night. Tomorrow we drive to Portsmouth and take a ferry to Brittany. Then we head across France and surprise my big sister. She and her man live near the Swiss border.

'If Ross is following us, he's bound to head for Dover, then for Geneva and Berners Bank, just as fast as he can. Let him. If we don't go there ourselves until next Thursday, maybe, by that time, he'll have decided we're not coming.'

'*Some chance of that!*' I thought.

'Some chance of that!' Prim said. 'But yes, I'll buy that idea. We might as well travel in comfort. Let Ross do the chasing!'

We turned off at Darlington, but as an added precaution, we decided not to stop in one of the hotels in town. Instead we headed for the outskirts, until we came upon a place not big enough to call itself a village, appropriately named Middleton-One-Row. It was big enough to have a nice road-side inn, the kind that's always popular with reps. There was one room left, twin-bedded. I looked at Prim, questioningly. She nodded, so I booked us in. The owner was a cheerful chap, and his chef did a remarkably good salmon *en croûte*, even at that time of night. Afterwards, we had a couple of pints with our host. His name was Peter and he seemed glad of the company, but at a quarter to midnight, we said goodnight and left him to close up.

Our room was nicely furnished, with a real *en suite* bathroom, not one of those partitioned-off jobs in the corner, the kind in which you try to pee quietly so your partner won't hear.

We lay side by side on our twin beds, each of us staring up at the ceiling. 'My brain's still travelling at 100 miles an hour,' said Prim. 'What a day this has been! Pure mayhem!'

I propped myself up on an elbow and gazed across at her. 'Do you have any other kind? It occurs to me that since I met you, my feet have hardly touched the ground.'

'I don't know about that,' she said, pushing herself off her divan and coming to join me on mine, 'but I do know that this will be the fourth different bed that I've slept in in the last five nights.'

I thought about that one, reached behind her, under her shirt, and unclipped her bra, one-handed. 'True. It's a bit like the Grand Prix circuit, isn't it. D'you think we should start giving them marks out of ten?'

She unzipped me and eased her hand inside my jeans. There wasn't much room in there any more. 'Not *them*, Osbert,' she whispered '*Us*. I reckon it's time for a test drive.' She leaned over me, pinning me down, and kissed me, disengaging herself with difficulty from my Levis, and going to work on the buckle of my belt.

'There is one thing, though,' she said, as I began to ease her out of her clothes. 'I've been off the pill for two years, and being a nurse, I know about cycles. Right now, if you even point that thing at me, I could get pregnant. So I hope that with all these propositions you've been throwing at me, you're carrying a supply.'

My face fell, just a second before hers. 'Christ,' she laughed. 'Nineties man!'

'Meets Sixties woman!' I retorted.

We lay there, half-undressed, shaking our heads and laughing, until Prim jumped up, half out of her tights, and hopped back across to her bed. She was almost there when I had a brainwave.

'Hold on, this is a reps' hotel. The Gents is bound to have a slot machine.'

We rifled through our change until we found four pound coins. Silently, I padded downstairs to the gents' toilet off the hallway. My heart rose as I saw the machine on the wall. It fell again, just as quickly.

Peter's is a popular hotel with reps; but just as popular, it seems, are the reps who use it. The machine was in perfect working order. It was also perfectly empty.

In which we plan to score high marks on the high seas but end up cast adrift.

'I wonder where Ricky Ross is waking up,' Prim said, as she stretched luxuriously, arching her back and squeezing the last of the sleep out of her body. She's the best str-e-e-e-tcher I've ever seen. When she does it she looks like a lioness, with her blonde mane and her golden skin.

'I hope the bastard's been driving all right,' I said, 'and that right about now he drops off to sleep at the wheel and totals himself.' I really meant it, and it must have sounded that way too, for Prim looked at me in surprise.

'If only life was that simple,' she said. She propped herself up on an elbow and grinned across at me. 'What's the game plan for today, lover-boy? Want to look around the shops this morning before we head south. Like Boots, maybe?'

'I could nip out now, if you like,' I said, experimentally.

She snorted. 'The Grant Prix circuit's closed. What time's breakfast?' I looked at my watch. It was almost quarter past nine.

'We've got about fifteen minutes to get down there.'

Prim showered while I shaved, and so we were able to make it with about five seconds to spare. We both felt guilty about keeping the chef from his break, so we settled for cereal and coffee.

Peter, it seemed, had taken to us. He was sorry to see us go, but Prim cheered him up when she said we'd look in on the way back. I muttered that when we did, all the facilities had better be in working order. He stared at me for a few seconds, until at last he grasped my meaning. 'Ah,' he said, mournfully, 'that's the trouble with outside suppliers.'

Rather than head south straight away we drove back into Darlington. It's a nice town, distinctive, with a market in its centre set out around a high tower. After I'd been to Boots, we found a travel agent and looked up ferry times from the south coast ports. 'I've never seen St Malo,' I suggested. The travel agent assured us that there would be plenty of space on a night crossing in midweek, so that was it.

We had nine hours to get to Portsmouth, and we used them all, driving at a steady pace, bypassing Leeds and circling south of Birmingham till we found the M40. We chatted as we travelled, when we weren't singing along to Jan's Abba tapes. (The woman's never been the same since she saw *Muriel's Wedding*.) We tried to talk about the future, but for both of us the crystal ball was obscured by the dark shadow of Ricky Ross, and our task in Geneva.

'If you've finished with nursing, honey,' I asked Prim as we crawled through Newbury, 'what are you going to do? Not, I say again, that you need to do anything.'

She shook her head, then shrugged her shoulders. 'I don't know, I really don't. All I do know is that I have to do something, but it has to be something really different.'

'How about marrying me and having babies?' The words

jumped unbidden from my mouth. I twisted the mirror and stared in it to make sure that it was me who had said them.

'Woah, Oz, woah,' she said. 'All in good time. It's only been five days, and we haven't even had that test drive yet. Your application still has to be approved.'

I must have looked downcast, because she squeezed my thigh. 'A couple of years down the road, if we can still stand each other, then we can talk about things like that. But is that what you really want?'

I took a hand off the wheel and stroked her soft cheek. 'Right now, Springtime, what I want is you. Anything else is a bonus.

'Tell you what, let's get the next few days over with. If we're still alive in a week, we'll have the rest of our lives in front of us!'

We drove on in silence for a while. Talk of test drives, and our developing, if frustrating, relationship made me think about ferry crossings. Jan and I went to London once. There's something about making love in a British Rail sleeper. I wondered if it might be the same on a cross-channel ferry. My Dad's house has cupboards that are bigger than railway sleepers but those narrow berths were an experience . . . especially with both of us crammed into the lower one.

We got to Portsmouth with two hours to spare. The travel agent was right, up to a point. There was plenty of vehicle space, with no buses booked on board. But there were absolutely no spare cabins. I looked at Prim as we stood at the booking window. 'Am I being punished for something?' I asked her. 'Are you? Has your Mum had a word with the Bloke Upstairs?'

In terms of Grand Prix circuits, the Club Class lounge on a Channel Ferry is strictly a pedestrian precinct.

We sat side by side in our reclining aircraft-style seats, the Fetherlites redundant in my wallet, and held hands through the night, all the way to France.

In which we arrive on a movie set and thwart a daring escape bid.

I like motoring in France. I don't know my left from my right at the best of times, so driving on the 'wrong' side of the road is no big deal for me.

There is this theory that to get to anywhere in France from the Channel ports you have to go through Paris. It's rubbish, of course. We hung about in St Malo for a while, just to get the feel of it, then headed south to Rennes. Using a map which we'd bought at the terminal we plotted a route more or less alongside the Loire, until we picked up the Autoroute which led to Lyon.

We made a couple of stops along the way, and Prim gave me yet another surprise. I may like France, but when it comes to speaking the language, I'm about as useful as Harpo Marx. Prim turned out to be fluent. 'It was Africa,' she explained. 'French was the main language where I was, so I had to pick it up.'

The day grew hotter as we went further south, until the information signs along the road were showing an outside temperature of 28 degrees. To make it tolerable we drove with the windows down and the sunroof open, but even at that, touching the steering wheel felt a bit like handling hot bread straight from the oven.

'Where does your sister live?' Prim asked as we pulled into a service area, to make another pit stop, and to buy food to take to Ellen's. Arriving empty-handed is not the done thing in the Blackstone family.

'A place called Pérrouges. I've never been there, but she says it's nice. Sort of old, she says.'

We found it without too much trouble, but when we got there we could barely believe our eyes. It turned out that my sister's home is in a piece of living history, a walled townlet with cobbled streets narrow enough to offer shade nearly all day, and hardly a building that's less than two hundred and fifty years old.

'Jesus,' said Prim. 'It's a movie set!'

Naturally, I'd forgotten to bring a note of Ellen's address, but my tour guide solved the problem by going into the town's tiny hotel and asking the receptionist where the Scots family lived. It wasn't far – nowhere in Pérrouges is far – just round the corner and down a twisty alley.

We knew the house before we got there. When they handed out the lungs, our Ellen was right up at the front of the queue.

'Jonathan!' The shout seemed to fill the narrow alleyway, bouncing back and forth off the stone walls. I jumped. It was pure reflex. When I was a kid, Ellen's bellow could freeze my blood from two hundred yards away. Close up it could emasculate an elephant. The sound was still echoing, on its way, no doubt, to frighten distant wildlife, when my older nephew came diving head first out of a low window, about thirty feet away. He did a perfect rolling landing, winding up on his feet, and kick-started a sprint. His trainers threw up puffs of dust as he raced up the sloping pathway towards us. He made to shimmy round us, head down, but I grabbed his shoulder. At first he tried to wriggle out of my grasp, and only when he found it was too strong for him, did he look up.

'Hello there, Wee Man. What have you been up to then?'

His mouth dropped open, answering my question in the process. It, and half of his face, was stained by the juice of berries.

'Uncle Oz! Uncle Oz!' He was so surprised that he forgot all about his escape bid, and his predicament. 'Mum, Mum!' he shouted, back down the alley. 'See who's here! See who's here!' Jonathan is only just turned seven, but he's showing signs already that he's inherited his mother's lung-power. I let him go and he ran back to the house, crashing through the door this time, rather than the window. A second or two later there was the sharp, unmistakable 'Splat!' of palm on bare leg, and a second after that the sound of a howl being stifled as Jonathan gasped out his news through the string of retribution.

'If you're making up stories again . . .' said Ellen as she stepped outside.

It had been over a year since I'd seen her. The first thing I realised was that there was more of her to see. Ellen's always been a square-built sort of girl, but France had straightened out what curves she had. I wouldn't say she'd got fat . . . no, to be honest, I would. She'd got fat.

She stared at me. 'Oz, you *bugger*! You might have let me know!' Jonathan appeared again by her side, sniffling and smiling at the same time, pulling his wee brother Colin along behind him.

I gave her a bear-sized hug. It's only when I see Ellen after a break that I realise how much she means to me. She hugged me back and looked up at me. If it had been anyone but Ellen, I'd have said there was a tear in the corner of her eye.

'Hi, Sis. I know we should have called, but it was a spur of the moment thing. Ellie, this is Prim Phillips, my girlfriend.'

You know right away how my sister feels about someone. If she has doubts, it shows in a narrowing of her eyes that she doesn't even know is there. She looked at Primavera, wide-eyed, and grinned. I have to say that even after a day's drive through France, Prim looked fantastic. The sun had given her skin an extra glow, and had picked out shiny highlights in her hair.

'You poor lassie,' said Ellen, 'come on in.'

The house was fantastic. Not huge, but big enough for a young family. It had a stone floor and walls, which made it wonderfully cool, and beamed ceilings, yet the important parts were modern. The kitchen, to which we followed Ellen, was lined with hand-built cupboards, and fitted out with every available appliance. A Pyrex bowl sat on the work-surface, half full of strawberries. Around it there lay piles of green husks.

Ellen pointed at it, still outraged. 'See that wee so-and-so. They were for tonight.' She glowered at her older son. 'So help me God!' Jonathan, reckoning he was on safer ground with me around, chanced his arm by smiling.

'It's all right, Ellie,' I said. 'We've got some more in the car.' I cuffed Jonathan, very lightly, around the ear. 'None for you though, pal.'

'Allan still at work?' I asked, innocently, and was concerned to see a shadow cross her face.

'Of course,' she said. 'Allan works every hour God sends. Allan volunteers for extra work. Last week he was away so early and home so late that he didn't see his kids at all.' She tried to sound casual, but she didn't fool me. My sister was not a happy lady.

I didn't want to get into the domestics, so I changed the subject. 'How are you getting on with the language?'

'Bloody awful,' she said. 'Stuff that, though. How's Dad?'

'He's great. I might as well tell you straight off; he's got a new interest in life. Auntie Mary.'

Ellen's face lit up again. 'That's great. I've been hoping that would happen. And how about Jan? Is she still with the German?' Ellen did not approve of Jan's relationship.

'Slovakian, Sis. She's Slovakian. Aye, they're still going strong.'

'And you two. How long have you been . . .'

We were still talking in the kitchen when Allan came in a couple of hours later, just after nine, but by that time the kids were in bed, our kit was in the spare room, and a meal had been prepared. '*Coq au Vin*' Ellen called it, muttering something about 'shaggin' in a Transit', but it looked like chicken in red wine sauce to me.

I try to make excuses for my brother-in-law, especially to my Dad, but I always wind up admitting that he's a selfish, boring get. Allan is not the sort of guy you'd invite out to the pub. He was surprised to see us, of course, but not the sort of surprise that gives way to a big smile, like Ellen's did. He barely hid his irritation at our disruption of his routine.

We ate outside in their small courtyard. Ellie asked Prim about Africa, and to be polite, I asked Allan about his job. He gave me a lecture on the state of the oil industry; I told him that I always judged the state of the oil industry by the number of rigs tied up idle in the Firth of Forth. Finally, as soon as half-decent manners allowed, my brother-in-law offered the 'early start' excuse and went upstairs.

Later, as Prim and I undressed in the tiny guest room, we thought we heard the sound of my sister's raised voice. 'See if I ever get like him, sweetheart,' I said. 'Make sure you shoot me before you leave, will you.'

In which an unhappy sister lends us her car and plots her own escape.

We decided that French Grand Prix should be postponed until another night.

Neither of us said anything, but we knew that it just wouldn't have been right in that unhappy house, under that roof. Instead, we lay together in the big iron-framed bed which almost filled the room, Prim in her nightshirt, me in my boxers, making our plans for the last stage of our journey, and trying not to dwell on the danger which might be lying in wait for us.

Next morning, when I wandered downstairs at seven o'clock for a glass of water, Allan was gone.

Over breakfast, with Jonathan packed off to school and Colin sent into the courtyard with a bun and a football, Ellen tried to keep her brave face on it, and I tried to go along with it. But it was no use.

'What is it, Ellie?' I asked her. 'D'you feel homesick, or what?'

She shook her head. 'No, wee brither. I feel bored. I feel

uncared for. I feel abandoned. Try to imagine what it's like living here. The place is lovely, sure, but so what. It's in the middle of nowhere, the natives are unfriendly. Bloody Hell, the place even has a wall round it. It's a place to visit, not to live, and yet I'm stuck here full-time with nothing to do but eat pastries and go quietly out of my mind. Look at the size of me, Oz. I'm like a bloody bus.

'How would you fancy this for a life? How would you, Prim?' Prim rolled her big eyes, and shook her head, solemnly.

'But Ellie,' I said, 'shouldn't you have thought all this out before you bought the place?'

She glared at me. 'I didn't buy it, brother. Allan did. He took the job, the company came up with this and he said okay. You don't think he consulted me about any of it, do you!'

I watched her as she savaged her third croissant. 'You know what, Ellie?' I said. 'I reckon that's mostly shite. You were brought up in Anstruther, for heaven's sake. That's hardly a bloody metropolis. Yet you could handle that, and, if everything else was okay, you could handle this.

'But we both know that right now, if you were living in the middle of the Champ d' Elysée, you'd still be bored out of your tree, and we both know why.'

But she wasn't ready for such fundamental truth. She shook her head and stood up, to fetch more coffee from the big range cooker. 'Enough about me,' she said, sitting back down at the table.

'Are you going to tell me, finally, what it is that's brought you two out here? And don't say you just came on holiday. You're a creature of habit, Oz. You take your holidays in July, like the rest of Scotland.'

Normally, Ellie's the third person in the world, alongside my Dad and Jan, that I'd have trusted with our problem. But all of a sudden I wasn't sure. She had problems of her own.

'Are you working up to telling me something bad about Dad?' she probed.

I shook my head. 'No, not at all. It's nothing like that. Look if I told you you'd think I'm mad.'

She looked me dead in the eye. 'Oz, remember when we were kids? Who did you come to when you were in bother? And who sorted it out for you? As for being mad, what's new?

'So come on boy. Out with it.'

So, just as I had with Jan and my Dad, I told her. I left out not a scrap of detail, from the size of Willie Kane's organ, to the size of his wife's betrayal. When I had finished, my sister was smiling. 'It's just like when you were Jonathan's age.

'You know, Prim, this bugger never got into ordinary bother like other kids. He did it in the grand style. I remember one summer: the man next door grew garden peas, on stalks, and they were right up against the boundary fence. This yin here, he reached through the fence, and he stripped all the peas out of nearly all the pods, but left them hanging there. When the man's wife went out to pick her peas, all she found was empty pods, hangin' there looking pathetic, like blown green condoms. There was hell to pay. He'd maybe have got away with it too, only he kept the evidence in a basin in his room!'

All of a sudden she was serious. 'Are you sure you're right about this man Ross?'

'As sure as we can be.'

'And you can't go to the police?'

I shook my head. 'He *is* the police. We'd wind up in the nick ourselves, and my client's business would be bust. There is the other angle too.'

'What's that?'

'If we can avoid Ross, and get the money back to Archer,

we collect ten per cent commission. That's ninety thousand, Ellie.'

'I'm a teacher. I had worked that out!' She shot me her old familiar glower. Everything was all right again.

'So you reckon that Ross'll have come after you.'

'Sure. He isn't just after ten per cent. He's after the lot.'

'So what's your next step? Geneva?'

I nodded.

'Right. If he's there he'll be looking out for Jan's car. So you two take mine. Just you drive right up to the door of the bank and march straight in. Once you've got the money, don't come back here. Head north. I'll take Jan's car back. It's time the kids saw their Grandad again.'

'What will Allan say about that?'

She looked at me, and it was as if I was back in the school playground. 'Not a bloody word, unless he wants his legs slapped!'

In which we cross the border and reach our objective.

Ellen's car was a farty wee Peugeot diesel, so short of horsepower that when the air conditioning clicked on, you felt a 'clunk', and the beast slowed by about five miles an hour. But it *had* air conditioning, and on the baking Autoroute as we headed for the Swiss border, that was real consolation for the loss of Jan's nippy wee Fiesta.

It isn't very far from the east side of Lyon to Switzerland, barely as much as an hour, even in Ellen's clunker. It was still morning when we crossed the border. I'd never been in Switzerland before, but I had seen Swiss drivers in action on the Autoroutes, and so I was extra careful.

We pulled into the first parking area we could find, to study the street map of Geneva that we had bought back in France. The place looked a bit smaller than Edinburgh. I was pleased, because it meant that Berners Bank should be relatively easy to find, but concerned, because I figured that the smaller the place, the easier we'd be to find.

Dawn had told us that the bank was more or less in the city

centre, in a street which bore its name. We found the index on the back of our map, and sure enough, there it was, Rue Berner, grid reference H6.

If Lyon is only a stone's throw from Switzerland, Geneva is only a spit from the border. We had hardly started down the road before the countryside was giving way to built-up areas. As we descended, in the distance we could see, beyond the city, the blue water of Lake Geneva, and beyond that the towering massif of Mont Blanc.

The first thing that struck me about Geneva was the flags. I don't think I've ever seen as many flagpoles in my life, or as many colours flying upon them. It's a real international city, just as much as London or Paris, and in some ways even more so. After all, the Red Cross is based there, and the World Health Organisation, and even, I read once, the World Council of Churches. *Appropriate*, I thought, feeling the stirring of my Calvinist roots.

Prim navigated us smoothly along the broad green avenues, taking left, then right, then right again. We missed Rue Berner first time around, but a laborious loop brought us into it at last. It was a big, wide street, with two-way traffic, and very definitely no parking. We drove down it as slowly as we could, shrinking into our seats as we looked around for any sign of Ricky Ross, but seeing none.

Berners was about four hundred yards down the street, its name picked out in beaten copper on a sign above a dark, narrow doorway. 'There it is,' said Prim, her voice hushed but excited. 'Do you see him?' she asked.

'No sign of him, as far as I can see.'

'What'll we do with the car?'

At that moment, I didn't have a clue, but just then the answer presented itself, a big blue 'P' sign above a doorway a hundred yards ahead. I swung the car in, took a ticket from an automatic machine and found myself steering sharply down and round a spiralling ramp which opened out eventually into a long neon-lit garage. We found a space, parked and just sat there, our hearts pounding, breathing heavily.

'This is it,' I said, trying to sound confident, but, I'm sure, sounding scared instead. 'Ten minutes and it'll be done.'

Prim nodded. 'Or we will,' she said, brightly. I didn't need to be reminded of that.

'There's still time to back out,' I said, quickly, to myself as much as to her. But I knew there wasn't. Sometimes, a man has to do . . . and all that. To steel myself, I thought ahead, of what it would be like when the thing was over, and Archer had the money back, and Prim and I could get down to some serious living together.

'Okay,' I said, at last, my loins as girded up as they were going to get. 'Let's go and get Archer's cash.'

Prim drew me to her, and kissed me. I could feel her hands trembling very slightly. 'I love you, Oz Blackstone,' she said, for the first time. 'Nothing can stop you and me.'

'I love you too, Primavera,' I said, grinning like an idiot, 'and you know what? I think you're right.'

She reached into her handbag, fiddled with her purse, and pulled out half of a five pound note. 'You'll need this.' I read the serial number aloud, 'AF 426469. Remember, that's the number of the account too.'

Apart from the map, we'd picked up a few other things in France. On the basis that even the most basic disguise might help, we'd bought floppy sun-hats, blue for me, white for Prim, and Vuarnet sun-glasses, a good brand that were going to cost Ray Archer plenty on my expense account. Finally, realising just in time that nine hundred thousand sterling might be just a shade bulky, we'd found a good size duffel bag. It was still stuffed with waste-paper packing, and we decided to leave it that way, looking full, so that out on the street we'd look even more like a couple of plonker tourists.

There was a lift up from the garage, to a narrow glazed door which opened directly out on to Rue Berner. We peered through the glass. Outside, the pavements on either side of the street were thronged, with business people rather than tourists. This was a commercial centre, with nothing to attract sightseers. We pulled on our sun-hats, then our shades.

'We should have taken the ones with the false noses and moustaches,' said Prim, giggling, very slightly nervously, but looking, I thought proudly to myself, absolutely sensational in tee-shirt and shorts. We looked at each other for reassurance and, taking a deep breath, stepped outside.

In which we do the business and Berner rings the bell.

The air was a lot cooler than it had been in Pérrouges, even in the morning. As the business people bustled by us, some of them in fairly heavy clothing, we realised all of a sudden how out of place we looked.

'Come on,' I said, picking up the pace until I was almost at a trot. Those last few yards to Berners were the most nervous of my life. Every step I took, I was tensed for a shout, or a heavy hand on my shoulder.

But nothing happened. Unimpeded, we reached the narrow entrance to the bank and almost fell inside. We took off our redundant sunglasses and hats and stuffed them into the duffel bag.

When I think of a bank, I think of a line of tellers behind counters, usually in a high-domed airy hall, where every whisper about the sad state of my account carries to the inquisitive ears of everyone else in the room.

I'd heard the term 'private bank' before. I even know of one in Edinburgh. But until I set foot in Berners I had no idea what the term really meant. There was a short hallway off the street, with an unmarked door, closed, to the right and a second door at the end, opening and welcoming. We stepped inside. For a second I had the strangest feeling, that somehow I was back in my Dad's front room. The furniture was similar, of the same vintage, and arranged in much the same way, around a fireplace, with an embroidered screen in front, not unlike my Mum's. The only major difference was a big rosewood desk, set before the curtained window.

We stared at each other. The room was empty. We looked around for a bell, something to ring, and call 'Shop!'

We didn't see a camera, but it must have been there, because when the door in the far wall opened and the man stepped in, he was smiling a greeting before he'd even seen us. He stretched out a hand and said, 'Good Day'; or rather, he said, 'Bonjour'.

'*Oh shit*,' I thought, but Prim shook his hand, returned his smile, and said simply, '*En Anglais, s'il vous plaît.*'

'Of course,' said the banker. He was a tall thin bloke, grey-haired, with a complexion that was so sallow it was virtually cream-coloured.

'I am Jean Berner. How can I help you?' I had the strangest feeling that he knew the answer already.

'We wish to make a cash withdrawal,' said Prim, 'from numbered account AF 426469. I believe that these represent the key.' She took out her half of the fiver from her purse. I unbuttoned my shirt pocket and produced the other half.

Berner took the two pieces of banknote from her and checked each number. 'That is correct,' he said. 'But you are not the young lady who opened the account.'

'No,' said Prim. 'That was my sister. But the arrangement was that possession of the note gives the bearers authority to operate it.'

He nodded. 'Of course. How much would you wish to withdraw?'

'Nine hundred thousand pounds, sterling,' I said.

Berner stepped over to the desk, produced a key, unlocked a central drawer and took out a sheaf of computer printouts. It looked completely out of place in that room as he leafed through it. 'But that will leave a balance of only forty-eight thousand,' he said. 'Our minimum deposit level is fifty thousand in sterling.' I looked at him, astonished. Even allowing for interest on the lump sum, Wee Willie must have salted away at least another thirty K that no-one knew about.

'In that case, close the account, please,' said Prim. 'We'll withdraw it all.'

If I was a banker and someone came in and told me that I'd lost a private account worth nearly a million squigglies, I'd be pissed off up to my neckline. Jean Berner's smug half-smile never wavered. I found myself wondering whether he regarded sterling as second-class money, and was glad to be shot of it.

'You will wait here, please.' He oiled his way back through the door, still carrying the printouts and Prim's fiver.

As the door closed behind him, Prim gave a wee jump of joy. I thought she was going to shout out loud, and somehow, with a video camera in the room, I didn't want that to happen. So I caught her in mid-jump and pulled her to me in a hug. She looked at me surprised, and gave me her most delicious grin. 'We're . . .'

I kissed her, to stop her mouth. 'We're on Candid Camera in here, so careful what you say and do.'

Still she smiled. 'Wow,' she whispered. 'You really are paranoid. He's gone to get our money, Oz. Relax.'

'When we step out of Ray Archer's office with our ten per cent, partner, then I'll relax,' I whispered back. 'Until then, this is just too easy, and he's just too pleased with himself.'

We stood there, hugging and kissing, and throwing in the odd bump and grind for the cameras.

Berner returned in a shade under five minutes, carrying a canvas satchel and an A4 form. And the bugger was still smiling. He put the bag on the desk and opened it wide for us to see inside. 'There you are,' he said. 'Nine hundred and forty-eight thousand pounds sterling. Now if you will each sign this withdrawal form . . .'

'Count it, please,' I said, really niggled by that smile. He looked at me, as if he was disappointed in me.

'But M'sieur, this is a reputable Swiss bank.'

'Oui, M'sewer,' I said. 'And I am a suspicious Scots bastard! Indulge us.'

With the sigh he would give to an awkward child, Berner unpacked all the money from the bag and piled it on the desk. There were nine large bundles and one smaller one. 'This money is in Bank of England fifty pound notes,' he said, picking up one of the larger bundles. 'Each one of these contains one hundred thousand pounds. He riffled through the bundle, holding it up for us to see. I worked out how thick two thousand fifty pound notes should be and nodded. He riffled through each of the others in turn, showing us that there was no newsprint laced in there. Not that I thought for a moment there would be. I just wanted to do something, anything to rile the guy. No chance. He was still smiling when he finished his riffling. He began to pack the satchel once more. Our wee duffel bag looked pretty silly beside it. When he was finished, he clicked its catch shut and snapped a small padlock into place. As we signed the form he produced a key, and held it out to Prim, together with the two halves of her fiver.

'Thank you very much,' he said. 'I hope that one day your

organisation will do business with Berners again.' We looked at him, puzzled. My old friend the hamster started running around in my stomach.

'Now for your surprise,' said Berner. 'You do not have to go to Lausanne to meet your colleague. He is here.' He reached under the rosewood desk and pressed a button. We heard a bell ring.

'Come on love,' I said picking up the heavy bag and taking Prim by the hand. 'Let's quit this town,'

Without an 'au revoir' to Berner we headed out of the room towards the exit. But the small door off the hall was open, and the hall wasn't empty any more. It was full: full of Rawdon Brooks.

In which Hansel and Gretel are right up against it in the forest.

He stood there, wrists limp no longer; instead he was tall, surprisingly wide-shouldered, narrow-waisted, and very trim in a beautifully cut jacket. There was no trace at all of the effete character we had met in the Lyceum rehearsal room. This Rawdon Brooks looked very dangerous, and I had no doubt at all that he was.

'So you made it at last, little people,' he said in a fruity, friendly voice, loud enough for Berner to hear through the open door. 'Come on and I'll tell you about the change of plan.' He was dressed immaculately, grey slacks accompanying his jacket. Again I flashed back to our first meeting, and realised what a consummate actor the man was. '*Which is the real him?*' I asked myself, until I saw the answer in his eyes.

His hands were clasped together in front of him, with an overcoat draped over them. He flicked the coat to one side, letting us see the silenced gun. After that we weren't about to argue. Her jerked his head towards the door. Prim, white-faced, walked past him and opened it, and we stepped out into the street.

All that stuff about being safe in a crowd, God, what rubbish that is. Brooks stepped close behind us and dug the gun into my back. 'Right,' he said in a voice that, suddenly, wasn't at all friendly. 'Walk in front of me, Oz. Primavera, take his arm. Now young man, remember this. You do just one thing wrong, and she gets it first, then you. Now do as I say. Walk!'

I could tell he wasn't in a negotiating mood. I walked, with Prim holding my arm, keeping the leisurely pace of a tourist, making certain that I didn't do *anything* wrong. He walked in silence until we reached the end of Rue Berner. 'Turn left,' said Rawdon. We did as we were told. All of a sudden, the pavement was even more crowded, but narrower. Brooks moved up alongside me. 'Right, Miss Phillips,' he said. 'Now it's the other way around. You do anything wrong and Oz gets it first, then you.

'Now we're going down this road until the next traffic lights, then we cross.'

As we walked, I realised that something strange had happened. The hamster wasn't running around in my stomach any more. Instead it felt as if it was encased in a block of ice. I had passed way beyond plain scared; now I knew what truly terrified felt like. I think I may have spoken to him to stop myself from passing out. 'Tell us, Rawdon,' I said. 'What tale did you spin Berner?'

He laughed, but it was as cold as his voice. There was triumph in it, triumph over me, triumph over Prim. He had my girl and me in his power and suddenly I hated him for it. Truly, I'd never hated anyone in my life before. The ice began to melt. Something I had been told years before by a soldier pal came back to me. 'Anger overcomes fear.' It doesn't, but it helps. I concentrated on my hatred as hard as I could.

'That was so easy,' he said, maddeningly self-confident. 'One is an actor after all. It's one's job to make people believe. I told him that I was a policeman on an Interpol operation with two Special Branch colleagues. We were off to pay off an informer who'd helped us round up some terrorists. I told him that the money was in the account that poor little Kane used dear Dawn to set up.

'I said that I'd travelled down first, and that you two would come down later with the banknote, pick up the cash and then rendezvous with me in a hotel in Lausanne. Only your car had broken down on the way, and I wasn't sure when you'd arrive, so I'd cancelled the hotel in Lausanne and come to meet you at the bank.

'I arranged with Berner to give you a little surprise. He'd allow me to wait in his anteroom until you two arrived, then when you'd done our business, he'd press his bell and I'd appear out of nowhere. It worked a treat, didn't it! One of my better productions, I'd say. It certainly gave my audience a start.'

Suddenly it all came back to me, what Dawn had said about him, and the College of Cardinals. 'Willie Kane cried it all out on your shoulder, didn't he. At the theatre club. He told you what he'd done for Dawn, about the bank account, about the money he'd stolen, about the key. Gay men are such good listeners after all, aren't you!'

We had reached the traffic lights, and the crossing indicator was flashing. 'Go on,' he said digging me in the ribs with the gun. 'Right,' he said, once we were on the other side of the street, 'that's where we're going, to that park down there. So we can decide what to do with you.' He added that as an afterthought, but we both knew that he'd made up his mind.

'You really are a good detective, Oz,' he said. He was

rubbing his power into us now, the bastard. 'That's just what happened.'

'But how did you get into Prim's flat? When I phoned, it was a woman who answered.'

He laughed softly. 'Did you really think so?' I thought back. A high voice. An arch tone. But in hindsight, no, not feminine: effeminate.

'Poor little Willie. When Dawn told him it couldn't go on he was distraught. He had stolen the money by that time. Even if he had given it back, his career would have been over. If he'd gone back to that wife of his, she'd have torn out his fingernails as a punishment.' He paused.

'She was there, you know, on the night. Just as I parked my car she came out, looking furious, having given the errant husband one last piece of her mind.

'The little chap asked me to come and see him, you know. He hadn't a clue what he wanted any more. So I persuaded him that he needed something new, something different. I told him to get undressed, lie down, and close his eyes, and that I'd make everything all right.' He laughed, an awful cold sound. 'And didn't I just.'

Geneva, they say, is famous for its parks, and the one towards which we were heading was probably its biggest, with a wide grassy area leading up to thick woodland. It was the middle of the afternoon, and for all its size it was uncomfortably empty. The forest seemed to go on for ever, and it looked very dark indeed. I suspected that on the other side there was nothing but the lake, since, above the tree-line, I could see the spume of the great Geneva fountain. All in all, it didn't look like the sort of place where you'd want to go with a man with a gun. But we had no choice: Brooks shoved us roughly through the gates.

'But you didn't find the fiver, Rawdon, did you?' I said, as we stumbled towards the woods.

'No indeed. Hard as I looked. And I never would, but for the strangest piece of luck. The very next night, dear PC McArthur came to the club. He was actually smiling! Unusual for him. I asked him what the joke was, and he said that his inspector was in terrible trouble because he had allowed a witness to take a piece of evidence away from a murder scene. A five pound note he said. A young couple, he said.

'And then, the morning after, you come barging into the Lyceum, all bright-eyed and full of investigative zeal. I had the whole picture then.'

We were more than halfway across the grass, nearing the woods. 'That policeman who questioned you before us,' said Prim. 'He never existed, did he?'

Brooks laughed. 'Of course not. Just a little something to set you off a-worrying about little sister.

'Once I knew you had the note, I knew that eventually, you'd wind up here. With the company in recess, it was just a matter of coming down here and waiting. Although I did think you'd have got here sooner.'

'So what happens now?' asked Primavera, direct as always. It was a question I'd been avoiding.

'Ferry crossings are really insecure things, you know,' said Brooks. 'You can take an unlicensed gun abroad in a car without worrying about being searched. You can even take really high quality heroin through, and a hypodermic.'

'*A bit of a junkie*,' Dawn had said. 'So that's it.' I think I may have snarled at him. 'We're going to have an overdose.' A picture flashed, unbidden into my mind: that poor dead lassie from years back, in that close, with me, in uniform, on guard at its mouth. I could see her, as clear as day.

'Precisely. You'll just be another couple of dead addicts. And when they find you, sooner or later, there'll be nothing to identify you. I think there are foxes in there too.'

We had reached the woods. 'Right, Hansel and Gretel, hold hands and go on ahead. But don't forget the gun.'

He drove us on through the trees, like animals. It grew darker and darker in there, with no sign of the other side. The traffic noise was distant, too. No, this was no copse, this was an urban forest.

At last we saw an area up ahead, where the trees seemed to thin, and where more light was allowed in from above. 'Enough,' said Brooks. 'This'll do. Now: Oz, dear boy, drop the bag. Then, both of you, turn around.'

We did as we were told. The big bastard just stood there, smiling at us, almost laughing. It was the way he was enjoying it, that was what was working on me. He was going to kill Prim, and he was looking forward to it.

He threw his raincoat on the ground and reached into the side pocket of his blazer with his left hand, pulling out a thin metal box. He flicked up the lid with his thumb and held it out for us to see. There it was, right enough, a hypo, primed and ready. 'I cooked it up in advance,' he said. 'There's enough in there to see you both off, believe me. It's a relic of a rogue consignment I confiscated from a member of the company in Edinburgh last year. The fool was going to take it. It's quite pure, uncut.'

A slow, wicked, leering smile, spread across his face. 'Right, to the performance. Oh, how I love live theatre!

'Let's see. Who goes first?' He looked at us, from me, to Prim, and back again. 'You, Oz, you've drawn the lucky bag. Primavera and I will be your audience. But worry not; it will be only a short time, before you are together again.

'Come here, both of you.' We stepped towards him. Fear was beginning to conquer anger, after all. Death is helluva final, when you look at it up close. He held the box out to Prim, keeping the gun on me.

'Take it,' he said, smoothly. 'Dawn told me that you are a nurse, so find a vein and give him half of the barrel.'

Prim looked mesmerised as she took the syringe from its cottonwool bed. She stared at it as she held it up. She gave it a wee squeeze, like they do in the movies, sending some of the juice spraying upwards. She beckoned me. 'Come here darling,' she said, softly, hypnotically. I felt myself drawn to her. The ice was melted, the hamster had gone. I sensed rather than saw Brooks looking at me, anticipating.

And then, quick as a cat, she jammed the syringe into the fleshy base of his right hand, and started to depress the plunger.

He screamed in pain, and dropped the gun. He stared down in horror as the syringe began to empty. Suddenly he unfroze. He tore his wounded hand away from her and yanked the needle out, throwing it as far from him as he could.

I remember once reading an article by some journalist on the tender topic of male sterilisation. Arguing in favour, he wrote that the after-effects of the procedure were no longer-lasting and no worse than a sharp blow in the stones from a soccer ball. Clearly this was a man who had never played football.

I remember my Dad once saying of an infamous serial killer, 'Hanging's too good for that bastard. It's a good kick in the balls he needs.'

And that, right there in the heart of the Geneva woods, was what I gave Rawdon Brooks, as he stood staring at his hand. Only it wasn't; it was worse than that. I gave him, left, right and centre, the legendary Oz Blackstone toe-poke, which may not look elegant, but when perfectly delivered, as this one was, can send the ball, plural in this case, flying further, straighter and faster than the finest instep delivery. I'll never know for sure, but I like to think that I tore them clean off.

He didn't scream. He howled. It was a primal sound, like a bear with its paw caught in a man-trap. I saw Prim staring at him, her mouth wide open in awe at the depths of his agony.

For good measure, as he stood there, clutching his person, knees turned in in the classic manner, I stuck the head on him. I'm not as good at that as I am at the toe-poke, but this was a pretty fair example. My forehead caught him on the left cheekbone, stunning me slightly and rocking him backwards.

I waited for him to go down, as reason told me he must. I stood back and waited for him to crumple. I mean he was a man, and I'd just nailed him with a blow from which not even the strongest guy can recover.

Yet he was still on his feet, the great bastard. His eyes were rolling, his cheek was swelling, his chest was heaving, but he was still on his feet. He reminded me bizarrely of Charles Laughton after his flogging in *Hunchback*, only Esmeralda was nowhere in sight. As I stood there watching him, I became transfixed. When his hand shot out and caught me round the throat, I didn't move. It wasn't until he began to squeeze that I realised how strong he was. Within a second or two my eyes began to swim. My hands went to his wrist, but his grip was locked on tight.

I was thinking about nothing other than him, and dying. The two muffled plops from my left hardly registered. What *did* register was Brooks' hand loosening its grip as he straightened up and fell backwards. His blazer had fallen open, and I saw the sudden bloom of red on his chest.

I looked behind me. Primavera stood there, as I had never seen her before. Her hands were locked together around the run in a markswoman's grip. Her eyes were cold and hard. And then all at once, they softened, and she started to shake.

I grabbed the gun from her and jammed it into a side pocket of the satchel. On the ground, Brooks rolled over, scrambling around, trying to get to his feet. Christ, was there no stopping this guy!

'Come on!' I yelled at Primavera, dragging her back to the real world. 'Let's go!' I grabbed the satchel, and realised for the first time that I still had that stupid duffel bag slung over my shoulder. I threw it away and grabbed her hand, pulling her behind me as we plunged out of the wood, back towards the green space of the park. For a while I thought we were lost, but at last we saw light ahead. As we cleared the woods, we looked at each other. Behind us we could hear the crashing of pursuit.

'Come on!' said Prim this time. 'Let's get back to the car. He doesn't know where that is, or what it looks like.'

'Can you remember the way?'

'I think so. Come on. Run!' We raced off across the grass, towards the gates. Handicapped as I was by the weight of the bag, I could still keep pace with Prim. Or maybe she was hanging back for me; I didn't have the breath to ask her.

We had turned into the street and were racing along the pavement when I looked back over the fence into the park and saw our pursuer break out of the woods. It wasn't a run as much as a shamble, more like Quasimodo than ever. His left eye was closed tight, and his shirt front was soaked in blood. He was loping along, almost doubled over, but he was loping helluva fast.

'Leg it, for Christ's sake,' I gasped. 'Here comes the Devil and he is pissed off!'

We sprinted through the pedestrians, knocking the wee ones aside, excusing ourselves around others. From the sounds of outrage behind us, I guessed that Brooks was clearing everyone out of his way. 'Why isn't the heroin stopping him, if it was meant to kill us?' I gasped.

'Because I just stuck it in his hand, not in a vein. Just shut up and run!'

When we reached the traffic lights, the pedestrian crossing was showing the red man sign, and the vehicles were flowing fast and freely. I grabbed Prim's hand and tugged her along the pavement, off towards the next corner and Rue Berner, looking, searching as we ran, for a gap in the traffic. At last, a chance appeared. We darted out between two cars, did a frantic shimmy in the middle of the road and made it to the other side.

We stopped, and looked back. Brooks was glaring at us across the street. His good eye looked wild, and his chest was heaving, but his eyes were still dead set on us. 'God, the heroin must be fuelling him,' gasped Prim.

If it was, it made him start straight across the road after us, looking neither right nor left.

If you've ever heard a dog, a big dog, being hit by a vehicle, you never forget the sound. But if you've ever heard the noise of a human being run over by a big vehicle, that's something that will give you nightmares for weeks afterwards.

There's the squeal of brakes and the awful thump, but then there's a tearing, dragging, cracking, crushing sound, and an awful last gasp. We were legging it up the pavement, when we heard it all. Gradually we slowed to a halt, like we were in a film and the camera was breaking down, until, reluctantly, we turned around.

It was a tourist bus, from Bathgate, of all places. When we saw him, Brooks was still moving under its wheels, his head and bloody chest sticking out. The rest of him was hidden, fortunately, under the bus, but around him, a crimson pool was starting to spread.

Instinctively, Primavera started towards him, but I took her hand, holding her back. 'No, honey,' I said, as gently as I could. 'You're not a nurse any more, remember. We've won. Now let's just get ourselves out of here.

'You and I are going home. I don't know about you, but I am absolutely knackered.'

In which the boat sails and our ship comes in.

We almost melted the wee Peugeot, but we made it to St Malo just in time to catch the night crossing. And this time there was a cabin available; a tiny cabin, but one of our very own, with a shower and two berths.

A Grand Prix circuit: small, but very definitely Formula One.

'Primavera, Primavera . . .' I moaned her name in the dim glow of the emergency light. She leaned her head towards me, kissing my chest, biting my nipples gently, responding to my touch and moving her self against my hands.

'Where have you come from?' I asked, wallowing at last in the perfection of her body, in her firm, full, big-nippled breasts, in the amazing narrowness of her waist, in the rounded curve of her hips, in the flatness of her belly, in the thick nest of wiry blonde hair at her centre, shining and sparkling as she moved.

'I've always been here,' she said, and she kissed me with her lips of velvet, as she had never kissed me before. 'I believe in destiny. You're part of mine, I'm part of yours. We were set on a course towards each other.'

'And will we go on together, we two, Springtime and Oz?'

'Who knows? *Right now* we're together, and that's what counts.'

I crouched above her, burying my face in her belly. As I flicked my tongue in and out of her navel, she gasped and arched her back. 'I want you now. I need you now. Come into me now.'

I placed a finger across her lips. 'Time enough,' I said, although she could feel that I was more than ready. I bent and kissed the inside of her thighs as she spread them wide, licking my way towards her. She moaned again. 'Now, Oz, now.'

'Yes, Primavera, yes!' I covered her and she took me into herself with a supple movement, into the sweetest embrace I had ever known. We lay entwined, barely moving. Her tongue was in my mouth again, her fingers wound through my crinkly hair. She pulled my head back and looked at me with smouldering eyes. 'You pass the audition. The job's yours!' she hissed.

Then her eyelids flickered and she began to shudder, gripping me tight, inside, tighter than I had ever imagined. Her fingers dug into my back, and she cried out, once, twice, again, again, again, again. And then I realised that two voices were calling out and that one of them was mine. I was lost. As I thrust into her and as she grasped me with her thighs and held me there, we were washed, on the high seas, by wave upon wave of sensation, by a feeling that every nerve-ending in our bodies was being bathed in soothing oil.

At last, we lay still. Her eyes were closed, and there was a sheen of sweat on her face. I licked it off; she tasted salty and sublime on my tongue. I felt myself start to subside, but she held me inside her. 'No, don't go,' she sighed. 'I want to keep you there for ever.'

'That's all right with me,' I said. 'I can't think of a better place to be. Primavera Phillips, you are the most beautiful, wonderful woman I have ever met, and I love you.'

She smiled up at me in the darkness, and smoothed damp hair away from my forehead. 'And I love you too, Oz Blackstone,' she murmured. 'It's been a crazy week, but this . . . this is like a dream.'

'Yes,' I said, 'like a dream I've had before.'

In which we find another stiff in Prim's bed, a sort of justice is done and there is a twist in the tale.

We made it back to Edinburgh on Sunday, via Portsmouth and points north, including Peter's hotel in Middleton-One-Row, where the three of us got completely stupid drunk, and, as I recall, Prim and I did something even stupider involving the absence of condoms.

The last few hours of the weekend, we spent tidying up the loft, before we enjoyed the unimaginable luxury of making love and sleeping together in our own bed, even if we did have a clearly contented iguana for company.

Next morning I phoned Archer, got through to him personally and in the most solemn voice I could manage, made an appointment to see him at three-thirty. Then I called Jan, and, putting aside my aversion to pubs at lunchtime, arranged to meet her, and Ellen, and the kids, who were all still at her place, in Whighams at one o'clock. That gave us some time to kill.

'Oz,' said Prim, as we lay in bed, under the light from the belvedere, 'sooner rather than later, I've got to go back to my flat, to pick up the rest of my things.' I didn't want to go back there, and neither did she, but she was right. It had to be done.

It felt strange parking in Ebeneezer Street. It was the place where I'd met Prim, yet I felt uncomfortable, still a stranger. It was *her* turf, not ours.

She must have read my mind. 'Oz, love,' she said as we climbed the dusty stair. 'Would you mind if I sold this place? Or would you think I was rushing things?'

I looked over solemnly. 'Maybe you should hold off,' I said, and then I kissed her. 'Until tomorrow. We've got a few things to do today.'

She unlocked the door and went to step inside, but I held her back. 'Hold on,' I said, laughing. 'Let me check the bed. Just in case there's a body in there.' She grinned as I looked round the bedroom door.

There was a body in the bed. It was Miles Grayson. But it was a brand new bed, and fortunately, he was very much alive. Dawn lay on his far side, hunched down as if she was trying to hide. I don't know which of us went pinker faster. 'I see you took our advice,' I said to her.

'Oz!' said Miles, the sound of his voice bringing Prim bursting into the room. 'Where the hell have you two been? Dawn's been worried about you.'

'So I see,' said Prim, archly, but with a smile.

'We just nipped over to France for a few days. To sort of, get to know each other, like.' A sudden thought struck me. 'Here, while we were away, we had this terrific idea for a film script. Come for dinner tonight and we'll tell you about it. We owe you a beer anyway.'

'Yes,' said Prim to her sister. 'And bring the rest of my clothes while you're at it.'

I flipped a card from the breast pocket of my Savoy Tailors'

Guild suit on to the bed. 'That's where we live. See you tonight. You be bad now!'

The whole team was gathered in Whighams when we got there, filling one of the low alcoves. There was a glass of draught Coke waiting for me, and a glass of white wine for Primavera. She jammed herself into a corner, on the far side of Jan. I sat down between my nephews and my sister and gave them all hugs. 'Everything all right, Ellie?'

She smiled at me. 'We'll see, Oz. We'll see. I'm going to stay at Dad's for a while, to see if I can get something of my old shape back and to see if Allan comes for me. If he does, I'll decide then whether I'll go back or not. The bugger's got to want me though.'

She whispered in my ear. 'Is this it then? Are you happy?'

'Ecstatic.' I whispered back.

'Good. Jan isn't, though.'

'Eh?'

'You don't have a clue about women, do you, son?'

That was too deep for me. I finished my Coke and went up to the bar for another round. As the barman was filling the tray, an Armani suit appeared by my elbow.

'Did you hear about Ricky Ross?' said Dylan, looking uncharacteristically solemn.

I looked at him, puzzled. 'I've been away. What about him?'

'Suspended. See your murder in Ebeneezer Street? It turned out that Ricky was screwing the victim's wife. Now she's been charged with the murder.

'We checked every detail about Ebeneezer Street that night. We found out that our traffic boys handed out a ticket to a car parked on a double yellow line there, just about the time that Kane was killed. It turned out that it belonged to his wife. She admits that she was there, but she swears he was alive when she left. I don't believe her though. We'll see whether the jury does.

'After we pulled her in she screamed bloody murder and shouted for Ricky. When he said he couldn't do anything she told us everything about him and her. He said that he'd encouraged her to leave the wee chap, and that he'd been blazing when she said she wanted him back. She even suggested that he might have done the murder.

'There's nothing to substantiate that, but being implicated in a murder inquiry's enough. He's out, and that's for sure.

'I'll tell you something, Blackstone, just between you and me. If you ever repeat it, I'll deny it all. Ricky really fancied you for it. He thought that you and the actress girl had set it up between you.'

His voice dropped to a whisper. 'You had a break-in at your flat, aye?'

I nodded, wondering. 'That was Ricky,' he said. 'I nearly shit myself when he told me he'd done that.'

'Nice of him. I don't feel sorry for him now. Here, I hope we're in the clear now. Ricky's theory was pure mince, you know.'

Dylan smiled again. 'Aye, you're okay. The Chief sorted him out on that. Your girlfriend's sister's in Miles Grayson's film, isn't she?'

'That's right.'

'Aye well, Sir James had a phone call last Monday evening, from Grayson. His secretary told me. She said that Grayson sounded really steamed up. The call lasted for about five minutes. When it was over, the Chief called Ricky in and sorted him out.'

I smiled at him. 'See truth, eh? Stranger than fiction.

'Here, Mike, did you ever find that fiver? The one that Prim spent.'

He laughed. 'You bugger! Aye; at least we think we did. We checked everything in town that looked like a grocer, and eventually we found a Bank of Scotland Fiver torn in two and taped back together in a place off Broughton Street. Is that where she spent it?'

I shrugged my shoulders. 'I wouldn't know. I wasn't with her all the time. What was your problem about that anyway?'

Dylan glowered. 'The Chief started that panic off too. He did a snap inspection of CID. Some stupid bastard of a DC let slip about your girlfriend picking up the fiver and the old fella tore Ricky up in front of everyone. So when he'd gone, Ricky put the thumbscrews on me. I'll tell you, if I hadn't found it, I'd have been back in uniform.'

I shook my head at the poor dupe. He hadn't even had the wit to take another fiver and cut it in half. I felt sorry for him. 'Here's a tip for you, then, to make up for it. Someone tried to kill my girlfriend's sister the Sunday before last. Hit and run, up in Auchterarder. The trouble is, outside the family the only people who knew that she was there were the film crew, and the police.

'We didn't report it, because she's in the movie and couldn't stand the publicity. But just for fun, why don't you check the car-hire companies and see whether anyone hired a medium-sized navy blue or black saloon, maybe a Mondeo, that day, then brought it back damaged, either very late at night or first thing next morning. I'll bet you'll find someone did, and that it was Linda Kane. Dig deeper and I think you'll find that Ricky told her that Dawn was at her folks' place.'

He looked at me, crest well fallen. 'Cheers Mike,' I said, and carried my tray back to the table.

And that was it. When we'd finished our drinks, Jan, Ellen and I had a mass exchange of car keys, then Prim and I went off for a reunion with the Nissan, which Jan had parked on the west side of Charlotte Square, only a hundred yards from the pub.

I was going to walk to Black and Muirton's but Prim said, 'No. Not with all that cash.' So we drove round the square and off along George Street. I ask you, who ever finds a parking space in George Street in the middle of the afternoon? We were all the way down in Heriot Row before I spotted a vacant bay.

'Right waste of time that was. I've got as far to walk back,' I said, jerking on the handbrake, and reaching into the back seat for the satchel of cash.

It felt cold and hard against my ribs. Gun barrels do, being metal and all. When they've a big silencer on them, it's even worse.

I looked into her eyes, saw myself reflected in them and knew what yet another word looked like. This time it was 'incredulous'. It's the look that comes with discovering that, however well you *think* you know someone, however close you are, you can never know them completely, never get completely inside their head.

'I'm sorry, Oz,' she said, quietly, almost tearfully, 'but I just can't let you.'

'Prim.' It came out as a croak. 'What do you mean?'

'I mean, my lover, that you and I are not as alike as you think. I know that not once have you ever thought of the possibility of just holding on to all of that untraceable cash, and using it to shape the rest of our lives.

'On the other hand, since I put those two bullets into old Rawdon, I've thought of nothing else. And even before then, the notion was more than tickling my fancy, it was giving me orgasms.'

I let go of the bag, dropping it back on to the seat. 'Come on Prim. Isn't a half-share of ninety thousand enough.'

She shook her head. 'No it bloody well isn't. I told you right at the start, five per cent wouldn't do.'

I looked down at the gun. I don't know much about safety catches, and I hadn't a clue whether this one was on or off. I slipped my left hand round her shoulders but she pulled back, digging the silencer in even harder. 'I mean it Oz. I can't let you do it. We were nearly killed for that money, and I shot a man because of it. It's gone past the stage of being someone's possession. It's a prize and we've won it.'

I looked at her, afraid to ask her just one question. 'And would you shoot me to keep it?' I'd seen enough lawyers in action to know that you never put a question to a witness unless you were certain of the answer.

So instead I said. 'You really mean it?'

She nodded. 'Yes,' she said, in a quiet voice.

'You're saying you want us to tell Archer that someone beat us to it, then take all of this untraceable money and bugger off somewhere warm for a few years, secure in the knowledge that even if he twigs, he won't be able to do anything about it other than watch his ship sink or have a whip-round among the boys to cover the loss.

'Is that what you're saying?'

'Yes.' It was barely a whisper now.

I looked at her, long and hard. I was really angry with her, for the first time in my life.

'In that case,' I said, slowly and evenly, 'what the hell d'you need the gun for?'

Her smile, her wonderful smile, flooded across her face.

She took the automatic from my ribs, held it up, pulled the magazine from the butt and showed it to me. It was empty.

I glowered at her. 'There's just one thing,' I grunted.

'What's that?' she said leaning forward and kissing me.

'Wherever we go, Wallace goes with us!'

A Coffin For Two

This book is dedicated to Salvador Felipé Jacinto Dali i Domènech, too crazy to die, and to Kathleen Pallares who told me where to find him.

1

'Senor Oz! Are you there, please?'

I don't believe that I sighed a lot in Scotland. I like to think that if someone asked me something, or if the phone rang, I answered as quickly and as pleasantly as I could.

Of course there were exceptions, like the time my mobile went off on the bedside cabinet just when I thought that my girlfriend Tomorrow – she was called Alison really – was about to lose her nickname at last. She gasped, under my skilled and delicate touch. She gasped again. Her eyes widened, and as they did, something else seemed to narrow. 'This is it,' I thought. 'Is this it?' she whispered. And then Mr Motorola sang his shrill, insistent wee song. The moment was gone, never to return.

I remember sighing then. Truth is, I remember swearing.

But by and large, the Edinburgh version of Osbert Blackstone was a happy, obliging soul, who never minded being disturbed, and who was always glad to see a pal.

'Oz! Please! Are you there!' The familiar voice, crying up from the pathway thirty feet below, had an unfamiliar, insistent tone.

I sighed; and I scowled. As I did, I caught my reflection in the mirror propped against the terrace wall. For an instant, I wondered who that sour-faced bloke was: in that same instant I realised that what Primavera had said was true. The Spanish version of Oz was well on the way to becoming a real slob.

I blinked hard and pushed myself up from my sunbed. A few months before I would have jumped up, but now three and a half kilos of extra baggage slowed me down.

'It's okay, Miguel,' I called out as I stepped towards the seaward wall. 'I'm here.'

I leaned over the wall, feeling my back, bum, and legs washed by the soft warmth of the autumn sun. Our Catalan neighbour stared up at me, open-mouthed, wide-eyed, and apparently, now that he had attracted my attention, speechless. He stood in the shadow of the building, dressed as always in dark trousers and a white polyester shirt with its sleeves rolled up to the elbows. Behind him, beyond the fringing trees, only a few white tops flicked the big blue crescent of the Bay of Roses, on which half a dozen wind-surfers were struggling in vain to gather some momentum in the Indian summer conditions.

Although Miguel is as amiable a bloke as you'd ever hope to meet, when you catch him off guard his natural expression is sombre. However I'd never seen him looking scared before. There was no mistaking it. The unofficial Deputy Mayor of St Marti d'Empuries looked as if he had had the fright of his life.

'What's up?' I asked him. My brain felt sluggish, the aftermath of half a bottle of Miguel's house *vi negre* over lunch, half an hour's sleep, a couple of beers and half of a heavy discussion, interrupted, just at the right moment, by his shout.

'Can you come down please, Senor Oz,' he said, wringing his hands with anxiety, a gesture which I might have found comical, had it not been for the expression on his face. Normally he's a faintly amusing guy in an unconscious sort of way. Looking up at me from the pathway, he was about as funny as the Callas scene from *Philadelphia*.

'Sure, but what is it?'

'Is my son.'

'What! Has something happened to him?'

He shook his dark head, violently. 'No. He is all right. But you know, he likes to be, what's the word, archaeologist?'

'Si,' I said, slipping unconsciously into Spanish.

'Just now, he find something. By the church, in front of the Forestals' House. Can you come an' look, please. There is no one else here. Everywhere is closed. And I need a witness.'

'Okay, man, okay.' I picked up a towel from the terrace floor and tied it round my middle, then stood up straight. 'I'm coming down, but what is it? What's Jordi found?'

His long face twisted even more. 'Is a body, Senor Oz. It is a body.'

2

'This isn't working Oz, is it.'

Primavera put her drink on the tiled floor of the terrace, and propped herself up on an elbow. She was wearing the bottom half of a yellow bikini, and a sad and disappointed frown. There was something about the frown which made me forget all about the rest of her.

In most people's lives there comes a moment when they are convinced that they have discovered perfection on two legs.

Invariably, absolutely without exception, they are wrong.

Nobody's perfect. I know that now. But when first I clapped eyes on Primavera Phillips, I really believed that she was that one unique being. I went on believing that, all the way through our incredible adventure, right up to the moment when she saved our lives in that wood in Geneva, and beyond that . . . for a few more days.

Yes, I thought the sun shone out of every orifice in Prim's body, until the moment when she put her proposition to me; the moment when, sat there in my old Nissan, with our client's nine hundred and something thousand quid in a bag in the back ready to be returned to him, she stuck that gun (okay, it was empty, but just for one moment . . .) in my ribs and proposed that we should keep the lot. It came as a total surprise when she showed me that she was susceptible to greed and lust just like everyone else.

She really would have taken all of the money and run, leaving our client up to his neck in the ordure. For a while I almost ran alongside her. When you have that amount of dough in your hands, never being able to come home again doesn't seem like much of a problem.

That was when my mum put in an appearance.

As I pondered the opportunity of being a near-millionaire, I saw her there in my car, quite clearly, over Prim's shoulder. Just like Prim on the terrace, she was frowning and shaking her head with that sad resignation which came over her whenever I had done something really stupid, or when she had caught me in the act of it.

When I was a kid in Anstruther, my maw had a great knack of showing up at the very moment when I didn't want to see her. Wee Oz and mischief tended to be synonymous, and my wrong-doings seemed to draw her like a magnet. I looked at my vision of her, over Prim's shoulder in the car, and I remembered that awful pre-pubescent time, when inexplicable curiosities started to stir, questions that had never occurred before, about how boys and girls are different, and why, exactly.

There I'd been, crouched at the bathroom door, peering through the keyhole with one wide eye at my sister's white bum and tanned thigh as she stepped carefully into the bath, managing without knowing it to answer none of my questions.

She hadn't coughed, said 'ahemm' or anything. My maw wasn't a theatrical person. I'd simply known that she was there from the way the hairs had prickled on the back of my neck. I fancy still that I heard a very quiet 'pop' as I unglued my eyeball from the keyhole and turned round.

She had worn the same expression then, a sad disappointed frown. She hadn't said a word, just shaken her head and turned away.

Mac and Flora, my dad and maw, weren't smackers. In all our childhood, they never laid a finger on Ellie or me. They didn't even shout at us . . . well, hardly ever. Whenever either of us transgressed they simply let us know, beyond the shadow of a doubt, that we had disappointed them; we knew that they didn't love us any the less because of our sin, but that it had made them sad because they loved us so much. That hurt more, and had a more curative effect than any leathering, I can tell you.

So I looked over my lover's shoulder at my lost mother's frown, and I knew that Flora Blackstone hadn't raised the sort of lad who could run off with someone else's money and live with himself thereafter. I realised, in a split-second spasm of remembered grief, the extent to which I'd missed her since she died. I realised too that I did not love Primavera Phillips more than I'd ever loved any woman who ever lived.

I still love her, though, and no mistake. In the end, after a very short, slightly heated discussion, we compromised. We did what my dad, Mac the Dentist, would have done in the same circumstances. I know this, because afterwards, I asked him. 'Sure as hell, son,' he said. 'I'd have screwed the bastard to the wall too.'

Instead of heading into the sunset at high speed, like the thieves we would have been, we went to see our client. We told him the whole story of what had happened in our pursuit of his stolen money. We told him of the risk we had taken, and were taking still, in withholding information from the police. We told him how close we had come to dying, and of the grisly end of our would-be murderer.

As he sat there, white-faced, we told him, finally, that we reckoned that a third of the recovered proceeds was a reasonable price to pay for our continued shtumm.

And he agreed. On the spot, with barely a blink. I guess that when you're facing bankruptcy, disgrace, maybe even an extended holiday in Saughton Prison, and two people walk into your office and offer you your life back, you know exactly what it's worth to you.

So there we were, Prim and I, with well upwards of three hundred grand in a bag, and with the world as our mollusc. On top of all that we were in lurv. Maybe each of us had cast aside our rose-coloured spectacles, but still we only had eyes for each other.

Without any disagreement, we decided that we would

regard our windfall as a gift from a grateful friend, and that the Tax Man could have his cut out of my stiff invoice to our grateful client. However, just in case the Tax Man didn't agree with us, we decided that we should go to live out of his clutches for a while. We decided that we would go on a voyage of discovery, not just in search of new places, but of ourselves, of what we would become as a couple.

So I began to wind down my private enquiry business, leaving all my clients in good hands, with the proviso that one day I might be back. Prim put her flat in the hands of the estate agents, with instructions to sell. I paid off the loan on my loft and put it in the hands of Jan More, my childhood friend, youthful lover, and potential step-sister, with the request that she rent it out and send me some of the proceeds.

Next, with the same sorrowful reluctance I guess I would have felt on seeing a child off to boarding school, I delivered Wallace, my faithful companion and loft-mate, into the hands of my dad, the only other man I could think of who was daft enough to take on an iguana as a pet.

There followed an almost endless round of hugging, selective kissing and general goodbyeing: in Edinburgh to a smiling, tearful Jan and her lesbian lawyer girlfriend Anoushka Turkel; in Anstruther to my dad and Auntie Mary, Jan's mum, the two of them an official couple at last, and to Ellie, gathering her two boys around her as she cut herself loose mentally from her useless, uncaring husband; in Auchterarder, to mum and dad Phillips, living happily in the time-warp that was Semple House, and to their younger daughter Dawn, the actress, as idyllically happy as Prim and I with Miles Grayson, her new leading man.

Finally, all goodbyes said, we fuelled up the nearly-new, one-careful-lady-owner Frontera Ozmobile and headed south . . . without the faintest bloody idea of where we were going.

We had taken much the same route into France a few weeks earlier, terrified, excited, fleeing – or so we had thought – from a relentless and murderous pursuer. This time was different. This time we sat on the dockside in St Malo, newly landed from Jersey on a sunny Wednesday morning in July, with the cheque book for our new joint account in Grindlay's Bank clean, crisp and virgin in our luggage, and with our gold cards gleaming in our pockets.

'This is it, partner,' I said, giving Prim's hand a squeeze. 'Decision time. Where's it to be? The Côte d'Azur? Tuscany? Greece?'

She wrinkled her amazingly cute nose. 'Been there. Done all of them. Still got the T-shirts.'

'Back to Switzerland?'

'No!' she said, firmly. 'Never again. Ever!' I nodded in agreement, breathing a sincere sigh of relief. Switzerland is the one place I never want to see again either.

'France is expensive, even for us,' she said. 'Even though I speak the language. Spanish can't be too difficult to pick up, though. Yes, let's try Spain.'

I pondered her choice. I'd been to Benidorm. 'Which part?' I asked her, doubtfully. 'It's a big place. They say Seville's nice, though,' I added, trying as always to be constructive.

She looked at me, wrinkling her eyebrows this time as well as her nose. 'Seville? In mid-summer? No, my love. I want to be able to get up in the morning and look at the Mediterranean, and I don't want it too hot to got out during the day.'

'Sod it! Let's just drive. We'll know when we get there.'

So we headed out of St Malo, more or less due south, picking our way carefully round Rennes, gasping as we climbed over the soaring bridge across the river in Nantes, and on towards Bordeaux and thenToulouse, more grateful with every kilometre for the air-conditioning which the Frontera's one careful lady owner had been thoughtful enough to instal.

I wanted to stop just past Toulouse, but Prim, doing her best to be excited as a schoolgirl, insisted that we drive on until she could see the Mediterranean. It was touch and go, but as we approached Narbonne, we took a curve and there it was, the last of the daylight glinting on its flat-calm waters as it stretched out silver-grey in the distance.

We found a hotel in the old French town: it looked nothing fancy from the outside, but the owner's eyes lit up as I flashed my gold card, and he showed us to his best room, en-suite, overlooking a leafy avenue, and with an impressive four-poster bed.

'Oh yes,' said Prim, as she saw it. 'I think I'm going to like this.'

She did. So did I. Very much.

The next day shaped the next part of the rest of our lives. Yet it began just like any other in our new existence. We made love – you can't practise hard enough, I always say – readied ourselves for the world outside, and had breakfast. Prim settled our bill with her card, said goodbye to our host in her excellent French, and followed me out to our car.

I watched her as she climbed into the Frontera. God, but she was beautiful; her denim shorts emphasised the curve of her hips and the tanned smoothness of her legs, her breasts swung heavily in her sleeveless cotton shirt as she pulled herself up into the high front seat. She smiled at me with her big brown eyes, a shaft of sunlight glinting through the glass roof on the tips of her blonde forelock. Just as I had every day of the incredible weeks since she had come into my life, I fell in love all over again.

'Don't take all day,' she called with a hint of a laugh. I vaulted, almost, into the driver's seat and as I strapped myself in she leaned across and kissed me. 'Let's go,' she whispered. 'Today we'll find what we're looking for. I can tell.'

We headed west out of Narbonne, down the autoroute towards Perpignan. We had been in too much of a rush the night before to appreciate the way the French landscape changes as you approach the Mediterranean. Now, driving along only a few miles from its coast, we were struck by the red rocks and soil and by the relative lack of vegetation, other than the ordered rows of the Languedoc vineyards. Prim pointed away up to her right, where a big sign in a field proclaimed that we were in Fitou country.

'Driving through France is a bit like being lost in a wine-list, isn't it,' she muttered.

It was as if the mountains jumped out at us. I swung the Frontera round a long curve, and there they were, a new, sudden, skyline, taking our breath away in simultaneous gasps.

'Big buggers, these Pyrenees, aren't they?'

For once Prim was lost for a reply. She just sat there, staring ahead, her mouth slightly open, fingertips to her lips. I had never seen her awestruck before. Somehow it was nice to know that she could be.

There had been overnight rain, and the morning was bright and clear, early enough still for there to be no heat haze to obscure the view. They stood out jagged against the blue sky, with the sun lighting their eastern slopes, their ravines and their valleys showing as dark shadows cast by its glare.

They towered over us as we crossed the plain around Perpignan, until at last the road began to rise, taking us ever more steeply into their foothills. Just like the mountains, the border would have taken us by surprise too, had we not reached an autoroute pay station a few miles earlier. What did take us by surprise, though, was the big Aztec monument overlooking the vehicle lanes.

It seemed for a while that we had more chance of finding an Aztec than a border guard. If we had been expecting a fond farewell from France or a big hello from Spain, we would have been disappointed. There was no one in sight at the French control point. I drove through slowly towards the Spanish station, where a man in uniform sat, smoking a cigarette and reading a newspaper. He didn't even look up as Prim waved our passports.

'Hasta la vista, Jimmy,' I called as we headed into Spain down another steep incline, away from a pass, the possession of which, I guessed, had been a strategic imperative for centuries, and which was guarded now by a man with a fag and the sports section.

A few miles along the road we came to a service area. 'Pull in there,' said Prim. A command, not a request.

I expected her to make for the 'ladies' sign, but instead she headed into the shop, emerging a couple of minutes later with a map, and two litres of bottled water. 'Let's do some exploring,' she said.

Her expression was so intense that it made me laugh. 'There's more to Spain than this, love,' I said.

'I know,' she said. 'But one piece at a time, okay? I don't want to leave those mountains behind just yet.' She spread out her map, located our position and traced a line with her finger. 'The next big town's called Figueras. Let's go past that, and head for the coast. Here, move over and let me drive.'

There was more than a hint of childish excitement about her enthusiasm. This was a new Prim, not the capable, well-organised woman I knew, whose every decision was weighed carefully and reached logically. I looked at her, and I loved her even more.

'Okay,' I said. 'Gimme the map.'

She handed it over, and we swapped seats without getting out of the car, clambering awkwardly across each other, managing to avoid the obstacle of the big gear lever. I strapped myself into the passenger seat and we headed off, abandoning the autopista – the more you learn about Spanish drivers, the more appropriate that name seems to be – as the autoroute becomes in Spain, and taking to the punters' free-of-charge highways.

I spread the map out on my lap and retraced our progress from the border with a finger. 'This road bypasses Figueras. If you take the first exit south of that, and head east, then . . .' She cut me off with a nod and a smile.

Past Figueras, we followed the signs for Roses, but found instead a place called Ampuriabrava. It was a huge marina rather than a town, a modern, concrete Venice, a network of wide canals with houses jammed together along their banks, each with a mooring rather than a garage. Prim pulled the Frontera to a halt and we climbed out, into the rising heat of late morning. We stared down one of the canals. There was a boat moored outside every house. I pointed to one of them, a long, three-masted schooner.

'See that?' She nodded, slightly awestruck once more. 'Well, my lovely, we think we're rolling in it, but I'll bet you we couldn't buy half of that bloody thing.'

'No,' she agreed. 'But only you would think of buying half a boat.' We headed out of Ampuriabrava in silence and followed the map south.

We found St Marti with our stomachs rather than with any navigational skills. We had driven through a narrow, dull town called San Pedro Pescador, then past kilometres of half-filled campsites, without, in all that time, clapping eyes on the Mediterranean, when all of a sudden a village loomed up before us, standing walled and rugged on a hill, with an ancient church as its crest.

Prim swung the car into an empty space at the roadside. 'Come on,' she said. 'Let's take a look.'

'Thought you wanted to be by the sea.'

She shrugged. 'Right now I want to be beside a toilet. After that . . . I don't know about you, but I'm bloody hungry. Anyway, if that map's right the sea should be just beyond the village.'

I looked around. There were scores, maybe hundreds of cars by the side of the road and in the official parks. More than a few had wind-surfers on their roofs.

A tarmac path sloped up toward the village. Arm in arm we followed it, under a stone arch that looked a few hundred years old, and into a tiny square with a red monoblock walkway that still looked brand new.

I read the street sign. 'Plaça Petita. Wonder where the big one is?'

It wasn't far. The red-brick road led us on up a narrow alley, shaded even from the midday sun. All of a sudden we were aware of a buzz of sound. As we reached the mouth of the alley it grew until it was almost a roar.

The pathway stopped as suddenly and unexpectedly as it had begun. We stood at the mouth of the alley and looked out into the square which was the heart of the tiny village.

It was filled with dozens of round wooden tables, and four times as many cane chairs. They sat out on gravelled earth, under huge parasols. Some were all white, others had a blue stripe. Spread out together they made the place look as if it was covered by a patchwork marquee.

The tables were jammed together tight and almost all of them were in use, by a congregation of the most casually dressed people I had ever seen in my life. All ages, all shapes, all sizes, none of them wearing many clothes. At least a dozen waiters danced nimbly among them, bearing trays of drinks and food. One of them swept past us, swinging three plates of fat, grilled sardines, slaked with garlic and olive oil, under our noses.

The square was bounded on three sides by old stone buildings. Every one of them housed a restaurant and bar, and each one seemed to own its own area of ground on which tables were set out, packed together tightly with just enough room to allow access. Above the parasols rose three young trees, with birds singing in their branches.

The old church stood at the head of the square. Its single great round window seemed to look down on the village like a benevolent eye. I couldn't help myself; I smiled up at it, and nodded. I stood there for a while, beaming, trying but failing to pick out a dominant language among the noise.

At last Prim squeezed my arm. She grinned too. 'A bit different from that concrete boatyard, eh? Come on.' She pulled me up the path, which was gravel now, into the heart of the square, looking around for an empty table. 'Over there,' she said, pointing to her left, towards a space near the entrance to one of the restaurants, dragging me behind her as she made for it.

The waiter stepped up just as we got there. He was a tallish bloke, about my height, forty-something but with jet-black hair, and a long face which broke into a pleasant smile as he drew back one of the cane chairs for Prim. It didn't strike me until later that he was less bronzed than I had expected a Spanish waiter to be. In fact it stood to reason, since he spent most of his summer under the parasols.

I was reaching into the back of my brain for my High School Spanish when he beat me to it. 'Français? Deutsch? Anglais?' he asked. At once I realised why I hadn't picked out a language among the hubbub. It was because there were so many of them being spoken at once. I shook my head as I sat down. He looked puzzled until Prim said, 'Écossais.'

'Ah,' he said, his smile widening. 'Scottish!'

I know quite a few English people, but I only give this tip to the ones I like. So pay attention. When you're travelling in France or Spain, always say that you're a Jock.

'This your firs' time in L'Escala?' the waiter went on, loosened up more than a bit.

We both looked puzzled. So did he, for a moment. 'You not staying in L'Escala, no? It is the next town,' he explained, waving loosely towards the south, 'beyond the ruins of Empuries.'

Prim shook her head and gave him her best schoolgirl smile. 'We're not staying anywhere yet. We're still considering where to stop. But right now we're only thinking about lunch.'

He smiled. 'Of course. I am sorry. The menu.' He bowed slightly and presented us with two thick brown folders, with leaves encased in plastic, each page with a wee flag sticking out to denote the language. We headed straight for the Union Jack.

So, on our first day in Spain we sat under the parasols in St Marti, eating salad and pizza, washed down with cold, gold beer. It was mid-afternoon when we paid the waiter and stepped between the tables, now mostly unoccupied, and out into the sun.

Most of the people leaving the restaurant had headed up another gravel path which led round the side of the church, past a two-storey villa with mosaic patterns on its walls, and with an almost flat roof. We followed them slowly in the heat, Prim with her arm wrapped around my waist. As we passed the house, the path took a sudden downward slope and there it was, the Mediterranean, spread before us at last. We stood beside a low wall bounding a crescent-shaped viewpoint, and gazed out dumbstruck.

I love views. All my life my favourite has always been the outlook from my bedroom in my dad's house in Anstruther, across the Firth of Forth towards the May Island and beyond to the Bass Rock. But the first time that I stood beneath the crest of St Marti d'Empuries and gazed around the great crescent of the Golf de Roses, it took my breath away.

Looking north, Prim and I recognised at once the high-rise apartment blocks of Ampuriabrava, which we had seen close up earlier that day. Beyond, like white pearls set into the side of the mountain which rose steeply from the sea at the distant mouth of the bay, were the villas of the town of Rosas. A strip of golden beach ran round the circumference of the bay, almost from its northern tip, until it was cut by the promontory on which we stood, and from which a long stone pier jutted out three hundred metres into the sea. The water was blue and calm.

We followed it as it curved south, past the remnants of an ancient sea wall, past the Greco-Roman ruins of which, we learned later, St Marti had been the forerunner. The semi-circle of the great bay was completed as the beach ended in another rocky rise. The town of L'Escala stood on its southern tip, no more than two kilometres away from where we stood. Its houses and shops seemed to shine, gleaming white in the sun. We looked for high-rise blocks but saw none. As with St Marti, the bell-tower of its church was the highest point on its skyline.

We must have stood there for five minutes, struck silent by

the simple symmetrical beauty of the gulf, watching the motor cruisers as they cut white lines through the blue surface of the mill-pond sea.

At last Prim gave me a squeeze. I looked down at her. She was as lovely and happy as I'd ever seen her. 'This is it, Oz,' she said. 'This is where I'd like to be.'

I laughed. 'Christ, love, we haven't been in Spain for half a day yet.' I protested, but my heart wasn't in it; because I knew that I felt just as she did.

Logic has nothing to do with it. Places are like people. There are millions of them, and you encounter new ones on a daily basis, but every so often you see one and you fall in love with it. That's how it was the first time I saw my loft in Edinburgh. That's how it was the first time I saw Wallace, my iguana, in Pet City. (It didn't even matter when I found out that he was a bloke.) I looked once again across the bay towards L'Escala, and I thought about all the places and people I loved. Anstruther, Edinburgh, my dad, my poor mum, Ellie, my nephews: the place felt comfortable among them all.

So I wrapped my arms around Primavera, and I kissed her, ignoring the raised eyebrows and half-smile of a fat Germanic type a few yards away. 'You sure?' I asked.

'Sure as I've ever been about anything.'

'For how long?'

She smiled. 'Who knows? That's the thing about this trip. Voyage of discovery, remember. Let's find somewhere to stay tonight, and take a longer look tomorrow.'

I looked back up the hill, towards the Casa Forestals, as the flat-roofed villa seemed to be called from the sign by its door, and St Marti. 'That's no more than a hamlet. There may be nothing there.'

Even Prim's shrugs seem optimistic. 'We'll never know until we ask,' she said, taking charge. 'Let's go back up and see our multi-lingual pal. He'll tell us what there is.'

The square was quiet as we climbed back up to the village. I checked my watch. It was three forty-five; respite for the bars and restaurants before the evening rush, I guessed. Our waiter friend was seated at one of his own tables, at the door of his establishment. For the first time I read the name above the door. 'Casa Miñana – Snack Bar.'

He stood up as we approached, with a smile that struck me as more than simply professionally friendly. He offered us a table. 'You like to drink? I am afraid that the kitchen is closed for two hours, but maybe a sandwich is possible.'

My partner, now in total command, shook her head. 'No more food. But two beers, yes please.' She sat down and I followed. He disappeared into the dark interior of Casa Miñana, re-emerging a minute later with two frosted globes of Spanish lager.

'Thank you,' said Prim. 'We were wondering; we'd like to stay around here tonight. Do you know if there are any rooms available?'

He frowned. 'Normally there are zimmer . . . sorry' – he corrected his linguistic lapse – 'rooms there, and there.' He nodded towards two other buildings on the square. 'But is summer, and all is occupied. You try L'Escala, yes? There are places there. Hostal Garbi, is very good.'

Prim nodded. 'Thank you.' He must have read disappointment in her eyes, for his face fell. All at once it brightened up again.

'Unless you like to stay here for a few days. My family, we have a few apartments we rent in the summer. They are all occupied, but there is another next to them. A Dutch man, he asked me to try to sell his apartment for him, and he say that if anyone want it I can rent it. If you want to stay for maybe a week, I could let you have that.'

My Scottishness surfaced. 'How much?'

'The owner say forty thousand pesetas for the week.' He paused, and my mental arithmetic worked that out as two hundred quid. 'Is very cheap for St Marti in July.' Suddenly he grinned. 'Cheaper than we rent our apartments. Which is why . . .'

Prim smiled back at him and finished his sentence. '. . . it's still empty and you are only telling us about it because yours are full.'

He blushed slightly and shrugged his shoulders. 'Is business,' he said, disarmingly. 'Would you like to see it?'

Prim and I nodded spontaneously, and simultaneously. The waiter lobbed the tray on which he had brought our beer, and which he still held, across to a much older man who had appeared in the doorway as we spoke. The veteran caught it deftly, without a word, and took a pace outside.

'My name is Miguel,' said our new friend, as we stood up. 'Miguel Miñana. This is my father. His name is Jaume.' We introduced ourselves and shook hands formally with the two Miñanas.

Miguel motioned us to follow and led us away from the snack bar, up towards the church then round to the left. We realised for the first time how small St Marti is, no more than three narrow, brick-paved alleys, linked at the foot by a fourth and opening out at the top into the square, and the area in front of the church. Our escort stopped at a plain yellow-painted wooden door at the top of the most distant alley, which even then was no more than thirty yards from the head of the square, defined by the low stone wall in front of the church. I looked up at the building, and took a wild guess that it was, maybe, two hundred years old.

'This is it,' he said, unlocking the door with a key from the vast bunch which hung on his belt. He stepped inside and switched on a light. A narrow stone stairway rose in front of us. 'Is up here, at the top,' he said, starting to climb. 'Very nice apartment. All new furniture, new kitchen, almost everything new. The owner and his wife not speak any more. That is why he want to sell.'

The stairway took three turns before we came to the apartment. No other doorways opened off it, but it was lit by three slit windows one above the other on successive levels. There were two keyholes in the brown-stained front door, each concealing a heavy, three-bolted double lock. Finally after much sorting of keys, Miguel unlocked them both, stepped inside and threw a switch. There was a hum as the motorised shutters, which covered every window, rose as one, letting the sunlight spill into the flat.

'Is very good, the way it faces,' he said. 'The sun only comes in the windows at the back, but unless you roll out the blind, you have it on the terrace all day. And this is the highest apartment on this side of the village, so it has no one can see in. You look round. See if you like.'

Both Prim and I had been expecting something old-fashioned. But at some point in the last twenty years or so the place had been gutted and rebuilt. We stepped into a big living area, with cream tiles on the floor and pristine, white-painted walls.

Doors on either side led into two bedrooms, the one on the left, en-suite. The other bathroom, and a spacious fully-fitted kitchen with washer-drier, fridge-freezer, halogen cooker, microwave and even dish-washer were set on either side of the entrance, and had good-sized windows which looked back down towards the square.

The living area was quality furnished, with two wide wood-framed sofas, with big, soft, pale blue cushions, a single chair, a round dining table set, and a sideboard. A television and video sat on a corner table, beside a big open fireplace, with, I noticed, a Sky satellite decoder, minus card. The stuff in the bedroom was of the same style and standard. I guessed that at some point while they were still together, the Dutch couple had gone to the local furniture store and bought the lot *en bloc*.

The living room and both bedrooms opened out onto a big balcony. In the larger bedroom Prim drew the muslin curtains aside, threw the double doors open and stepped out. 'Oh!' she cried out loud. 'Bloody hell!' So did I. The terrace was L-shaped, since the smaller bedroom, on the right, was set back from the line of the living room. A quick count of its floor tiles told me that it was around five metres deep and at least twelve wide. It stood above the tops of the trees which lay on the slope to the north of St Marti, giving a panoramic view which stretched from L'Escala on our right, right across the bay and on to the spectacular skyline of the Pyrenees with which Primavera had fallen in love that morning.

Miguel was standing behind us. 'You like, eh,' he whispered, with a smile. 'You know, I think this is the finest view in all of Catalunya.'

I must have looked puzzled. 'Ah,' he said. 'You think that you are in Spain, yes?'

I must have looked even more puzzled. 'And so you are,' he went on. 'But you are also in Catalunya. Spain is many places, many provinces. Here we are Catalans first, Spanish second. We speak Catalan first, Castellano second . . . although a few will not speak Castellano at all. We have our own flag, like the Spanish flag, the same colours, but different.' He laughed. 'We even have our own taxes . . . although many people, they don' pay them!'

Prim tugged his sleeve. 'You said forty thousand pesetas for the week?'

'Yes. I can take Visa if you like. At this time of year Catalunya runs on Visa.'

She looked at me. A question. I nodded. An answer.

So we went back to the snack bar, paid the man with one of our shiny gold cards and moved in there and then. In time to catch the last of the evening sun, stretched out in our cossies – initially, at least – on the sun loungers which we had found with the rest of the terrace furniture. In time to discover that Miguel had been right when he said that our balcony, bounded by a low wall topped by a wooden rail, was completely private. There's nothing on earth quite like sunbathing in the salty air of the Mediterranean with the warmth caressing the length of your body. But don't just take my word for it. Ask Primavera.

Our voyage might have been over for the moment, but there was still plenty of discovering to do. We spent the next week exploring the region: the incredible detail of the excavated Greek and Roman cities of Empuries, the homely L'Escala with the narrow streets of its old town sloping down to a pocket-sized sandy beach, and its expanding marina where we encountered another expatriate Scot, running a very good restaurant with her Catalan husband, the neighbouring town of Torroella de Montgri, with its baking hot square and its leafy avenues . . . sorry, ramblas. In the process we found at least a dozen good places to eat, since neither of us was in a hurry to learn about supermarket shopping in Spain.

On our seventh night in St Marti, as on all the others, we brought our evening to an end at a table outside Casa Miñana, enjoying the buzz of the people and the cold of the draught Estrella beer. As our friend passed by with a nod and a smile, Prim stopped him with a touch on his arm.

'Miguel.' She hesitated, for about half a second. 'What would it cost to buy the apartment?'

He looked down at her, suddenly solemn. So did I. 'To buy it?' he repeated.

She nodded.

He glanced across at me, then back at Prim, all the time scratching his chin. 'An apartment like that, in this village,' he said at last, 'it cost maybe fourteen, maybe fifteen million pesetas.'

I gulped. Millions of anything have that effect on me. I looked across at Prim, watching her concentrate as she converted mentally to sterling.

'But the Dutchman,' Miguel went on, 'he say to me, get me nine million and I will be happy.' He paused. 'That is with the furniture, the cups, the saucers, everything.'

We both liked Miguel, he had befriended us, and given us a couple of mines full of useful information about places to go, things to see, and even places to eat – not a hint normally thrown out by a restaurateur. But both of us looked at him as if he was Tommy Cooper at his funniest.

'Nine million!' I gasped, when at last I could. 'For a top

quality, furnished two-bed apartment in an exclusive village, with one of the finest views in Europe. Christ, Miguel, that's forty-five grand in real money. Forgive us, but what's the catch?'

He smiled and shrugged. 'Senor Oz, Senora Prim, I assure you there is no catch. Things between the Dutchman and his wife are very bad. She is not a good woman. She run off with another man, but she wants all his money. He say to me that the more he sell the place for the more he will have to give her. So he say to me to find someone I like, someone who will enjoy the place, and who will not tell anyone in the village what they pay for it, and to sell it to them for nine million.

'You are interested, yes? If you need a *hipoteca* . . . Sorry. How you say? Mortgage, I know a man in a bank.'

Prim looked at me and nodded. If I had said no I would have been deeper in the shit than the Dutchman. So instead, I said, 'Yes, we're interested. No, we don't need a mortgage.'

Miguel beamed. 'Good. That is very good! I will phone the Dutchman now and tell him.'

He disappeared into the bar, leaving us staring at each other, stunned. 'Can you believe it?' Prim whispered.

'Just,' I replied, 'but to be on the safe side, we'd better find a lawyer, pronto.'

Miguel reappeared five minutes later, still smiling. 'Everything is okay. Nine million is okay. He says he hopes you have better luck there than he did. Before he left he gave me power of attorney, so I can go to the *notario* with you to pass the *escritura*.'

He had read my mind. 'But you, you should have a lawyer. Just so everything can be explained to you.' He passed me a card which he had been holding between his fingers. 'You go see this man. He is in L'Escala and he is lawyer for a lot of British people here. He is very good, very honest.'

His name was Ray Lopez, half Catalan, half English, all lawyer. We saw him next morning, and found that a phone call from Miguel had beaten us to it. Sr Lopez looked into the local and regional registers and pronounced everything as 'Appropriate, Senor y Senora,' and five days later Sr Osbert Blackstone and Sra Primavera Phillips were joint owners of the apartment of their dreams.

The dreams continued through the summer. Every morning we walked along the three-kilometre road to L'Escala, for coffee in the open air, either at the Casablanca by the beach, or at El Centre, beside the old church. Most afternoons we spent swimming in the sea and sunbathing on the beach below St Marti, or lying naked on the beds on the terrace. On alternate nights we would cook for ourselves, at home, or eat out, at one of our growing list of restaurants, occasionally with members of our circle of English ex-pat acquaintances which had developed out of a couple of introductions made by Ray Lopez.

Weeks turned into months as we enjoyed our idyll beneath the Spanish sun. It was there, on the twenty-first of September, that I clambered over the milestone of my thirtieth birthday. In the course of it all, we became sybarites, Prim and I. Without our realising it our voyage had turned into an exploration of the limits of self-indulgence, and in the process we were turning ourselves into different people.

I suppose that it had begun to dawn on us both, but as usual, it was Prim who said it first; on the terrace, in the still-hot autumn sun, on the day after my birthday.

'This isn't working Oz, is it.'

I took a swig of my beer, from the bottle as usual, and frowned back at her. 'What the hell do you mean? We've got quarter of a million in the bank in Jersey, we've got a house a lot of people would kill for, in a place we both love. We screw each other's brains out every day . . . like half an hour ago for example. We've got no ties, no worries, no responsibilities. And you lie there with the Piz Buin glistening on your brown bosom and tell me that it isn't working.'

She clenched her jaw. 'Well it isn't. We've found our place, sure. We've had our holiday, too. But it's got to stop sometime.'

She had thrown me into a grim mood. I resisted. 'Why has it got to stop?'

The frown grew deeper. 'Well . . . our cash won't last for ever.'

'No? Where we have it, we're earning a minimum of fifteen grand investment income. Jan's starting to bank another four-fifty a month in rent of the loft. That's twenty K without touching our capital. So!' My voice rose of its own accord. I'd never snapped at Prim before. Come to think of it I don't remember ever snapping at anyone before. 'Why isn't it working?'

She swung her legs round and sat on the edge of the lounger, pulling her knees up to her chin. The frown had gone, replaced by what looked like a plea in her eyes. 'Because I, at least, need ties, need worries, need responsibilities. I need to be doing something. And so, if you'd think about it, do you.

'When we met you were dynamic. You couldn't stop moving if you tried. You swept me off my feet.'

'As you swept me,' I said. 'As you still do.'

'Fine, but if we become stagnant there will come a point when I don't. Oz, we're too bloody young to opt out. You say we can live on what we have now, but if we have kids . . . when we have kids . . . what then? What sort of role models would we be?' She was in full cry now. 'Remember that English bloke Trevor. The one we met at Gary's restaurant. The fellow who's been here for years, doing little or nothing, but knowing everything. How'd you like to have him for a father?'

'Aw, come on!' That was a sure sign that she was winning the argument. She knew it, and she closed in for the kill.

'The last couple of months have been great, sure. But I've got to the stage when I'm conscious that all I'm really doing is sitting on my steadily widening arse watching you doing the same thing. And am I wrong or is the sex not *quite* as magic as it was at the start?' She had me there.

'Oz, we have to think about what's ahead. It'll be winter soon, even here. It's time we got back to work.'

With a very ill grace, I gave up. 'Okay, so what'll we do?'

She beamed at me. 'Why don't we do what we've shown we're good at? Investigations.'

I stared at her. 'Investigations? Here? But we barely . . .'

She waved a hand, as if she was brushing me aside. 'Let me finish. I mean investigations here for people in Britain. You were a private enquiry agent in Edinburgh. There's no reason why we can't do the same thing in Spain for people in Britain. All we have to do is widen the definition a bit. If a UK company wants some market intelligence we'll do that. If a lawyer wants a witness interviewed, we'll do that. If a travel company wants resorts checked out we'll do that. If a parent wants a missing kid found, we'll do that.' All the time she spoke her smile was getting wider, and her eyes brighter.

'We'll place small ads in British newspapers,' she burbled, 'in the business sections. Something like "Phillips and Blackstone. Spanish Investigations. You want to know? Let us find out. Replies to a box number." We'll use the *Telegraph*, *Sunday Times*, *Scotsman*, *Herald*, and a legal magazine. We can mailshot the big law firms in London and Scotland, through a post office box here. It won't cost all that much to try, and I'm sure it'll be a winner.'

I looked across at her. I was on my fourth San Miguel of the day. The light in her eyes was beginning to hurt mine.

'Couldn't you just get a job nursing?' I said wearily. 'In Gerona or Figueras, maybe. Couldn't we just buy a bar that I could run? That we could both run?'

She looked at me. Now the brightness of her eyes had turned into lasers, cutting me open. 'Sure we could do that, Oz. I could go out every day and force myself to do a job I swore I'd never do again. Then I could come home at night – or worse still, be there all day – to watch you sat on your barstool, pontificating and turning into a replica of that arsehole Trevor.

'You said it all really: "Couldn't we *just* . . ."' She twisted the word like a knife. 'You meant find something, anything, to occupy our time. Well, you can become a cabbage if you like, Oz, but I won't stick around to watch. If we're going to stay here long-term, and I'd like to, we have to get a life that makes the most of our strengths, rather than indulges our weaknesses. Laziness is an easy vice to pick up. I can see it taking hold of you, and I can feel it growing in me.'

I finished my San Miguel in a single swallow, took another from the ice bucket, twisted off the top, and stared across at her, unsmiling. Temper tantrums were strangers to me. I had a feeling that I was about to say something very bad, something about once a nurse always a sergeant major, something about not trying to run my fucking life. It didn't occur to me for a second to look for a funny line to divert her with laughter. It didn't even occur to me that I might have looked a wee bit ridiculous, lying there naked and quivering with petulance.

I took another swig of beer, then a deep breath, as if I was fuelling the tirade to come.

'Senor Oz! Are you there, please?'

3

'Okay, Miguel. Give me a couple of minutes and I'll see you at the church.'

He nodded and I turned away from the wall. I was alone on the terrace. Prim's lounger was empty, although a bisected crescent in the cushion marked the spot where she had been sitting.

I stepped from the sunlight into the cool darkness of the living room. She was leaning against the bedroom door. I looked at her big brown eyes. The lasers had been switched off, and normal sparkling conditions restored, with perhaps an added hint of contrition.

As I came up to her she reached out for the towel around my waist, unfastening it and using it to pull me towards her. I felt two hard nipples warm against my chest, as her mouth reached up for mine. I kissed her, a bit warily still.

'I'm sorry, love,' she whispered, 'sounding off like that. But I really do want it to work for us. Can we give it a try?'

I looked down at her.

'Please?' she said, very quietly.

My conversation with Miguel had already done something for my lethargy level. That wide-eyed look was enough to do the rest. 'Okay, partner. Let's try it out. But it's Blackstone and Phillips, mind, not the other way around.'

Primavera beamed up at me. 'Tell you what,' she whispered. 'Let's call ourselves Blackstone Spanish Investigations. My mother doesn't expect me to live in sin forever, you know.'

I gulped. Marriage, for us, was a bit like death. Probably on the agenda, only we weren't sure when.

She let go of the towel and grasped my bum in both hands. 'And now, since we've nothing better to do before dinner . . .'

I disengaged her. 'Ah but I have,' I said. 'I have to meet Miguel, now. You draw up the ads. We can fax them to Jan tonight and ask her to place them.'

She nodded. 'Okay. What did Miguel want, anyway? I couldn't hear.'

'It was about young Jordi. He's found a body.'

'Oh,' said Prim. 'I see.'

4

Finding a body in St Marti is not, actually, all that uncommon an occurrence.

The village has renewed itself time and time again, on the same site, over the last couple of millennia. Even the church isn't any more than a few centuries old . . . or most of it, since there is a stone over the door which dates back over a thousand years.

People have lived there pretty well continuously all that time, and nature being what it is they've died there too. All that history is lying there in layers beneath the surface, and you don't have to scratch too deep before you begin to find it. Every time the locals dig up a drain or lay a cable there's a fair chance they'll find an ancestor.

During the previous few weeks the town council of L'Escala, which is responsible for the village, had put men to work on the area in front of and alongside the Casa Forestals, the foresters' house, clearing and levelling the site, making it ready to be transformed into a paved public viewpoint.

I could see Miguel pacing about restlessly in front of the church as I stepped out of our yellow front door, back into the sunshine in my shorts, sandals and Runrig T-shirt. To my surprise, he was smoking a cigarette, something I'd never seen him do before. Yet the Miñana family had been in St Marti for as long as their records went back, so I guessed that it was the possibility that young Jordi's find might have been his great-great-great-great-great granny that was making him so twitchy. Something else surprised me. In the bright light of day, he was carrying a black, rubber-bound Ever Ready torch.

He turned as I approached. 'Ahh, Oz. Thank you for coming. I am sorry if I interrupted your siesta. You do not bring Senora Prim? No. Is good.'

I smiled at his concern for my beloved. After the year she had spent as a nurse in an African war zone, not to mention our escapade in Switzerland, I was pretty certain that there was nothing beneath the soil of St Marti to make her bat an eyelid.

'No problem, Miguel. So, where's your old Roman warrior?'

He gave me a strange look. 'Over here, come on.' He led the way across the crown of the square, towards the excavations around the foresters' house. It was late afternoon on a Monday in late September, one of the very few occasions on which the hub of St Marti is likely to be completely deserted.

'When did Jordi do his digging?' I asked.

'This afternoon, once the men had finished work for the day. He likes the archaeology. He says that he wants to go to study it at university. My father says that like us he should work in the bar and on our farm, but I say, we'll see.'

He beckoned me on, round to the side of the tall house, to the narrow area which lay between it and the church. The ground was uneven, littered with stones and clumps of dried yellow soil, with the remnants of vegetation wound through it. The workers had marked the walls of the church and the house to show where, eventually, the line of the new viewpoint would be.

Miguel pointed to a patch of ground in the shadow of the house, almost against the wall. 'There it is. Look.' I followed his pointing finger, bending to see better.

It lay just below the level to which the men had been digging. I could see what young Jordi's sharp eye had picked up, and how he had gone about exposing it handful by handful. It was the lid of a stone coffin. It had been pulled aside, exposing about half of the width of the chamber, but not recently, for despite young Jordi's excavation I could see that it was still partly full of soil.

The body was there all right. The skull grinned up at me, its big teeth standing out and its eye sockets full of dry yellow earth. It was a big skull, and the bones of the shoulders seemed wide. I guessed that this had been a man, and probably an important one at that, to have merited a coffin, since most of the early inhabitants of St Marti had been buried in shrouds. I looked down the length of the skeleton, as the boy had exposed it. All the bits seemed to be there as it lay stretched out on its bed of clay. Something on the left wrist caught my eye. I leaned a bit closer. It was a bracelet, about an inch and a half wide, with a finely worked design showing where Jordi had rubbed away the dirt.

I stood up and looked at Miguel. 'Okay,' I said, 'You were right. It's a body. Now what do you want me to witness?'

He looked at me still frowning. 'Eventually, I want you to say that there was nothing there but the bracelet when we find him. The archaeologists are very suspicious. They may say that there was something else and that Jordi took it.'

'Why me?'

'Because I trus' you, that's why.'

I smiled at the compliment. Then an idea struck me. 'I'll get my camera and take a photo. That should satisfy them.'

A look of horror flashed across his face. 'No, no! You must not. There is something else. Look again.' Hesitantly he handed me the torch.

I took it and knelt down beside the stone coffin, noticing for the first time how deep it was. I shone the torch inside, looking more closely at the centuries-old skeleton, beginning to feel a wee bit ghoulish.

For an instant, a strange flash caught my eye; it could have been gold or silver. I couldn't be sure, for the stone lid cast a dark shadow. I swung the torch back slowly until its beam found the bright metal once more. My stomach turned over. The torch-light shone full on a man's wristwatch. It had a black face with gold hands, and gold roman numerals and a stainless steel back, with what looked like 18-carat gold plate around the edge of the face. Its strap was black leather, and looked as if it was partly rotted.

A sudden wave of fear swept over me. It might have got out of control had I not realised almost at once what had made it spring up. The watch was an identical model to one which I had given my dad nine months before, as a Christmas present: Giorgio of Beverley Hills, Swiss made, water resistant to three atmospheres. I was pretty sure that Giorgio didn't have a branch in Catalunya . . . or at least that he didn't in the days when they were still burying people in stone chests.

My grip on myself didn't last long. The sound of your own scream confined and magnified within a stone coffin is – Oh God, how I hope it is – a once in a lifetime experience. I just couldn't help it. I jumped up, banging the side of my head on the edge of the lid, rolled over and scrambled away from the thing, looking, I suspect, like the old film of Jackie K 'hauling ass' out of that limo in Dallas.

I lay on the ground, staring up at Miguel, aware that my mouth was hanging open, but unable to do anything about it . . . like speak.

He looked at me, with scant sympathy, I have to say. Alongside my reaction, his earlier agitation was stoic by comparison. He didn't say a word, but I knew that there was face to be lost in the situation, so finally I gave him what I hoped was a wicked smile, and rolled back towards the open grave. In my hurried withdrawal I had dropped the torch. I reached down and picked it up, then lowered myself once more through the opening.

Imagine the worst morning you've ever had after the night before. The wildest stag party – and let's not be sexist about this – or hen night, you could ever imagine, when things have got really out of control, you've ended up guttered in some disco, and, as you wake up, you really can't remember a thing about the person next to you, the face you see on the pillow next to yours. Go on, give free rein to your worst nightmare.

Nothing like it.

Inside the coffin, a second skull grinned at me, eye to eye, no more than a foot away, like that face on the other pillow. Unlike the original tenant, yellowed with age, this one was still more or less shining white. The beam of the torch reflected off a gold filling in one of the back teeth, and off the steel of a bridge set on the lower jaw. I forced myself to stare at it dispassionately, fighting hard to master my horror. I succeeded, and at last I was able to play the torch down the rest of the body. It lay on its side, pressed against the coffin wall. It was clean, if you could use that word for something that was well down the descent into corruption, because the earth which had spilled in through the open lid, covering most of the original skeleton, had not piled up beyond its right limb. Relics of clothing, unspeakably stained, still hung on the bones. There were strands of a shirt that had probably been blue, and trousers that might once have been cream. A black leather belt was still looped around the waist, the weight of its heavy, rusted metal buckle pulling it down against the bony spine. There seemed to be no jewellery, other than that Giorgio watch. I shone the beam on and around the hands, looking for a wedding ring but seeing none.

I looked back up at the skull. A few wisps of fair hair still clung to its dome. 'Afternoon,' I said. 'Sorry to disturb you. I'll be off now.'

I hauled myself out of the coffin for a second time, under control this time, and stood up beside Miguel, with a quick glance over my shoulder to confirm that the square was still empty.

'I see.' I didn't think there was much more to be said.

'Yes,' said Miguel. 'Is terrible. What are we going to do?'

I looked at him in surprise, my eyebrows shooting halfway up my forehead. 'I reckon that "Call the police", sounds like a pretty good answer to that one.'

He gasped, and his face became a mask of fright. 'Ah no, not that. That would be terrible. The tourists would not come any more. All the families in the village need them for the money, for the businesses.'

'Come on, man,' I said. 'It wouldn't be that bad.'

He nodded his head violently. 'Oh yes it would. This is a quiet place, a peaceful place. Most of our tourists come every year, from all over Spain, and Europe. Many of them have children. Others are old. They will not come back to a place where something like this can happen. Where people can be killed and buried.'

'How will they know about it?'

He looked at me as if I was daft. 'From the newspapers, the television . . . and not only in Spain.'

He had me there. I could see the headlines. 'Fresh Stiff in Pre-historic Coffin.' Yes, even the *Lothian Herald and Post* would run that one. But even at that . . . 'Listen, Miguel,' I insisted, 'the season's almost over. It'll all have been forgotten by next summer.'

A very obvious question struck me suddenly, right in the teeth. 'Eh, you don't know who that is down there, do you?'

He shook his head this time, and so violently that I thought it might come off. 'No, no, no! But the Guardia Civil, they will find out, then they will find out who did it, and there will be a trial. In Spain that takes a long time, and all that time there will be *periodistas* here, asking questions, taking pictures. The families, they will go away, and the wrong sort of people will come instead.'

He paused, chewing his lip nervously. 'The Guardia Civil, they will investigate everyone in the village. They will ask questions and they will find things out that maybe some will not want found out.'

I pointed to the coffin. 'You mean someone here might have . . .'

'Oh no, I know everyone in this village, and around it. I promise you, no one who lives here would have done that.

No, I mean that they will find things out about our businesses, that maybe someone no pay as much tax as he should, that maybe someone no pay any tax at all.'

As a self-employed person, I understood that concern. 'Ahh. I'm with you,' I said. 'But even at that, Miguel man. This is murder we're talking about. That bloke didn't climb in there himself. He was put there.

'This ground used to be hidden from the village by a thick hedge, until the workmen took it down to prepare for the viewpoint. I'd guess that someone killed him up here, went to dig a grave, then hit the stone coffin by accident and had the bright idea of shoving him inside.

'Almost certainly that guy down there has a family. They deserve to be put out of their misery. And whoever murdered him deserves to be caught. What if he's killed more than one, and uses St Marti as a graveyard? Tax man or no tax man, we can't just cover the thing up and pretend that it isn't there.'

Miguel looked at me, slightly shocked. 'Oh no, of course not. I do not mean that we should do that. Is not possibly anyway. It was Jordi who found this, remember. Even if I told him not to do it, he could not stop himself telling his friends at school about what he had found.'

'Does he know what's inside?'

'No, he did not see the other body. Only the old one. But that is enough. He is very proud of being an archaeologist. Also, is the law that when you find something like this, you must report it.'

I turned and took a few steps away from the coffin, until I could see down the square. A waiter had appeared outside the Esculapi and was busying himself pulling his tables to the side and hosing the gravel underneath, to keep down the dust.

'So what do you want to do?' I asked Miguel, quietly, over my shoulder.

'I want to move the other body. Tonight. Out of here, away from St Marti, somewhere else, where it will be found.'

'You're crackers, man!' I tapped the side of my head.

'Maybe. But will you help me?'

I gave it a couple of seconds' thought. 'Of course I will. No one ever accused me of being sensible either.'

5

'You're going to *what*!' She had been straddling me on the bed; suddenly she sat bolt upright.

'I'm going to help him,' I repeated, staring up at her. 'What else should I do? The guy's beside himself with worry about it, and he's got no one else. Shifting that lid will be a two-man job, and Jaume's far too old for it.

'Remember, Miguel's the reason we're here. He's done us a huge favour, and if he's got a problem, it's up to us to help him out. We're part of this community now. If Miguel says he knows what's best for it, then even though it scares me shitless, I just think I have to go along with it.'

Prim frowned at me, and resumed her ministrations with Dettol-soaked cotton wool to the graze on my right temple, where I had bumped it on the coffin. I had come home unaware of the line of blood trickling down my face.

'But won't that make you both accessories after the fact, or something like that?'

'I'd rather not think about that, thank you very much.'

'Well what about this poor man?' she said, severely. 'From the way you described the condition of the skeleton, he can't have been dead for all that long. Almost certainly, he'll be on someone's missing persons list. What about his family? Don't they have rights?'

She dabbed again, a wee bit too hard, I thought, making me wince. 'Easy on the antiseptic, love. They've got the same rights today as they had yesterday, but you could argue that thanks to Jordi and Miguel they're nearer today to having them fulfilled. Miguel isn't talking about burying the guy again.

He plans to leave him in a place where he's likely to be found.'

'Such as?' My arguments were having little or no effect on her disapproval level.

'Well, hardly in the middle of the road, but in a place where he won't be too hard to find yet where realistically he might have been since he was killed.'

She seemed to brighten up a bit. 'I see. Then you and I might go for a walk one day and sort of trip over him. Accidentally. Yes?'

I wasn't so sure about that idea, but I said 'Yes,' anyway.

'Okay then,' she said, grudgingly. 'D'you want me to come with you tonight?'

I shook my head. 'I think that would make Miguel uncomfortable. Anyway, two of us stumbling around in the dark will be quite enough.'

'When are you meeting him?'

'Three o'clock. I'll try not to wake you, going out or coming back.'

She shook her head, shot me her best 'Daft bugger!' expression, and kissed me gently in the middle of the forehead. 'Fair enough, but make damn sure you do one thing.'

'What's that?'

'Have a shower before you get back into bed!'

She jumped off me and headed for the bedroom door. 'Change of subject,' she called back to me. 'Come on and I'll show you our advertisement. I've got it written out.' I followed her into the living room. We had added a writing bureau to our inherited furniture, to accommodate my lap-top and printer. The fall-flap was down and on it lay a sheet of paper. 'There you are,' said Prim, standing over it. 'What d'you think?'

I scanned it, murmuring as I read.

Blackstone Spanish Investigations
Legal, Business, Personal
Member BEAA
Write Box No xxx

I looked through it again. 'Seems all right. I've kept up my membership of the British Association, so that's okay too.'

'Good. I've done this covering note to Jan.' She handed me another A4 sheet. I read again.

> Dear Jan,
> Could you could place the following for us as a small ad in the business sections of *The Times*, *Guardian*, *Herald*, and *Scotsman*. To run every second Friday. Just deduct the cost from rent cheques.
> All the best
> Primavera and Osbert

Not the way I'd have put it, but then I didn't write it. I nodded and fed the two sheets into the slot of our Spanish-made telefax, dialled Jan's number and pushed the button. A few seconds later, the line engaged and the message rolled through. Prim hugged me, smiling, looking gorgeous in simple jeans and blue T-shirt.

'Aren't you excited? "Blackstone Spanish Investigations". It's the start of a new era. Wait and see, Oz my darling, it can't fail.' She reached out a hand and took the car keys from a dish on top of the bureau.

'This calls for a celebration,' she said. 'Today's catch should be in the fish shops by now. I'll take a run into L'Escala and pick some up. D'you want some more beer?'

I shook my head. I was beginning to share her enthusiasm for our new business venture. Maybe, at the same time, I was beginning to lose my enthusiasm for San Miguel as an all-day refreshment. 'Pick up some diet drinks and fizzy water instead. I had a bit of bother squeezing into that coffin!'

She laughed and headed for the door. I watched her from the kitchen window as she hauled herself up into the Frontera, which was parked beside the church, and drove carefully out of the village. As the big boxy car disappeared out of sight, I turned away, with a strange feeling coming over me. My passing sanctimony about beer forgotten, I reached out automatically and took one from the fridge as I passed.

I strolled back into the living room and out onto the balcony. I looked out to sea feeling nervy, jumpy. Suddenly I realised what was odd. It was the first time in weeks, no months, that I had been completely alone, without Prim in the next room, or waiting upstairs for me. Until that moment we had done everything together, apart from our daily ablutions, and even then Prim wasn't always too fussy about shutting the door. I smiled at the thought, and it reminded me of her first meeting with Jan, in bizarre circumstances.

And then I thought of Jan, and realised that I hadn't heard the sound of her voice since we had left Scotland. A fax is a wonderful tool, but it can make you forget what that Cockney bloke went on about on telly . . . you know the fat, bald wee guy who used to talk about 'vachas', whatever they are . . . that 'it's good to tork'.

We had two phones, the one with the fax, and a cordless job with a charger on the bedside table. I sat in a cane chair on the terrace in the yellow evening sun and dialled Jan's number. A great wave of gladness washed over me as she answered with her usual business-like 'hello'.

'Hi there, gal. How goes it? D'you get the fax?'

'Yes, I sure did. I was just about to phone you. Doesn't "please" translate into Spanish, then? I'm your accountant, Oz, not your bloody secretary.'

'Sorry.'

'A phone call would have been nice.'

'This is a phone call.'

'I meant before the fax. You're using me, Osbert, you and Prim. Don't tell me she didn't write it anyway. You've never been as concise as that in your bloody life, boy.'

'Sorry, Jan, sorry, sorry, sorry.'

She sighed. 'Ah, you're forgiven. But you should have talked to me first. There's all sorts of things to be thought through.

Like tax, for example. Are you going to stay over there indefinitely?'

'Looks like it.'

'Then you should apply for official resident status. That means you won't be paying tax in the UK, even if you bank all your income in Jersey, which you should. What about your Post Office box number. Who's going to empty that?'

I gulped. 'Good question. Can we have them forwarded on to another box number here?'

'I'll check for you.'

'Thanks love,' I said, sincerely. Jan's efficiency had brought me down to earth. 'Listen, this is only a thought, but would you like to be part of the business, if it takes off? You could handle UK contacts.'

I could almost hear her shaking her head, two thousand kilometres away. 'I don't think so, sunshine. Like I said, I'm your accountant. That's enough for me. Why don't you ask your sister?'

I grunted. 'Ellie? I could do, but what if she goes back to France, and Allan?'

'Hmmph! When did you phone your dad last?'

Guilt shot through me. 'About two months ago. Why?'

'Because Ellie's not going back to France. She says she's made her mind up. She's found herself again, she says. She's losing weight, she's doing some supply teaching, and she isn't missing Allan a bit. And good for her. I always thought he was a creep . . . and so did you, only you'd never admit it.'

Jan's news made me sit up in my chair. 'Course I wouldn't. He was my sister's husband. Ellie wouldn't have thanked me for telling her she'd made a mistake. Some things, you have to find out for yourself. She might have phoned to tell me, though.'

'Christ!' She snapped the saviour's name down the line. 'Just when I thought I was listening to the new, mature Osbert Blackstone, you say something like that.

'Oz, a few months ago she wouldn't have had to. Nor would

I. You'd have asked. If this is what being in the money's done for you then I don't like it. It seems like you've buggered off and forgotten about us all. You admit that you haven't called Mac in two months . . . not even to check on your iguana. I didn't have to ask you that, by the way. Mum told me, and guess who mentioned it to her.

'You haven't spoken to your sister since you left either, not even to ask about your nephews. As for me, well I know I don't count any more, but it's a bit much when you send me fucking faxes rather than phone me.

'Look, don't get me wrong. I'm pleased for you and Prim. It's just that I don't like seeing you turning into a selfish git, that's all.' Finally, the line went quiet.

'I see,' I said. 'You haven't left anything out, have you?'

She laughed. Thank God, she laughed. 'Och I'm sorry, Oz, it's just . . .'

'Don't be sorry. You're right. Prim told me much the same thing today, if less directly. That's what the business idea's about. What d'you think of it, anyway?'

She pondered my question. 'It should work. You should charge forty quid an hour to private clients, and sixty quid to professionals and corporates. Do your invoicing out of Jersey, to minimise tax problems. I'll set that up for you. Yes, the whole thing sounds like a nice wee earner. Be careful about employing people in Spain, though. I've heard that can be a bugger.'

Her enthusiasm had cheered me up. 'We'll look into that. We have friends here who can advise us. You go ahead and place the ads . . . please.' I paused. 'But enough of that stuff. How're you doing?'

'Fine.'

'How's Anoushka?'

'Fine.'

'No patter of tiny feet yet?'

She gasped, then spluttered. 'You bastard, Oz! Only you could say that and live.'

'I won't push my luck, then. How's your mum?'

'Don't ask me. Try phoning your dad and asking him.'

As if she could see me, I nodded. 'Next call. I promise.'

'Okay, get on with it, then.'

'Yes, Boss.' I paused, as something from the past gripped my stomach. 'Hey, Jan.'

'Yes?'

'I . . . Oh, it's just what you said about not counting any more. You're wrong. You do.'

'I know, Oz. See you.' There was a click, then a buzz.

I'd never failed to keep a promise to Jan, and so I dialled my dad as soon as the line cleared. A child answered, with a bold, 'Anstruther 9671.'

'Jonathan?'

'Yes.' He paused. 'Is that you, Dad?' he asked, uncertain and sounding far from overjoyed.

'Impossible. It's your Uncle Oz.'

'Uncle Oz! Uncle Oz!'

The wee chap and I always got on like a house on fire. 'Yes indeed. And how are you sir? How's Enster?'

To my amusement he dropped into an East Fife accent. 'Fair braw,' he shouted.

I laughed. 'Just don't let your mum hear you talking like that or it'll be slapped legs for you, my lad. Is Grandad there?'

'No, but Mum is. Mum!' The shout almost deafened me. 'It's Uncle Oz.'

In the distance, I heard the rushing of feet.

'Oz? Is everything all right?' Somehow that made me feel really bad.

'Of course it is, Sis. Anyway that's my line. How's it with you?'

'Never better. Well, not for a few years, at least,' she said. She sounded determinedly cheerful. 'I'm not going back to Allan, Oz. It's nothing to do with bein' stuck in that museum in France, either. I just don't love him any more. I've settled in back here, I'm getting teaching work in St Andrews and Jonathan's settling in fine at the primary. He's in Auntie Mary's class. That reminds me, have you spoken to Jan lately?'

'Yes, a minute ago. How are Dad and Auntie Mary getting on, now that they've come out of the closet? Are they being lambasted in the pulpit every Sunday?'

Ellie laughed. 'Naw! The whole town thinks it's great. I'd forgotten how popular our father is around here. Everybody loves him; Mary too. They're the Anstruther couple of the year.' She paused. 'Just like you and Jan, once.'

'Eh?' I'm not taken by surprise all that often, and hardly ever by my sister.

'Make no mistake,' she said. 'The wifies in the bakers used to say exactly the same things about you two that they're saying now about Dad and Mary. "Made for each other, that pair." I've heard it said. Last Saturday, and ten years ago. Exactly the same words, by the same big fat woman. Remember Mrs Scorgie?'

I chuckled. 'Remember her? I used to pinch her apples when I was a kid.'

'It's a funny thing, life. The difference between Dad and Mary and you and Jan is that they've come together out of bereavement, while you two had it easy from the start. That's probably why you grew apart.'

I thought about what she was saying. 'Don't be so sure,' I murmured at last. 'Jan and I are just the same people. It's our worlds that changed. We've never stopped being fond of each other, just like you and I haven't. We just grew up and fell in love with different people.'

I paused. 'That's history, though. Back to you and Allan. You've really decided that it's all up with you two, then?'

'Aye,' she said, firmly. 'I've got a sort of litmus test for relationships, Oz. I ask myself, "if I died tomorrow, who would grieve for me the worst?" I think of the boys, of Dad, and of you. But I don't think of Allan in that context, not any more. And the truth is, if it was him that snuffed it I wouldn't even get my hankie out. I'd just phone the undertaker in France and tell him where to send the bill afterwards.'

'Christ, Sis, that's a bit tough.'

The laughter had gone from her voice. 'He's giving me no reason to think well of him. I had a recorded delivery letter from an Edinburgh solicitor this morning, requiring me . . . would you believe it, to resume conjugal relations with him in France, or to send the boys back to his care, otherwise he's going to start an action for custody against me, in France. He's a resident, so he can do that, apparently. And French courts are notorious for taking the father's side in cases like this.' She snorted. 'Conjugal relations, indeed! I hadn't had any of those for two months before I left.'

I was taken completely by surprise. I had reckoned that Allan would hardly have noticed that Ellie was gone. I said as much.

'For a while that would have been right. But Allan has ideas of how life should be. Very important job, designer house, designer family. We were part of his environment, the kids and I. Now that he realises that it's been changed, and not by him, he doesn't like it. Hence the threats.'

'Does Dad know?'

'I showed him the letter. He just shook his head and said, "Tell him to fuck off." But it isn't as easy as that. I get a lawyer, she tells his lawyer to fuck off, they translate that into Latin, it all gets very expensive, and the next thing you know the kids and I are the lead story on *Reporting Scotland*.'

I frowned. 'Money isn't an issue. The kids and you are.' I reached a decision. 'Listen, we're only five hours away from Lyon. I'm going to see the bastard.'

'No, Oz. Stay out of it.'

'Sure,' I laughed, 'just like you've always stayed out of it when I've been in trouble. I'm going, Ellie.'

'But what will you say to him?'

I laughed even louder. 'I haven't a clue. I suppose I'll try to act as an honest broker between you, to talk him into being reasonable. If that fails, I'll probably just offer to kick his fucking head in.'

My sister grunted. 'I should have done that a couple of years ago. Too late now though. Look, brother, if you're determined, then thanks. I love you for it. Dad'll be pleased too.'

'What? That I'm taking an interest?'

Ellie hesitated. 'To be frank, yes. He's worried about you and Prim, long-term, lying out there vegetating.'

'Then tell him to stop. The signs have been spotted and action taken. We're starting a business. Jan'll fill you in on it. Tell Dad something else from me too.'

'What's that?'

'Remind him that the telephone is a two-way device.' Ellie laughed. Our father was notorious for never making telephone calls. I guess that was where I had taken it from. 'Listen,' I went on, 'since Dad's not there, how's the other dinosaur?'

'Wallace? As green as ever. Jonathan's adopted him. He takes him for walks in the garden, on a lead. I'm worried about my older son. He's turning into a cut-down version of you.'

I laughed. 'He should be here tonight then. He could come on my adventure.'

'What's that?'

'I can't tell you over the phone. We get too many crossed lines here. But just think of Burke and Hare!'

6

Until I eyeballed a skull at close quarters, I used to think that there was nothing as savage as the grin of a monkfish, cooked whole and taken straight from the oven.

Prim had returned from the *peixateria* – sounds so much more interesting than fishmonger, doesn't it – beside the roundabout on the way into L'Escala, with two of the sublimely ugly fish, gutted but otherwise intact. We had cooked them whole, as we had seen it down in Meson del Conde, the restaurant on the lower side of the square, in a rich tomato and onion sauce, with sliced potatoes boiling in the juice.

Prim's nursing experience came into play as she took them off the bone. All I could do was admire her skill, and stare back at the fish as they looked at me reproachfully, their huge mouths stretched in wicked smiles.

After that, we had an early night. Prim, unwakeable by an earthquake, fell into her usual depth of sleep while I dozed fitfully, dreaming occasionally of my dad, dressed as a pirate for Hallowe'en, my nephew Jonathan, in a suit and speaking into a mobile phone, and Jan sitting cross-legged on the harbour wall at Anstruther, gazing out to sea through my big binoculars, with the wind ruffling her hair. As I looked at her, she lowered the glasses and turned towards me. 'I know, Oz,' she said. 'See you.' Then she went all fuzzy and turned, somehow, into Prim.

I was awake a couple of minutes before 2:55 a.m., the time at which I had set the alarm to ring. I cancelled it, slipped out of bed without waking Primavera – as if there was a chance –

then put on my oldest jeans, sweatshirt and trainers, and went outside.

This time, Miguel was waiting for me out of sight, against the wall of the Casa Forestals. I didn't see him at first, not until he stepped from out of the shadows, scaring me half to death. Until that moment, it hadn't occurred to me that there was a full moon and a cloudless sky. Luckily it had occurred to Miguel. He had even catered for it. He beckoned me over to where the skeletons lay. As I stepped towards him I could see that he had set up a makeshift screen, a rough wooden framework covered with dark cloth. Behind it, we were screened completely from any insomniacs in the village.

The moon cast some light on the grave, but Miguel had added to it by wedging his torch between two rocks and directing its beam on to the coffin. 'We have to move more earth, then lift the lid,' he said. He handed me a funny sort of tool, a cross between a pickaxe and a shovel, with a short handle. Clearing the earth away didn't take long, but raising the stone lid was a different matter. Since its original disturbance, soil had worked its way between the lid and base and had been turned by moisture into a form of cement. It took us twenty minutes of muffled chipping and levering with the sharp end of our implements before we could get the thing to budge. At last we swung it up and over, lowering it gently to avoid any chance of it breaking. The beam now shone full into the open coffin, reflecting on the white of the younger skull, and on the replica of my Dad's Giorgio watch.

'Okay, Miguel,' I whispered. 'That was the easy part. Now tell me, how the hell are we going to shift this poor bugger without him turning into a jigsaw puzzle?'

He looked at me, puzzled himself for a second until he caught on. Then he smiled, looking macabre in the torch light. I shuddered. Miguel has long canine teeth. I glanced up at the moon and looked furtively at him for signs of sprouting hair, or fingers turning into claws. 'Like this,' he said, and produced a bolt of black cloth, just like the one from which our screen was made.

Carefully, he spread it inside the coffin, beside the ragged skeleton. 'Now,' he said, 'we take care, and we roll him over into the sheet. See?'

I did as I was told. Together, very delicately, we reached behind and under the body, and very slowly, rolled it over into the waiting black shroud.

It worked. Almost. The skeleton moved in one piece. The skull stayed where it was, grinning at us as wickedly as one of those bloody monkfish. That almost did me in. Just for a second, I thought that the fish was going to make a return appearance. But I mastered the rising sensation at the back of my throat, as Miguel reached down and pulled the skull into the sheet, then wrapped it fully round the body.

We lifted it out, holding either end taut like a sack, and carried it down to the Miñana pick-up. A long crate lay in the back. 'In there,' said Miguel. Very gently we laid our pal in his new, temporary, coffin.

Carefully, we smoothed out the marks where he had laid within the stone box, checking to make sure that not as much as a toenail was left behind. We replaced the lid, ajar like Jordi had found it, and putting some of the earth which he had removed back inside for luck. Then we dismantled our screen and smoothed out our footprints.

'Come.' Miguel signalled me to follow. He was in full command now, as we climbed into the Toyota truck. He allowed it to run down the slope, away from the village before switching on the engine and engaging gear. We drove quietly through the wooded track, then out on to the road and away from the village.

'Where are we going?' I asked.

'Not far, but far enough. To the woods behind L'Escala.'

The journey took less than five minutes. He headed towards the town, but instead of going in, swung round past the hypermarket and on, up towards an area called Riells de D'Alt, where Prim and I had never ventured. He simply drove until the road ran out, then a bit further, into the edge of a wood, running the truck between the first few trees so that it was out of sight. Eventually he drew to a halt and reached for the torch.

He jumped out of the car, surprisingly nimbly and shone the torch on a deep ditch at the edge of the tree-line. It might have been intended for drainage, or as a firebreak, or both. 'Over there,' he said. Following his lead, I helped him unload the crate from the back of the truck and carry it across to the long trench. Together we lifted out the black sheet, and its contents, then lowered it into its new resting place.

'Okay,' said a coolly efficient Miguel I had not known before that night. 'Now pull.' Together we tugged the shroud, and the skeleton rolled out. We arranged the bones carefully, to avoid any suspicions that the body might have been moved.

'That's good enough. Now, some wood.' He plunged back into the wood, with me on his tail. As quickly as we could we gathered fallen branches and other debris and placed them over the bones in a makeshift cover.

At last, Miguel stood up and beamed: a sardonic smile of satisfaction. 'There, Oz. Now they can find the poor man, any time they like. And tomorrow before the men from the town hall came to work, I will call the mayor and tell him that my son has found a body from the Romans. All will be as it should.'

He looked at me. 'We work hard. You want to go for a drink now.' As I looked at him in astonishment he reached behind the driver's seat of the truck and produced a flask and two clean glasses. In the moonlight he filled each with strong, smooth new red wine. We looked east as we drank, at the first intimation of the new day, away out on the edge of the sea.

We finished the flask in half an hour. Miguel spent the time telling me of his national service. He had served his time in the Spanish navy. Towards the end, his ship had been ordered to North Africa, to help in rescue and recovery following a Moroccan earthquake.

'After that, my friend, tonight's work was, as you might say, a slice of cake.' He threw the last drops of his wine on the ground, as if to bless the poor sod we had just reburied.

'Come, or the Senora Prim and the Senora Maria will think we went to the place beside the go-karts.'

'What the hell is the place beside the go-karts?'

His smile lit up the dying night. 'Ah, Senor Oz! I see there are things you still have to learn about L'Escala!'

7

I was aware, but only dimly, of a nose, buried in my chest and sniffing.

'Badedas,' said Prim, approvingly. 'So you did have a shower before you got back in here.'

'Course,' I murmured, and rolled over.

'I love the smell of Badedas,' she said, following me. 'It turns me on.'

'What doesn't?' I whispered in her ear, as I settled on my back, far too tired for any serious exertion, but far too interested to stay asleep.

Afterwards, I knew I was really in the good books when she brought me breakfast in bed. Sliced tomatoes, and a baguette, bought as dough in a batch and baked in our own oven. We ate together, sitting up, looking out of the open terrace door across the sun-washed bay, with our naked backs cool against the wooden headboard.

'It went all right, then?' asked Prim, at last.

'Mmm,' I said, wiping a sliver of tomato from my chin. 'He's gone, the poor bugger, and St Marti is saved for tourism, saved from the attentions of the coppers and the tax inspectors.'

She looked up at me. 'Er, where did you put him?'

'Up behind Riells, in the back of beyond.'

'Are you sure you'll be able to find him again, in the daylight?'

'Sure. In a couple of days we'll be able to go for a walk, like we agreed, and just sort of accidentally stumble over the poor bugger.' *If the dogs haven't found him first,* came as an afterthought, but stayed unspoken.

'Can't we go today?'

I shook my head. 'No, we should give him a couple of days to . . . settle into his new surroundings. Anyway, I've got something else to do today.' I glanced at the time. It was five minutes past midday. 'Scratch today; make it tomorrow.'

We had been so busy cooking and enjoying the monkfish the night before that I hadn't told Prim about my conversation with Ellie. She listened as I explained about my sister's decision, her husband's ultimatum, and my decision to involve myself.

'You don't mind me driving up to Lyon, do you?'

She squeezed my arm and rubbed her forehead against it. 'Course not. Any sister of yours is a sister of mine. Allan's a prat and a boor, and he needs to be told so. Let him know too that if it does get to court, he needn't think he can rely on outspending her.'

I smiled. That was what I'd hoped she'd say. Then a mischievous thought struck me, and I nudged her. 'Hey, what you said about sisters. If Dad and Auntie Mary get hitched, will that apply to Jan too?'

She looked at me, sideways. 'Given Jan's circumstances,' she said at last, with a grin, 'I think it can.'

All at once she stretched herself, as only Prim can, a real stre-e-e-etch, arms straight above her head, back arched, breasts thrust out, and looked around the room. 'Ugh!' she shouted, suddenly enough to startle me, and pointed towards the doorway to the living room. 'Those!' My sweatshirt, jeans, socks and jockeys lay where I had dropped them before taking my Badedas shower. 'My God, think where they've been. Oz, they're for the wash right now.'

She jumped out of bed, pulling on her towelling robe, and trotted around to my pile of discards. Gingerly, she picked them up, patted the pockets of the jeans to check for change and keys. She paused, then reached into the right hand pocket. 'What's this?' she asked, holding it up.

Right at that moment, I had no conscious memory of how the watch had got into my pocket. But I knew at once what it was, and from the look on my face, Prim guessed in the same second where I had found it.

'Euchh!' she cried, and tossed it away from her, on to the bed. 'Horrible! Clean it up for God's sake. Better still, get rid of it.' Without waiting for my reaction she disappeared towards the kitchen, carrying my clothes.

As I thought back to my adventure, it came back to me through the foggy curtain which Miguel's new red wine had cast over the later part of the evening. How the body's left hand had fallen out of the shroud as we lifted it into the crate, and the watch with it. The disgust with which I had thrust the bony extremity back beside its arm. The hesitation with which I had put the watch into my pocket, meaning to return it later to what was left of its owner.

I picked it up, from where Prim had thrown it, and looked at it, as closely as I could manage on a full stomach. The face and back were dirty but there was no sign of corrosion. The leather strap was in better condition than I had thought, although there were a few scraps clinging to the inside. I tried desperately not to consider what they might be.

I took the watch through to our bedroom, and set to work on it, with soap and a nail brush. The dirt was dried on, but after a few minutes it began to loosen, and with more vigorous rubbing, and polishing with the small towel which hung on a ring by the bidet it was soon shining, looking for the most part brand new. Only the leather strap still looked a bit tired. I took the thing out to the terrace and examined it in daylight, front and back. There was no doubt: it was exactly the same model that I had bought for my father. The black face which he said was a bugger to read in anything but good light; the steel back, engraved with the maker's name, his crest, and a number. I peered at it. '930100,' I read aloud.

'What?' asked Prim from the living-room doorway. 'And for God's sake put some clothes on. Standing around in the buff after midday doesn't fit with our new work ethic.'

I grunted and held up the watch. 'There's a number on the back. These things don't cost enough to be exclusive, though. Chances are it's just a piece of designer flash.'

'Mmm.' She followed me as I headed for the shower. 'What are you going to do with it? Put it back.'

'Hardly. Not now that I've cleaned it up. Right now, I don't have a bloody clue what I'm going to do with it. Although throwing it in a communal dustbin seems like a good idea.' Leaving that thought aside, I shoved it away into my sock drawer, out of sight . . . and, after a while, out of mind.

8

Naturally, I asked Prim if she wanted to come to Lyon, but I didn't try too hard to persuade her when she said, 'No.'

Our serious discussion two days before had made me realise just how much we were living in each other's pockets, and given me a nostalgic urge to do something on my own, just to remind myself what it was like. I was pretty sure that Prim felt the same.

I did no tourist driving heading for Lyon, but followed the autoroute all the way, sticking to the coast past Narbonne this time, on through Montpellier and Nimes, finally heading north after the Orange junction.

Although I had never stopped in Lyon before, I knew that Allan worked at the head office of Sprite Oil, in the heart of the city. I had no intention of giving him advance warning of my visit, so I stopped at a filling station near Vienne to buy a street map, and check the address in the telephone directory.

Lyon is a big place, and like many of the major French cities, a river runs through it. By the time I reached my destination the Rhone seemed like an old friend, since I reckoned that I had crossed and recrossed it at least four times on the journey. Its smell was strong in my nostrils when I found Allan's office, just where the phone book and the map said it should be. I was prepared to give my French a whirl, but the receptionist's English made it unnecessary. Going on for three months in Spain, my Mediterranean tan shining gold in the light reflected from the building's big glass walls and, she still clocked me as a Brit before I'd opened my mouth.

'Good afternoon, sir. How can I help you?' She was a nice-looking girl, with a wide smile and curly brown hair.

'I'd like to see Allan Sinclair, in your marketing department.'

'Of course. Who shall I say is calling?'

I smiled at her. 'I'd rather you didn't. Could you just tell him it's someone with a message from his wife.'

The receptionist nodded, dialled a number then spoke rapidly in French. The only words which jumped out clearly at me were, 'sa femme'. After a few seconds, she looked up at me again. 'Would you wait over there, please, sir. In that room.'

I thanked her and followed her pointing finger to an obscured glass door at the side of the hall, behind which was a small office with a view down to the river. I had been waiting for almost ten minutes when the door opened and my brother-in-law appeared. Quite suddenly it dawned on me that as a professional interviewer I had prepared badly for this one. I had no idea what I was going to say.

Allan solved my problem for me by kicking things off and making me mad in the process. He arched his eyebrows, and looked at me down his nose – or should that be up his nose, because he's three inches shorter than me – in that 'This is too tiresome' way of his. This is a guy who could make you feel unwelcome in your own house.

'What are you doing here?' he asked. 'I was told that it was someone from Ellen.'

'So?' I said, belligerently. 'Listen, Allan, if I'd said it was me, then all of a sudden you'd have been in a meeting. I know you, pal.'

He shuffled his feet and started to reply, but I beat him to it. 'Anyway, I do have a message from my sister. She's not coming back to France, Allan, or to you. I'm sorry, chum, but that's it. Now, what she wants, what we all want is that you should face up to it and accept it.'

He hunched his shoulders. 'Why should I? She's my wife, dammit. She made vows, that sort of thing. Now she's broken them, and she's stolen my sons.'

Allan had always got on my tits, even from the days when

he and Ellie were newly engaged, but I was doing my level best to keep to my honest broker role. That crack got to me, though.

'Am I hearing this? Are you calling my sister a thief?'

He held up his hands as if to ward me off. For an instant it had been necessary. 'Okay, taken them, if you prefer. But she did. She just took the boys and left me a note on the kitchen table. No warning, no nothing.'

I looked at him. 'Allan, I spent one night in your house in France, and I could see the warning signs. You were just too fucking blind.

'It's time you opened your eyes and faced up to some truth about yourself. My sister's bright, man, as bright as you. She's dynamic, if anything more so than you. Time was when she had ambition too. Yet you stuck her away in that place in the middle of nowhere, with no other function than to look after your kids and make your meals.

'When was the last time you took the boys to the seaside, or took Ellie to the theatre? I know the answer, Allan. Never. You imprisoned her over here, pal. Now she's escaped.'

My brother-in-law looked at me, huffily. 'She felt enough for me to marry me, Oz.'

For the first time, I began to feel sorry for him. 'True, Allan. Because you're good at your job. You felt you should have a wife, so you looked at the women you knew and you picked Ellen. Then you marketed yourself to her, like a barrel of oil. But you never had a fucking clue what being a partner's about. It's not something you are, it's something you become. You have to work at it. It's taken me thirty years to realise that. It's bloody hard work too, I'll tell you. You both have to make the effort. Ellie did, but you never had a fucking clue. So now she's given up, and you only have yourself to blame.'

I looked at him. 'Tell me honestly, Allan. Do you think that you and she were ever really in love?'

He sat down on one of the wooden chairs set around the

room's small table, and looked up at me, for quite a long time. Finally he did something that for him was really very strange. He smiled. I hadn't seen him do that since Jonathan was born. 'It's funny that you of all people should ask me that. When Ellen and I were engaged, I used to think that you were a waster. A scatter-brained, self-indulgent waster, without a career plan, and with no idea of where you were going in life.'

I laughed. 'Life's a Mystery Tour, pal. Didn't anyone tell you?'

But he held up a hand to shut me up. 'Yet there was one thing about you of which I was really jealous. I used to look at you and Jan, the way you were together, the way you touched each other without even knowing you were doing it, the way you looked at each other, and I wished that I could be like you, in love like that.

'I supposed that once you were married, that was what did it. I was wrong, though. I was proud of Ellen, and I did my best to give her the best, but I never could feel that way you and Jan used to look, or the way you and what's her name looked when you turned up in Pérrouges, just before Ellie left.' He paused. 'You didn't persuade her to go, did you?'

I shook my head. 'No, man. You did that yourself.' I felt thoroughly sorry for him now. And a lot more reflective than I had been half an hour before.

'About that lawyer's letter, Oz,' said Allan. 'That was temper and pride on my part. Tell Ellen I'm sorry about that; I shouldn't have tried to bully her. We can sort out a separation agreement, but between ourselves. As long as I can see the kids when I like.'

I interrupted him, right there. 'No, not just when you like. Jonathan and Colin are best with their mother, all right, but they deserve a father too, even if he does live a long way off. You can stop being a husband, Allan, but you can't stop being a dad. I know yours wasn't around, and I know you used to treat mine as if he wasn't there either. Well, you should look to him now. You've got a lot to learn about dadship, and you won't find a better role model than Mac Blackstone.'

'I hear you,' he said, standing up. 'Tell Ellen from me that it's okay.'

'No, sir,' I answered, firmly. 'I'm just the bridge-builder. Tell her yourself. Phone her tonight, then as soon as you can, take some time off from this place and visit her and the boys. Sort everything out between you. Think about this as you do it, Allan. You and my sister don't belong together any more. You probably never did. But maybe there's someone out there for you, someone to make your eyes light up. Who knows, there might even be more than one!'

My failed brother-in-law smiled again. 'One step at a time, Oz, eh. But I'll call Ellen tonight, that's a promise.'

Allan stretched out an arm to usher me to the door. 'How are you and Prim doing anyway? Still together, I take it. You haven't come from Scotland to see me, have you?' He looked at me, working a few things out for the first time. 'No, surely not: not with that tan.'

But I wasn't listening to his small talk. I was looking at his left wrist.

'Allan,' I asked at last, 'where did you get that watch?'

He glanced at me. 'Familiar, is it? Last time I saw your dad, I noticed the one he was wearing. I saw the same model in Jenners, so I bought it for day-to-day wear. Did you think I'd pinched Mac's?'

'Don't be daft. No,' I lied, 'it's just that I bought my dad his in a jeweller's shop. I thought it was pretty exclusive, that's all. Can I have a look at it?'

He shrugged, unfastened the strap, and handed it over. I walked over to the window and looked at the steel back. It was smeared by wear, but a quick rub with my thumb cleaned it up. I read the number on the back. '921428.'

'Okay?'

'Aye, sure, Allan. What did you pay for it?'

'One ninety, I think.' That was a relief. Dad's was ten quid cheaper.

With the air cleared my brother-in-law was more relaxed than I had seen him. 'Do you want to hang around and eat with me tonight?' he asked. 'You could give me some tips about being single.'

I shook my head. 'No thanks. No hard feelings, but you've got a call to make and I've got a home to go to. I don't have an overnight pass!'

I hung around Lyon for an hour or two, after I left Allan's office. I sent postcards to my dad and to Jan. Finally I phoned my sister, reckoning that I'd killed enough time to let her get home from teaching or from picking up Jonathan from school, whichever was on her agenda for the day.

Ellie was more than delighted when I told her that Allan was seeing sense and would phone her that evening. Her relief came down the phone in waves. 'Thanks a million, brother,' she said. 'I was really worried that he was going to dig in his heels. You didn't have to lean on him too hard, did you?'

'No. Not at all. The guy doesn't exist in the same world as you and I, Ellie. I just made him realise that you can't live in his any more. He's got the message now. You should be able to sort things out between you from now on.'

'Let's hope so. I'll do my best. But I'm not going back, Oz, come what may.'

'No, and he won't expect that.'

She chuckled. 'Imagine. You being my minder. What would Mum have thought?'

'She'd have been astonished. Simple as that.'

'She'd have been proud too.' Ellen paused, as each of us thought of our mother. 'I owe you one, Oz,' she said.

'Bollocks to that, Sis. You're still well in credit when it comes to us looking out for each other. You can do something for me, though. Send me some new photos of you and the kids. I'll send you some of Prim and me, and of where we live now. It knocks Pérrouges for six, I'll tell you.'

'You sound as if you've really settled in there, son.'

I laughed. 'We sure have. We're real locals now. We know where all the bodies are buried!'

9

I made it back to St Marti just after 9 p.m. Casa Miñana was closed for the day, but there were still some open-air diners at the tables outside Meson del Conde and the Esculapi, most of them in heavy sweaters against the cool of the autumn evening.

The apartment was in darkness when I opened the door. I wondered whether I had missed seeing Prim at one of the tables, until I found a note on the sideboard.

Dear Oz
I'm taking the Carrilet into L'Escala, then on to the Trattoria.
If you don't show up there by 11, I'll take a taxi home.
Lurv
P

I folded the note and smiled. The Trattoria was one of our favourite places. It was very well situated in L'Escala's big modern marina, from which the local anchovy fishermen still set out at night, single-handed in their small boats, to haul in their plentiful catch. L'Escala calls itself 'The Town of the Anchovy', but don't let that put you off.

As with Gary's restaurant, behind the church in L'Escala, quite a few of the Trattoria's customers are British, on account of the co-proprietrix being a Jockess, and so we had got into the habit of going to one or the other whenever we felt the need of some ex-pat company.

I found Prim at an outside table when I arrived, having parked the car just across the street, chatting with, or being chatted up by El Patron. A beer and a menu lay in front of her. I asked for one of each for myself. 'Sure,' said Juan. The name makes him a member of a minority group in L'Escala, where most of the men seem to be called Jordi or Jaume. He smiled. 'My wife is off tonight, so you have me. Is still okay, though, yes?'

I gave him a doubtful look.

'How did it go?' asked Prim, when we were alone.

'Okay. Sorted. No fuss. No problem. Lyon's a nice place. We should go there sometime.' I looked up as Juan's son brought my beer, then I drained half of it in a single swallow, and gave him a nod which meant that another would be in order soon.

'So how was your day?'

'Good. Busy. I phoned the British Consulate in Barcelona. I figured that we'd better find out a bit more about Spain and its institutions if we're going to start up in business here. We have an appointment with him on Friday, 11 a.m.'

I looked at her in surprise. 'So at last we're going to Barça.'

She nodded. 'Next we had a fax from Jan. It's a proof of our ad. It's in the *Scotsman* this week, then the *Times*, *Herald* and *Guardian* on successive Fridays.' She dug deep into her bag and produced two sheets of fax paper folded together. I opened them: the first was as Prim had said, a copy of our ad as it would appear. The second was a note from Jan which made me look again at the first.

Dear Blackstone Spanish Investigations

Your ad is attached, as requested, but with one amendment. Some of your customers might have urgent needs. In that case a box number will be too slow, so I've put my phone number on as the contact point. That way, you can action anything that's urgent right away. I'm in most of the time. If it gets too busy I can always put the answer phone on.

Jan

I checked. Sure enough the ad read 'Phone/Fax' and Jan's telephone number. 'Good girl Janet,' I said.

'Yes,' said Prim. 'I don't know if Ms Anoushka Turkel will like it, though. It's her phone too.'

'Nah. Noosh won't be a problem.'

Prim shot me a long look. 'No,' she said. 'I suppose she will be in favour of anything that keeps you and Jan 1300 miles apart.'

'Don't be daft.'

'Who's being daft? You're Jan's ex, and now your dad's going steady with her mum. Noosh is an insecure person and that doesn't help.' She reached across and punched me lightly on the chin. 'Just as well I'm not, eh.'

I made a face. 'You've no reason to be . . . either of you.'

I decided that it was time to change the subject. 'So was that the extent of your busy day, making a phone call and receiving a fax?'

Primavera pouted. 'No! I did some ironing . . . yours too . . . then tonight I went to see someone in L'Escala. Remember the Wilsons, the couple from London we met at Maggie Clark's pool party, then had dinner with at La Bassa?'

I nodded. 'Sure, Phil and . . .'

'Yes. Well, it came back to me. He's a jeweller. I phoned them on the off chance that they were here, and they are. So I went to see them and showed Phil the watch you brought home.'

I sat bolt upright, so fast that I thought I'd thrown my back out. 'You did what!'

She shot me a pitying glance. 'Don't worry, I didn't tell him where it came from. I only said you'd found it in the village. He recognised the model. It's a limited edition produced for the British and American market. Sold all through last year and the year before, then withdrawn. Each watch is individually numbered. Depending on the efficiency of the retailer, you could identify the owner from the serial number.'

She looked so pleased with herself that it seemed a pity to deflate her. 'And why the hell would I want to do that? Bearing in mind where it came from, that is.' She stared at me. I went on, 'Suppose the body is found and identified by teeth or clothes or whatever? Suppose I turn up with the watch, all bright and shiny? I'd be in the frame for murder!'

'You could always say you found it in the village, like I told Phil.'

I shook my head, sadly. 'Prim, the guy's been dead for a year. We've been here for less than three months.' An awful thought came to me. 'Jesus, have you got it in your bag?'

'Yes,' she whispered. 'Shall I drop it on the floor, and leave it here?'

'Sure, you do that so that Juan or his son find it, and take it to the police. Then the body turns up and it's them in the nick!

'No, there's only one thing to be done. Tomorrow, we're going for a walk, and we're going to stumble over the body, accidentally. Then before we call the police, we're going to muddy up that watch and give it back to its rightful owner!'

10

The phone rang early next morning, around 8:30 a.m.. Well, it was early for us. I swung myself around to sit on the edge of the bed and picked up the portable hand set from its cradle.

'Hola,' I mumbled, expecting it to be one of the many wrong numbers generated by the L'Escala exchange.

'And hola to you too, son,' said Mac the Dentist. 'Rub the sleep out of your voice, for fuck's sake. What's happened to the old rise and shine Oz? Jesus, here am I, all ready for a day's drilling and filling and you're still sounding like last night's washing up.' As an irregular user of the telephone my father has no idea of proper etiquette. Under that heading I include niceties like not phoning before breakfast.

'Sorry, Dad,' I croaked. 'I had a busy day yesterday. I did eight or nine hundred miles.'

'Aye, I know. Your sister told me all about it. Allan phoned her last night, like he promised you. They had a civilised conversation, he said he was sorry about that lawyer's letter, and he spoke to the boys . . . well to Jonathan, at least. Wee Colin hadn't a clue who he was; he thought it was you, in fact.

'The upshot is, he's agreed to a separation. Ellen spoke to Jan's pal Noosh, and she's going to draw up an informal agreement, recording the date of the split and the arrangements for custody and child support. There's a half-term holiday next month. He's going to take time off and come over then, to see the kids and sign on the dotted line.'

I grunted. 'That's good. I don't think as badly of the guy now, you know. He just needed to be made to see past his own pressures and his own needs. He's a workaholic; the truth is that a family's just a distraction to him.'

My dad grunted. 'Aye, that's probably so. Tell you, though, he'll get a shock when he sees our Ellie again. So'll you, for that matter. The wee fat barrel is no more. She's lost at least a stone and a half, she'd had a decent haircut and she's started taking care of her appearance again.' He paused. 'You've done more than you know for your sister, son. She told me that if you and Prim hadn't turned up in France, and made her see what was happening to her, she'd probably never have got out of her rut. She'd just have drifted quietly into a miserable middle age. Now she's young again.'

I smiled at the thought. 'Ahh, that's good. But how about you? How are you and Auntie Mary getting on?'

'Perfectly well, son. Perfectly well. As a matter of fact, I've more or less moved in with Mary. For the moment at least, while Ellie's in Anstruther. It's better for the boys to be alone with their mother. I'm Grandad, and I want to stay that way. I don't want them to start thinking of me as any form of dad, and if we were all under the one roof that could happen. I'll move back in when Allan gets here, as a sort of chaperone if you like, but until then I'm leaving the three of them to get on with it.'

There was a silence on the line for a couple of seconds. At last I asked him the obvious. 'So? Or are your intentions strictly dishonourable?'

'Cheeky bastard,' my dad growled. 'You're in no position to ask me that, after you and Jan built up our hopes for years. But since you have asked, I'll tell you. We're going to let Ellen get herself sorted out, and fixed up with a place to live. She's looking for a permanent job, in Fife, Dundee or Edinburgh. Meantime, Allan's going to sell the house in Pérrouges and move himself into Lyon. When he's done that, she'll get herself a flat somewhere handy for her work.

'Once all that's taken care of, Mary and I will expect you and Jan to chum us to the Registry Office in St Andrews, as best man and bridesmaid.'

I beamed, wide awake now. 'That's great. When d'you reckon? Around Christmas, maybe?'

'Possibly. But not a word to a soul, apart from Jan and Primavera. If it leaks out in advance I'll have your balls for paperweights.'

'Promise. See you at Christmas, then.'

'Before that, I hope. Here, have you spoken to Jan lately?'

'Aye. On Monday, in fact. She sounded fine.'

'Mmm,' said my dad. 'I rather think she is. See you when I see you.' He hung up.

As I replaced the phone in its charger, I felt an arm slip around my waist and pull me back into bed. 'Was Mac saying what I thought he was saying?' Prim asked.

'Yup. I'm going to be best man. Around Christmas.' I rolled around and squeezed her bum, friendly like. 'How about making it a double event?'

She wove her fingers into my chest hair and tugged, hard enough to get my attention. 'Like we've agreed, there's no rush. A year or two down the road we can think about that.'

'Come on now, darlin'. A year or two's a long way off.'

'Exactly.'

'The point my dad was making . . .'

She cut me off, frowning. 'I can guess. It was that you and Jan dithered around so long that eventually you went off the idea. Well, I'm going to allow us time to find out whether the same could happen to us.'

'Hey,' I said. 'What's with this "I"? This is a "we" thing.'

Her frown vanished, and she reached down. 'I wouldn't say that, darling. Not at all!'

With one thing and another, it was early afternoon before we set out on the walk which we had discussed over supper in the Trattoria. I went for my morning run, part of my routine since catching sight of my spreading middle in the mirror a few days before, then swam in the sea with Prim, before lunching at Casa Miñana on Catalan salad and chips . . . well, you can't give everything up.

Miguel smiled as he brought our meals, and nodded towards the Casa Forestals. The town hall's site workers had gone, replaced by half a dozen earnest young people in shorts and T-shirts. 'The archaeologists,' he said, loud enough for the diners at the other tables to hear. 'They have found a Roman body. They are very excited. It has a bracelet, an' they think this means that he was a very important man. A governor, maybe. They think they may know who he was. It was on Catalan television last night. Is very good for St Marti. It means lots of extra visitors this weekend. Lots of extra business. Very good.'

When we set out for L'Escala, finally, I was still swelled with inner pride over my contribution to the local tourist industry. To make our search as authentic as possible we walked all the way, along the walkway behind the beaches, then following the road past the garages, heading up towards the Hiperstel supermarket and the entrance to the town.

That was where it got difficult. I remembered Miguel making a turn, but suddenly I was faced with a choice of three. I picked one with absolute certainty. We headed along the straight road, past villas on either side for almost a kilometre, before it ran out in open country, with only a bare, tree-less hillside in sight. We retraced our steps, with Prim grumbling not a little, and looked along the second option, which we decided ran too close to the first to be a likely choice. Finally, we made the third turn. There before us was a white building with 'Tenis-Bar' emblazoned along its side.

'This is the one,' I said. 'I'd forgotten about that bar.'

'Better you hadn't told me that,' muttered Prim, looking flushed, hot and sticky. 'Is it open?'

Sadly it was closed. We headed along the road, following my path of three nights before. The first part of the road was made up, but in common with much of that sprawling part of outer L'Escala, the tarmac soon ran out. I remembered the teeth-jarring bumps in Miguel's pick-up as we walked along the hard, rutted pathway. The trees began to appear fairly early on in the gardens of villas built on either side of the road. All but a very few were empty, their owners back at work in France, Belgium, Germany, or maybe Barcelona. Eventually, the houses simply came to an end. There was a small development of apartments on our right, then nothing but trees.

'Is this it?' asked Prim.

'On a bit yet,' I said. 'Miguel drove till we were out of sight of any houses.' We trudged on until the trees before us were so thick that no truck could pass, or no moonlight could penetrate. 'It has to be around here. Maybe we were nearer the edge of the forest than this.'

Beside me, Prim shivered in the warmth of the afternoon. I knew that she was remembering, like me, the last time we had been together in a forest, and how narrowly we had escaped with our lives. 'I don't like this, Oz,' she said. I had never heard her sound scared before.

'No. Me neither. Come on.' I led her quickly away to the right, to where the trees were thinnest and the light brightest. All at once we could see the edge of the wood, and the bare brown fields beyond. I looked around, and all of a sudden I saw two pines, close together, thirty yards away. 'There.' I pointed. 'I'm sure that's where Miguel stopped.'

We hurried across and stood between them. The fields sloped down, and looking northwest we could see the great Pyrrenean skyline, carved in its blue background, with lines of snow on its highest peaks. Much closer stood two old barns, converted into discos, and on the far side of the road to Bellcaire, the go-kart track.

The drainage ditch – never a fire-break, as I could see in the daylight – was only a few feet away. I took Prim's hand and led us to it. Together we looked down its length.

There was nothing to be seen.

'Oh, for Christ's sake, Oz!' She exploded. 'After all that, you've brought us to the wrong place.'

I shook my head. 'No! This is it. We must have put him

further down than I thought. Come on. Let's walk down the length of it. But remember, act casual. We can be seen from over there.'

Hand in hand, we ambled casually down the fringe of the wood, on the edge of the ditch, expecting with every step to find a skeleton, and planning our 'shock, horror' reactions for the benefit of anyone who might have been watching us from a distance. But there was nothing. Not a trace, not a scrap, not a sign. Eventually the ditch simply stopped.

Silently, we turned and retraced our steps, bumbling along with growing dismay. Eventually we found ourselves back at our starting point. 'Well, smartarse,' said Prim, ironically. 'Still so confident?'

I was not amused, and was about to tell her so, when something caught my eye. A few feet beyond us, the ditch sloped downwards towards the town out of our sight. Just on the curve I saw that a number of twigs and broken branches lay on its northern bank.

'Look there,' I said, pulling her with me as I moved forward again, no longer giving a stuff about onlookers. We reached the wooden debris in a few strides, and stared into the ditch. It was empty.

'But this is it,' I said. 'I'm certain. We put a few branches over him to cover him, and make it look as if he could have been here for a while. Some bastard's beaten us to it.'

Prim let my hand go and knelt beside the ditch, then leaned in and picked something up, something that had been half hidden by a stone. She held it up and gazed at it, appraisingly. 'Big toe,' she said at last. 'I was good at anatomy. You're right. Someone's found your body.'

'In that case,' I said. 'I suggest that we get out of here . . . fast. Because we've just sent a signal to anyone who might be watching this place that we are after it too.'

11

For all that it's a small town, with an off-season population that would fit into the Wheatfield Grandstand at Tynecastle Park, with a few seats left over, L'Escala has its own radio station.

We listened to the first hourly news bulletin after we made it back to St Marti. It was in Catalan, but we could follow enough to be sure that there was no mention of a body having been found on the outskirts of town. There was nothing in the Costa Brava section of *La Vanguardia*, or *L'Avui*, which we bought in town before catching the Carrilet home. There were big stories about the important Roman find in St Marti, with a photo of Miguel and young Jordi in *L'Avui*, but nowhere was there any mention of the former occupant of the stone coffin's top bunk.

We strolled round to the square after dinner on the terrace. Miguel had been right about the extra visitors. They had begun to arrive already, in droves, and we had trouble finding a table outside Casa Miñana. When we had, Miguel brought us two beers automatically. I motioned to him to the spare seat beside us.

'Prim and I went to visit our friend this afternoon. The one we saw last in Riells on Tuesday morning. I found his watch and I wanted to give it back to him.' A brief look of panic flashed across our friend's face, for an instant. 'The trouble was, he's gone.'

Miguel gulped, but otherwise managed to stay impassive.

'You haven't heard of him being moved anywhere, have you?'

He shook his head. 'No. Nothing,' he said, quietly. 'I was sure he would be found. There are shepherds up there, with dogs.' Beside me, Prim gave a barely noticeable shudder. 'But not this soon.'

He paused. 'We will look at the newspapers for the next day or two, and at the *Empordan*, the newspaper for here, when it is published. If there is nothing in that, my wife has a sister who has a son who is married to a woman who is in the municipal police in L'Escala. I will ask my wife to ask him to find out if the police know anything. But I will be . . . I'm sorry, I don't know the word.'

'Discreet, Miguel,' said Prim. 'The word is discreet!'

12

There was nothing about the missing skeleton on Radio L'Escala next morning either, or in the daily newspapers.

We left for Barcelona at 8:30 a.m., found Avinguda Diagonal without any great difficulty, parked and made it comfortably to the British Consulate in time for our appointment. It was another pleasant morning, with the temperature only in the low seventies, but it was hot indoors, and the air conditioning in the fourteenth floor suite was welcome. We were amazed to see that only the private offices had this benefit, and imagined the discomfort of the poor punters queuing in the real heat of July and August, watching the staff, cool behind their thick glass screen, while they sweltered in the reception area.

We were received by the commercial counsellor, a decent chap called Hal something. We explained our backgrounds and our idea. He gave us the thumbs up straight away.

'Good proposition,' he said. 'Most people looking for business information come to us, and we don't have the manpower to deal with them all promptly. I'll be happy to refer people to you. I don't think that your fees will frighten many off. As for the legal and personal stuff, I don't know of anyone who does that, so you should be on a winner there too.

'If I were you, once you're up and running, I'd think about reversing the process, and offering a British market information service to Spanish customers.'

Hal echoed Jan's advice that we should seek resident status straight away. 'From what you've said, you can show a level of income, so you'll have no problem.'

He gave us a series of names and addresses and was able to make a couple of appointments for us. We spent much of the rest of the day in government offices, filling in forms and signing papers, and by mid-afternoon we had gone most of the way to becoming Spanish residents.

'You know,' said Prim, as we strolled down the Ramblas, celebrating our imminent new status, 'it must be two years since I was in a city as big as this. Let's do the tourist thing with the rest of the daylight.'

So we visited the Sagrada Familia, then the Olympic Stadium. We meant to take in Nou Camp, the vast home of Barça football club, but there was a league game on that evening. The man on the gate laughed at me when I asked if there were any tickets.

It was just after midnight when we rolled into the apartment, knackered and very well fed, having dined on the way home at Mas Pou, one of our favourite restaurants. As soon as I switched on the light, I saw a sheet of fax paper lying curled on the phone. I picked it up and read its very short message.

Oz/Prim
Phone me, soon as you get in. You're in business.
Jan

Prim peered at it. 'Exciting,' she said, shivering a little. The air temperature had turned colder as the evening had worn on. 'Go on, then. Call her.'

I looked at my watch. 'It's a bit late, even though we're an hour ahead.'

'Can't you see. She says as soon as we get in.'

'Okay. But I'll blame you if we wake them up.'

I needn't have worried. Jan was bright as a button as she answered the phone. 'About bloody time, Oz,' she said, almost as soon as I'd spoken.

'Sorry, but we're just in. It's been a long day.'

'Aye, sure, I'll bet the last bottle of Rioja went on for ever.'

'House red, actually, my dear. But you're right. So what's the story?'

She paused. 'I had a call this afternoon, from a man in Edinburgh who'd spotted the ad. His name is Gavin Scott, and he wants to talk to you about a commission.'

'That's great. Give me his number and I'll phone him.'

'No. That's the point. He insists that he has to meet you in person, to brief you on the project. I said you'd see him at three o'clock on Sunday.'

I gasped. 'You said what!?'

'Come on, Blackstone, are you serious about this business or not? I offered to take the brief, but he said that he wants to meet the man on the ground in Spain. His business schedule is very busy so he asked if you could make it this weekend.'

'How the bloody hell am I supposed to get to Edinburgh for Sunday?' I spluttered. Prim stared at me, astonishment written all over her face.

'Let me see,' said Jan. 'I think they're called aeroplanes. Don't worry about the cost. Mr Scott said he'd pay your expenses if you took the commission.' She laughed. 'Listen to you there, gasping for air. Blackstone Spanish Investigations, indeed. I suggest that you start investigating airline timetables, bloody quick. Call me tomorrow, and let me know when you'll arrive in Edinburgh. Love to Prim. Goodnight.'

I hung up. 'Well?' demanded my partner. As succinctly as I could, I passed on Jan's message.

'He's not asking much, this man Scott, is he,' said Prim. 'We're invited to that Catalan Society party tomorrow, as well. Still, Jan's right. In business you respond to the customer's needs. Especially,' she added, 'if he's paying for the flight.'

'I suppose so,' I muttered, and reached for the telephone directory. 'Break out a couple of beers. I've got some phoning to do.'

13

Finding a flight turned out to be easier than I had expected. The KLM desk was still open when I called, and they had seats on their 4:05 p.m. flight to Amsterdam, linking with an Air UK transfer that would land me in Edinburgh at 8 p.m. BST.

Rather than take the car out of play for two days, Prim ran me to Figueras to catch a fast train to Barcelona with a connection that would take me right into the airport.

It was a weird feeling, saying goodbye to her in the station. My trip to Lyon had been one thing, but this would be the first night we had spent apart since the beginning of our relationship. 'Miss me,' she ordered.

'I promise,' I said, meaning it with all my heart. 'Don't enjoy the party.'

'Listen, you know I wouldn't be going, only Janice insisted when I called her to cancel.'

We kissed, and I walked into the station, with the beginning of a strange feeling creeping over me. I supposed that in all my life, it was the first real experience of loneliness.

The flight was fine, with a mercifully brief stop-over in Schiphol Airport, just long enough to buy aftershave for my Dad, perfume for Ellie, alcohol for Jan, chocolate for Auntie Mary and toys for the kids. Oh yes, and long enough also to make one phone call.

Jan was waiting right at the international arrivals doorway in Scotland's capital airport, as I emerged with my hold-all slung over my shoulder and my duty free clinking in its bag. She stood there, looking more like Jane Russell than ever in black slacks and white shirt, her shoulder-length hair swept back off her forehead.

I laid my burdens down on the concourse and we hugged for all we were worth. 'Hello darlin',' she said quietly. 'By God, but you look brown. Are you that colour all over?'

I grinned. 'What's the point in having a completely secluded terrace if you don't get your arse sun-tanned?'

We kissed hello. A big wet one; none of this both cheeks stuff. This was Jan and me.

'You sure it's okay, you two putting me up for the night like you said?'

She shook her head, as I picked up my luggage. 'Change of plan. You don't have long at home, so we're going across the river. Mac and Mary are expecting us for supper. I said we'd be there for nine-thirty.'

My stomach growled in anticipation of the prospect of Auntie Mary's cooking. 'Is Noosh coming?'

'To my mum's? You must be kidding.' I didn't press the point. Although Jan and her mum were reconciled, Anoushka had never been welcome in Anstruther.

Jan led me out to the unexpected cold of the evening, to the red Fiesta that I knew so well, and we were off, heading towards the Forth Bridge and Fife, and towards our parents.

The kids were still up when we arrived there, twenty minutes ahead of schedule, thanks to Jan's flat out driving. On the way I had told her about St Marti, how we had found it, and how we had settled into the community. It was a monologue, interrupted only by the occasional glance at Jan as she drove across country, at the beautifully straight profile with which once I had been so familiar.

I repeated the story over supper at Auntie Mary's almost word for word, only this time I produced the photographs to back it up . . . having extracted all the snaps of Prim with her shirt off. Eventually, Ellie took Jonathan and Colin off to bed, promising to wait up herself for me for a longer blether.

After they had gone, we sat around Auntie Mary's fire, she

and Dad, and Jan and me – plus Wallace, my faithful iguana, moved in, it seemed, along with my dad, and sleeping serenely on the window seat – talking about a Christmas wedding. 'Now remember, you two,' my father lectured us. 'When it happens, we want it kept quiet. Just a registry office ceremony and that's it. The four of us, plus Prim, Ellie and the kids will go for lunch afterwards, but that will be the extent of the reception.'

'Fair enough, Dad,' I said. *'Aye, sure, that'll be right,'* I thought, glancing across at Jan, and knowing from the look in her eyes that she was thinking exactly the same as me. We would discuss this between ourselves at a later date.

Mac the Dentist looked across at the two of us. He opened his mouth as if to say something profound, then thought better of it.

'Time I went home,' I said, seizing the moment. 'I want a chat with my sister.' I kissed Auntie Mary and Jan goodnight, patted my dad on his bald spot, then lugged my bag round to the big house looking out to sea.

I took a good look at Ellie as she opened the door for me. Dad was right. The fat wee wifie I had found in France was gone. My sister, with her waist back and her new haircut, looked better than she had since she was twenty-one. And there was a gleam in her eye that I couldn't remember ever seeing there.

'You're doing great, Our Ellie,' I said, at last, as I settled into dad's armchair clutching a coffee which she had brought me. 'It does my eyes good to look at you.'

'Not just *your* eyes, brother,' she said. 'I am having an affair.'

You could have knocked me down with a Lightbody's celebration cake. 'You're what?' I couldn't help it. I laughed. 'Who with?'

'Grammar, Osbert. With whom, please. With a guy at the school where I'm teaching part-time. He's separated, like me. He's one of your chauvinist types. I reckon he thinks he's using me. The truth is that it's the other way round. I am feasting on his body, but when I've finished all the white meat, he'll be getting the push, believe you me.'

I managed to restrain my laughter this time. 'Well, just you be careful. Take no chances until you've got everything sorted out with Allan. He's seeing reason right now, but if he finds out that you're playing away games before the separation agreement's even drafted, he might change his mind.'

She nodded. 'Don't worry; the same thought occurred to me. I've decided to put Ross into cold storage until everything's taken care of. If he doesn't like that, well tough on him. Actually,' she said, 'I might just leave him in the freezer for good. The truth is I don't like him that much. It was just that I needed to be made a fuss of, even if I did know all along that he was only doing it to get his end away.'

I gazed at her in the lamplight, hugging my mug of coffee, not knowing quite what to make of my new, capricious sister. 'You know, Ellie, after Jan and I decided that we weren't right for each other, and I was bouncing about like Zebedee in the *Magic Roundabout*, whispering "Time for bed" in the ears of as many women as I could, I used to lie awake on my many nights alone, and think about you and Allan. You weren't long married then, and very solid and responsible . . .'

'And boring, Oz, don't forget boring.'

'. . . yes, okay, and boring. But still I used to lie there and wish I could be like you, able to make a single commitment.'

I smiled at her. 'Now look at us. We've turned almost full circle. I'm settled down with Prim, in the sort of solid relationship I used to dream about, while you've cut yourself adrift from all of that. Just be careful of one thing, though, sister. Don't let yourself become like I used to be.'

It was her turn to smile. 'Promiscuous, you mean? Don't worry, as well as you I've got two sons and a father to protect me against that. If I'm indulging myself just now, it's for the good of my morale, not just because I've a need to get properly laid.'

She paused. 'Anyway, what about you and Prim? You've got that solid relationship, you say. But is it what you want, or is it what you think you should have?'

'Of course it's what I want. Prim's a fantastic woman. She changed my life from the day I met her. She's changed me.'

'Aye,' said Ellie, looking at me as if she was reading me, 'she has that. She's started you thinking again after all these years. And you're more mature, too. Not so long ago you'd have run a mile rather than get involved between Allan and me. That's good.'

I frowned at her. 'Come on, sis. I'd like to think I'd always have stood up for you.'

'Sure,' she responded, quickly. 'But before, you'd have just picked up the telephone, and told Allan he was an arse; or if you were really pumped up, maybe you'd have gone and thumped him. But you wouldn't have got involved, not like you did. You've changed all right, and I've got to credit Primavera for that.'

She sipped her coffee. 'But tell me something I've always wanted to know, Oz, about you and Jan. What happened to the two of you?'

Taken by surprise, I stared for a while out of the bay window. 'Time?' I ventured at last, but without conviction.

'Bollocks,' said Ellen, with a laugh. 'Do better.'

I tried again. 'Okay. I suppose that at some point we decided that with the way we had grown up together, and become a couple, it had all come too easy for us. I suppose that we decided that we were drifting towards marriage because it was expected of us, and maybe because it was the soft option. I suppose we just decided that it was wrong. We never had a great debate about it. It just . . . worked out that way.'

'Mmm,' said my sister, pressing herself back into the sofa. We sat in silence for two or three minutes, until she looked across at me and whispered, 'Oz, is that really true?'

I looked deep into my mug, as if it was a window to the past. 'No,' I said, for the first time in my life. 'The truth isn't that we decided anything. I did.

'At university, everyone had a steady. That was the way it was, and so there was no pressure on Jan and me. But at some point in my very short police career, I looked around at my contemporaries, and the way they lived. There they were, young guys like me, tear-arseing around in their time off, scoring women like trophies. There was one guy we called Comanche, because every time he made a new conquest, he used to cut off a curl of her hair – and you know what I'm talking about – and bring it to work with him next day.

'I looked at those characters and I told myself, "This is how normal young men live." And I began to feel abnormal. At that point, Jan was the only girl I'd ever slept with, and I thought to myself, "What if we get married, and at some point I come to regret all that missed experience? What if I start to fancy the grass on the other side of the hill, enough to go grazing?" I was afraid of that, Ellie. Maybe I was afraid of the hurt of losing her, so I ensured that I never would, by pushing her away.'

'But there was something else too, Oz, wasn't there?'

'Yes.' It came out in a hoarse whisper. 'I really did want to graze, from the start. I just couldn't suppress it. Sex with Jan was good, but it was rarely great, and never all that it might have been. Both of us knew that. But then how could it have been? We only had experience of each other.'

I gazed across at her. 'I did it very gradually, disengaging myself, until it was how it was and she had settled for being best friends. Of course, I never told her what I've just told you. I've never admitted that to anyone before . . . not even me.'

'What about love, Oz? How did you make yourself stop loving her?'

'I never even tried. I never did stop. I'll always love Jan, but in a way that's different from anyone else. I'll always be there for her, except for . . .'

'Except for the times when she might need you the most.

When was the last time you slept with Jan?' asked Ellie suddenly.

'Last March, before I met Prim. We had a sort of arrangement.'

'Yes, I know about it. Jan and I had a girlie night. She had a few drinks and told me about it. Occasional grazing rights on each other, to use your analogy. Only now you've closed the pasture. So don't tell me you'll always be there for her, brother, although I know you'd like to mean it. How can you be, when you're living in Spain, in love with another woman?'

She looked at me, with a very straight face. 'Oz, if you want to do what's best for Jan, you should cut her out of your life completely. Maybe both of you should have done that years ago.'

She paused. 'Let me ask you something? Just suppose that instead of Jan More it had been Primavera Phillips that you grew up with, and drifted towards marriage with. Would things have been different then?'

'Stop!' For a second I was afraid my shout might have wakened the boys. 'You're doing my head in. Things are as they are, and that's it. As for cutting Jan off, no way could I do that. But if that's what she wants, it's open to her.

'As for you, get back into your glass house, with your fancy man, and stop throwing stones!'

14

I took my nephews to St Andrews next morning, in the back of my dad's beloved and exceptionally low mileage old Jag, with Jonathan on a booster seat and Colin in his car seat attachment. I called Auntie Mary's to ask if Jan wanted to come too, but she said that the supermarket was at the top of their agenda.

I took them into the castle, and showed them the bottle dungeon, and the mine and counter-mine, telling them the same tales of John Knox and the wars of the reformation that Mac the Dentist had told their mother and me, but leaving out any mention of the Cardinal's body hanging in the great window, or of burning martyrs down yonder on the Scores.

We wandered down towards the old course. There, on a whim, I took Jonathan into Auchterlonie's and bought him his first golf clubs, a junior three wood, seven iron and putter, smiling at the realisation of the pestering they would cause my dad after I was gone.

Finally, having shown them the ruin of the cathedral, told them more spooky stories, and treated them to multi-coloured ice creams from Janetta's, we headed back over the hill to Anstruther, leaving enough time for Colin to be sick before lunch.

'You'll keep Christmas free then,' said my dad quietly as I said goodbye, to him and to Wallace, at Auntie Mary's front door, with Jan waiting outside in the Fiesta.

'Sure I will.'

He gave me a hug. 'No fuss, remember. Good luck with the new business.'

'Did you get the renewed message from Mac about quiet weddings?' Jan asked, as we headed out of town. 'I did from Mum.'

I nodded.

'What are we going to do, then?'

'What else? I've told Ellie to book the village hall for the afternoon as soon as we know the date.'

Jan beamed across at me. 'That's my boy. Who do they think they're messing with, eh!'

As we skirted Kirkcaldy it started to rain. 'First I've seen in four weeks,' I said. I tilted up the glass roof, and breathed deeply to enjoy the smell of the moistened dust by the roadside, and of the dampening fields.

'D'you miss it?'

'I've made a point of not thinking in terms of missing. Thanks for arranging last night, though. I really enjoyed it.'

'Did you and Ellie sit up late?'

'Late enough. She's sorted, okay. Has she been talking much to you?'

Jan laughed. Her rich, deep laugh. 'Do you mean has she told me about her illicit nookie? Oh, yes. But don't you worry about it. She's grazing, darlin', that's all. Just grazing.'

I looked across at her in surprise, but her eyes were on the road.

'So,' I said at last. 'Where are we meeting BSI's first client?'

'At his house. He lives in Milton Bridge, just outside Penicuik. He faxed me a map showing how to get there.'

'Mmm. So what does he do for a living, this Mr Gavin Scott? I can't say I've ever heard of him.'

Jan shook her dark head. 'Your clients have been mostly lawyers till now, so that doesn't surprise me. The header sheet on the fax he sent me came from Soutar's, the advertising agency in Leith. I've got a small agency on my client list, so I was able to check him out.

'Soutar's is the biggest in the business north of the border, and Gavin Scott is managing director. The chairman is a Tory life peer, but Mr Scott is the main man. He and his wife, also a director, own all the shares. He bought the business for a song ten years ago when it was on its uppers, and he turned it around. He's in his early forties, very well respected and very rich. According to the *Insider* magazine top people survey the Scotts drew down £300,000 between them in salary last year, and the same again in dividend.'

'They're not short of a pound then,' I muttered. 'I should have flown first class. Is there any other background on them?'

'Only that he's a member of the Scottish Arts Council. He was appointed last year.'

Gavin Scott's map was clear and accurate. It led us straight up the driveway of Westlands, as the sign at the entrance named the property. The house itself wasn't all that big, but there was a stable block to the side, and beyond a paddock, in which a woman and a girl, wearing Barbour jackets, were exercising steaming horses in the rain.

My new client answered the door himself. Jan had been intending to wait in the car, but I insisted that she came with me. Apart from anything else, I had never met this man; a witness might be handy.

'Mr Blackstone, Ms More. Come away in.' Gavin Scott was a stocky bloke, an inch or two shorter than me but thicker in the chest. He had wiry black hair, flecked with grey at the sides, and eyes that shone with a real intensity. My instant impression was that he made me feel comfortable.

'Bugger of a day, isn't it,' he said as he showed us through a panelled hall and into the sitting room. I looked around. As in the hall, much of the wall space was taken up by paintings, a mix of portraits and landscapes, oils and water-colours, all of them looking like originals, and if I was any judge, expensive.

Scott jerked a thumb towards a window at the end of the room, through which we could see the paddock. 'You must think my wife and daughter are mad, out riding in the rain, but the horses need the exercise.'

A thermos jug and three cups lay on a low table. Our host

poured the coffee and offered biscuits, which we declined. 'Thank you for acting so quickly, Mr Blackstone,' he said, as we settled into the yellow velvet upholstery. 'Once I've decided to do something, I'm the sort of bloke who wants it to happen yesterday. Your ad was a godsend. It came just at the right time.'

'That's good to hear,' I said. 'Would you like me to tell you a bit about myself, and about my associates?'

He shook his head and smiled. 'No need. I've checked you out. I have a friend in the police force, DI Michael Dylan. After Ms More explained your background, I asked him. For reasons which will become obvious, I didn't give him details of *why* I was asking, but he gave you a glowing report. Two glowing reports, in fact; both on you and on Ms Phillips.'

I concealed my surprise. I knew Mike Dylan, all right. I thought he was a bampot, and until that moment I had believed that he held the same opinion of me.

'Mike said that Ms Phillips' sister is involved with Miles Grayson. Is that right?'

'Dawn? Yes. She's an actress. She and Miles have just finished a movie together. They're off in the States now, starting work on another.' I wondered which had impressed Scott more, Dylan's OK or our vicarious connection with the mega-rich and famous.

'Very good. Now, to business. Take a look at these.' He stood up and walked around behind the couch on which Jan and I were seated. We turned, watching him. Behind us stood a tall easel, and on it was what we took to be a big landscape-style picture covered by a white dust-sheet.

'Behold,' said Gavin Scott, dramatically. He switched on a single spotlight set into the ceiling, and whipped off the sheet with a flourish.

Jan and I gasped, in unison. The colour of the picture seemed to explode into the room. It showed a golden desert stretching into the distance. In the background were the white skulls of four horses, with in their midst the unmistakable skeleton of a giraffe. A woman stood in the middle distance, dark-haired and laughing, yet somehow transparent, as if the reflected light of the desert sand was shining through her. Everything caught the eye, but in the foreground, as if he was marching out of the picture, was the dominant figure: a toreador, wearing a blue hat and carrying a red cape. His uniform was full of sparkling colour, but it was his face more than anything in the rest of the picture which grabbed the attention. He wore a smile, yet it was the saddest smile I had ever seen. His eyes were bloodshot and the left one was lightly hooded. From it, a single tear ran down his cheek.

Jan and I rose together from the sofa, as if in respect for the work. We stared at it, both of us philistines when it comes to really fine art, but open-mouthed nonetheless.

'What is it?' I was able to gasp, eventually.

'That, Oz . . . I can call you Oz, yes? . . . is the big question.' Scott replaced the dust sheet. I was glad. I had heard the legend that men who looked at Michelangelo's statue of David were likely to be driven mad by its beauty. Until that moment, I had found the concept laughable.

Jan and I settled back into the couch opposite our client. 'Earlier this year, in late June, in fact,' he said, 'my wife Ida and I, and our daughter, were on holiday in Begur, in Northern Spain. I believe it's near where you're based, Oz.'

'That's true,' I agreed, 'though I've never been there.'

'We were visiting friends, an old agency client and his wife, who live there full-time. We played a bit of golf at the Pals club, where David Foy, my chum, is a member. One day when we were there we met an English bloke. We bumped into him again by coincidence in Begur, a few days later, and then a third time, at the golf club.'

He paused, as if to let us absorb what he was telling us. 'On the third occasion, he looked as if he was leading up to something. Eventually, he came out with it. He told us that a very exclusive dinner party had been organised for the next evening, at a very exclusive restaurant in a place called Peretellada.

'He said that apart from the host there would be seven seats, and that every place would be filled by informal invitation. We asked him if he was going, but he said no, that it was miles too rich for his blood. It was for high rollers only, he said, because at the end of the night, there was to be an auction. A single lot, the nature of which would not be revealed until after the dinner had been served. He said that if anyone rather than an invited guest turned up, the dinner would be cancelled and the auction would not take place. Then he asked David if he would like the last seat at the table.'

He smiled. 'David's the perfect host. Without a moment's hesitation he said that he couldn't possibly accept unless I was invited too. The guy went out and made a phone call, then came back two minutes later. I was in.'

Scott picked up the jug and refilled our cups. 'We didn't tell our wives where we were off to, just that it was the local boys' club. Instead we sent them and our daughter off to eat in a swank beach-front place at Llafranc, and headed out ourselves, in full evening kit. The restaurant in Peretellada was a very posh affair, inside a big medieval hall.'

I nodded. 'I know the one you mean,' I said. 'I tried to go in there in shorts once. Never got past the door.'

Scott laughed. 'I can imagine. Anyway, the dinner was in a private room. Our host was waiting for us in the cocktail bar, with champagne. He was an Englishman, and he introduced himself as Ronald Starr, "with two Rs" he said. The six other guests were from all over Europe. There was a Dutchman, a German, an Italian, a Belgian, a Swede, and a Swiss. Starr introduced us all. When it came to me he said that I was a late entrant, and that I had been allowed in because I was Scottish, and not English.

'Once the niceties were over with, he led us through to our dining room. The picture was there, just as you see it now, covered up on an easel.

'We made polite conversation over dinner, all of it in English, since that was our common language. No one spoke much to Starr, other than to be polite. I think that we had all decided by this time that he was in the property business, and that the picture would be of a villa he was trying to sell to the drunkest bidder.

'For that reason no one drank much. We all finished dinner as quickly as was decently possible, all of us keen to see what the hook was, then get out of there. Pity, really, since it was a bloody good meal, and all the better because someone else was paying.' He paused, with a grin.

'Finally we all said, "Bugger the coffee and petit fours, let's get on with it." Starr nodded and said, "Fair enough." He stood up and walked round to the easel, stood beside it and said, "Gentlemen, you have all been invited tonight to give you the opportunity to bid for a painting entitled, 'The Toreador of the Apocalypse', a hitherto unknown original work by Salvador Dalí. The picture has always been in private hands, and I am here as the agent of the owner. There is no provenance, other than the signature, and naturally that will be reflected in the price expected. You may have ten minutes to examine the work and satisfy yourself as to the signature and to the quality. After that bidding will commence." And then he whipped off the sheet and turned on the lights.'

'What happened?' Jan gasped, literally on the edge of her seat.

'The German, the Swede and the Belgian each took one look, thanked Starr for dinner and left. I think David Foy would have gone too, but I was hooked. I know art, I was our creative director before I became full-time MD. I've studied Dalí too. The signature looked absolutely authentic, and the sheer blinding quality of the work backed it up.

'After ten minutes, Starr tapped the table and we sat down to bid. Bids were in dollars. He opened at one hundred and fifty thousand. The Dutchman nodded, but backed out as soon as the Swiss said a hundred and eighty. I came in at two hundred. There was no one else. I felt David Foy tugging my sleeve, but I ignored him.

'The Swiss was a fat, arrogant, super-rich bastard, the sort who'd have paid a quarter of a million dollars just for a story to tell the folks back home. He wouldn't have known a Dalí from a Donald Duck. We went to three thousand in steps of twenty thousand. I had stopped thinking by then. He hadn't. He kept adding more tens, just for the hell of it. Until he bailed out at my bid of four hundred thousand dollars, US. Two hundred and sixty thousand, in sterling.'

I whistled softly. I had never been in a room with that much painting before, other than in an art gallery.

'I didn't tell Ida till the next day. Then I had to. We didn't have two hundred and sixty grand in personal cash; our big dough is in property or pensions. So I had to make it a business purchase, and for that I needed Ida's name alongside mine to authorise a banker's draft, and have it DHL'ed out to us.'

'How did Mrs Scott react?' I asked, anticipating the answer.

'She went crazy. We were bound for the divorce court, till she saw the picture, which had been locked up overnight at Peretellada. Then she was okay. She came with me next day, to meet Starr at the Hotel Aiguablava, pay him and collect it. We sent half our luggage back by courier and brought the Dalí home in the back of the Range Rover. As soon as I was back in Scotland I got hold of a couple of my painter chums from the Arts Council and asked them if they would authenticate it for me as a Dalí. That's where the real problem began.'

Scott looked at me, earnestly. 'I know my stuff, Oz. The technique is right, the canvas is old enough. Instinct and experience tell me that's a Dalí. More than that; it's a bloody masterpiece. The trouble is I can't find anyone with the balls to agree with me.

'The so-called experts say that absolutely everything Dalí did is catalogued, apart from doodles on napkins or on the back of menus. They say it's impossible for a great work of that type to have existed in secret. They say that Dalí was an egomaniac, and that everything he did was for his own greater glory, or that of his wife, Gala. That's her in the picture, by the way, the ghostly woman: She's a recurring figure in most of his mature work.'

He paused again. 'The art historians did tell me something though. Something that worries me. Dalí gave up painting after Gala died. But there's a rumour that before he died himself, he signed blank sheets of paper, and canvasses with backwash on them.

'So far, there'd been no trace of any turning up, but the best guess that I've been given is that this is the first, that somewhere out there is a genius forger, and that the only genuine thing about "The Toreador of the Apocalypse" is Dalí's signature.'

Scott stood up and walked back round to the easel. He removed the dust-sheet again, and again the work leapt off the canvas at us. He pointed at the bottom right-hand corner. 'Look at the signature. Look at that big "D", distinctive, almost like the thistle in the Scottish Nationalists' party crest. Look at the structure of it; it's a work of art in itself.

'I want you to go back to Spain and find out the truth for me, Oz. I have to know whether it is a terrific forgery, and I've been conned, or whether I'm right and it's the real thing.'

He smiled. 'If it turns out that it is a fake, then its value will be written down to zero, and the business will have incurred a capital loss. It won't be a total loss, since we can offset it against capital gains elsewhere, but I hate to think what I'm going to tell the shareholders at the AGM. Ida and I still own forty per cent of the company, but if I've blown a quarter of a million of their dough the majority could fire me.

'On the other hand, if the Toreador is authentic, as my heart tells me it is, and you can prove it, then potentially, I've made millions, and I'll be a hero.'

Scott looked at me earnestly. 'So, do you accept the commission?'

I nodded. 'Certainly.' I reached into my document case, and produced two sheets of A4. 'This is a letter of engagement, setting out our terms. If that's okay, please sign both copies and keep one for your records.'

He scanned them quickly, then picked up a pen from the coffee table and signed them both. He reached into his back pocket and produced a folded cheque, and a business card, which he handed over together with my copy of the agreement. 'There's three thousand, on account. My ex-Directory number here, and my mobile number are written on the back of the card. Keep me posted, regularly.'

Scott stood up. 'I have something else for you.' He reached out and picked up a long buff-coloured tube which I had noticed, standing upright by the fireplace.

'I've had the picture scanned and copied in colour. It's in here, along with a list of the names of the other people at the dinner, as far as I can remember them. I can't imagine that they'll be much help though.'

I took the tube from him. 'Can you give me a description of Ronald Starr?' I asked.

He scratched his chin. 'Nondescript is the best I can do. British, almost certainly English, middle-aged, medium height, medium build, dark hair going to grey, navy-blue blazer, grey slacks, white shirt, dark tie with a golf club crest.'

'How did you know it was a golf club?'

He smiled. 'It had fucking golf clubs on it, didn't it.'

'Touché,' I said. 'There is one other thing. Can you remember the name of the English bloke who made the introduction in the first place?'

Scott nodded at once. 'His Christian name, yes. He told us his surname, but it's gone, completely. But his first name I know for sure. He was called Trevor.'

15

'Scott might not have realised, but I saw you twitch,' said Jan, as I drove us back towards Edinburgh. 'That name, Trevor; it meant something to you, didn't it?'

I shrugged, as expressively as I could at the wheel of the Fiesta. 'There must be a few English ex-pats called Trevor up and down the Spanish Costas. I just happen to have met one.'

'Yes, but when he described the man: fifty-something, bald, cultured accent, walnut tan. You reacted to that too.'

'Okay,' I grunted, reluctantly. 'I didn't want to get Scott excited, that's all. The description matches, virtually point for point. About five feet six, bald as an egg, and with the sort of tan that you see on a Brit who's been in Spain for a few years. His accent's affected, the sort you can adjust to fit almost any occasion. My man Trevor normally dresses like the second engineer in a down-market inshore fishing vessel. I've seen Pals Golf Club. Looking like he does, you wouldn't get into the car park. But I suppose that his costume could be as adjustable as his voice.'

'It's a good starting point, then,' said Jan, cheerfully. 'Assuming that he is the same Trevor, he should be able to help you find this man Starr.'

'That's true. And I suppose I should be grateful; I hope this job's always as easy. I'll go in search of him on Tuesday.' I paused. 'Meantime, this is still Sunday, it's after five o'clock, and I'm on expenses. Let's go and eat somewhere . . . unless you're expected home, that is.'

Jan shook her head. 'No,' she said. 'I'm not expected. You're on.'

I turned the car on to the Edinburgh bypass and headed east, towards the A1, then on down to the ribbon village of Aberlady, one of our old favourites, where we stopped at the Old Inn. Even on a Sunday it was busy, but they found a table in the corner and squeezed us in. We tossed a coin to see who would drive home. I lost.

'So,' Jan said, sipping a tasty Rioja, while I toyed with my Strathmore Lemon. 'You're back in business, Oz. I wonder if all your commissions will be like this one.'

'I don't imagine so. In fact I hope not. I'm not optimistic of getting a result for Mr Scott. That's a hell of a picture, but there are some helluva good painters in northern Spain. If the rumour about signed blanks is true, then the best our client will do is to crystallise his capital loss, and throw himself on the mercy of the shareholders at the Annual Meeting.' I paused. 'It's "our" commissions, by the way. I know what you said earlier, but if you're going to be involved in BSI, I insist that it's as a partner. The business must have someone in Britain, and you're her. Financial Controller, and no arguments.'

She smiled. 'Hadn't you better talk that over with Prim?'

'Primavera will agree. So must you.'

She looked at me, with a delicious smile. 'Christ, but I can't get used to you being decisive! Okay, I agree.' She extended her hand; we shook on it.

'Well,' she said, 'if I'm in, we'd better take some decisions; for openers about how the business should be set up, for tax-sheltering and other purposes.'

I made a face. 'I'm not worried about avoiding tax. That's not why we went to Spain.'

'So why did you?' asked Jan, quietly.

I looked at her, across the table, as she started on her dressed Dunbar crab. Enormous, it was. Funny things have happened to the marine life down that way since they opened Torness nuclear power station.

'Good question. Because it was there, I suppose. Because

we could afford it.' I laughed. 'And yes, I suppose to avoid the possibility of paying tax on Ray Archer's gift, even though we knew he'd have to show it as a trading loss, and that he could never declare it as a payment to us.'

I took a spoonful of my Provençal fish soup. 'I suppose there was another reason, on top of those. To give ourselves a start as a couple in completely new surroundings, away from all the influences we'd known until then.'

'Like me, for example.'

She took me by surprise. 'No, of course not,' I said, defensively.

Something flickered in her eyes. 'Okay,' she said, in a voice which, whether she meant it or not, was loud enough to carry to the next table. 'Nor, I suppose, was it simply a case of suddenly finding yourselves moderately rich and deciding to indulge yourselves by lying in the sun and copulating all day long.'

For a moment the territory felt distinctly uncomfortable. 'Sorry,' I murmured. 'I thought that was what I just said we decided to do.'

She laughed, and at once I was comfortable again. I looked at her as she attacked her crab, and I remembered Saturday evenings, more than a decade in the past, and the seafood stall in Crail harbour; other generations of crustaceans, still steaming from the boiling pot. Jan and I as sixteen-year-olds, country kids with ruddy faces, and tight-muscled thighs from our beach and coastal walks, tearing into them, bare-handed, as later we tore heartily into each other. I snapped myself back to the present and turned my attention to my own meal, quickly.

'It's funny to think of a man like Gavin Scott being conned,' said Jan, finished at last.

'Not really,' I countered. 'Scott's a gambler by nature, I'd say. Look at his track record in business. He staked the lot on buying Soutar's and it's paid off. Once a punter always a punter. On top of that he's an art enthusiast; he'd call himself an expert. A painter and a punter combined: some combination.

'You have to understand, love, that there's a whole Dalí industry out there. If you spend any time in Catalunya you can't avoid it. It's all around you. You'll find Dalí prints in all the souvenir shops, and you'll find special prints of signed work in the more up-market places. There's a Dalí museum in Figueras, and it has hundreds of thousands of visitors each year.

'The great man is buried there, you know. In the cellar. I've seen his tomb. The museum itself is spectacular. It's a work of art in its own right; by Dalí, about Dalí. Paintings, displays, objects: the whole experience draws you into it, makes you part of it.'

'Christ, Oz,' Jan chuckled. 'You sound like a disciple.'

'I suppose I am, in a way. You visit the place and you can't help it. The man was just crazy, but wonderfully crazy, larger than life. How can I put it? If you visit the place and you're in tune with it, you can sense that in death he's become part of it.

'I'm no expert, and that's how the place took me. So imagine someone like Scott, caught up in the spirit of it. He told us he'd been there, but I knew that even before I asked him. So imagine him, given the opportunity to have a piece of Dalí as his own, and not just any old piece, but an undiscovered, signed work which he's told is genuine, and from the look of it, could be the real deal.

'Gavin Scott doesn't see himself as having been conned. He sees himself as having taken a gamble, with a limited downside and one which might still pay off, if you, Prim and I can come up trumps for him.'

Jan raised her right eyebrow, a gesture I had known since childhood. 'If we do, maybe we should ask for a cut of the winnings.'

'Absolutely not. Been there, done that, got the scars. We set decent fee levels, we bill by the hour, and we do not, repeat not, become personally involved with our clients. This may be a three-way equal partnership, but this is the one area in which Oz is laying down the law.'

She looked at me and smiled. 'Christ,' she said. 'First you play big brother for your big sister. Now you're getting assertive with me. After a lifetime of pretending to be Tonto, you've turned into the Lone Ranger.'

I stared back at her, conspiratorially, from under hooded eyebrows. 'It's the Spanish influence at work. Incidentally after the *Black and White Minstrels*, *The Lone Ranger* is the most politically incorrect TV programme ever made. In Spanish, Tonto, as in His Faithful Indian Companion, means stupid. But I'll stop short of turning into the masked man, if you don't mind. Kemo Sabay, phoneticised, translates roughly as smartarse . . . and . . .'

'. . . nobody loves a Smartarse,' we said, in unison.

16

Jan was still grinning as we left the Old Inn and headed up to town. She settled comfortably into the passenger seat as I drove through the night.

The yellow lights of Edinburgh bore down on us quickly as we listened to a Tom Waits tape which she had plugged into the cassette player. 'You sure Noosh doesn't have a problem about me staying?' I asked once more as I turned off London Road and headed into Holyrood Park.

'None at all. Hey Oz,' said Jan suddenly, as we passed St Margaret's Loch, and its geese, curled up asleep on its grassy banks. 'How come you never ask me about your loft, and about your tenant? Never once have you asked me who I've put in there, or for references. Why is that?'

'Simple. I don't want to know. I loved my loft. Still do. If I have a mental picture of the person living there, I'm afraid that I'll start to feel jealous. Then I might get nostalgic for it, and even out in Spain, I might feel homesick. Does that make sense to you?'

She nodded. 'Perfect sense. You don't want anything to disturb the Spanish idyll.'

'No,' I protested. 'That's not it.'

'Oh no. So you're still the same old softie at heart, then.' For a while, there was silence in the dark. 'Let's drive past it anyway,' said Jan, finally.

I swung out of the park, made the turn at the foot of the Royal Mile, then turned again. Less than a minute later, I could see the old building, with its belvedere, a familiar part of the Old Town nightscape.

'Stop there,' said Jan, quietly, as we reached it. 'Just pull into your parking space. There's nobody in.'

I did as I was told, without thinking. Something about Jan's voice had my complete attention. She stepped out of the car as soon as it came to a halt, taking her jacket from its hook by the hand grip and reaching into the pocket.

I followed her. 'Jan, what is this?' I asked at last.

She gazed at me, across the red roof of the Fiesta. Her face had an odd look, and even at that distance, I could see that she was trembling. 'Anoushka and I have split up, Oz.' She kept her voice steady with an effort. 'I'm your tenant.'

I felt my jaw drop for an instant, and snapped it shut. 'But . . . When . . .'

'About a week after you left for Spain.'

'Why?'

She turned towards the door, beckoning me to follow. 'Come on. I don't want to talk out here.'

I followed her into the building and up the twisting stair which led to my old home. She unlocked the door, then stepped straight into the toilet, off the tiny hall. I was in the kitchen opposite, watching the kettle and waiting for it to boil, when she emerged. Her face and eyes were clear of make-up.

Standing in the doorway, she smiled at me awkwardly. I pulled her to me and hugged her. 'Jan, love. Why didn't you tell me before?' She wrapped her arms around me and put her head on my shoulder, pressing her eyes hard against the wool and cashmere blazer that I had picked up from my dad's.

'I couldn't. I didn't know how to tell you.'

'Who else knows about it? Christ, I can't believe that we went through last night and I never picked up a hint.'

She gave me a quick hug, released me and stepped across to the work-surface, reaching out for the coffee jar. 'Only Ellie knows so far, and she promised not to tell a soul, not even you. I'm still working out what to say to Mum. All that grief I put her through, making her realise that she had a gay daughter. Now . . .'

I took her face in both my hands and turned it up towards me. 'My old girl, just tell her. She's your mum, and she loves you. End of story.'

On the counter, the kettle hissed steam, until the thermostat cut out. I took the jar from her and made coffee for us both, reaching into the fridge for the milk without even looking.

'Come on,' I said. 'Upstairs and tell me all about it.'

She led the way up to the living area, turning the dimmer switch to raise the wall lighting, an array which I had planned myself. Everything was as I had left it, almost. The furniture was still there, but slightly rearranged. The sofa-bed was on the other side of the room from where I had liked it. The desk faced away from the window. The curtains were tied back with neat bows. But up on the raised sleeping area, the bed was still in the same place, with, above it, the ladder which led up to the belvedere, where Wallace and I used to sit in serenity, my dinosaur sunning himself while I read the Sunday papers.

I took the occasional chair, facing Jan as she slumped into the sofa.

'Honest to god, love,' I said. 'I hadn't a clue. I mean, your telephone number's the same . . .'

'It's my business number, remember. I had it transferred the day I moved in.'

I sipped my coffee. It was still piping hot. 'So what happened? Did Anoushka find someone else? I thought she doted on you.'

Jan shook her head, and turned her gaze away from me, looking at the glazed French doors which led out to the tiny balcony. 'Noosh didn't find anyone else, Oz. I did.'

I gulped. To my complete surprise, my old friend the hamster began to run around in my stomach. 'Eh?'

'I found me again, Oz. I found Jan.'

I stood up and walked to the doorway, almost forcing her to look at me. 'What do you mean?' I asked her, gently.

'I suppose it was you leaving that made me look at myself. While you were here, I think you helped me cling on to my own self. The fact that you and I went back so far, and that I could still count on you, helped me to hold on to my own personality, and assert myself every so often.'

She must have caught a flicker at the corner of my mouth. 'Oh, I don't mean that you were here to give me a good shag if Noosh and I had a fight and I felt like really getting even with her.' She laughed softly; Jan has a lascivious chuckle which for some reason always makes me think of brown sugar. 'Yes, boy,' she said, 'I admit it, I used you like an old pair of gardening gloves.' She paused, and her expression became earnest again.

'But don't you get the idea that I had turned to Noosh on the rebound, after you started to push me away. She seduced me, Oz, like I told you way back, and I loved it. The sex was great at first, ten out of ten. After a while it settled into a consistent eight, but that's higher than most straight couples score. Satisfying and without risk. Nothing wrong with that, and I'm not being defensive in the slightest.'

I nodded. 'Understood. So what happened, after I left?'

'It started even before then,' she said, 'when I saw you and Prim together for the first time, and realised how it was going to turn out. It wasn't like that when you had other girlfriends. I knew they wouldn't last. This time, I began to feel alone, and I began to look at my relationship with Ms Turkel.'

She took a deep breath, and when she spoke again there was a momentary, and uncharacteristic tremor in her voice. 'As soon as I did, I realised what I had become. She was the dominant partner. I was the subordinate. It may have been two names beside the doorbell, but Noosh saw us, in straight terms, like she was the husband and I was the wife. We split the overhead down the middle, but I was the housekeeper. From the start that went without saying. I had been able to live with it because I was earning good money, and contributing, able to tell myself that we were equals; but that wasn't how Noosh saw it and that wasn't what she wanted.'

Jan put her coffee cup on the floor. (I couldn't help it; I glanced down fleetingly to make sure that it wasn't going to topple over and stain my carpet. Happily she didn't notice.) She stood up and took a step or two across to stand beside me, to link her arm through mine.

'Oz my darlin',' she said. 'I'd never before been dominated by anyone in my life. That was why you and I were so great as youngsters. Neither of us ever dreamed of possessing the other. I never thought of you as *my* boyfriend or of me as *your* girlfriend. I was always Jan, her own woman. You were Oz, your own man, and I loved you.'

She squeezed my arm. 'So with you, my pit prop, taken away, I looked at Noosh and me and I realised what I was. In that instant, it all fell apart. I waited until you and Prim were gone . . . I had Ellie and the kids to distract me until then . . . and I told Noosh how it was. She didn't like it, and we had a row. I said I realised that she couldn't change, so that was it.

'I moved out and into the loft. Originally I just meant it to be for a couple of weeks, while I found somewhere else, but I like it here. How about selling it to me, once Noosh gives me my share of our flat? I don't imagine that Prim will fancy me being your tenant on a long-term basis.'

I laughed. 'There's the shorter term question of how she'd feel about me sleeping on the sofa-bed tonight. But hold on, I'm still getting my head round this.' I turned her towards me and slipped my arms around her waist. Her body, held gently against mine, was oh, so familiar. 'You've no regrets? You've had no second thoughts?'

'None. I'm Jan again. Like I said, my big problem now is what to tell my mum, how to tell her.'

I smiled at her. We were almost eye to eye, since Jan still had her shoes on. 'No problem. Just tell her exactly what you've told me.'

'Apart from the bit about you giving me a good shag every so often?' she murmured.

'That's up to you. You're your own woman again, remember. Here's a thought, though. Dad and Auntie Mary are a team now. You should tell them together. I can promise you, based on long experience, that there's no better listener than my old man.'

She thought about it and nodded. 'You're right. I'll do it. Even the bit about you know what, if slightly watered down. Tomorrow, I'll take you to the airport, and then I'll head straight back up to Fife.

'Thanks, darlin',' she said, 'for being there yet again. Tell you this, if Mac's a great listener, then the skill's hereditary.' She kissed me, like she had the evening before, at the airport. Without even thinking about it, I kissed her right back.

And then I kissed her again. All of a sudden I wasn't thinking about anything, except Jan, that seafood stall in Crail once more, those harbour walls in Anstruther, coastal walks, and later times in the loft, when I'd be alone in the evening and the entry phone would ring.

We looked at each other, our eyes inches apart, the air between us smoking with memories. My heart was in charge now. I flicked an eyebrow as if nodding back in time. 'Just now,' I whispered, 'about you and me. You said, "loved". You used the past tense.'

'Did I?' she answered my unspoken question. 'Then I meant "love". How could I not? I'm Jan, and I haven't changed.'

17

'So where does this take Jan and Oz?'

I lay face down on the bed, my chin buried in my knotted fists, my eyes focused on a scratch in the headboard. Euphoria was dissipating as practicality took hold, and as I contemplated the scattered pieces of my so-certain future.

'Not one step forward,' she answered. 'Not one step back. But, by God, it was good, wasn't it.' She lay beside me, her shiny brown hair tousled and fallen over one eye, the way it always seemed to after we had made love. 'I like being a strong and independent woman again.'

Of course, the inevitable had happened.

I'll never believe for one second that Jan had planned it that way. Still, we had kissed again, and it had taken on a momentum of its own, until the neat bows tying back the curtains had been slipped, and we were easing each other out of our clothing, as we had done on countless occasions over the last fourteen years.

Yet this was unlike any of those innumerable matings in the past. There was a maturity to it, a gentleness, a patience, on my part and on Jan's, of which I had never been aware before, and maybe for my part never capable. It was long and slow and smiling and joyful, two old friends meeting again after believing they never would, until at last we climaxed together, as never before, Jan bucking and heaving beneath me and crying out, wide-eyed, in absolute triumph. Eventually, we had fallen asleep in each other's arms, awakening hours later, still entwined.

I rolled on to my back and Jan slid on top of me, her long

legs covering mine, propped up on her elbows with her hair falling towards my face.

I let my eyes roam. 'Nice tits,' I said, by way of morning conversation.

'Nice love handles,' she replied, taking a grip of my extended waist with her right hand and squeezing. 'They're new. I think I like them.'

'Don't,' I murmured. 'They're going.' Her face fell, just for a moment, before she slammed her smile firmly back into place. 'No,' I said, hurriedly. 'I meant I've started exercising again.'

'Sure,' she whispered, 'but they are going, aren't they? Back to Spain, to find out whether Gavin Scott's Dalí's a fake or not.'

'Aye, and to sort out a few other matters too. But let's not talk about that.'

'No,' she said, lowering her lips to mine. 'I've got other things in mind.'

Afterwards, as the gleam of orgasmic triumph in Jan's eye began to soften once more, we lay in silence for a while, gazing up at the slivers of Monday morning sky which showed through the glass of the belvedere. The rain had gone, and the autumn sunshine was back.

I broke the quiet, reaching across and rubbing her nipple with the flat of my thumb. 'You remember I had a long talk with Ellie, on Saturday night?' I asked her.

'Mhm.'

'She told me that I should cut you out of my life, for your sake.'

'Funny, that,' said Jan. 'She told me that I should cut you out of mine, for my sake. What did you say to her?'

'I told her that you'd have to wield the knife for both of us. What did you say?'

'I said . . .' She paused, and looked up at the sky once more. 'I said that you can't cut your heart out and expect to go on living.'

I didn't have a funny line to follow that. So I said, 'Ellie cares about you and me, but she doesn't really know us; like not *really*.'

She wrapped her arms around me again. 'No. No one really knows you and me, except for you and me.'

'Only,' I cautioned her, 'all of a sudden I'm not sure that I know *me* any more.'

Jan propped herself up on an elbow and looked down at me. On occasion she may fart quietly in her sleep, but I've never known anyone who looks, invariably, as beautiful as she does when she's newly wakened in the morning.

She fixed me in the eye and spoke, slowly and deliberately. 'In that case, Osbert Blackstone, the one and only true love of my life, the sooner you get back to Spain and find yourself again, the better it will be.'

I started to speak, but she put a finger across my lips. 'No pressure. No demands. No ultimatum. I'm saying nothing other than this. For the first time I've made love with you in the knowledge that you were living with another woman. But it'll be the last. I'll always love you, and I'll always be your best friend, but I can't be your second best woman. You'll always love me too, I know. But you have to work out how you want it to be. Like it's been for the last few years, as best of friends . . . except without the occasional bit of the other . . . or like we were before that. Agreed?'

I nodded my head on the pillow. 'Agreed.'

'Good,' she said, running her hand down my belly and leaning over me again. 'But for now, since we're here . . .'

18

Eventually, I shaved, showered and dressed, then, leaving Jan stretched out in the bath, I went out to fetch our breakfast. My old pal Ali, the open-all-hours grocer at the top of the close, looked up in surprise when I walked into his shop. In fact his eyebrows shot up so far that I thought he would dislodge his turban.

Until I left for Spain, Ali and I had been team-mates in a five-a-side football club which played at Meadowbank every Tuesday night. The lads and I had a theory that Ali's turban was stitched into his scalp, since he never took it off, not even in the showers.

'Oz, pal. Hullawarerr, how yis been?' he bellowed as I walked in. Ali was born and raised in Scotland. His complexion and head-dress may be sub-continental Asian, but his accent is pure Rab C.

'Hullawrerr to youse, China,' I responded. 'I's been fine.'

'So ah see,' he said, taking a closer look. 'Yis're fuckin' darker-skinned than me noo. How long are yis here for?'

I checked my watch. It was just leaving 10:30 a.m. 'About five and a half hours.'

'Is yer lass back wi yis?'

'No. Prim's in Spain. We're living there now.'

'Aye, ah ken. Yis sent me a postcard, mind.'

The wheels were turning under that turban. 'So have yis been stayin' in the loft?'

I decided to cut the interrogation short. 'That's right, sunshine. With Jan, my old school chum. She's living there now. Tall girl, dark hair; shops in here according to the label on her washing up liquid. Now we'd like breakfast. So it'll be four of your freshest rolls and half a pound of your spiciest Lorne sausage, please, my good man. Oh yes, and a *Daily Record*.'

Ali glanced at his watch, as he selected four rolls from that morning's batch. 'Breakfast!' he said. 'At half past ten! You'll be in the *Daily* fuckin' *Record* yirself, the wey you're goin' on, pal.'

Jan was in the kitchen when I got back, in her dressing gown, with her hair wrapped in a towel.

'Go on,' I said, kissing her shiny nose. 'Get yourself sorted. I'll make breakfast. Incidentally, shouldn't you be working today?'

She shrugged her shoulders. 'I don't have any meetings, so I'm okay. You know what the self-employed life is like. I'll do a double shift tomorrow. So I'm yours for the day, or at least till you catch your plane.'

'Good,' I said, 'for there's something I'd like to do in town, while I've got the chance. So you get your legs and stuff upstairs and get dressed. I'll be about ten minutes with the rolls and coffee.'

It was a mild morning, so we ate in canvas chairs out on the pocket-sized wooden balcony. As the last of the coffee went down, Jan grabbed my *Daily Record* and handed me three envelopes, already opened. They were all addressed to Blackstone Spanish Investigations.

They were all follow-ups from the other enquiries which Jan had fielded on the previous Friday. One was from a firm of Glasgow solicitors, looking to have a statement taken in Tarragona from a potential witness in a civil court action. The others had come from manufacturing companies looking for information on the sales potential for their products in Spain.

'Interesting,' I said, as Jan studied her horoscope. It always amazes me how intelligent people can fall for that crap. 'I can do the interview, no problem. Prim can tackle the other two. They'll be desk research mainly. Hal, at the consulate, will be able to give us some of the information, and probably the contacts who'll give us the rest.'

'That's fine,' said Jan, 'but just remember that Gavin Scott comes first.'

'Sure.' I took her hand and looked out across the roofs of the Old Town, towards the crests of Holyrood Palace. 'All this, the last few days,' I said. 'It's doing my head in, you know. A week ago, Prim told me I was well down the road to vegetation. She was right. She came up with the business idea. She, more than anyone, put me on that plane.

'Look at me now, seven days later. Sat on another terrace, with another woman. And you know, don't you, that part of me wants to stay here?'

Jan gave my fingers a squeeze. 'Sure, darlin',' she said, in her lazy drawl. 'But all of you's got to want it or it's no good. Okay, so you and I took each other by surprise last night. But we've slept together often enough before.'

She caught my smile. 'Okay, maybe not often enough.' She laughed, then was serious again. 'Still, it shouldn't have casual consequences for either of us. Make no mistake, I know what I want, bottom line, and I know why. But I'm not going to tell you what this is. Not now, anyway.

'Whatever direction you decide you want your life to take, you can't be ambivalent about it. You've got to be certain, and you've got to be certain for the right reason.

'I haven't a bloody clue what your reason will turn out to be, but I'm sure that you'll find it. Even then, there'll be no guarantee you'll get what you want, but I know that you won't unless you're completely committed to it.'

Jan reached out and touched my cheek, holding my gaze. 'Remember those birds we used to watch from the beach when we were kids, the gulls and the ducks, floating on the sea just behind the crest of the tide, getting closer to land, but never quite allowing the waves to bring them in to shore? Well, my darling, no more drifting on the tide. It's make your mind up time.'

I smiled at her, but I wasn't laughing. 'Two days ago, I thought I had; but maybe I was just treading water. The Mediterranean's different, remember. No tides.'

She stood up and stepped inside, drawing me with her. 'Now, what's the thing you want to do uptown, because time's getting on?'

I folded the chairs and carried them inside as Jan closed the French doors. 'Okay,' I said. 'I want to go to a jeweller's.'

I told her no more than that, all the way up from the loft, through Waverley Station and out into Princes Street. I could tell that I had her interest, but typically, she refused to ask me anything about my purpose.

Finally we reached Laing's, in Frederick Street. 'Okay,' I said. 'I'll tell you now. This is a bit of detective work of my own.' I led her inside and asked for Gregor, the manager. 'He's one of my Tuesday football pals,' I explained to Jan as he came bounding down the stairs at the rear of the shop.

His eyes lit up as he saw us, and I could tell that he was anticipating a diamond sale. I put him right at once, as he greeted us. 'I'm after nuggets of information,' I said, 'not gold.'

'Christ, Oz,' he groaned, 'that's corny. But tell me about it anyway.'

He motioned Jan and I to chairs at one of their fitting tables, and sat down with us. 'Remember that watch I bought last year for my dad?' I asked him.

'Sure. Giorgio of Beverley Hills. A good line for us.'

'Glad to hear it. They've all got serial numbers, yes?' Gregor nodded. 'And they're guaranteed, obviously,' I went on. 'So, are the serial numbers registered with the guarantee, or are they just for show? In other words, can you identify the purchaser just by looking at the back of the watch?'

'Yes, assuming that all the paperwork's been done. Why? Has your dad been getting unwanted mail from Giorgio?'

'No, nothing like that. The thing is, I found a watch just like it in Spain, and I'd like to return it if I can. A guy out there told me that those watches were made for the UK market only.'

'And America.'

'Mmm. But assuming it is UK, if I give you the serial number could you come up with a name and address?'

He scratched his chin. 'If we sold it, I can tell you straight away. But it's probably odds against that. What's the number?'

'930100.'

He stood up. 'Give me a minute.' He trotted back up the stairs to what I assumed was his office, reappearing a few minutes later. 'No, it isn't one of ours,' he said. 'But the first letter of the serial number tells me that it is a UK watch, and the second that it was sold in the West of England.

'I can't make any promises, Oz, because the manufacturers have no obligation to give me information about other people's customers. We're significant buyers, though. I shouldn't imagine I'll have any bother. Will you be at Meadowbank tomorrow night?' he asked. 'I should have news by then.'

'Sorry. I'm going back to Spain this afternoon. But you can fax me, one way or another.' I scribbled my St Marti number on a scratchpad which lay on the table.

'Sure, I'll do that,' he said. 'It's a pity you can't stay longer. Our Tuesday night game's got too serious since you left. Anything else I can do for you, while you're here?'

I nodded, and pointed towards a display case beside our table. 'Since you ask. See that gold necklet? You can wrap that up for me.' Gregor's eyes lit up again.

Buying jewellery in Laing's is always a pleasant experience. Very few shops these days have the knack of making the customer feel special, but theirs is one that does. I replaced my card in my wallet and slipped my purchase into the pocket of my jacket, as Gregor showed us out into Frederick Street. 'I'll give you information any time you like if that's what comes of it,' he said, waving us farewell.

We walked casually back the way we had come, pausing to window-gaze in the specialist Waverley Shopping Centre. It was dead on 2 p.m. by the time we arrived back at the loft. 'Better head for the airport,' said Jan, in a matter-of-fact way, as we stood, looking out of the window once more.

'Yes.' I paused. 'Listen, I can get a taxi.'

She threw me one of her most dismissive looks.

'Okay,' I grinned, 'but I had to offer.' I picked up my bag, and Gavin Scott's print, in its tube, and we headed for the door.

Half-an-hour later, Jan pulled up at the airport. We looked at each other. It had all been said. Well, almost. 'Whatever,' said Jan. 'I love you.' We kissed.

'Whatever,' I said. I took the long box from my pocket, ripped the paper from it, took out the necklet and fastened it around her throat. She looked at me in surprise, but didn't say a word. The gold seemed to shine even brighter.

She smiled and touched my cheek. 'Think of it this way. At worst we'll be step-brother and step-sister . . . or maybe at best.'

19

My flight landed in Barcelona ten minutes early, and so it was just after nine-thirty when I stepped through the blue channel and out into the concourse. The arrangement had been that I would catch the last train to Girona and take a taxi home.

But there she was, copper tan, sun-gold blonde, bright-brown-eyed. My Primavera.

All the way home I had thought of my weird weekend. My reunions, my serious conversation with my sister, and the Shane Warne googly that Jan's rediscovered emancipation had thrown into my comfortable, complacent life.

I was certain that I loved Prim. I was certain that I loved Jan. I was certain that sometime very soon I was going to have to make a painful choice. That was where my certainty ended.

Somewhere in there, there was something profound, something meaningful, something which gave me the answer. The big overwhelming reason leading me to the decision which I knew I had to make, a situation which I had not as much as contemplated only twenty-four hours before.

My eyes were closed for most of both return flights, apart from the occasions when I was shaken by the flight crews so that I could decline their offers of drink, token food and duty-free that I could buy cheaper in the shops in Spain. But was I asleep? Oh no. All the way back to what I had called home when I left it, my mind was racing, full of thoughts of Jan, our night together, and of the many nights in our past.

I had no idea what I was going to say to Prim, or even how I would feel when I saw her. For that matter I had no idea how I would look to her. Would the truth be written in my eyes, or betrayed by the way I spoke to her?

I still had no answers to any of it as I stepped out through the International Arrivals doorway, to find her there, in the front of the crowd. I was surprised, and in there was a tiny flash of frustration, for some little devil inside me had worked out that if she hadn't been there I would have had an opportunity to throw a moody, to begin an undermining process, a distancing of myself from Prim and her love.

But when I saw her my smile broke out, in spite of itself. I heard myself say, 'Hello love, I wondered if you'd be here, in spite of what we agreed.' And my arms, burdens and all, spread out to enfold her and to return her hug.

She kissed me and whispered, 'Welcome back. I've been cold these last two nights without you.'

'Hah,' I heard myself say. 'Think yourself lucky. You might have been in Anstruther.' My first tiny half-lie.

She took my arm, just like Jan had done, as I slung my bag over my shoulder. 'What's that?' she asked, intrigued, pointing at the long tube, which I was carrying sloped like a rifle against my neck, as we emerged into the warm, humid, evening air and crossed the road to the car park.

'I'll show you when we get home. It's too awkward to open it now, but it has to do with our commission.'

Because I had declined the aircraft booze, I was able to drive us back up the autopista to L'Escala. We sat in silence for the first part of the journey, for the ronda north through Barça is a bit of a bugger to find, and you can get seriously lost if you take the wrong option.

But eventually, we were through the city and safely on our way. 'So how is everyone?' asked Prim, as the Frontera's lights cut a swathe through a bank of mist.

'Everyone's fine. Dad and Mary are as happy as I've ever seen them. My nephews are exhausting. Wallace is being spoiled rotten. Oh yes, and my sister's got a bit on the side.'

'What!' Prim sat bolt upright and turned towards me in

her seat, until she was caught by her seat belt. There was a huge grin on her face, as if she found the notion preposterous.

I couldn't help but feel slightly offended, on Ellie's behalf. 'You heard me,' I said. 'What's so funny about that?You haven't seen my sister in going on three months. She's quite a piece of work now, I can tell you.'

'I'm sure she is. It's just that I didn't expect . . .' She trailed off, and out of the corner of my eye I could see her smile. 'I suppose I shouldn't be surprised, though. After all, you Blackstones are fast workers.'

Suddenly I was back in the loft. 'That's what you think,' I muttered, almost, but not quite, to myself. I couldn't hold it in. I was thinking of the passing of most of a lifetime, and of the confusion that had run through it.

She looked at me, puzzled, as I stared at the road ahead. 'Oh, don't be huffy. If Ellie's got a new light in her life, that's great. God knows, my own sister's had a few torches in her time.'

'Aye,' I said. 'We're talking about the Hampden floodlights there, right enough.'

'Oz!' Now it was Prim's turn to flare up. 'Look, what's got into you?'

There it was. My opening. My chance to spill the beans, to confess all about the night before . . . and maybe throw Prim's life, and mine, down the crapper.

'Och, I'm sorry, love,' I said at last. 'Two flights in a day. It's too much for me. As a matter of fact one's too much. Flying stresses me out, and it takes me a while to get back to normal.'

Suddenly her hand was on my sleeve, then stroking my cheek. 'Full of surprises, aren't you. I didn't think anything stressed you out. Never mind, I'll cure it once we get home.'

I flashed her a weak smile. 'Tonight, my love, I'm a rat. Food and drink come first.'

'My God,' she laughed. 'It has been a tough day.'

Casa Miñana was closed up tight when we got back to St

Marti, just before 11:15 p.m., but they were still serving food at the tables outside Meson del Conde. We chose a place well back from the doorway and sat down, without even taking my bag upstairs to the apartment. We ordered sardines followed by chicken and chips, and I told the waiter to keep the beer coming.

Suddenly I was hungry and thirsty at the same time. Prim watched me as I demolished my sardines, then what was left of hers, and set about my half chicken. 'When did you last eat?' she asked.

'Breakfast,' I said, without thinking.

'Let me guess,' she said. 'Rolls and sliced sausage.'

'Got it in one,' I said, finishing my third beer. 'From Ali's.'

'I thought you said you were in Anstruther?'

'That was Saturday night.' I don't think I paused, or batted an eyelid. 'Ali's isn't all that far from Jan's.'

'No,' she said, 'I suppose not. How is Jan, anyway?'

'Blooming. We're plotting our parents' wedding.'

'I'll bet. And how's Noosh?'

'Okay. She's advising Ellie on her separation agreement, or her firm is.'

'Mmm. That's good.'

'*Sure is*,' I thought. '*I didn't tell her a single lie there.*' 'Not fucking much!' an invisible wee red devil on my shoulder whispered in my ear.

'By the way, Dawn phoned yesterday morning,' said Prim, 'from Los Angeles. She's at Miles' place. She sounded really happy. What a difference from the girl we met at Auchterarder a few months ago.'

'I'm pleased to hear it. But don't let's get back to talking about sisters, eh.'

'No, I suppose not. But the cow woke me up. They had just got in from a party. It was nine-thirty in the morning here.'

I finished my chicken and attacked my next beer. 'How

was the party you were at? That Anglo-Catalan thing on Saturday.'

She shrugged. 'It was okay. Quite interesting, I suppose, although I was the only person there aged under fifty, apart from someone's son.'

'Who was that?' I asked.

'A couple called Miller. He's visiting them for a couple of weeks. His name's Steve. He's in the motor business, in Brighton.'

'So what was interesting about the night? Him?'

She shot me a piercing look. 'Don't be silly. I made some new acquaintances. D'you remember that lady we've seen at the Trattoria? Very tall, slim, blonde.' I nodded.

'I was introduced to her. Her name's Shirley Gash. She's fantastic. She had this amazing little man with her. I'm not quite sure where he fits in. She announced him as a house guest. His name's Davidoff, would you believe. Sounds like a Russian Prince. Unfortunately he looks like a Transylvanian gypsy. You might meet him. We're invited up to Shirley's for drinks tomorrow afternoon. Apparently she lives in a big house up on what they call Millionaires' Row. Janice says she's a widow.'

I did in some more beer, chasing but not killing my thirst. A refill appeared automatically, with our coffee. I was working at it, and I had almost reached the mellow stage, when the shout came from the doorway of Meson del Conde. 'Primavera, my love!'

We both looked up together, but something made me look at Prim, rather than at the shouter. Even under the tan, I could see her flush. He came towards us between the tables, a medium sized chap, wearing a professional smile and a silk shirt with a gold Benson and Hedges pack in the breast pocket. Behind him a different couple, well old enough to have been his parents, stood by the entrance to the restaurant. I recognised them as part of the ex-pat wallpaper.

He leaned over Prim and kissed her, on the cheek, but for

a little longer than politeness dictated. 'Lovely to see you again,' I heard him whisper. I had taken an instant dislike to him, and that just made it worse.

Primavera leaned back in her chair, back from him, and looked up at me. 'Steve,' she said. 'This is Oz Blackstone, my boyfriend. He just got back from Scotland tonight. Oz, this is Steve Miller.'

I like to think that I'm a friendly guy, but on the odd occasion when someone does get up my nose, I just can't help clearing it. I stood up, slowly. Miller held out his hand. I shook it, squeezing more powerfully than was necessary.

'*You know, Steve,*' a voice in my head said, '*there's nothing more annoying, even to a placid bloke like me, than some smarmy bastard coming up and slobbering all over your girlfriend, just as if you weren't there. Now piss off before I take a pop at you.*'

'Hello, Steve,' I said, instead. I nodded towards the two bodgers in the doorway. 'Is that your band?'

He looked at me, bewildered.

'Sorry,' I said. 'You're no rock n' roller, eh?'

He looked down at Prim. 'I think I'd better go.'

'No comment,' I said.

Prim scowled at me. 'Steve,' she said. 'I . . .'

'No really, I think I should. I don't want to cause trouble.'

'Wise man,' I said. He gave me what was meant to be a hostile look, then turned and made his way back towards his parents.

Prim waved goodnight as the three Millers disappeared around the corner. Then she turned to me. 'What the hell was that about?' She shot it at me, as soon as they were out of sight.

'Good question,' I said. 'Who did he think I was? The invisible fucking man?'

She held up her hands. 'Okay, enough. You've had a hard day, and you're a bit pissed. Let's call a truce and go home.'

I bent down and kissed her on the cheek, just where Miller had kissed her, but for a significant moment longer. Then I kissed her full on the lips. 'Truce it is,' I said. 'One more beer, and it's a deal about going home as well.'

She sighed and smiled. 'All right. But only one.' She made signs to the waiter, ordering another for herself in the process.

'Oh, by the way,' she said, 'there was a fax coming through just as I left. I didn't have time to look at it, though.'

'Fair enough,' I replied as the beers arrived, then promptly forgot about it as I made a conscious effort to bring my mind back to Spain, to Prim, and to what I had thought was my real world, until the day before.

I could see that she was still upset. I reached out a hand and ruffled her hair. 'Hey, sweetheart. I'm sorry.' I wasn't, of course. I had enjoyed seeing off Mr Miller. 'I'm sure he's a very nice bloke. He just caught me on the raw, that's all.'

Pouting, as only she can, she looked at me, sideways. 'Boys,' she said with a sigh. 'I don't know.'

It was almost 1 a.m. when we climbed the stairs to the apartment. I didn't think I was all that pissed, but somehow I managed to get Gavin Scott's tube tangled between my legs just as we got to the front door. I sprawled forward and lay on the steps, grinning up at Prim. She shook her head, took my bag from me, stepped over me and unlocked the door.

'I can see this is going to be my lucky night!' she said as I stumbled in behind her, laughing, slapping her lightly across the bum with the tube.

'D'you want to see what's in it now?' I asked.

'Tomorrow. I'm off to bed.'

'Okay. Me too.' I followed her into the bedroom and began to undress, throwing my clothes on to the chair. I was stood there in my jockeys when the garlic from the sardines began to make its presence felt. I swallowed a couple of Breath Asure pills, then wandered through to the kitchen in search of the Normogastryls. I found them in the cupboard, and dissolved a couple as a pre-emptive strike against nocturnal heartburn.

They had been the last tablets in the tube. As I swallowed the alkaline remedy, I stepped on the pedal bin, to discard it.

The kitchen light was directly overhead or I might not have noticed. The liner had been changed recently, and the bin was almost empty . . . save for several discarded cigarette ends, and a scattering of ash. I picked one out, and looked at it. Benson and Hedges.

I don't know the guy who stormed through to the bedroom, brandishing the offending butt. Whoever he was, he wasn't good old lovable, can't be riled, takes everything in his stride Oz Blackstone. This was a steamed-up, hypocritical, petulant clown, who didn't stop to think whether he was genuinely jealous or simply latching on to an excuse.

Prim was almost asleep when the shout came from the doorway. 'What the fuck is this?'

She rubbed her eyes. 'Eh?'

'Who do we know that smokes Bensons?'

'Oh shit.' She sounded weary, but she pulled herself up in bed. The guy in the doorway didn't have the wit to realise how desirable she looked, just at that moment.

'Now listen carefully,' she said, 'because I'm not going to repeat this. Yesterday afternoon, a few of us who had been at the party on Saturday met up for lunch in the square. There was Shirley Gash, a lady called Tina, Steve Miller and his parents. Just as we were finishing our meals, it looked as if it might rain, so I invited them all up here for coffee. Steve and Tina both smoke. I expect that if you root about some more in the bin you'll find some Marlboro stubs as well.

'Is that clear,' she shouted, suddenly. 'Or do you want to count your bloody condoms?'

The alien in the doorway vanished, leaving me stood in his place, brandishing a fag-end and feeling very, very stupid. I dropped the stub into the waste-basket in the corner, stepped across to the bed and opened the drawer of the cabinet on my side.

I reached in and took out the Fetherlites, which had lain there since Prim had decided that she had been on the pill for long enough. I opened the pack and looked inside. 'Funny,' I said, in a normal Oz voice, if a bit fuzzy around the edges, 'There's six here. I thought I only had five.'

She reached inside my jockeys and grabbed me firmly by the balls. 'Fine,' she said, 'but if you don't stop all of this nonsense, they will be nothing but reminders of a distant past. Now say, "Sorry, Primavera."'

I didn't hesitate. 'Sorry, Primavera.'

'Apology accepted,' she said, without slackening her grip. 'Now come here.'

She had my undivided attention. There was nothing else I could do.

20

There was a pink thing on the floor beside the bed, shapeless, like a discarded nylon pop sock. I was lying face down, my head hanging off the mattress, so that when my eyes swam slowly back into focus, it was the first thing I saw.

In those waking moments, I felt disorientated, and unsure of where I was. It was a lonely feeling. When you're thirty years old, and have no experience of loneliness, that can be scary.

At last I could see properly. The pink thing was a used Fetherlite, lying on the tiled floor, shrivelled and knotted beside its foil wrapper. My eyes swivelled round like a chameleon's, and spotted five left in the packet which lay open on the cabinet. '*Whose idea was that?*' I mused, until I remembered that it had been mine.

'What time is it?' I croaked. My mouth was full of ashes, and a wee man with a couple of hammers was playing a xylophone tune inside my head. There was no answer to my question. I reached behind me and beyond. Prim's side of the bed was empty and the quilt was turned back.

I swung myself out of bed with an effort and looked at the clock radio. Eight forty-five, it told me: not too bad. The bathroom door was closed, and from inside I could hear the sound of the shower. With instinct driving me to find something resembling a disciplined routine, I pulled on my running shorts, stepped into my trainers, and ventured out into the morning, jogging at first, then upping my pace until it could almost have been described as running.

The first mile was murder, but once I had paused to urinate

like a true Continental in the bushes by the track-side, things gradually became easier. Three or four miles later, I felt like someone I recognised, even though I was sat on the ground in front of the church, my chest heaving and my body pouring out sweat that probably tasted a lot like draught Estrella Dorada. The wee man with the hammers had gone, and my mouth was moist again.

I left my steaming trainers, socks and shorts on the stairs, outside the front door, and stepped back into the apartment. The doors to the terrace were wide open, and Prim was outside, leaning over the patio table, looking undeniably tasty in her cream cotton Bermudas.

I crept up behind her and put my hands on her hips. She jumped and sniffed, without turning around. 'Don't touch me,' she warned. 'At least, not till you've showered.'

I stepped back from her, aware suddenly that a small puddle was forming on the tiles around me.

'Do you feel better now?' she asked, her back still to me.

'A thousand times. It's the only real hangover cure.' I paused, and leaned over to scratch the back of her right thigh. 'I'm sorry about last night, love.'

'Why?' she said, turning at last. 'You were magnificent.' She smiled. 'Oh, you meant about earlier on. That's okay. You redeemed yourself.'

I looked over her shoulder, at the table. Upon it, Gavin Scott's print lay unrolled, weighted down by four mugs.

'What is it?' she asked. 'It's fantastic.'

'You should see the original. Let me shower and dress and I'll tell you the whole story.'

I disappeared into the apartment. I washed my face thoroughly in hot water, then lathered my stubble. Looking in the mirror, I remembered my last shave, and where I had had it. I closed my eyes and let a picture of Jan form in my mind. She smiled at me, sadly, shook her head, then faded away.

Fifteen minutes later I stepped back on to the terrace,

smooth-chinned, showered and dressed, my eyes still a touch blood-shot, but otherwise presentable. Our standard breakfast of tomatoes, bread and cheese, and hot coffee, lay on the table. Scott's print of the apocalyptic toreador was spread on the floor.

As we ate I told Primavera the story of our client's bizarre gamble, and of our commission to try to ensure that it paid off.

'Are we up to this, Oz?' she asked, when I had finished.

'Course we are. Listen, woman, you were the one who proposed this business venture. Don't go wobbly on me now.'

She pursed her lips. 'No. You're right. After that last thing we pulled off, Phillips and Blackstone are up for anything.' She thought for a minute or two. 'Right,' she said at last. 'Here's what we do. The first priority is to find this man Trevor. We've met him once, in Gary's; so we begin by going back there. At the same time, we should take this print up to the Dalí Museum in Figueras and let the curator there have a look at it.'

I held up a hand. 'No way!' Stopping Prim in full flow is not easy. You certainly don't say, 'Excuse me.'

She glared at me, but I stuck to my guns. 'We can't do that, for Christ's sake. How do you think the curator might react if we show up on his doorstep with a print of an alleged Dalí that doesn't appear in any catalogue of his work, and isn't mentioned in any biography of the man?

'At the very least, he'd throw us out. At worst, he'd think we were forgers and would call the Guardia Civil. You and I have applications in the pipeline for resident status. I doubt if they'd be confirmed if we were banged up in Figueras nick!'

She looked at me, her 'man or a mouse' glare. 'Nonsense. We've got our letter of engagement from Mr Scott. We can show him that.'

'Sorry, but that's cobblers. Who's Scott to him? What would that letter mean?' I eye-balled her across the table. 'Anyway, there's another scenario. What if Scott's picture is the real thing? A genuine, uncatalogued, unknown Dalí? I've seen the original, and it's some piece of work. You might think that the print looks great, but believe me it's two-dimensional in comparison.

'He said it himself. If it's genuine, it'll be worth millions. So, if it's genuine, how come it shows up in Ronald Starr's very discreet, very private auction in Peretellada? And how come our client picks it up for a trifling two hundred and sixty thousand? I'll tell you why. Because stolen works of art will sell for about one tenth of their true value on the black market.

'I doubt if it's occurred to our client, or he wouldn't have given me this print to wave around the countryside, but if Gavin has bought himself a genuine Dalí, then it's a pound to a pinch of pig-shit that it's stolen goods.'

She looked at me. 'So should we take it to the police?'

'Fine, let's do that. Let's tell the Guardia the whole story. Then a few things might happen. They might simply laugh at us, and that would be all right. Or, they could confirm that the thing is a fake and start a hue and cry looking for the forger who's putting the Dalí industry at risk. Last but not least, they could authenticate it and issue an international warrant for our client's arrest on a charge of handling a stolen masterpiece.'

Prim surrendered, with an ill grace. 'Okay, Mr Clever. So what should we do?'

I paused, savouring my victory. 'We should find Mr Ronald Starr, and ask him the questions that Gavin Scott left unasked when he bought the picture, because he wanted the thing so much that he just switched his brain off. If he was an agent at the auction, who was the principal? And how did he or she come to own it? While we're looking for Starr, we should ask a few general questions about Dalí, and about anyone who might be up to imitating him.'

'Ask questions of whom?' she asked, grammatically.

'Of other artists, of course. And I think I know where to

find some.' I reached across and squeezed her hand. 'You were right about one thing, though, my dear one. It starts with Trevor. Tonight, we're dining out.'

'Okay,' she said, 'but the rest of the day we spend getting this business of ours into shape. You said that you had other correspondence.'

I nodded, and retrieved my document case from its pocket in my flight-bag, in the bedroom, where Prim had dropped it the night before. I showed her our three enquiries, and talked them through with her.

'Yes,' she said, 'you should do the one in Tarragona. I'm not so sure about taking on both the others though.'

'Why not?'

She frowned. 'They both want quick responses. We don't want to spread ourselves too thin.'

'Listen,' I said. 'These are both Edinburgh companies. If we give them a prompt effective service, they might tell their pals about us. If we give them the bum's rush, or crap service, they're sure to tell their pals about that. If we find ourselves short of hours in the day, then we hire casual help.'

'Yes, but what about admin, and invoicing, and so on?'

'No problem. I've persuaded Jan to come in with us, to handle finance. She'll do all our billing in Scotland, routed through Jersey, and she'll handle first responses to enquiries, like she did with these and with Gavin Scott. That's okay with you, isn't it?'

There was a silence for a while, which worried me for an instant, until I realised she thought I'd take her approval as read. 'Yes, of course,' she said finally. 'I've got no problem with that.' She paused. 'Shirley Gash might help us. Not that she needs the money, but she did say that she's desperate for things to do with her time.' She stood up from the table. 'I'll get the computer, and we can draft our responses to these people.'

I watched her as she strolled back into the living-room and picked up the lap-top. All at once my eye fell on a piece of paper on the floor. 'Hey,' I called to her. 'We forgot about that fax from last night. Bring that too.'

She nodded and bent to pick it up. 'It's from someone called Gregor, at Laing's,' she said, glancing at the heading. She read on down the page. By the time she re-emerged on to the terrace, her mouth was hanging open in a silent gasp, and her eyes were wide with surprise. She handed me the fax without a word.

I read it aloud.

Hi Oz,
I had an immediate response from the manufacturers to your enquiry. Giorgio of Beverley Hills gentleman's wristwatch, serial number 930100, was sold on February 22, last year, by Jackson's of Bristol.
The registered owner is Mr Ronald Starr, of 126 Glannefran Hill, Mold, Clwyd, Wales. He should be pleased to hear from you.

'Pleased!' said Prim, huskily. 'I'd have thought that even "astonished" would be an understatement!'

21

I leaned on the terrace wall, freshened-up coffee in hand, gazing out across the sun-washed mountains. 'Christ, Ms Phillips,' I said, over my shoulder, 'but we're some investigators, are we not. Imagine, finding Ronald Starr as quickly as this.'

Behind me, Prim laughed ironically. 'Sure, it'd be great, if he wasn't dead. And also, if we hadn't lost him again. Or had you forgotten that?'

'You must be joking. Misplacing a skeleton is not something that slips your mind after a few days.'

I turned and sat down beside her again at the table. 'You realise, don't you, love, that Gregor's fax makes this a completely different situation. For openers, it means we're looking for someone else.'

'Possibly,' she said, 'but not necessarily.'

'How d'you make that out?'

'Maybe the man in the coffin *was* the host at Gavin Scott's dinner?'

I shook my head. 'Look, Scott's evening at Peretellada took place late in June, three months ago. Suppose the auctioneer was killed the day after, and the body buried up there by the church. When Miguel and I saw it, the skeleton was clean. Like, I mean there were no . . . bits . . . on it.

'Now I know we've had a hot, humid summer, with a few heavy rainstorms at night. I know the coffin lid was open. I know that with the movement of earth you get around here, it wasn't buried that deep for all that it was a Roman relic. Yet still; you're the one with the medical background. You tell me, could that corpse have deteriorated to that extent in such a short time?'

She thought about it for a while. 'I'm a nurse, Oz, not a pathologist. I'm no expert in rates of decomposition. However, I have worked in Africa, in a war zone, and I have come upon bodies that had been lying in the open for up to four months.' She shuddered. 'None of them were in the condition you describe. Even with vultures and other scavengers, none of them were as clean as the skeleton you described. There were always . . . bits . . . left.'

She paused. 'Okay. Starr bought his watch a year and a half ago. Maybe the man in the coffin stole it before he was murdered. Maybe the real Ronald Starr was the man at the auction.'

'Maybe,' I said. 'In theory that would be good news. It would mean that we have a UK address for him, where we can at least start looking.

'But just let's stick with the possibility that the guy in the coffin was the real Ronald Starr. The skeleton is missing, remember. What if the police have it? What if, even as we speak, they are hard at work trying to identify it by dental records?'

'How would they know where to start?' Prim asked, almost in protest.

'They can look at dental techniques and materials used, and take a fair guess about where the work was done. Then there was the belt, and the scraps of clothes. Maker's labels would tell them his likely nationality. Once they have that . . . plain sailing. I have a dentist pal. He gets asked for patient records far more often than you'd think.'

I looked at my partner for a few seconds, letting my arguments take hold. 'Suppose we turn up with Ronald Starr's shiny watch at or around the same time as the Spanish police identify his skeleton? Don't you think that they, and the British police as well, would give us some funny looks?'

'True,' said Primavera.

'Thank you. Now here's the really scary one. Let's say we have the authentic Ronald Starr in that stone box, since last year. Yes?' She nodded. 'Right. Then, three months ago, at Gavin Scott's dinner, the host introduces himself as Ronald Starr. Let's discount completely the possibility that there might be two Ronald Starrs with two "R"s along this small stretch of the Costa Brava.

'What we're left with is the certainty that Ronald Starr Mark Two knew he didn't have a rival for the name. My guess is that the man we're trying to trace isn't just a con-man, or an art-thief. He's a murderer.' I gulped as I said it. So did Prim.

'Where does that put Trevor?' she asked.

'God alone knows. It could put him at the graveside, holding a shovel. Although he needn't necessarily know about any of that. But let's not kid ourselves that you and I can pick out a murderer simply by looking him in the eye. Bitter experience tells us that's not the case. No, the one certain thing is that when we approach Trevor, we'll have to do it very carefully.'

'I couldn't agree more,' said Prim. She stood up, and began to wander around the terrace that had become our office. My eyes followed her. She really was devastating: beautiful, dynamic, bursting with energy. A few days before I had asked her to marry me. What sane man wouldn't have?

At last she turned towards me again, her back to the sea. 'Oz, is there any way we can find out more about Ronald Starr? We really need to know all we can about him. Dead or alive, this whole affair seems to fit around him.'

'Sure,' I agreed. 'The problem is how we can do that, without arousing suspicion, or drawing attention to ourselves.' I thought about it, until a small idea switched itself on, like a dim light bulb, in the back of my brain. 'There is one possibility. Back home, I used to do some work for a credit control company. Those guys get everywhere. They have databases like you wouldn't believe. Another of my football pals works there, and he owes me a couple. I could ask him if his outfit has a file on Mr Starr.'

'Good,' said Prim, resuming command. 'You do that. Meantime, let's draft those responses to our other clients. We don't have all day. We're due at Shirley's at two-thirty.'

22

I called my pal Eddie just before lunch-time by his clock; by ours it was thirty-five minutes before we were expected to arrive for afternoon drinks with Shirley Gash.

Eddie is a creature of habit. He works in a big glass office in Edinburgh's new financial district, each day in his working life taking hundreds of dispassionate decisions, any one of which, he knows, may result in some poor wee woman he has never met and never will meet being refused extended credit to buy a new washing machine, something which is probably essential if her six kids are to have clean clothes every day, or a new cooker, essential if their meals are to be cooked properly.

Eddie hates his job, but he does it anyway, because it's a job, and because within his decision-making limits he is allowed to exercise a tiny element of his own judgement, which might sway the balance occasionally in the poor wee woman's favour.

Like many guys in his position, Eddie has a safety valve. Every working day, he and four pals take a taxi along the Western Approach Road, past the brewery, to the Diggers, where each of them has two pints of McEwan's eighty shilling ale, and a pie, for lunch. Actually, the Diggers isn't called the Diggers, not officially. The name above the door is Athletic Arms, but it's straight across the road from the Dalry Cemetery, thus . . .

I could picture Eddie, slipping on his jacket with an eye on the clock, cursing as the phone rang.

'Two-one-four-three.' He growled his extension number at me.

'Eddie, hello. It's Oz.'

'Blackstone! Where the eff are you? I spoke to Gregor last night. He said you'd been in buying gold jewellery for this absolutely gorgeous big brunette, but he thought you were heading back to Spain.'

'I was. I did. That's where I am now.'

'With the gorgeous big brunette, you lucky bastard?'

I coughed. 'Aye, the weather's lovely. A few clouds in the sky, temperature in the low seventies. Just about par for the course.'

'I see,' said Eddie. 'Not with the gorgeous big brunette. So what can I do for you, you horny bastard, if it's not a lift to the football you're after?'

I glanced across the terrace. Prim was sat at the table, checking the faxes which she was about to send to our three potential clients. She gave me a quick grin.

'That magic database of yours,' I said to Eddie. 'You're forever boasting that it's the best in the business.'

'That's right. All human life is here, my man. Even you. In fact I looked you up for fun this morning, after Gregor said he'd seen you. You seem to be doing very well.'

'Pleased to hear it. Listen, I've got a name. Mr Ronald Starr – two Rs – 126 Glannefran Hill, Mold, Clwyd, Wales. I need info about him, if he's in your computer.'

There was a pause at the other end of the line. 'For fuck's sake, Oz. Have you never heard of the Date Protection Act?'

'Of course.'

'Well . . .'

'I don't think it's a problem.'

'Hah! It's a problem, all right. A major league problem. A go to jail problem.'

'Not if the subject's dead, surely.'

Eddie hesitated again. 'I'm not sure about that, even. But this guy Starr, are you sure he's dead?'

'Either that or he's got helluva thin over the last few months. Skeletal, even. Look, Eddie, I don't want financial info. Only some background stuff: married or single, occupation, employer and when was the last time that any trace of him showed up in the system.'

A great exhalation of breath came down the phone line like a roar. 'Christ, I don't know, Oz.'

I sighed, as loudly as I could. 'I hate to do this, Eddie, but d'you remember that time . . .'

'. . . when my mother had that problem, and you had a word with someone. Aye, okay. Enough said. Look, you don't want this just now, do you? Only the lads are waiting for me.'

'No, of course not. But if you can give me a call from home tonight.' I gave him my phone number.

'Okay,' said Eddie. 'Around six o'clock, our time.'

'Great. I'll be here. Be clear, man, this squares us.'

There was a growl. 'Too fuckin' right it does, pal. Too fuckin' right!'

23

'She's fantastic,' Prim had said of Shirley Gash. It turned out to be true, literally. Shirley is the stuff of fantasy, without a doubt.

I had seen her before, a couple of times at tables on the other side of the Trattoria, and on another occasion dining beneath the trees in the square at St Marti, with a man. I had been struck by her each time, but meeting her up close was something else.

'Come away in, folks,' she boomed from the top of the wide stone stair which led up to her front door. The villa's high, wide iron gate had slid open as if by magic as I had pulled the Frontera to a halt in the street, giving us access to a wide driveway.

Prim waved and trotted up the steps, with me at her heels, as always. At the top, she stood on tiptoe and kissed our hostess, on both cheeks.

'Shirley,' she said, turning to me. 'This is Oz; Oz Blackstone.'

'Hello, love. Great to meet you after all I heard from this one at the weekend.'

All at once I was engulfed, by arms and a flowery muslin wrap, and by a great bosom, encased in a peach-coloured swimsuit. I hadn't realised how big she was until then. She was at least as tall as me, slim enough, but strongly built, with breasts like racing airships, so she could never be model thin. I found out there and then that Shirley Gash is one of nature's great huggers. When that splendid woman, in her pastel colours, hugs you, it's an experience akin to falling into a field of sunflowers.

'Hi,' I said, when I could. 'Just as well we've been formally introduced, isn't it.'

She roared with laughter and threw an arm around my shoulders, drawing me into the villa. Rude as it was, I gazed around. I couldn't help it. This was not your average Spanish holiday home. Everything about it was on the big scale, as if it had been built to scale for Shirley . . . which in fact turned out to have been the case. The square entrance hall led to a huge living-room, beyond which I could see a roofed-over terrace, so big that it put ours to shame.

I was about to step through its double doors when she took my arm. 'No, this way, love. It's too nice a day to sit in here.'

She led me through a door at the back of the hall and out into the sunshine. I looked around, and whistled. Three tall, thick palm trees shaded a corner at the back of the house. Two more stood off to the side, with a hammock slung between them, and other mature shrubs and flowering bushes were set around the grassed over area. But the garden was dominated by the pool, around twenty metres long, I guessed, and rectangular in shape. It was surrounded by a paved terrace, beyond which, on the left, I could see a summer-house, stone-built like the rest. It seemed large enough for a family of four, with big arched wooden doors which opened into the pool area.

'Like it?' asked Shirley. I nodded, speechless.

'Clive, my late husband, and I,' she said, with strong traces of a Midlands accent, 'we built it together. He was in the furniture business, manufacturing and importing. He started the company from scratch and did very well. A few years ago he was killed in a helicopter crash. My son does most of the running of the business now, along with my brother, so I decided to hand the place in Staffordshire over to him and spend most of my time over here.' The mention of adult offspring made me look at her again, playing my 'guess her age' game. I lost. Shirley could have been anywhere between thirty-five and fifty . . . as, it turned out, she was . . . but the way she looked, at that first meeting, only a fool would have cared.

'How do you find living here?' I asked her, and not simply to make conversation.

'It's okay in the summer,' she replied, with barely a pause. 'But sometimes, in the winter, when it's quiet . . .' She looked at me, with a big open smile. 'Frankly, love, it gets on my tits. But when that happens at least I can bugger off back to the UK.'

She showed us to a group of garden seats, big double loungers, like wooden sofas, with thick cloth-covered cushions. Some of them were set in the shade of the palms. 'Make yourself comfortable, won't you. Clive had these made for us in the factory. They're placed so that you can sit in the sun, or sit out, whichever you prefer.' Since I had coated myself in Piz Buin before leaving the apartment, I chose the sunshine. Prim took a seat tucked away under the palm leaves.

'I've made up sangria and sandwiches,' said Shirley. She glanced at Prim. 'I don't know if he'll be joining us or not. You can never tell with that bugger.'

All of a sudden she cupped her thumb and middle finger to her lips and whistled. It was the sort of piercing sound that would put a line of bo'sun's pipes to shame; the sort of whistle that most wee boys dream of being able to do, but very few can; the sort of whistle which, up close, threatens the integrity of your eardrums. In theory it should have been one of the least lady-like things I had ever seen – or heard – in my life, yet in no way did it detract from the glamour of the larger than life Shirley Gash.

'Oi,' she shouted across the garden, in the general direction of the summer-house, 'are you coming out or what, you old bastard?' She gazed towards the big wooden doors for a while, but nothing stirred. Finally, she shrugged her shoulders and vanished indoors, to reappear with a big tray laden with a huge plastic jug of sangria, four beakers, and a plate piled high with baguette sandwiches.

The voice came from over my shoulder, taking me by surprise. 'Hope that wasn't me you were shouting at. I respond to "Adrian" most of the time, but never to "You old bastard".' Prim and I looked back, simultaneously, towards the house. A man stood there, smiling. The door offered little head-room and so he almost filled it, although he was of no more than medium height. He was wearing cream slacks and a shirt to match, with a tiny crest on the breast pocket. He had a neatly trimmed beard, and his dark, sun-tinted hair was cropped to around the same length, giving his head a sort of 'fitted' look.

'No,' said Shirley. 'I leave out the "old" in your case.' She turned towards us. 'Prim, Oz, this is my brother, Adrian Ford. He arrived on Sunday night for a week. Treats this place like a bleedin' holiday camp, he does.

'You off out to play again, then?'

Adrian nodded. 'I should get another eighteen holes in. I won't be home for supper, Shirl, I shouldn't think.'

'If you are, you're taking me out. I don't mind giving you a roof, but you know better than to look for me in the kitchen.'

'Course I do, Sis.' He leaned out of the doorway, kissed her, smiled and nodded to Prim and I, then vanished into the house.

Shirley stared after him. She was trying to frown, but I could tell that she was pleased by his attention. 'Bugger!' she muttered. 'Still, he is my little brother and I do love 'im. He's come over here as often as he can since Clive died, and since he got divorced. Five or six times a year; just to make sure I'm all right, he says. He means it too. He probably will be back this evening, and if he is, he will take me out for dinner. John, my son, says he's a bloody liability in the business, but fuck it, it can afford him.'

'Where does he play his golf?' I asked.

'At Torremirona, the new course up towards Figueras.'

She turned back to the sangria and poured us each a glass.

'I promise you,' she said, 'this isn't too strong. You can come a right cropper with sangria. All the bars make it differently. There's brandy in most of them, gin in others. Christ, I've had some where I've been sure there's been bloody strychnine lurking in there.

'This is safe, honest. Here,' she picked up the plate, 'have some grub.'

The sandwiches turned out to be filled with anchovies and *escalivada* – sliced peppers and onion fried in olive oil. They were all absolutely fresh, and the bread was still warm. 'D'you bake this yourself, Shirley?' I asked, half in jest.

'Yeah,' she replied, completely in earnest. 'I buy in the dough, freeze it, then just stick it in the oven when I need it. That's how bleedin' bored I can get out here. I mean, baking my own bread. If my Clive can see me now, he must be roarin' with laughter, wherever he is.' She glanced briefly downwards as she ripped off a handful of baguette.

'Go on, then,' she said, *escalivada* sandwich held ready for action. 'Tell us your story, then. Everybody's got one out here. We get all sorts of couples turning up along this part of the Costa; Brits, French, Germans. Hell of a lot unmarried, very few of them with too much to say about what they did in England. Most of them are knockin' on a bit, though. You two are the exception. You're the first pre-wrinklies I can remember settling down out here. So what brought you?'

I looked at Prim. She smiled and nodded very slightly, amusement in her eyes as she wondered what I would say. I think I surprised her by telling the truth. 'I was in the investigation business in Edinburgh. Prim and I did a job on a paid-by-results basis. We got a great result, got paid a lot, and thought we would move out here for a while.'

Prim nodded. 'That's right. But after three months, like you, we were beginning to get lethargic. Hence the new business.'

'Lethargic in three months! And you've got a bloke. I've been here three years, and all I've got for company is him across there. When he deigns to pay me a visit, that is.' She wiped her chin and jerked a thumb in the direction of the summerhouse, all in the same movement. 'So have you cut your ties with Scotland?'

'Yes,' said Prim.

'Not exactly,' said I, in the same moment.

'Oh yes?' said Shirley, looking at us, from one to the other and back again.

'What I mean,' said Prim, 'is that we agreed when we left we didn't want to live there any more. What Oz means is that we've realised that, apart from family ties, if we want to make this business work we must have a home base. That's about right, isn't it, darling?'

I couldn't do anything but nod. It was the truth, chronologically, and I could live with it, even if it didn't take account of subsequent developments. But for a moment, it did bring a picture of Jan back into my mind, and a pang to my stomach as my internal hamster did another lap of its treadmill.

'Shirley,' said Prim, judging that the moment was right, 'we might need the odd bit of research assistance with our commissions. We were wondering if you'd be interested in helping us. I mean the sort of research you can do by telephone, not knocking on doors at midnight,' she added, hurriedly.

Shirley looked at her in surprise, then beamed. 'You mean it?' she said. 'Too bloody right I'd be interested. When Clive was alive, I used to be involved in the business. But our John doesn't like having me around in the office. He says it undermines his authority. So my business year now consists of three board meetings . . . that's me and him . . . and a personal appearance at the staff Christmas party. I do a mean Shirley Bassey, mind.'

Without warning, she sprang to her feet, and for a moment, I thought that we were in for 'Goldfinger'. Instead, she put her hands on her well-rounded hips and looked across the garden, towards the summer-house.

'Hey,' she called out. 'At bleedin' last. The great man puts in an appearance. Get yer arse around here, Davidoff, and be sociable.'

Both Prim and I followed her gaze, across to the summer-house. One of the big wooden doors stood ajar. Moving at a leisurely pace, a figure emerged into the daylight. My first impression was one of total darkness, as if someone had cut a hole in the day. He wore a black silk T-shirt, black slacks with a razor crease, black shoes and black socks. His skin, that which we could see, was deeply tanned, and his hair though it was cropped into the side of his head, and into a sharp 'V' on top, had the same silky sheen as his shirt. Setting it all off, he wore a flamboyant black patch, silk once again, over his right eye. The other gleamed and flashed darkly.

He ambled round the pool, with determined disinterest, his mouth set in something akin to a scowl . . . until, in the shade behind the palm trees, he caught sight of Prim.

In a flash, he was transformed. The scowl became a grin of delight, the malevolent eye lit up like a small sun, and he straightened. His stroll turned into a brisk, almost military walk, as he bustled forward, ignoring Shirley and me.

'Primavera, my dear one,' he said. 'This great fool of a woman tells me that she had guests. I guess it is some of the unspeakable Belgians that she has here all the time. She does not tell me it is you, my brightness.'

He seized her hands in his and kissed them, pressing them to his mouth. Prim gazed, smiling, up at him. It was the first time I had ever seen her overwhelmed.

'Oi!' If there had been coconuts in the palm trees, Shirley's bellow would have shaken them loose.

'Stand up straight, you 'orrible little mongrel, and leave the lady alone.'

He did as he was told, although his shining gaze stayed fixed on Primavera.

'This is Oz,' said Shirley, heavily. 'Oz Blackstone . . . and listen carefully to this bit . . . Primavera's partner and lover. Oz, this, for what it's worth, is Davidoff. Don't ask me what his other name is.'

At last he turned his eye towards me. I could almost feel it as it ran me up and down. 'Listen to her,' he said. 'Who needs more than one name, my friend? I am Davidoff, you are Oz, and she, the lovely Primavera. These names are enough for us.' He turned to our hostess. 'And this, of course, is Shirley. Sure there are a million fucking Shirleys in the world, but I bet you don't find another like this lady.'

He spread his arms out in a great, expansive gesture. 'We four, we are all unique. You meet us you never forget us. Not like the unspeakable Dutch! They are all the fucking same, in their caravans with the bicycles fixed on the back, crawling along the roads like fucking tortoises.

'And Oz, my new friend, you are special above all men. You have a prize beyond jewels. You take to your bed this lovely woman, for whom even my body lusts without shame, even if it is also without hope. Spend wisely the days of your youth, my boy, for they are numbered, and they are running out.'

He was hypnotic, the man, his hands gesticulating, waving, swooping as he spoke. I looked at him, trying to guess his age, but he was even harder to place than Shirley. Davidoff seemed to have been fashioned out of leather. His dark olive skin seemed smooth as velvet, and it had a suppleness which made me suspect that it had been oiled. His hair, on closer inspection, looked almost certainly to be dyed, but there was no trace of shadow or stubble on his chin to confirm this.

The only thing about him which seemed to hint at significant age was the white of his eye. In fact, white was no longer an appropriate term. It seemed to have darkened as if to match the rest of him, to a shade of yellow which was almost approaching amber.

Abruptly, he turned back to Primavera, and bowed. 'Come my dear,' he said. 'Let me take you for a walk around Shirley's garden, and let me show you where she permits me to live when I am here.'

He held out a hand for Prim as she stood up. It was only when she stood beside him that I was able to gauge his height. He seemed to be elastic, for as she came to his side he seemed to stretch by a couple of inches, standing erect at around five feet nine. I shook my head in amusement as they moved off towards the pool and sat down once more, beside Shirley.

'Where did you find him?' I asked.

'Clive found him,' she said, shaking her head, 'or he found Clive. I was never sure which. He told me that they met in a bar, in-country somewhere, one day when he was out on his own for a drive. They got talking and they just hit it off. They bonded, I suppose you'd say. Clive invited him to stay in the summer-house whenever he felt like it. In return, and without ever being asked, he started to do odd jobs around the place. All sorts of things. Cleaning the pool, painting, some gardening.'

She pointed above our heads. 'See those palms? As they grow, every so often the lowest leaves go yellow and have to be cut off close to the trunk, with a saw. It's a hell of a job, but the old fellow manages it, no bother. He just shins up the things like a monkey and gets to work.

'After Clive was killed, when I came back and told him, he was distraught. He sat in front of the summer-house sobbing his little heart out, for about half a day. Then he got up and started to gather up his things. I said to him, "What the hell are you doing?" and he said, "I will go. You will not want me here now." I just told him. "Don't give me any of that macho crap. You're my friend too. That hasn't changed." So things went on as before.'

'How long has he lived with you now?'

She smiled. 'We've known him for six or seven years now, but he doesn't live with me. He comes and goes as he pleases, unannounced. He might stay here for a month, or two, then he buggers off and it'll be weeks before he's back.'

'What nationality is he?'

Shirley looked at me, quickly. 'Oh, he's Catalan, make no mistake. You're meant to assume that; he gets very huffy if anyone asks him that question. And whatever you do, don't call him Spanish.' She pointed to the summer-house. A small pole rose from the right-hand gable and from it, a small red and yellow striped Catalan flag fluttered. 'That's his personal standard,' said Shirley. 'When he arrives, he parks his little Noddy car up at the back gate, and runs that up the pole. Most times that's how I know he's taken up residence.'

She laughed. 'The old bugger. He's like a mobile gnome sometimes. He's all over Prim just now, but he'll go for days without saying a word. He's never up before midday, and never in bed before midnight. He wanders around but never gets in my way. I like to sunbathe in the buff, and he just lets me get on with it, pottering around, pruning the plants.'

I looked at her in surprise. 'Don't you . . .'

She shrugged. 'You sound just like my son John, the way you said that. Davidoff always says that at his age he's only a man in his head. According to him his balls don't work any more . . . like those of the unspeakable French, he says. Davidoff doesn't like any nationality, other than Catalans and British.'

'What age is he?'

Shirley sat silent for a moment or two. 'Gawd knows,' she said, eventually, shrugging. 'Look at him.' Together we gazed across the pool, as he ushered Prim into the summer-house, behind the wooden doors. 'I've asked him, but all he'll say is, "Older than you, cherub." I've tried to guess, but I can't get near it. If you see him normally you'd probably say he was going on seventy, but there are moments . . . like when he's quiet, when he needs a shave, when that bloody depressing Tramuntana wind's been blowing for three or four days, when the sun isn't shining . . . when you can detect a great sadness in him. When that comes over him, you could believe that he's a lot older than that.'

I stared at the door, which had closed behind them. 'And when he's not here, where does he go? Where does he live?'

She shrugged again. 'Gawd knows, again. I never ask, he never says. I look at him sometimes and I remember this cat that Clive and I used to have in England. He was ours from a kitten. He had an electric cat flap, and a magnetic key that fixed on his collar. We fed him and looked after his vet shots and everything, and he came and went as he pleased. Quite often, when he came in he'd be stinkin' of fish or cat food. We knew that he had another home, that someone else was feeding him and enjoying his company, as well as us, but we never found out who it was.

'Sometimes I think that Davidoff's like him, that there's another Clive and Shirley somewhere, none of us knowing about the other.' She grinned. 'But so what. He's a one-off and I love him, and when he's around, I never feel like buggering off back to Britain.'

We sat in silence for a while, staring at the closed doors. 'He must know a lot of stuff,' I ventured eventually. 'About Catalunya.'

'Christ, yes. But he doesn't talk to just anyone. You're all right, though. He likes you.'

'How do you know that?'

'Because he didn't ignore you. That's what he does with most people, first time he meets them.'

As she spoke, the wooden door creaked open again, and Prim emerged, smiling, with Davidoff at her heels.

They rejoined us arm in arm. Prim sat down again, and Davidoff beckoned to me. 'Come on, my boy,' he said. There was something about him that made me think of *Zorba the Greek*, and Anthony Quinn's great line to Alan Bates, '*Let me teach you to dance.*' Then I realised what it was. His English, good as it was, was overlaid by a slight but distinct American accent, as if he had extended his vocabulary and polished his grammar by watching movies. I stood up and followed him, a Theodorakis tune playing in my head.

We strolled along the side of the pool. 'Like I told you, young Mister Oz,' he muttered, 'you are a lucky man to have a woman like that. She makes my blood boil like it has not for many years. You must take nothing for granted, if you are to hold on to her.'

'Seems to me,' I said, 'you're pretty lucky yourself, to have someone like Shirley for a friend.'

'That I know. But then so is she, to have someone like Davidoff to look after her, and to help her get over Clive.' He sighed. 'Not that she will ever do that. Her son, John, he is no help to her. When he visits Shirley, I go away. Adrian, he is all right. He's a nice guy, but John, no. He is such a prick. He thinks he knows everything, that one. He pushes Shirley away from the business even although it is hers, and he makes her feel useless.'

I glanced at him. 'We've asked her if she'd like to help with some work we've got.'

'Ah, that's good. You could tell, then, how lonely she can be. That's kind of you.'

'Not entirely. We really do need help. All of a sudden we've got quite a bit of work on our hands.' I stopped at the deep end of the pool, not far from a Bouganvilla which exploded from the garden wall.

'Davidoff,' I began. 'You must know all there is to know about Catalunya.'

He laughed. 'The only man who thinks he knows everything about Catalunya is the President of our Government . . . and he is wrong. But Davidoff knows more than anyone else. How can I educate you?'

'What can you tell me about Dalí?' I asked him, feeling unaccountably nervous all of a sudden.

He turned to fix his eye on me. 'You ask about Catalunya, and you ask about Dalí. That is interesting. Dalí was probably the least typical Catalan there has ever been. The average Catalan man, he keeps himself hidden from outsiders, he is reserved among strangers, he is tight with money, he is not flamboyant in any way. As a race, Catalan men seem to feel an inferiority.

'Dalí was the opposite of all these things. He is the most famous Catalan there has ever been, more famous even than Carreras. It's good you are interested in him.'

He paused. 'What did they say about him in his obituaries? Salvador Felipé Jacinto Dalí i Domènech, born on the eleventh of May, 1904, at number 20 Carrer Monturiol, Figueras. Died in his apartment in the Dalí Museum on the twenty-third of January 1989. A genius, self-proclaimed, yet also by acclamation. The greatest surrealist artist of all time. He was larger than life, he was a showman, he was a great egomaniac, he was an internationalist, and he was generous to a fault. Everything that normally the Catalan is not.'

I stared at him. 'You knew him?'

He smiled. 'I could tell you everything there is to know about Dalí. But it is better that I show you. Yes, Oz. Someday soon I will show you.'

He walked me back to join Shirley and Prim. 'Now,' he said, 'it is time for Davidoff to rest. The little vampire must go back to his box to prepare for the night.' He blew a kiss to Primavera, turned on his heel and walked, straight-backed, off to the summer-house.

24

'You know, Oz, you men will never cease to amaze and amuse me.'

Prim was at the wheel of the Frontera, driving along the beach-front of Riells as we wound our way home from our afternoon with Shirley Gash and Davidoff. She shot a sidelong, smiling glance at me.

'What d'you mean?'

'It's your attitudes. This male thing you have about perceived rivals. You're like bloody lions, all of you. I thought you might have been different, my Oz, but you're not.'

I growled, deep in my throat, grinning at her.

'No, seriously,' she said. 'You men, you sit there, at the head of your pride – Christ, you even call me your lioness, on occasion – looking ever so sure of yourselves, but all the time really insecure: because every time another young lion comes along, you react instinctively to him as a threat, someone who has to be seen off. Look at the show you put on with Steve Miller last night. That was a classic example of it.'

That riled me. 'Come on, that guy is a balloon.'

'Of course he is,' she countered. 'He's a smarmy, conceited prat who thinks he's God's gift to women. But did you consider for a minute that I might have been capable of working that out for myself, and of seeing him off? No you didn't. Your involuntary male reflex came into play. "Cor', there's another young lion after my lioness. Better see him off sharpish." Straight away your chest was puffed out, your eyes were burning, and your whole posture was aggressive.'

'And you women, you resent that, do you?'

'On one hand, yes; because it implies that you men see us as possessions. On the other hand, no; because it's good for our egos, and because secretly most women are taken by the thought of men fighting over them, even if it is only handbags at ten paces. But that's not my point.'

'Then what is?'

'That it's an ageist thing.'

'Eh?'

'Think about it. You ran Steve Miller, a guy your own age, right out of town because he showed an interest in me. Yet this afternoon, Davidoff kissed my hands in the most seductive way imaginable, and you laughed. Then he walked me round the garden and into his boudoir, and you sat there chatting to Shirley.

'Why? Because he's an old lion, as old as Methuselah, and so you didn't perceive him as a threat. You felt vulnerable with Steve and complacent with Davidoff, and you were dead wrong, twice.'

I laughed, although something told me I shouldn't. 'You fancy Davidoff, do you?'

'Don't make a joke of it,' she snapped. 'Steve Miller repels me, Davidoff is fascinating. He's charming, wise, considerate, and flattering. Guys like Steve shape themselves to suit the circumstances and to gain their own ends. Davidoff is constant, unshakable and ageless, and he's got the gift of making a woman feel wanted for herself, not just for her . . .' She paused, searching for her words.

'What he tells a woman, by his whole behaviour towards her, is that if she permits him to please her in any way, she is bestowing a great honour upon him. That's a hell of a lot more romantic than the slobbering kisses of a dozen Steve Millers, I can tell you.'

'Mmm,' I mused. 'Shirley says the old fella's balls don't work any more.'

She withered me with her glance. 'There's more to it than

balls, my man. Jan and Noosh would be the first to tell you that.'

I felt my skin flush, and it must have showed, even in the car, because her look became quizzical. 'You still haven't come to terms with that, have you?' she said, with a note of surprise in her voice. 'Your ex taking up with another woman. I don't suppose there can be a bigger blow to the male ego than that.'

She parked the car outside our apartment. She didn't know it, of course, but she had given me the perfect feed, the perfect opportunity to tell her of the sea-change in Jan's life and of the confusion into which mine had been thrown as a result. I suppose if I was as honest a bloke as I've always liked to think myself, I would have taken it. But right then, Flora Blackstone wasn't looking over Prim's shoulder, telling me to do the right thing.

For all that, I should have told her as soon as I got off the plane, back there in Barcelona airport. But I didn't, as I couldn't then, because I wasn't ready.

You might think that it's every young man's dream, to be in love with two really gorgeous women. Wrong. Actually it's a nightmare, because all the time you know that sooner or later, you'll have to choose. Worse, one of them – God forbid, both – might choose for you. Whatever happens, down the road someone gets hurt. Chances are everyone gets hurt. Chances are, when the smoke clears, you wind up sleeping in a mostly empty bed, back in the life of carry-out kebabs, frozen pizzas, and too many bevvies with the lads.

I knew all this, but I still . . . or was it because of it . . . I climbed our winding stair and kept my trap shut. You see, I still didn't know the answer, the reason that Jan had talked about. It was in there, but I just couldn't find it. To my great relief at that moment, though, Prim must have thought that she'd gone too far, since she chose to resume our discussion of the functionality of Davidoff's nuts.

'Anyway,' she insisted. 'He would tell Shirley that, to make her feel completely comfortable around him. Think on this, too; even if it is true, there might just be a few women who would welcome the challenge of reviving them.'

With that remark, I decided that a tactical sulk was called for. The strategy seemed to have worked, for no sooner was the door closed than Prim wound her arms around my neck, pulled me to her and kissed her.

'Just in case you were getting the wrong idea,' she murmured, unbuttoning my shirt, 'I'm not thinking about trading you in for an older model.' She unzipped my cotton trousers. I couldn't help it; I flipped the waistband button of her Bermudas.

'Mmm,' she whispered, with the beginning of the wicked smile that I knew so well. 'Now that's no challenge . . . no challenge at all.'

She rose to it, nevertheless.

Afterwards, as we lay outside in the evening sun, I thought back to Prim's theorising on the drive home. 'Hey, what you were saying earlier,' I teased her. 'Since you're so hot on ageism, how come you left me alone with Shirley, after the welcome she gave me?'

She laughed. 'One, because Shirley's still too much in love with her husband to look at any other man, two, because underneath that outrageous front, she's very much a lady, and three, because I trust . . .'

She stopped as the telephone rang, and as I jumped up to answer it.

'Oz, s'at you?'

'S'me, Eddie. Any luck?'

'Luck's got luck all to do with it. I told you our database is the best in the business. Your man Starr's on it . . . in a way.'

'Eh? What d'you mean in a way? He's either on it or he isn't.'

'Aye well,' said my pal, 'that's the thing. He's on the blacklist. He owes his credit card companies a few hundred and the interest's mounting by the month. According to his file, Starr is a lecturer at Cardiff College of Art. He's single, aged thirty-four. He was a tenant at the address you gave me. It's a college house, apparently. But for over a year now, the credit card company's had mail returned from there, stamped "gone away".

'There have been no transactions on his cards for about a year now . . . no attempt to use them, I mean, because they've both been pulled. But Oz, the daft thing is, he's in credit at the bank, and he has a building society account with thousands in it. Both those accounts are frozen, pending court actions against him in Wales by the Visa and Mastercard operators. They both got judgements last month, and they're on the point of enforcing them.'

'Did Starr defend the actions?'

'No. The bailiffs for the pursuers couldn't serve the writs, so they had to place a public notice in the local press advising of the hearings. No one turned up on the day, though.'

'What about the art college? Do they know anything about him?'

'The database doesn't say anything about that, Oz.'

'Does it list a next of kin?'

'No.' Eddie paused. 'Look, what's all this about, China? 'Cos if you're certain that this guy's Hovis, and it looks as if you could be, you should report it.'

'Ahh,' I said. 'It's not quite as simple as that. I've just had information that he is, but I'm not in a position to prove it. What you've told me is very useful, though. It clarifies one or two things.'

'So what more d'you need to prove it?'

'A body would help, Eddie. See you. Thanks.'

As I hung up, Primavera appeared at my shoulder, slipping on her dressing gown, and with mine slung over her shoulder. For the first time, I noticed the gathering cool of the autumn evening.

'What did he have?' she asked.

'From what he told me, Starr seems to have vanished last year. That makes it all the more certain that our pile of bones is him. Eddie did have something new to add, though. The man was an art teacher, in Cardiff.'

'That's interesting. So how will we follow that up?'

I tied the cord of my robe. 'I guess by calling the Cardiff College of Art. Maybe the people there will be able to tell us more about the probably late Mr Starr.'

'Excellent,' said Prim. 'That gives you something to do tomorrow. Meanwhile, we have an earlier engagement, remember. Dining at Gary's, in search of Trevor.'

I gave her a pretty good grimace. 'After what we've learned so far, I'm not sure I want to find him. Still, there is one plus point.'

'What's that?'

'We can put dinner on expenses.'

25

I never have found out what Gary's surname is. I don't know of anyone else in L'Escala who knows it either; simply because no one I've met has ever asked him. That's the sort of place L'Escala is.

Although it's only a few kilometres away its attitudes, compared with those in St Marti, are light years apart. In the village where Prim and I made our home, the rare outsiders who manage to buy property and choose to become permanent residents find themselves subject to direct, and not very discreet enquiries, until their backgrounds and much of their intimate business is known.

In L'Escala, though, a poncho-wearing stranger could ride into town on a sway-backed burro, stay for a year, kill all the local bad guys and ride out again, without anyone knowing as much as his name, unless he had chosen to give it.

All we knew of Gary was that he was a nice bloke who ran a restaurant. We had learned second-hand from Shirley that he had arrived in town a couple of years before, had liked the place and had decided to stay and open a business.

He was waiting for us in his pocket-sized dining room, at the top of an alley behind the church, his hand out-stretched in greeting, and a smile of welcome on his face, when we arrived just before 9 p.m. 'Hello there. Dead on time as usual. It really helps, your being able to come now. I've got Maggie and five friends booked in for nine-thirty, so I'll have you well under way by then.'

We were used to the ways of Gary's, a one-man operation where everything is bought fresh and cooked fresh, and where evenings are planned with military efficiency, and run that way until the last course is served to the last table, and everyone can get pleasantly pissed.

Prim had made our menu choices by telephone when she booked, and so, even allowing for his timetable, we were able to relax over a beer with our host before we ate.

We talked about this and that; our new business venture, Gary's opening schedule for the winter months, and the success of the tourist season which was just winding down . . . something many Catalan business owners do not care to discuss in public, just in case the tax hombre may be listening at the next table. But we didn't rush to ask any questions. We had agreed that in the circumstances – since our discovery about Starr had changed the nature of the game – that tracing Trevor was a subject to be handled with care. Also, Gary had told Prim earlier of his booking for six, and we had decided to sit tight, on the off chance that our man would be one of the number.

Our salmon steaks were on the table when the sextet arrived. We looked up as they entered, one by one; Maggie, whom we knew, a German couple named Manfred and Lucy, whom we had met there before, and the three Millers, parents and son. Maggie gave us her usual generous 'Hello', Manfred and Lucy came along to our table to shake hands, but the Millers settled into their places at table, with the briefest of smiles.

Prim kicked me under the table, and, her hand out of sight under her napkin, pointed across in their general direction. I took the hint, rose from my place, and walked over to Steve. I tapped him on the shoulder. 'About last night,' I said, trying not to choke. 'I'm sorry if we got off to a bad start. I didn't mean all that crap (*lie*). I had a few beers too many on top of a heavy day (*truth*).'

He reached round and offered a handshake. 'That's okay, Ozzie, old chap,' he said, loudly and magnanimously . . . there's nothing worse than an arsehole like him being magnanimous to you. 'No harm done.'

When I sat down again at our table, I could see the effort with which Prim was suppressing her grin. She knows how much I *hate* being called 'Ozzie'.

The ice was broken, though, and our two tables soon became an informal arrangement of eight, with the inevitable increase in wine consumption to which that leads. I had given up hope of us getting any more out of the evening than a good meal and a good bevvy, when all of a sudden, we had an ally.

'Hey, Gary,' called Maggie, in her sharp, northern accent. She runs a service company for villa owners, and her success is built on being able to arrange absolutely anything. 'That chap Trevor Eames. 'Ave you seen him lately? Only Steve 'ere wants to fix up some sailing lessons when he comes back at easter; and Trevor does that, doesn't he?'

'Yes, that's right,' said the restauranteur. 'You won't find him just now, though. I know for a fact he's away crewing, on a big sailing boat out of Ampuriabrava.'

'When will he be back?'

Gary sucked in his breath. 'I'm not sure. You never can be certain with these casual trips. But from what he was saying, I wouldn't look for him to be around before next week.'

'Oh dash,' said Maggie. 'Steve goes home on Friday.'

I saw my chance and stepped into it. 'Tell you what, Steve,' I said. 'Prim and I have been talking about learning to sail. Why don't we look him up when he gets back, and make an arrangement for you while we're about it?'

'Would you, Ozzie old chap? That'd be great. I'm due back on April two next year, for a fortnight.'

'Zero problemo, Stevie son. D'you know where this Trevor lives, Gary? He is the bloke we've seen in here, isn't he? Wee chap, bald head, skin like a walnut.'

Our host looked up from the bar, where he was sorting out the bills, and nodded. 'That's the man; that's Trevor. Never at a loss for a word. But I'm sorry, Oz, I don't know where he lives, only that it's somewhere in L'Escala. He has a boat in the marina, though, with a little day cabin, and with a couple of dinghies which he uses for teaching strapped to the roof. You'll usually find him around there, when he's in town. It's called *La Sirena* something. *La Sirena Two*, I think. I've got no idea where his mooring is, though.'

'Thanks, Gary. We'll start looking for him next week.'

'Okay. If he comes in, I'll mention it. Do you want me to send him along to see you in St Marti?'

That was pushing it. 'No, that's okay. There's no guarantee we'd be in. We'll find him ourselves, don't you worry.'

26

We managed to escape from our extended dinner table without doing ourselves too much damage, and so my morning run was a much less harrowing experience than that of the day before. I even completed a few feeble push-ups in front of the church before heading back up to the apartment.

When I came in, carrying my trainers this time, having judged them safe to be allowed indoors, Prim was showered and dressed and looking pleased with herself. She didn't even wait to be asked. 'I've been on to international directory enquiries. The number of Cardiff Art College is on the pad beside the phone.

'And we've had a fax confirming theTarragona commission. They want a report by the beginning of next week, if possible. The client has arranged for you to do the interview on Friday.'

Thinking again about my trainers, I tossed them out on to the terrace. 'No problem. Have they given us details about the subject?'

'Yes. She's Spanish.'

'Christ, that's a small detail they haven't mentioned before. Still, we are called Blackstone Spanish Investigations, so they're entitled to make the assumption.'

Prim nodded. 'That's right. So we just hire an interpreter and put translation costs on the bill.'

'Sure, but where will we find an interpreter for Frid . . .' I caught her eye, and her smile, and read her mind.

'Davidoff.' We said the name in unison.

'D'you think he would?'

'We can only ask,' said Primavera. 'But if *I* ask him, I think he might.'

We ate breakfast on the terrace as usual, then tossed a coin to decide who would wash the dishes and who would call Cardiff College of Art. I won.

The man on the switchboard told me that the principal's name was Mrs Adams, and put me through to her office. Her secretary turned out to be a more formidable obstacle to clear. 'I'm sorry, but the principal is a very busy person. "Confidential matter" is not good enough.'

'Okay. I'm a private investigator. I'm making enquiries on behalf of a client about a member of your staff. Mr Ronald Starr.'

'Hold on, please.' Her tone didn't change but I could tell that I had cleared the hurdle. She was back on the line in less than ten seconds. 'I'm putting you through.'

'Mr Blackstone?' Mrs Adams had the rich deep voice of a Welsh rugby commentator. I wondered about Mr Adams. 'You say you're making enquiries about Ronnie Starr?'

'That's right.'

'Mmm. Do something for me when you find him, will you. Tell him to get back here and empty out his bloody locker!'

For a second I thought she was about to hang up. Maybe she had been, but I stopped her. 'Hold on, Mrs Adams,' I said quickly. 'If I'm right you might as well clear out his locker yourself.'

I held my breath, waiting still for the hum of a broken line. 'You think Ronnie's dead?' she asked, at last.

Perhaps I had gone too far. 'It has to be a possibility. When did you hear from him last?'

'I haven't heard from the man since the day he left us, in June last year. I did expect him back in October, to start a new contract. But he didn't appear. No letter, no call, nothing. I was keeping his job open, and his college flat unlet. He let me down. Left me with a roll of students and no one to teach them. I even had to get paint on my hands again.'

'Mrs Adams,' I ventured, 'can you tell me a few things about Ronald Starr? What was his speciality?'

'He was a painting tutor. Good all-rounder, but his main interest was surrealism.'

'Was he a good painter?'

'Exceptional,' she barked. 'I've no idea why he was teaching, really. He could have supported himself by painting professionally. In fact he should have. He was that good.'

'His own work, it was surrealist too, yes?'

'That's right. The chap had a tremendous range. His colour choice was fantastic, the way he blended them together. He could make a canvas sing.'

I began to tremble. All of a sudden, the jigsaw seemed to have fewer, much bigger, pieces. I pushed it a bit further. 'When he left, last year, d'you know where he was going?'

'Yes,' she said, heavily. 'He told me he was bound for the north of Spain. To paint, and to research the Catalan surrealists. The king of them all, of course, was Dalí. Ronnie Starr worshipped him. He seemed to know his whole portfolio, off by heart. He could mimic some of it as well.' Her booming chuckle startled me. 'He could do a great soft watch, could our Ronnie!'

27

When I called Gavin Scott on his mobile, he was in the middle of a meeting. When he called me back fifteen minutes later, I could hear other voices in the background.

'Sorry, Oz,' he said. 'We've got a major business pitch this afternoon. You rang in the middle of the dress rehearsal. You got something to report already?'

'Yes, Gavin. It's nothing concrete, but let's just say that a pretty strong possibility has opened up. You might not like it, though.'

I heard him take a deep breath. 'Try me, anyway.'

'Okay. Let's start with the man named Trevor that you described to us. Does the surname Eames mean anything to you?'

There was a few seconds' silence, then, 'Yes! That was it. Trevor Eames. That's how he introduced himself the first time that we met.'

'Okay, that's a good start. We've found him. At least we know where he is. He's out on the Med for the next week or so, helping sail some rich German's schooner. As soon as he's back we'll see what he can tell us.'

'That's great,' said Scott. 'Quick work. Now what's the bad news?'

It was my turn to take a deep breath. 'There's bad, and there's worse. It looks as if your Dalí isn't a Dalí after all, but a brilliant fake by a very gifted painter.'

'Who?'

'Ronald Starr,' I said. 'He was a lecturer at an art college in Wales, and a real student of Dalí.'

'What! The guy who was the host at the dinner?' Scott's voice was raised. In the background, the hum of his colleagues' conversation suddenly fell silent.

'This is where it gets worse, Gavin. Ronnie Starr disappeared from his job, and from everything else, over a year ago. We don't know who your mysterious auctioneer was, but we're pretty certain that he wasn't the real Starr.'

'Why are you so sure?'

'Because we have very solid reason to believe that Ronnie Starr is dead.'

Via satellite, I heard Gavin Scott gasp. 'Hold on a minute,' he said. 'You lot,' he called to his staff. 'Leave me alone for a bit, please.'

Down the line I heard the sound of shuffling, mumbling, and finally, a closing door. 'Okay, be more specific. Are we talking heart attack? Accident?'

'No, I don't think so. We're talking violence. We're talking about Ronnie Starr being talked into painting your undiscovered Dalí masterpiece, then being murdered, before the picture was sold to you at that bizarre auction.'

'Jesus!' There was another long pause. 'What should we do now? Should you go to the Spanish police?'

'Absolutely,' I said. 'If I had any sense, I probably would. So it's just as well I haven't, because your door would be the first they would knock on.'

'Why, for God's sake?'

'Well, for starters, because I doubt if the way you bought a quarter of a million pounds' worth of picture, then transported it out of Spain, is entirely legal.'

Scott spluttered. 'Come on, Oz. I acted in good faith.'

'I'm sure you did. I bet you didn't get a VAT receipt though. Spanish IVA taxes on your buy would be around eight and a half million pesetas. Alternatively, the Customs and Excise could do you for evading duty. It's a case of take your pick, although maybe they could both do you.

'If that's not enough, think on this. I'm not in a position to prove that Starr was murdered. But the evidence could turn up any day now, if it hasn't already. Then the police have a scenario where you tell them that you paid over a quarter of a million for a painting by a murdered man, at a phoney auction. All they have is your word and your friend Foy's for that.'

'And Trevor Eames . . .'

'. . . who may be implicated in the murder. He's going to back you up, is he? Sorry, without the phoney Ronald Starr, what they'll see is you being offered the picture by the real one, knocking him on the head, and using it as a scam to steal four hundred thousand US from your own company. As for Foy, he's your pal. How likely are they to believe him?'

'Oh shit!' The sound of heavy breathing bounced off the satellite. 'What am I going to do, Oz?'

'Burn the fucking picture and forget you ever heard of me?' I offered, helpfully, but knew that was a non-starter as soon as I said it.

'Then I really would have embezzled a quarter of a million from my own company. Besides, Oz, I couldn't bring myself to do that. I hear what you're saying about this guy Starr having painted this picture; but suppose, just suppose that you're wrong. Suppose this is what it was said to be at the auction, an authentic Dalí, but privately owned and therefore unknown. What if I burned it, then found out that it was the real thing, and that it could be authenticated?'

'And if it turned out that it had been stolen?'

The reply came without a moment's hesitation. 'Then I'd return it to the owner, assuming he claimed it . . . provided that its existence is acknowledged to the world. Oz,' said Scott, 'I want you to carry on, if you're prepared to. The brief is still the same. Find out the truth about this picture, one way or another. Will you do it, or is it too dangerous for you and your partner? If the Toreador can be authenticated, I'll pay you a bonus.'

I glanced across at Prim. I knew what she would say. 'Okay, we'll carry on, but without a variation in terms. Forget the bonus. I do need two things, though. I know you weren't keen on me approaching your friend Foy. The way things are going, I think I have to talk to him now.'

There was a moment's hesitation, but finally Scott said, 'Okay. As I told you, David felt terribly guilty about involving me in the auction. I wanted to spare him involvement, but if you think it's necessary, carry on. What's the other thing?'

'I want you to get details for me of the bank where your draft was cashed, and the account through which it was processed.'

'Okay,' said our client. 'I'll get you that as soon as I can. Look after yourself.'

'No worries,' I assured him. 'I hope your people get the business today. You may need it to pay our fee. This could be a long job.'

28

While I spent the rest of the morning drawing up work plans for our two commercial commissions, Prim took the car and drove up to Shirley's, on Millionaire's Row, above L'Escala.

She returned two hours later, flushed with a cocktail of flattery and success. 'For you, my lovely Primavera, and for my friend Oz,' she mimicked in a Hispanic-American accent, 'it will be an honour and a pleasure. No, more than that, it will be an adventure.'

She laughed. 'Tarragona! Davidoff has not been to Tarragona for forty years. When I come into middle age, I decide that Barcelona was as far south as I wished to venture. Now that I am old, even Girona seems like too much trouble. But to Tarragona, and with Senor Oz. Yes, that will be an adventure.'

She finished her monologue and looked at me. 'One interpreter hired and ready for action. He is even, and wait for this, going to get himself out of bed before midday for the occasion. You can pick him up at nine o'clock. Shirley says that it's an easy two-hour drive to Tarragona down the autopista. Your appointment with Senora Compostella is at midday, so you'll have plenty of time.

'I guarantee you one thing. You'll have plenty of chat on the way down. Shirley said to me she hasn't seen Davidoff come out of his shell like this since her husband died.'

'I'm looking forward to it,' I said. 'Maybe I can quiz him about Dalí on the trip.'

I thought back to Prim's mimicry. 'Have you worked out yet how old he might be?'

She shook her head. 'No, I still can't get close to it. There's a tremendous vitality about him, and with that jet-black hair and the sleek skin, you could almost see him being in his sixties. But it's that eye of his. He fixes you with it, and you feel that you could be staring into the mists of time.'

'Time,' I said. 'Yes, time. As in lunch-time. Fancy a salad down in the square? I really need to talk to Miguel.'

Prim nodded her agreement. We locked up the apartment and strolled round to the heart of our hamlet. The archaeologists were still having their effect on business, and the tables outside the restaurants were busier than we had been assured was normal for the time of year. Nevertheless, our usual table near the door was available, and Miguel showed us to it, handing us menus automatically, although we knew his carta by heart.

I motioned him to join us as we attacked our chicken, rice, and side-salads. 'Still many peoples,' he said, as he sat down.

'Yes,' I agreed, 'but none of them police, which would have been the case for sure if we hadn't moved our chum.' The smile left his face in an instant.

'Miguel, I think we know who the body was.'

'How?' he whispered, incredulous. I took the watch from my pocket and showed it to him discreetly, in the palm of my hand. He gulped in fright. 'You . . . How . . .'

'I put it in my pocket at one point, and forgot to replace it. We traced him from its serial number. Now we need to find him again. Have you had any word from your wife's nephew's wife in the local police?'

His face fell, a guilty look spreading across it. 'No, Oz. Not yet. To tell you the true, I have done nothing about it. I decide that the best thing was to forget about it.'

I shook my head. 'Maybe it was, but not any more. The guy was murdered, Miguel. He doesn't deserve to be tossed in a ditch and forgotten. Your tourist trade is safe. Now we owe it to him to try to ensure that he has a decent burial, and that whoever killed him is made to answer for it.'

He sighed. 'Okay, Oz, okay. I will see what I can do. I will speak to Santi and ask him to try to find out from Ramona if the local police know about the body. And don' worry Oz. I will be . . .'

'. . . discreet, Miguel. Yes, that's still a good idea.'

29

'Four weeks on Saturday.'

No 'hello'. No 'how are you?' No such pleasantries. The phone rang, I picked it up and that was all the voice at the other end had to say.

'Dad?'

'Who else?' came the cheerful growl.

'Aye, right, but what was that you said?'

'Is this a bad line or something? I said, "Four weeks on Saturday." This Saturday coming that is. Eleven-thirty, St Andrews Registry Office, lunch at the Peat Inn thereafter for the principals and families.'

I was aware that my mouth had fallen open. 'For fuck's sake, Dad. I liked it better when you were predictable. Whatever happened to, "Round about Christmas"?'

'Change of plan.'

'Christ, Auntie Mary isn't . . . Is she?'

'Cheeky bastard,' It was half growl, half laugh. 'The fact is, your sister's got a permanent teaching job in that private girls' school, what's its name, in St Andrews. She got the word on Monday afternoon. It's only fifteen minutes' drive away, so, with Jonathan settled in at the primary here, and wee Colin at nursery, it seems daft for her to be looking for a flat, when she can stay on where she is. D'you agree with that?'

'Completely.'

'That's good. It's all cut and dried anyway, but I thought I'd go through the motions of consulting you. The upshot of it all is that the way is clear for Mary and me to tie the knot, and for me to move into her house on a permanent basis. So.'

He paused and took a deep breath. 'Four weeks on Saturday.'

'That's a deal. We'll be there, don't worry. I take it that Auntie Mary's told Jan.'

'Of course,' said my dad. 'It all came together when she was here on Monday evening. Breaking her news to us.' He hesitated again, then, dropping his voice as if he was afraid he was within someone's earshot, he asked, 'Are you alone there?'

I nodded, as if he could see me. 'Yeah. Prim's gone shopping.'

'Right. That was quite a surprise, Jan's visit. Is there anything going on that Mary and I should know about?'

I tried to sound as incredulous as I could. 'Eh? What do mean, for God's sake?'

'Don't come the funny man with me, son. Jan, having dropped you off at the airport, comes home especially to tell us that she's been split up from Ms Turkel for the last couple of months, and that she's living at your place. We know that you stayed there on Sunday night; then Jan turns up wearing a new piece of gold, and looking like two million dollars. What d'you expect Mary and I to make of that?'

I tried a touch of bluster. 'Aw come on, Dad, how long have Jan and I known each other?'

'Aw come on, nothing. You're not playing games with the lass, are you? Or with Primavera for that matter?'

'No, Dad,' I said. I had never been able to bullshit Mac the Dentist. 'No games. It's just that I thought that everyone had settled down to live happily ever after, me included. Now the whole board game's up in the air.'

'Well, just you get it back on the table, son, and you remember this. People are not chess pieces.'

'I know that. I'm a people myself, remember. Last Sunday was a total surprise to me too. I had no hint that Jan was on her own again. And I'll grant you it's set me on my heels. Until then I was as happy as Larry, not a cloud in the sky. Why, last week I asked Prim to marry me, again. She said, "Fine, No rush. Let's wait a while." Now . . .'

'Aye,' said my dad. 'What about now?'

'Well, it isn't that I don't love Prim any more, that's for sure. And I've never thought of her as just another live-in. It's just that getting together with Jan last weekend . . . it wasn't like before. We're both older, and wiser for a start.'

'You're both grown up at last, you mean.'

'I suppose so. All that time she was with Noosh, I thought, "Fair enough, as long as she's happy." Anyway, she wasn't completely gone, if you know what I mean.'

'I know,' he rumbled. 'She told us that too.'

'Aye, okay. You could say that we were just using each other all that time. I don't know. What I do know is that we were always there for each other, up to a point, without ever asking ourselves any serious questions. When we were kids, Jan and I never discussed "us", quote unquote, you know. We just were. We didn't need to keep telling each other, "I love you." We knew it anyway.

'I still love Jan and she loves me, but she's got her life sorted out now. It could be that I won't fit into it. And like I said earlier, I still love Prim and we've got out lives sorted . . .'

'Except . . .' said my dad.

'Last week, if you'd asked me I'd have said I knew exactly what I wanted. I've got to work that out afresh, and make a commitment to it, without any guarantees that I'll get it.'

He was silent, but I sensed something. It was a long time since my dad had been worried about me, and it didn't make me feel good. 'Can I take it that you haven't told Prim everything about last weekend?'

'You can take it.'

'Then isn't it time you set out the whole board game for her?' he said.

There was undeniable truth in that, yet . . . 'I should. But we're involved in a bit of business that's taking up most of our attention. Plus . . . ahh, bloody hell, I just don't know what to do!'

'There's nothing new about that, son,' said wise old Mac.

'But at least now you care. Listen,' he continued, 'I think you have to put a time-frame on this. You're coming back for our wedding in four weeks. You'll have to sort yourself out by then. If Jan's the one for you, Prim deserves to be told. If what you have is what you really want, then you have to make that clear to Jan. I'm speaking as a potential step-father here, you understand, as well as your old man.'

A great wedge of truth hit me. 'I feel I should know the answer now, Dad,' I said, spontaneously. 'It's in there somewhere . . . and the reason for it. Like Jan said, what I want is one thing. But I have to work out *why* I want it, too . . . and that's the bugger.'

30

Davidoff was on parade as promised when I arrived at Shirley's at nine o'clock. He was dressed immaculately in uncreased black, scrubbed and oiled like a well greased wheel nut as he appeared through the garden gate at the side of the impressive villa.

Shirley stood in the doorway at the top of the stairs, chuckling and shaking her head as he strode solemnly down the slope towards me.

I greeted him with a '*Bon dia*', and a bow, holding open the passenger door of the Frontera. He returned both, then stepped up into the car, and slid into the back seat. I watched him, astonished, as he folded himself along its width, like a concertina.

Holding up his head to peer awkwardly from his single eye, he announced, 'I promised our lovely Primavera that Davidoff would be ready to leave at nine. I did not say that he would be properly awake. Davidoff needs his beauty sleep. You may rouse me as we get close to Tarragona.'

Just for a moment, when he referred to Primavera as 'our' my mind flashed back to her lecture on ageism, but I let it pass, waving goodbye to Shirley as the great black gate closed automatically behind me.

The radio was on as always as we headed down the hill, until a theatrical cough from the back seat made me switch it off. By the time we reached the autopista ticket station, fifteen minutes later, the only sound in the car was a gentle snoring.

Shirley had been right about the drive to Tarragona. Bypassing Barça to the east, the road was straight and fast.

Scenically, it was also very boring. Fortunately, after cruising at my customary fifteen Ks above the speed limit for just over an hour and a half, the Tarragona signs began to appear, and I was able to waken the wee man in the back with a clear conscience.

Nimbly, he slid over the gear lever into the passenger seat. As we left the autopista and neared the town, he grew animated. I suspected that he might even have been excited, but not about to let anyone know it.

It might have been forty years since his last visit, but Davidoff could still recall the way into the centre of town. I had bought a street map the day before and found our destination, but it was almost redundant as the old man directed me, right, left, then right again.

We parked in a public underground garage, emerging into the town's main square at around eleven twenty, with plenty of time in hand for our date with Senora Compostella. The day was overcast, but it was still warm enough to sit in comfort at a pavement café. Davidoff nodded his approval when I asked for a *cortado* – expresso with a little milk – ordering the same, but with a shot of brandy added.

As we passed the time, I briefed him on the subject of the interview and on the questions I had to put to our witness. The case centred around goods manufactured in Spain and supplied in Scotland, by a Scottish customer. The specification was in dispute, and Senora Compostella's evidence was crucial to our client's defence against the argument. If she gave us a strong enough response, there was a good chance that the action would never reach court.

She was ready and waiting for us when we crossed the square at midday and made our way up to the lawyers' office. I smiled as I walked into the room, not just to put the lady at her ease, but because all of a sudden it felt good to be back at work. This was my job, after all, wherever I did it. As I sat down opposite Senora Compostella, I realised that I had been away for long enough.

I could tell right away that she was going to be a good one. There was something in the cast of her jaw and the steadiness of her gaze as she looked back at us, unfazed even by my bizarre translator, that told me she would not prevaricate. I was right. Every one of her answers was on the button, making it clear that the pursuer's version of the circumstance was insupportable. Davidoff performed the translator's duties impeccably, making certain that the witness understood each question before accepting and translating her response.

The interview took forty minutes. When it was over, the lawyer's secretary retired for half an hour, before reappearing with a Spanish transcript. Davidoff checked it against my English notes and nodded. 'It's okay. This is what she said.'

Senora Compostella signed on the dotted line, we all shook hands and at one twenty-five Davidoff and I were back in the square, each of us puffed up with the pleasure of a job well done.

'This job of yours, Senor Oz,' said my temporary colleague, grinning at me, with his eye flashing wickedly. 'It's a nice way to live, yes. Meeting people all the time, persuading them to tell you the truth.'

I nodded. 'Not so long ago, I'd decided that it was a bore. But you're right. There are worse ways to earn your bread.'

'Speaking of bread,' he said. 'Follow me. My old body is crying out.' He led me out of the square, walking so briskly that I had to stretch my legs to keep up with him. We turned into a side street, then an alley off it, which opened eventually into a small square. Davidoff's eye lit up with pleasure as he looked into its furthest corner. 'Ah! It is still there. Wonderful.'

I followed him across to the narrow doorway above which a simple sign, 'Al Forn', swung slightly in a swirling breeze. We stepped inside, into what seemed to me to be just another smoke-stained old bar, with a counter down one side, and booths lined down the other. We were the only customers. As we slid into one of the fixed tables, Davidoff nodded to a middle-aged man, who stood at the end of the bar. He wore a red shirt and black trousers, with a yellow sash around his waist.

The waiter nodded, curious but professionally polite. Davidoff spoke to him in Catalan. I could tell from his inflection that it was a question, and also that it had had an effect, as the waiter's mouth dropped open in surprise. They conversed for a couple of minutes before, following a last guttural burst from my friend, the man nodded and headed off towards the kitchen.

'I just asked him if he is Mario,' said Davidoff, 'and then I tell him that last time I was here he was six years old and playing on the floor where he is standing now. This place has been in the same family for ninety years. Almost since . . .' He stopped, and shook his head. 'No more, though. Mario says that his son is in Barça, studying to be a lawyer.' He spat on the floor. 'Too many fucking lawyers today. Not enough tradition.'

Mario reappeared a few minutes later, carrying a tray on which was piled tomato bread, melon and cured mountain ham. As he placed them before us, a very old woman appeared in the kitchen doorway. Unnoticed by Davidoff, she stared at him, almost in disbelief, with her hand at her mouth. Then with a shake of her head, she turned and was gone.

I wondered about her, but the first slice of melon soon distracted me. 'Davidoff?' I asked between mouthfuls. 'When you were here last, forty years ago, what were you? What were you doing?'

He shrugged. 'Nothing much,' he said. 'I came to this place to speak Catalan. When Franco was around, it was against the law for us to use our own language. But still we did. Here and in places like it, where everyone was known and where the police could not come unnoticed. We would come here and we would speak, sing, recite poetry and debate, all in Catalan. Here we kept the torch alight.'

The eye misted over. 'That's history though. Noble, but still only history. Let's you and I talk about today. Oz, I have a confession to make to you.' It seemed to burst out from him. 'You have a rival. I am captivated by Primavera. I am insanely jealous of you, and maybe I would kill you if it made it possible for me to take your place.'

No adjective exists to describe my reaction. 'Astonished' certainly wouldn't do it justice. I stared at him, and realised that he was deadly serious. 'Well,' I said, when I could, for there was something about his matter of fact declaration that had unnerved me for a second. 'Maybe I should kill you first.'

He smiled. 'Maybe you should, my boy. But don't worry. I like you too much to do you harm. Primavera would not approve, anyway.'

I gave my best 'Who cares?' shrug. 'You never know. She'd be worth twice as much with me gone. Tell you what, I'm not afraid of competition. If you think you've got a chance, you have my permission to pay court to her. Best man wins and all that stuff.'

'Hah,' he laughed. 'Maybe with two bulls such as us competing for her it is Primavera who will be the winner. I accept your gracious gesture. Let us see.'

As we finished our ham, I glanced around. 'Did Dalí come here?' I asked.

'Oh yes,' said Davidoff. 'He came here. He put his sign on the place. A moment.' Beckoning me to follow, he slid out of the booth and stepped over to the end of the bar nearest the door. At its corner a square wooden pillar rose to the ceiling. It was as old as the building and glazed with the latest of many coats of varnish. The dark little man swung the door open, to see better, and began to peer at the far side of the column, feeling with his fingers. At last he nodded. 'Here. Look.'

I leaned in alongside him and looked at the space between his thumb and first finger as he pressed them against the wood. At first I couldn't see it, until I moved my head and found the right angle of light. There it was. The distinctive thistle-like

'D', the 'a', the 'l' and the final sweeping 'í' with its accent mark, carved carefully into the column, varnished a dozen times since it was cut, perhaps, but still marking the place where he had been.

I followed Davidoff back to our booth as Mario reappeared with coffee and brandy. '*La cuenta*,' said the lithe old man, and a few minutes later the bill was presented; nine hundred pesetas. Peanuts, we couldn't buy the ham for that in our butcher in L'Escala.

I dropped a thousand peseta note, and another two hundred for luck, on to the table. 'Good,' said Davidoff. 'Now come with me, and I will show you Dalí. You are my friend, so I will introduce you.'

I was puzzled as I followed him out of Al Forn and back to the car park, but he said nothing more. He stayed silent, too, on the drive back up the autopista, his attention being focused on industrial developments along the way, all of which were clearly new to him, few of which met with his approval. 'Ahhh,' he muttered as we passed a factory on the Barcelona ring road, 'they are raping Catalunya.'

We were north of Girona when he told me to leave the autopista. 'Come off here, and head for Palafrugell.'

I did as I was told, picking up the C255 and following the signs for La Bisbal and beyond. Around fifteen minutes later, with the clock showing almost four-thirty, we had just past Flaça when Davidoff sat bolt upright in his seat. 'Here! Look out, it's coming. A turn to the right.' I braked hard, and just in time, otherwise I would have driven past the tiny white arrow pointing to La Pera. The road was narrow, even by local standards, and twisty, a succession of blind corners leading up to a village which looked, as we approached, like an inland version of St Marti.

'Go round it,' barked Davidoff. 'Take the road to Pubol.' Again I did as I was told, circling La Pera and driving on for another kilometre, until the road petered out, ending in a circular, red ash car park. 'Okay,' he said, as we drew to a halt. 'Now I will show you where you will find the heart of Dalí.'

We stepped out of the big car, and once again I followed his lead, as we climbed up towards a collection of old buildings which barely qualified as a village. I could see a single street, and hear noise coming from what might have been a bar. There was a church tower, with a cross. Beyond them all there was another building; not huge, but imposing, and managing somehow to dominate the local skyline.

Davidoff stopped at the foot of the street. 'You have been to the place in Figueras, yes?'

'The museum? Sure. It's sort of obligatory, isn't it?'

He shrugged. 'So they say. You will have seen Dalí's tomb there.'

I nodded.

'A tourist attraction! Like the whole museum. His grave is part of a fucking funfair to bring visitors to the town. Deutschmarks, francs, dollars, pounds; that's what it is about. But that is not where the spirit of Dalí belongs. This is where it lives today. Come on.'

He bustled off, up the sloping street, with me on his heels as usual. We hadn't gone far before he turned into an opening on the right and led me up a few wide stone steps. There was a turnstile at the top. Davidoff stopped and nodded towards it. I took the hint, and handed over a two thousand peseta note. The blonde girl in the booth gave me two tickets, my change and a smile. I would have returned it, but my guide pushed me through the gate, following behind.

It was a solid stone building, three storeys high, and seventeenth-century, according to a stone over the main entrance on which the numbers '168' could be seen, the fourth having faded with time. It would have been wrong to describe it as a country house, yet it fitted into a category of sorts. Davidoff told me what that was. 'This is the Castle of Pubol,' he announced. 'Legend has it that Dalí gave this place to Gala, his wife. It is true that there she lived her later years.' He led me around the corner of the building, into a garden. While it couldn't have been called overgrown, it was filled with head-high shrubs, set around two parallel paths which led up to a shallow ornamental pool. The impression was one of controlled wilderness.

'Gala's real name was Elena,' said Davidoff. 'She was older than Salvador, but from the moment in 1929 when they met, he was enamoured of her . . . even though she was married to someone else at the time. They ran off, almost at once. They had to be together, for she was as crazy as Salvador was. Dalí worshipped her, he painted her, he indulged her. She invades all his work, and pervaded all his life.

'He promised her that one day he would give her a castle; then one day, by accident, he found this place. He bought it as a ruin, and he renovated it. He put his mark upon it.' Davidoff nodded around him. I followed his glances. The pool was lined with countless images of some composer or other; I couldn't put a name to him. Around the garden, amid the shrubbery, stood several huge statues of emaciated, distorted elephants.

'When it was finished,' he said, with feeling. 'He gave it to her, as hers alone. And he promised her that he would come here only at her invitation.' Davidoff chuckled sadly. 'But she did not invite him often. She had other, younger tastes, and she was able to indulge them here, without him around.'

He led me into the castle's courtyard and up an iron stairway, installed over the original stone steps, which I guess had been judged unsafe. It led into the first floor, a series of interconnecting rooms.

'This is where Gala lived her strange indulgent life. She would surround herself with young men. Like him, look.' We were in the music room. He pointed to a large photo set on top of the grand piano. It showed an ageless, painted lady, beaming with lecherous pride like a decadent Roman empress, as, beside her, a blond, cherubic young man played the same instrument.

We wandered through the fairly ordinary rooms, then up an internal stairway which led to the building's highest level. It was darkened, and filled with a series of display cases, in which an array of clothing was on show. 'There are some of her dresses,' said Davidoff. 'As you can see she was a small woman, like a bird, to the end.'

'She is dead then?' I asked, unsure of anything in this strange place.

'Oh yes. More than ten years ago. Come, I will show you something else.' He set off once more, at his loping half-trot. I followed down the stairs, out into the courtyard and back towards the garden. But not into it. He turned a sharp corner and as I stepped round behind him I found that we were in a garage; once a stable, I guessed, or even a kitchen. It was occupied.

The car was one of the most beautiful I had ever seen; but then I have a thing about classic American automobiles. This one was a Cadillac, a lovely, big powder blue creature, with leather upholstery. Its body work shone under the neon light above, and it was roped off, to keep away the greasy fingers of tourists.

'What . . .' I began.

'Gala lived her last years here,' said Davidoff. 'But she did not die here. When she became ill she was taken, in this car, to Dalí's house in Port Lligat, near Cadaques. And when she passed away, she was simply put back into this same vehicle . . . there, in that back seat there, and taken home.

'Come on,' he said. 'Now I will show you where the spirit of Dalí lies.' He walked slowly now, almost on tiptoe, as we went back into the castle. To the left a doorway led off the courtyard. He led me through it, and down another flight of stairs, of washed stone like its walls and ceiling, and like the great cellar into which it opened.

I looked at the crypt and I couldn't speak. Maybe it wasn't a lifetime first for Oz Blackstone, but it's a pretty rare occurrence, nonetheless. The place was filled with a soft yellow glow from up-lighters, serving to emphasise the colour of the stone. All but a small section of the floor was roped off, but there was no need to move about in this chamber to know what it was.

The far wall was curved, and there the light picked out a number of objects; statuary mostly, save for one. I'd never seen a giraffe before, not even in a zoo, but I guessed that this one was perhaps half-grown. It stood maybe eight feet tall, long neck crested by its small face, its spotted amber coat shining, stock-still; stuffed.

It held my gaze until I was able to tear it away to look at what lay immediately before me. There were two long rectangular slabs, each ten feet long, four feet wide, six inches thick, flat and standing proud of the floor. In the stone to the right a simple cross had been cut. Its neighbour was unmarked.

'This is the Delma,' said Davidoff. 'This is the grave of Gala, the inspiration of Dalí.'

'And this?' I asked, pointing to the second tombstone.

'This was for Dalí himself. This is where it is said that Salvador declared he would be buried, but he never was.'

'Why not?'

My little friend shrugged his shoulders. 'Who knows? Some say that he forgot how much he loved her. In the end, as always, he was as crazy as a bedbug. People could pour things into his mind. Whether this was poured or not no one knows, but when he died, the people of Figueras just announced that he had decided he should be buried in the museum there.'

'But how could they do that?'

'Easy. Because everything of Dalí belongs to a foundation now. They have the pow and when Salvador died, well, it was god's mouth to their ears. So in Figueras the flamboyant man lies. And Gala lies here by herself.'

His face twisted into a grimace. 'But what has happened since is not good. This place, her private home, has been opened as another museum, another tourist attraction. I do not like that. No one came here when she was alive without her asking them. Why should it be different now she is dead?'

He crossed himself, barely noticeably, and motioned me towards the doorway. We left in silence. The sun was shining into the courtyard when we emerged. 'Did you know Dalí?' I asked him.

He smiled, for the first time since we had come to Pubol. 'Everyone knew Dalí. Dalí belonged to all Catalunya. I guess he still does.'

I looked across the yard. Gala's castle even had its own souvenir shop. I wandered across and looked in at the postcards, posters, and other memorabilia. Among them was a large coffee table book of the artist's life and work, translated into French and English.

I went to pick one up, but Davidoff shook his head. 'No good. I know more than you will find in there. Let's go back to L'Escala. This has been a long day for me.'

'Why not end it,' I asked him, 'by coming to our place for dinner? I have something I'd like to show you.'

'Dinner? Yes. I would like that. First I must go back to Shirley's and sleep for a little. I must be fresh if I am to pay court to Primavera.'

31

Davidoff had never been to our apartment, so I promised that I would be waiting for him at the church at eight o'clock that evening.

I had never seen his car, but when it came chugging round the bend I didn't have to look to see who was inside. It was an ancient Seat 500, rear-engined, and revving away like a sewing machine in distress. Once its paint had been silver, but time and the *Tramuntana*, the cold north wind which drives the sand like rain, had turned it into a shade beyond conventional description.

It was a Noddy car with a roof on, one of those machines which you either love or want to deliver straight to the nearest crusher. I loved it, and so did Davidoff. He beamed with pride as he eased it from its flat out crawl to a dead stop, and as he climbed out and locked the door, I noticed that he had left it in gear. A wise precaution, I thought.

If the ancient had been spruced up for our morning outing, for the evening he was resplendent. He wore a black silk shirt, with a black cravat tied high at the neck, black leather trousers and black patent shoes which shone with a light of their own. His skin shone like oiled olive wood and his close-cut hair was slicked with dressing. To top it all off his eye patch was satin with sparkles set in it.

As he stepped up to me, hand outstretched, I caught a whiff of Bay Rum.

'Well met again, my young friend,' he said. 'May you rue the day when you permitted me to be the suitor of Primavera.'

I laughed. 'Strut your stuff, old man,' I said, probably a

little more brashly than I had really intended. 'The lady is waiting for us upstairs.'

Davidoff had brought with him a bottle of really good *Cava*, straight from the fridge. Not one of your Freixenets, which are all right in themselves, but a Mas Caro, vintage brut, which was better than most champagnes.

We did it justice on our terrace as a large sea bass steamed gently in a kettle on the stove, as the guacamole salad chilled in the fridge and as the candles in their sconces gradually took more and more effect in the darkening evening.

'You are very private here,' said Davidoff, oozing his snakelike charm at Prim and treating me to a show of tolerant disdain. It came to me that maybe I liked him so much because he reminded me of my old iguana flatmate. The only difference was that Wallace never tried to seduce any of my girlfriends.

'Yes, we are,' she replied, showing a leg through the split in her yellow skirt. 'It's very good for the tan.'

'You must be careful of your skin, my dear,' he cautioned. 'It is the most sensitive organ of your body . . . save one, of course . . . and you must treat it with respect. Use the finest creams and moisturisers, or the sun will age it before its time. I see on the beach the old ladies who were foolish in their youth. Now their skin hangs on them like ill-fitting sacks. *Cara mia*, I would shoot you now before I would see you become like them.'

We ate on the terrace, too, but in consideration of Davidoff's age, I lit one of our butane gas heaters and set it near him in the open doorway. He frowned at me as I positioned it, as if he thought I was reminding Prim of his years . . . which of course I was . . . but he didn't ask me to take it away.

My guacamole salad hit the spot, and Prim's sea bass was done to perfection. Our guest attacked them with an enjoyment that would have gladdened any cook's heart, and polished off his poached fresh figs in marsala by wiping the dish clean with his last piece of bread.

During the meal I tried to lure him back to the subject of

Dalí, but he refused the bait. Instead he spoke seriously of the Franco years, of the oppression of Catalunya, and of the brutality of the Civil War.

'I lost many friends,' he said sadly. 'I lost the sight of my eye too. A piece of shrapnel.'

I looked at him in surprise, at his first admission of his years. Wounded in a war sixty years earlier.

'You fought against Franco?'

'Yes. In vain as it turned out.' He looked at Prim with a flashing, gleaming smile. 'I was only a boy, you understand. But it was for my freedom as a man.'

'And did you stay here, afterwards?' She was staring at him, captivated as far as I could see.

'No. I could not bear it. My friends and I went to America. We worked there for most of the forties. That was when I learned most of my English, and picked up this goddamn strange accent.

'Eventually, Franco felt secure enough to let the exiles come back, although he still kept Catalunya under his boot. We were the only Spanish with the *cojones* to stand up to him.' He smiled at Prim, almost coyly. 'I hope your Spanish is not so good, Senora.'

She grinned, and I could have sworn she was flirting with him. 'Good enough, Senor. But Franco's balls must have been bigger than yours, because he died an old man, in his bed.'

Davidoff acknowledged her point with a nod. 'Maybe so. But remember, he had the military, and the garrotte. They were strong deterrents.'

He must have sensed that he had taken his courtship as far as he could for the night, for without warning he turned to me. 'Oz, my young friend. Earlier, you said you had something to show me.'

'Yes, but first, let's clear the table.'

When Prim and I had removed the last of the dishes, I switched on the twin spots which lit up the terrace at night, and picked up Gavin Scott's tube which lay in the corner to my right. I took out the colour photocopy, unrolled it, and spread it on the table in front of Davidoff.

'What d'you think of this?' I asked.

The old boy gasped. A great hissing gasp. His mouth dropped open. Until that moment, I hadn't thought it possible that anything could take him by surprise.

He put his hands on the picture, and I saw that they were shaking slightly. 'Where did you get this?' he whispered.

'The original belongs to a client of ours, in Scotland. It was sold to him at a private auction in Peretellada in June of this year, and offered as an unknown work by Dalí. Look, in the corner. It's signed, but undated. Blackstone Spanish Investigations has been hired to authenticate it, if we can.'

'Who was the owner of this original before your client?' Davidoff asked, beginning to recover from his surprise.

'We don't know. Our client was visiting a pal of his, a bloke called David Foy, an ex-pat who lives down in Bagur. They were invited to the auction by a guy they met at Pals golf club, another Englishman, Trevor Eames, who lives around here. The auction was run by a man calling himself Ronald Starr, who said he was an agent for the owner.'

'Yes?' said Davidoff, intense, captivated.

'The only thing is, we believe that the real Ronnie Starr was dead by then, murdered, and buried in a grave not far from here. The real Starr was a talented artist, and an expert on Dalí. Our theory is that he forged the picture, showed it to someone, and that that person killed him and stole it, knowing that there's always some fool out there ready to part with his money. Our client paid four hundred thousand US for it.'

'Jesus!' The word shot from Davidoff's narrowed lips as if it had escaped. His face was tense and his eye was blazing.

'We've heard a story,' I began, 'that before he died Dalí signed some blank canvasses, backwashes and the like.'

'No!' The little man sat bolt upright. 'I know the people who looked after Dalí before he died. He didn't sign no blank anythings. Towards the end he couldn't even wipe his own ass, let alone autograph canvases. The man buried in Figueras didn't sign anything from the day that Gala died. That I can tell you.'

I leaned over the picture again. 'Could it be older than that? Could it possibly be genuine?'

Davidoff's face creased into a smile. 'No, boy. This is a recent work. And the man buried in Figueras had nothing to do with it.'

'How do you know?'

'Because the vision is not the same. This is not his vision. He would not have seen something like this; it is too, too . . . sympathetic. That's the best that I can explain to you.'

'But it could have been Ronnie Starr who painted it?'

He shrugged. 'Or another artist. There are others, you know. Why don't you ask around?'

I nodded. 'That's what we plan to do.'

'Good,' he said. 'I'll let you go on with it.'

He rose to his feet and drew Prim with him, to kiss her on both cheeks, his lips just brushing the corners of her mouth.

'Now I got to go. You have given me a day I won't forget in a hurry, Senor Oz, but it is over. It is late and I must go. Before the sun comes up and catches me unawares!'

32

Davidoff left at a quarter to midnight. We heard his little car mewling its way into the night, down the track below our balcony. It was hardly out of earshot before we locked up and headed after him.

In the summer, you can tell the difference between the visitors and the locals in L'Escala. They pass each other in the streets; the former group heading home, the latter heading for the night-spots.

Apart from the diners, nothing much happens in La Lluna before midnight. It's only then that the boys and girls come out to play in the bar, and on the pool and speed-disc tables. Prim and I had found the place during the summer. On the doorstep of our thirties, we were older than the average punters, but still young enough not to stand out as oddities.

La Lluna, set back from the road just off Riells beach, is four establishments in one: restaurant, bar, games arcade and art gallery. All around the place, the walls are hung with the work of Girona artists. Paco and Dani, the proprietors, know their stuff, and more than a few of their customers go there with an eye on the pictures as well as the menu. We were among them, and had come to know that Friday night was when the painters came to drop off their work.

Paco was having a break in the doorway as we crunched our way across the gravel. He acknowledged us with a wave as we wedged ourselves on to two stools at the bar and ordered our drinks, then wandered over to say hello.

We shook hands. 'You are well, yes?' he asked.

'Fine, last time we looked.' I pointed to a very tasty still-life on the far wall. 'I fancy that. *Cuanto es?*'

Paco dug into the pocket of his apron and produced a card with prices scribbled on it. 'That one? It says here sixty thousand pesetas. But maybe you could have it for less. Manuel, the artist, he is here. Would you like to speak to him?'

I looked at Prim. She nodded, and Paco disappeared, into the dining room off the bar, returning after a couple of minutes with a stocky man of around forty with long, wild hair, round, bear-like shoulders and intense bright eyes. 'This is Manuel,' he said, 'the artist. From Girona. I leave you to talk.' He vanished once more, this time through to the games room, where the noise was mounting as a speed-disc game reached its decisive moments.

'You like the still-life?' Manuel asked, in good clear English.

'Very much. What's the medium?'

'Oil. On linoleum.'

My eyebrows rose. 'Lino?'

'Si. Linoleum is oil-based itself, so it should be good for painting. I do it as an experiment. Most of my work is experimental.'

He looked from me to Prim and back again. 'Fifty thousand,' he said.

'Visa?' asked Prim.

'Si, just tell Paco.'

'Deal,' she said.

'You choose well,' said Manuel. 'Just don't tell anyone what you pay for it. My work is on show in the galleries in Girona. They would ask for a hundred thousand for that picture.'

'*And it would still be a bargain,*' I thought . . . but I kept the thought to myself. Our new friend was a talented man. His brush work was strong and his colours vivid. Look at the still-life for long enough and you'd swear that it was three-dimensional, and that the glass, the bowl, and the orange were suspended in mid-air.

I decided that it was time to move on to the real business. 'Where did you study, Manuel?'

'In Figueras.'

'Oh. At the same college as Dalí?'

He shook his head. 'No, Dalí studied in Madrid . . . until they kicked him out.'

'Why?'

Manuel laughed. 'They say that he would not sit his examinations. The story is that Dalí declared that none of the examiners were fit to judge him. But others say that his work was shit in those days, and he did not want to be exposed.'

'Is he one of your influences?'

Manuel shook his head. 'No. You would ruin yourself as an artist if you tried to copy Dalí's style. No one has ever seen the world like he did. As far as I can, I try to be myself, with no influences. If I lean towards anyone, it is Miro . . . another great Catalan artist.'

'Do you know of anyone who can copy Dalí's style?'

'I know a few fools who try. None of them can get near it.'

'Someone told me,' said Prim, all innocence, 'that Dalí's supposed to have signed some blank sheets before he died.'

'A legend, Senora. If he signed them, they would be useless, for anyone painting on them would be seen through in an instant. There are people who can copy Miro, who can copy Van Gogh, who can copy Picasso. If it was worth it you could even copy Manuel. But no one can copy Dalí.'

I took a chance. 'Have you ever heard of a man named Ronald Starr?'

I glanced at him as he considered the question. 'No, Senor, never.' He looked genuinely blank.

'Mmm.' I glanced through to the dining room. There were empty tables in the corner. 'Do you have a minute to look at something?'

'Sure.'

While Manuel and Prim moved into the next room, I ran out to the car park, returning with Gavin Scott's tube, and a flashlight. 'What do you think of this?' I asked, spreading the copy on the table and shining the wide beam across it.

The artist leaned across the table, studying the copy, for almost five minutes. At last he straightened up, flexing his great bear shoulders. He smiled. 'What do I think? I think that I would like to see the original.'

'Do you think it could be a Dalí?'

He shook his head, but with a hint of reluctance. 'No. I see the signature, but I don't think so. I almost wish it was.'

'Why?' I asked, probing his wistfulness.

'Because whoever painted this is very dangerous, *muy peligroso*, with a brush in his hand. This person could forge anything.'

33

Manuel's still-life hung, in its heavy black frame, on the wall facing our bed when we woke next morning, just after ten.

'Well,' said Prim, propped up on her elbows and gazing at it. 'That was an expensive night out. Two hundred and fifty quid.'

'Worth every peseta, all things considered. We got a free assessment of Scott's picture thrown in.'

She nodded, acknowledging. 'I suppose so. Should we call him and tell him he's bought a fake?'

'No, not yet. I think we owe it to him to find out a bit more. I think someone owes it to Ronnie Starr, too.'

'So what's next on the agenda?'

'I thought we'd go down to Begur to see David Foy, while we're waiting for Trevor Eames to get back from his voyage. He's the only other person – apart from Eames – who's seen the phoney Starr.'

'Okay. What do we do? Call him first and make an appointment?'

I pondered that one. 'No, let's not. Scott gave me his address. Let's pay him a surprise visit.'

'Maybe we could take Davidoff.'

'I think not. We don't want to terrify the man.' I rolled over on to my front and tweaked her right nipple. 'Did you enjoy yourself last night, then? Being courted and all?'

She smiled down at me. 'Is that what he was doing? I'm flattered.'

'As if you didn't know.'

'Well . . .' she said, almost defensively. 'Davidoff's wonderful.

I don't care what age he is . . .'

'Seventy-five at least, from what he said about the Civil War.'

'. . . I've never met anyone like him. It'd be great to think that you'll be like him when you're old. But you won't. You'll have two point four children and a quota of grandchildren. You'll be straightforward and funny, like your dad, but you won't be dark and mysterious.'

I felt offended. 'No, and I won't be chasing after young women either.'

'That could be a pity. You know what they say about old fiddles!'

I couldn't resist it, I reached for her. 'Sure, but you can play a young one more often!'

34

We picked up a street map of Begur in the tourist information office, and found Starr's house without difficulty in the little inland town.

On the way down I had taken a detour, back to Pubol, so that Primavera could see Gala's castle, and her grave. 'So sad,' she had said. 'That she's left here all on her own. There's something, something . . . not right about it.'

The gift shop was open as usual. Because Davidoff wasn't there to stop me, and maybe to spite the wee bugger, I bought the Dalí book after all.

The Foy villa stood on its own at the top of a little hill. There was a Jag in the garage, and a Citroen Saxo in the driveway when we parked the Frontera in the street at three-thirty. The sky had been leaden all the way down, and as we arrived the first raindrops of the storm began to fall. We jumped out of the car and ran up to the front door.

The man who opened the door was around fifty, but looked very fit for it. He stood about six feet two, with a trim waist and a heavy chest. Frizzy, silver-grey hair rose from his high forehead. Not a man, I sensed at once, you'd be wise to cross.

'Si?' he said, staring at us in surprise.

'Mr Foy? My name's Blackstone, and this is Ms Phillips. We're working for Gavin Scott.'

His eyebrows narrowed. Very, very slightly, but they narrowed. 'Gav? What does he want? Have you come all the way from Edinburgh?'

I shook my head. 'No. We live here too, just a bit up the

coast. We're private investigators.'

He smiled. 'Private eyes, eh. Well, you'd better come in.' He held the big, white door wide for us and ushered us into the house, through to a living-room with a terrace which overlooked the distant Mediterranean.

'You're alone here?' I asked.

'My wife's next door, at the neighbours. It's her bridge afternoon.' His accent was difficult to place. North of England perhaps.

'How did you come to know Mr Scott?' said Prim, as Foy invited us to sit.

'I used to be a client. Jenny and I were in the rag trade in Glasgow and Newcastle, till we sold out and retired here. Gav and Ida still keep in touch.'

'They were here in June, yes?'

'That's right.' The smile returned. 'I think I can guess what this is about now. That picture, yes?'

'Got it in one. Mr Scott has asked us to find out more about it, to try to authenticate it if we can. That means we need to find the man who set up the dinner, and the auction. Have you encountered him again, since then?'

Foy shook his head. 'The mysterious Mr Starr? No I haven't.'

'How about Trevor Eames?'

'I see him occasionally at the golf club.'

'Is he a member?'

Foy grinned. 'To tell you the truth, I've never been quite sure. He's always in tow with someone or other when he's there, although he never seems to be buying. Never seen him on the course, though.'

'When he told you about the auction, didn't it strike you as pretty weird?'

'This can be a weird place, Mr Blackstone. There's more than a few people like Starr around here; not exactly kosher.'

I grunted. 'You can certainly say that about the guy who sold Gavin Scott that picture. For a start, he isn't Ronald

Starr. The real Starr was murdered, almost a year ago. We think he painted the picture that you saw at the auction. And our guess is that the guy who sold it bumped him off.'

'Fucking hell!' David Foy slumped back in his cane chair, all of the colour gone suddenly from his face. Then, just as suddenly, he jumped to his feet. 'I think you'd better go. I've got nothing to say to you.'

'Eh?' Prim and I stared at him, stunned by the change in his manner.

'You heard me. Hop it. Get the fuck out.' He jerked his thumb towards the door, menacingly.

Automatically I stood up, but Prim sat her ground. 'If you won't talk to us, Mr Foy,' she said quietly, 'would you speak to the Guardia Civil?'

'You wouldn't go to them.'

She looked up at him, with her sweetest, most beatific smile. 'Too fucking right we would,' she countered. 'Murder, fraud, maybe art theft: oh yes, they'll want to talk to you. They might even give you a bed for the night.'

He stared down at her, his forehead knitted, then across at me. Finally, he sat down again, in the cane chair. 'Okay,' he said. 'But none of this goes back to Gavin. Okay?'

'We'll see about that,' said Prim.

Foy ran his hands through his thick hair and looked across at us. 'The whole thing was a set-up. It started off as a laugh really. I bumped into Trevor at the club earlier on this year, just before Easter, and I bought him a drink. After we'd had a couple of bevvies, and got a bit relaxed, he started to talk about this chap he knew who'd come by this picture. It was a forgery, he said of a Dalí, but so good that even an expert couldn't put his hand on his heart and swear it wasn't the real thing. He said his mate had asked him to get him a few quid for it.

'He offered it to me first off, for seventy-five thou, sterling. I told him to fuck off. Then I thought about Gav. The auction was my idea. You know what Gav's like with pictures. Thinks he's a connoisseur, a real ace. I told Trevor about him, and I suggested that if the thing was that good, and he accepted it as genuine, then if we could get him bidding for it, he'd go through the roof.' He paused. 'A couple of days later, Trevor called me and said his chum wanted to talk about my idea. We met in the place at Peretellada. Trevor introduced the guy as Ronald Starr.'

'What did he look like?' I asked.

'Ordinary. Around forty. Medium everything. There was nothing about him that stood out.'

'Would you recognise him again?'

'Too right!' said David Foy, emphatically. 'I'd recognise anyone who owes me money.'

'What do you mean?'

'The bastard stiffed me, didn't he. We talked my idea through. Then the guy Starr took me out to his car and showed me the picture. I'm no bleeding expert, but even I could see it was the business. I began to regret not giving him his seventy-five grand. Not enough to change my mind, though. We agreed that we'd set up the auction, and that I'd fit Gav into it.'

I looked at him. I don't think I was smiling at the time. 'Some pal you are. So the meetings with Trevor at the golf club, they were all prearranged?'

'Yes.'

'And the other people at the auction?'

'All hired hands. The whole thing worked a treat. Mind you, Starr went further than I intended. Our deal was that he would fold at two hundred and fifty US, but Starr and his phoney Swiss took a chance and carried on up to four hundred.'

I shook my head. 'But why? What did you have against Scott?'

Foy shrugged. 'Gav thinks he's a real player. I just wanted to show him he was still small-time, that's all.'

'And what was in it for you?' asked Prim.

'Twenty per cent . . . which I never got.'

I smiled at him. 'Appropriate in the circumstances. What happened?'

'I haven't seen Starr since that night in Peretellada. We had agreed that the three of us would meet up there again, a fortnight after the pay-off, to divvy up. Trevor and I showed, but there was no sign of the other fella. Only a message that dinner was on him, and that he hoped we'd enjoy it.'

'Have you tried to find him?'

Foy grinned, ruefully. 'I wouldn't know where to start. I did employ some local talent to ask around, but they came up empty. Like you said, I suppose it serves me right.'

Prim and I nodded, simultaneously, and stood up to leave.

Outside, the short, heavy storm was over. Foy called after us as we walked down the drive. 'You won't tell Gav, right?'

Prim looked over her shoulder. 'You haven't given us a single reason why we shouldn't. What do you think we'll do?'

We left him, staring after us, with a king-size worry that hadn't been there half an hour earlier.

35

Next day we took a stroll round the marina in L'Escala. It was quieter than in July and August, many of the boats having been taken out already for the winter. But there were still hundreds moored in the big basin, and so looking for a single boat was like searching for one anchovy among the shoal.

It didn't help either that *La Sirena* turned out to be the most popular name for a small boat in all Catalunya. We must have found a dozen of them before we happened on what we guessed must be Trevor Eames' boat, moored sharp end in against the quay furthest from the shore.

It was an eighteen-foot sail-boat, with a single mast and a classic wheel, behind the steps leading down to its cabin. *La Sirena Two* was emblazoned on either side of the bow, and a pair of small pram dinghies were lashed, not to the cabin roof as Gary had said, but to the sides.

Everything else was lashed down too. We tried the cabin door, but it was locked, and the windows were curtained. It was pretty obvious that Trevor was still at sea.

On the way back to St Marti, Prim had an idea. 'We really should check out the place at Peretellada, shouldn't we. Just in case the phoney Starr was daft enough to have booked the dinner using his real name.'

'Fat chance, but yes, you're right.'

'Then why don't I,' she said, 'take Davidoff along there with me tomorrow, to ask some questions?'

I looked at her, right eyebrow cocked. 'Oh yes! After some more courtship.'

She grinned. 'And why not. A lady likes to be wooed. You

still don't quite realise that, do you?'

All of a sudden, I was miles away, thinking of Jan and my impulse buy in Laing's. All of a sudden, I was torn in two.

Prim dug me in the ribs. 'Hey.'

'Sorry. Of course I do. I'm just not very good at it, that's all.'

'Well, it's time you put in some practice.'

My conscience must have pricked me, for as soon as we reached St Marti, I dropped Prim off and without warning, headed back the way we had come. She was on the terrace when I returned, looking tense. 'What's up?' she said. 'Why the huff?'

'No huff,' I said, and handed her a small brown box. She opened it. Inside, on a white satin cushion, were the gold dolphin earrings which she had admired, pointedly, in a designer jeweller's window in L'Escala a few evenings before. From behind my back, I produced a single red rose.

'Sorry,' I said. 'I've been a bugger lately.'

Holding the rose in one hand and the earrings in the other, she rose up on tiptoe and kissed me.

'You may not be in the Davidoff class as a romantic,' she whispered, 'but I suppose you do your best.'

Somehow, that didn't make me feel any better.

36

As good as her word, my partner headed off for Peretellada just after noon next day, to pick up Davidoff from Shirley's *en route*. The rest of our Sunday had been slightly strange, with Prim preening herself in her new earrings and me feeling increasingly tense and guilty.

Fortunately, she had her period, for if she had been expecting me to make love to her, I think I would have been struggling to do her justice. That evening, we dined on pizza at Casa Miñana. Miguel wasn't there, but his father told me that he had gone for a drink with his wife's nephew in L'Escala.

Left on my own next morning, I was writing up reports on the two projects which Shirley had helped us research, when the phone rang. I picked it up and heard the fax tone. It connected and five pages were excreted. Four of them were new business enquiries from our second ad the previous Friday, and the fifth was an explanatory note from Jan.

Less than a minute after the transmission had stopped, the phone rang again. This time, there was a voice on the line. Jan's.

'Hi there. Did all that stuff come through okay?'

'Yeah, clear as a bell.'

'So how are you?'

'I've been better.'

There was a silence. 'I'm sorry,' she said, eventually. 'I was home at the weekend, and Mac collared me. He said he'd given you a sort of a bollocking . . . his words. It made me realise that it was really me who deserved it, and that I've been an unthinking bitch. I should have told you about Noosh and me as soon as it happened, and asked your permission to use the loft. I'm sorry.

'What I shouldn't have done was sleep with you. Prim's a great lass, Oz, and the two of you are perfectly happy. You don't need, and Prim doesn't deserve, me messing your life about.'

She paused again, then went on in a cold, flat, matter-of-fact voice I'd never heard before. 'You probably can't talk now. The only other thing I want to say is, forget that night ever happened, and forget all that stuff I came out with next day. You're with Prim, and it's for the right reason . . . you love her. I'll see you at the wedding . . . both of you.'

I sat there, my heart pounding, and a cold feeling gripping me. I had never heard her like this before, not even in the tense times in our twenties, when we were drifting apart. 'I can talk okay,' I said. 'Is that how you want it to be, Jan?' A vision of her, naked in the light of morning, appeared in my mind.

'Yes. That's how I want it to be. See you four weeks on Friday.' The words snapped out, then the line went dead.

There was nothing to do after that but go for a beer, even though it was still only lunchtime. I dragged myself down to the square, in something close to a daze. Half an hour before, I had thought I was as confused as I could get. I had been wrong.

I was gazing into my empty glass, my mind still bouncing between Edinburgh and St Marti, when I felt a hand on my shoulder. 'Hey Oz, you alone today?'

I looked up, brought back to my surroundings. 'Oh, hi, Miguel. Yes, Prim's away. So was I, just then.'

'If you like, I leave you alone.'

'No, no. Please join me.' I looked around. All the other tables were empty. 'You don't seem to have anything else to do.'

He pulled up a chair, and waved to the other waiter to

bring us two more beers. 'Is good I see you. I was going to come up to the apartment. My wife's nephew Santi is coming to see us. What he told me last night, I could hardly believe, so I asked him to come today and tell you himself. He finish work at one, and he come here for lunch. He be here any minute now.'

Miguel was right. Less than five minutes later we heard the scream of a moped with a straight-through exhaust, and a young man swung into the village in a cloud of dust. He parked at the edge of Casa Miñana's array of tables and shambled across towards us, pulling his crash helmet off as he did so.

Santi looked to be aged around twenty-five. From the colour of his jeans and shirt, I guessed that he worked on a building site. His thirst reinforced that guess. The first beer which was set before him disappeared in around ten seconds. Eventually, after we had ordered *bocadillos* for lunch, his uncle told him to begin his story.

He spoke no English, but his enunciation in Spanish was clear and I could follow most of what he said. Whenever I looked puzzled, Miguel filled in the blanks.

As I listened to what he told me, I could feel a smile spreading slowly across my face. After a while, I stopped him and turned to Miguel. 'Let me get this right so far,' I said, in English, knowing that Santi couldn't understand us. 'The day after I helped you evict our bony chum from up there beside the church, a farm worker found him and went to the local police.' My pal nodded.

'Santi's wife and another officer went up to look. They checked that it was true, and they reported back to their boss. When they did, the local mayor was in the room, and he went crazy over the idea of a body being found in his town.'

'That's right,' said Miguel, chuckling. 'He thinks like I do, that a thing like that in the papers get the town a bad name, that it bad for the tourists.'

I grinned at Santi as I spoke to Miguel. 'So he gives the

farm hand some money to keep quiet, and he tells Ramona and her pal to bundle the skeleton up and move it somewhere else?'

'Si. The poor guy, he being passed around like a parcel. At this rate he could wind up in Barcelona. Come to think of it, that where we should have taken him. They find lots of dead bodies there.'

I shook my head, helpless. 'Jesus Christ,' I chuckled. 'So what did they do?'

Miguel finished the story himself. 'At first,' he said, 'Ramona was going to take him to Estartit. But the mayor, he say, "No, that not fair." Instead he tell them to take it to Ventallo, eight kilometres along the road to Girona. They have no tourists. There, if they find a body, it not matter.

'So Ramona and her friend, they take a sack and they put the body in it. Then when it gets dark they take it to Ventallo. Not by the main road. There is another before that, a farm track. They leave it there, not far from the road and close to the town.'

'And they've heard nothing since?'

'Nothing.'

He paused, as the pair of us took in the latest stage in the odyssey of the late Ronnie Starr, and as Santi stared at us, absolutely bewildered. 'Did Ramona say anything else?' I asked.

'Si, she said that she took a good look at the body as they were picking it up. She said that it looked as if the back of the skull had been smashed in. She say that someone must have hit him with something.'

'Aye,' I muttered, 'unless you stood on him in the dark.'

My friend's mouth fell open, as he looked at me. 'You don' think . . .'

'No, don't be daft. Someone caved his head in all right. And I know why.'

There was no more funny side. 'What will you do now?' asked Miguel. I made a mental note of the 'you'.

'I'll need to think about that. But I guess we'll wind up taking a run along to Ventallo.'

37

'I think we're in the wrong business, Oz.'

'What makes you say that?' I asked Prim, curious. I had been asleep when she came in, but the sound of the shower had wakened me.

She stood in the doorway of our en-suite bathroom, grinning as she towelled herself off. 'It came to me today, that as investigators, in this country at least, we leave a lot to be desired.'

I frowned, feeling wounded by her slight. 'We've got a result in every commission we've had so far, and there are four more waiting to be tackled. I call that pretty good work.'

She tossed the towel into the big clothes basket and pulled on her robe. 'Maybe so, but it's tame compared to what I saw today. I tell you, Davidoff could make a horse talk . . . and in any one of several languages at that.'

She followed me out on to the balcony, and sat down facing me. 'Those people today! When we walked in they greeted me in English. But as soon as I started asking questions, the manager appeared and they ran out of vocabulary. The manager's French dried up as well.

'Then Davidoff stepped in. He was speaking in Catalan, so I hadn't a clue what they were saying, but I could tell that he was laying down the law. Pretty soon the manager went off and came back with his bookings register. The dinner was there. A private room for nine, reserved by Mr Starr, as we thought.'

'How did he pay for it?'

'The manager said he settled the bill in cash. He would, wouldn't he?'

'So you'd guess. Did Davidoff ask the manager whether he had ever seen this Starr before?'

She nodded. 'He told me that he hadn't.' She took my hand. 'So, was my trip worth it?'

'You were right,' I said. 'It was something we had to do, even if it doesn't take us any nearer the mystery man. You went there, and you found out what you had to. You got the result by the best means available, so don't sell yourself short as a detective.'

Prim laughed at my defence of our profession. 'Don't be so precious. How was your day anyway? This business of ours seems to be a success, so far, at least. I saw Jan's fax when I came in, and the four enquiries. Did she phone as well?'

'Yup.'

'How is she?'

'Fine, as far as I could tell. She sent her best. Said she'd see us at Dad's wedding.'

Primavera looked at me archly. 'Oh, so I am invited, then.'

'Of course. Stop being silly.'

'I'm not, it's just that whenever you've mentioned it so far it's always been in "I" terms. You and Jan, best man and bridesmaid. I was beginning to wonder whether I figured or not.'

Inside I was squirming. 'Look, don't be daft. Okay?'

She pouted. 'Who stole your scone? You're always like this when you have a sleep in the afternoon.'

'Och, I'm sorry,' I said, seizing my chance to change the subject. 'I had a couple of beers at lunchtime, with Miguel . . . and with his wife's nephew, the policewoman's husband.' Spinning it out as long as I could, I told her how the bones of poor Ronnie Starr had been run out of yet another town.

'My God,' she whispered, when I was done. She didn't see anything funny about it. Nor did I now that the beer had worn off. 'If you believe in restless spirits, his must be pretty frantic by now. What are we going to do?'

I spread my hands. 'What we did the week before last. Go

and look for him. I know roughly where he was dropped.'

'But we can hardly go wandering around the fields there,' she protested. 'It's a working village, not the sort of place where young couples go for an innocent stroll.'

She had a point. I thought about it, and a solution presented itself. 'Tell you what. Remember that restaurant we went to in Ventallo?'

'The farmhouse?'

'Yes. Let's go there again. Tomorrow night.'

She shook her head. 'Can't be tomorrow. Shirley's having a whist night. I said we'd go.'

'A whist night! With the over fifties!'

'You'll enjoy it. Adrian will be there too. I had a chat with him this afternoon, when I took Davidoff back. He's a nice chap.'

I laughed. 'Okay, I get it. I can talk to Adrian, while you're wooed by Davidoff.'

She smiled, but a touch defensively. 'Well! Indulge me, okay?'

'Okay,' I said. 'We'll go to Ventallo on Wednesday . . . after we have another look for Trevor Eames. His voyage can't be going on for ever.'

38

It was probably a blessing that Blackstone Spanish Investigations seemed to be welcomed by the market, and to be generating substantial momentum. Both Prim and I spent the best part of the next day, without taking a siesta and with barely a break for lunch, preparing responses to the enquiries which Jan had faxed through.

Prim was excited, because the investigation business was still new to her, and allowed her to use her considerable brain in an entirely different way from what she was used to in her nursing career.

I got a buzz from it too; partly because enquiries like these, and my interview in Tarragona, straight-forward factual work as they were, made me feel somehow that I was back in my real world after an extended lie-in, and partly because it allowed me to concentrate on something other than our pursuit of the two Ronald Starrs, skeleton and impostor, or on my disturbing conversation with Jan of the day before.

'Partner,' said Prim as I sorted through all of the paper which our day had generated, 'we are on to a good thing here. If this is what it's like after our second speculative ad, imagine what it's going to be like when we really get our marketing act together.'

'Eh?'

'You heard. Look, all we've done so far is stick a toe in the water, for no other reason than to keep ourselves occupied. In a very short time we've found out that the water's pretty deep.' She leaned across the terrace table. 'If we put together a sensible marketing strategy, with more focused advertising in the right journals, and with carefully targeted mailshots, we could build up a pretty respectable business in no time.'

I stared at her. 'Come on, love, how many hours are in the day?'

She stared right back at me. 'Eight times the number of people you hire.'

I couldn't think of a quick comeback to that one.

'We needn't just be hiring them here, either,' she said. 'Why shouldn't BSI work in both directions, like the guy in the Consulate suggested, handling investigations in Britain for Spanish clients? Come to that why should it restrict itself to Britain? With a little planning we could have a business dedicated to answering questions all over Europe, and providing information to order from a database, and . . .'

'. . . and hold on just a minute! Have you any idea what it would take to set up a business like that?'

Her stare had turned into a frown. 'We've got quite a bit at our disposal.'

'I don't only mean cash. I mean the time it would swallow, and the implications it would have for our lives. Have you any idea what's involved in running a business?'

'Yes. Hard work, self-discipline, dedication, reliability, quality standards: that sort of stuff.'

'Sure, and accountants, bankers, lawyers, health and safety inspectors, VAT men, office overheads, employee overheads, employees' statutory rights, customers you never get to know, customers you can't stand but can't tell to piss off in case they rubbish you in the market place, customers who don't pay their bills, overdrafts, ulcers: that sort of stuff.'

I shook my head. 'I could have done all that in Edinburgh, love, but I chose to be self-employed. I like being self-employed. I feel comfortable being self-employed. I don't want to run a business that has a hundred mouths to feed. I don't want to feel responsible for so many people's lives. I don't want to be able to go round the world on the air-miles I've racked up on business flights during the year.'

That frown of hers had deepened. 'Don't you have any ambitions?'

I laughed out loud. I couldn't help it, but she didn't like that; not one bit. I stood up and walked across to the edge of the terrace. 'Take a look out there. That's the Mediterranean. Those are the Pyrenees. This is a very comfortable home in a beautiful place in the sunshine. We have cash in the bank, and earning capacity. We can live here, or in Scotland, as we choose. All these advantages, all the parts of our lifestyle are wildest dream stuff for most of the guys I know. I'm thirty, and they're all reality. I reckon I'd be greedy if I had any more. Now you're saying they're not enough.'

She stood up and stamped her foot in frustration. 'Come on! You must always have a goal. Otherwise . . .'

'Otherwise what? Isn't being happy enough?' I paused, and smiled, trying to put out the flames. 'If you want me to have a goal, how about extending the Blackstone line? To tell you the god's honest, that's the only ambition I've got left.'

Someone must have filled my fire extinguisher with petrol when I wasn't looking. 'That's all the growing you want to do for the rest of your life, is it?' she exploded. 'Your bloody dynasty? You can have kids and be a business success too, you know.'

'But I'm a business success already, as far as I'm concerned. You and I, *we* are a business success.'

She shook her head. 'Oz, what will you be like when you're old?'

I looked at her, puzzled. 'Knackered, probably. I'll be like my dad, I hope, although he's still a few years away from old himself. What do you want me to be like?'

She stepped up and seized me by the shirt front. 'I want you to be fighting against being old. I want the flame of ambition always to be burning inside you.'

It dawned on me. 'You want me to be like Davidoff, don't you.'

For an instant, she looked defensive, then she tugged my shirt again, yanking out a few chest hairs in the process. 'And why not? Most men his age . . . whatever that might be . . . have given up the ghost, but not him. He looks after himself. He's fit, he's charming, he's funny and he's full of life.'

'Not all of him, according to Shirley.'

She flashed her eyes at me. 'Whatever the truth of that, he isn't a boring old fart. You could be one of those by the time you're forty.'

This was getting near the bone. 'Only if I'm bored myself, dear,' I retorted. The flames in her eyes went out instantly, and were replaced by hurt. I grabbed her and hugged, and she pressed her face against my chest, as if to smother any more anger. 'Sorry, Prim my love,' I said. 'This is a daft argument anyway. It shouldn't be about what I want, or what you want, but about what we agree together that we want.

'Tell you what. This weekend, we'll draw up a business plan, and maybe when we go back for Dad's wedding, we'll see about taking someone on in Edinburgh, to market the business for us. Long-term decisions can wait till then.'

She was mollified, but there was still tension between us when we arrived at Shirley's three hours later. We found that we knew all of the other guests. Ma and Pa Miller were among them, no longer in the shadow of Steve, now that he had gone back to England.

Fortunately, the whist turned out to be optional; good news for me since I hate card games of any form, and good news for Prim, since it meant that she could allow herself to be whisked into the garden by Davidoff with a clear conscience. I watched him nosing his *Cava* and nodding his approval as they headed for the door. When he was with Prim he always seemed a wee bit taller, his back a wee bit straighter, his shoulders a wee bit wider.

I heard his voice drift back to me. 'Ah, these unspeakable people. Had it not been for you, I think I would have gone today.'

'Where would you have gone to, Davidoff?' I heard her ask. 'Where do you live?'

I strained to hear the answer, but it was lost as Adrian Ford caught my elbow, with a cheery, 'Hello!'

I turned towards him, leaving Prim to her fate with a smile. 'Glad you could come,' he said at once. 'My sister didn't give me a choice about tonight. She said I was co-host and that was it.' He paused. 'Are you a cards man, Oz . . . or would you prefer a game of snooker?'

I grinned at Shirley's amiable brother. 'Anything but bloody cards,' I whispered.

'Excellent. Let's grab some food from the buffet, and I'll show you the table. Clive had it shipped over from England.'

The snooker room was in the basement level of the house, off the vast garage. In the corner there was a small fridge, from which Adrian produced two Sol beers. He uncapped them, handing one to me. 'No limes to suck with them, I'm afraid, though I always think that's a bit of a pose.' I agreed. Beer was beer, whether it was Mexican, Spanish or made in Fountainbridge.

Adrian's snooker seemed to be on a par with mine. After half an hour, there were still four reds left on the table, one for each empty Sol bottle on top of the fridge. 'I never could take this game seriously,' he confessed at last. 'Clive used to regard me as cannon fodder, and Shirley used to say that she could wipe the floor with the pair of us.

'Golf's my game, really,' he added, suddenly slamming the twelfth red into the right middle pocket. The white spun back behind the blue, on its spot. He rolled it away very gently, then edged a red along the cushion into the top left pocket, finishing on the black. It went down, followed by the last two reds, two pinks and all the colours.

I looked him in the eye as the last black thudded against the back of the pocket. 'Are you as big a bandit at golf?'

Adrian smiled, his beard spreading out in a funny kind of way. 'Not a bandit, Oz. I just don't like to show all I've got.

Bit like someone else around here,' he added, almost absent-mindedly. 'The thing was,' he went on quickly, 'I could hardly have screwed poor old Clive into his own table, could I. It wouldn't have been courteous. Old man, *you*'re a better player than he was. When we were down here I used to miss in a way that would set balls up for him to pot. You should always keep a bit back, whatever you do in life. Just a little extra in the tank, for when you really need it.'

I wondered about the ethics of that approach. 'Where do you play your golf?' I asked him.

'When I'm here, at Torremirona, mostly, although I've played all of the courses in the province at one time or another. Back home I play at the Belfry, off six.' Having seen his snooker, I wondered how genuine his golf handicap might be. 'How about you?' he went on. 'Do you play?'

I'm always modest about my golf, with good reason. 'I'm from Fife,' I said, 'so it's compulsory. I'm a member of Elie, like my dad, but I haven't been there very often of late. I've never played over here.'

'Mmm,' Adrian mused. 'Next time I'm over we'll have a game. It'll need to wait till then, I'm afraid, for my dance card's full for the rest of this week, and I'm going home on Saturday.'

'Too bad.'

'Yes,' he agreed. 'John, my nephew's coming out on Monday to see his mum, and to have a board meeting with her. They're directors of the company. I'm not; just a poor wage slave, I'm afraid, but John and I can't both be away at the same time. Or so he says.'

He glanced up at the clock on the flock-papered wall. 'I suppose we should really put in an appearance upstairs. Fulfilling one's social obligations and all that.'

As Adrian re-racked the crystallite balls, I wiped the cues and replaced them in their clips on the wall. 'Do I get the impression that you and your nephew don't get on?'

He smiled. 'Let's just say that things run more smoothly

when one of us isn't around. John runs the business now, although Shirl's the major shareholder. I keep a quiet eye on her interests, but mostly I let him get on with it. As long as he doesn't make any mistakes, I'm happy to stay in the background. Anyway, he doesn't pay me enough for me to do any more than I do at present. No bonuses, no profit share, no options. Just salary, pension and company car.

'Come on, let's rejoin the wrinklies . . . only don't tell my sister that's how I describe her circle of companions.' He led the way up the narrow, tiled staircase, back to the party. Shirley was in the kitchen, opening more *Cava*.

'Good,' she said. 'About time you two were back. Adrian, put the coffee on, love. Oz, could you do something for me? I owe those bloody card-sharp Millers three thousand pesetas, and I've left my purse up in my bedroom. Take a run up and get it for me, will you. It's the door facing you at the top of the stairs. You'll find it on the dressing table, I think.'

'Sure.'

As I crossed the hall, I glanced through the open garden door. It was dark but Prim and Davidoff were still outside, side by side on one of the big loungers. She was smiling and leaning slightly against him. I laughed to myself at his persistence as I trotted up the wide stairway.

When I found the light switch, I saw that Shirley's bedroom was on the same grand scale as the rest of the house. It had its own terrace, with patio doors, and a huge bed, covered in pink satin. The dressing table was against the far wall. Her cosmetics were arrayed neatly to one side on a silver tray. On the other side was a photograph, in an ebony frame, of Shirley, a few years younger and a few years lighter and a tall, dark-haired, distinguished-looking man.

The purse lay in the centre of the table. I crossed the room, picked it up and turned back towards the door. It was only then that I saw the picture.

It was hung above the bed. Even in the artificial light, its colours exploded out at me. Along the Firth of Forth on the east coast of Scotland, it's pretty well compulsory for aspiring artists to paint the Bass Rock. In Catalunya, it's the same with Cadaques, the fishing village with which Picasso, Miro and Dalí all had links.

There must be a million pictures of the place, with its bay, its square-towered white church and its encircling mountains behind. But none like this. It was big, a metre deep at least, and maybe one and a half wide. In the foreground the sea shone cobalt blue. The white church tower gleamed almost silver. On the slopes behind the town, the sun glinted on the green foliage.

I gazed at it, and as I did, the intensity of its colours reminded me of another picture; one which I had seen in Milton Bridge, in Scotland.

I leaned across Shirley's bed, looking for a signature. It took me a while to find it, for it was modest, and self-effacing. But eventually I spotted it, near the bottom left corner. It was small, but it was clear. I read the name aloud. 'Ronald Starr.'

I was shaking with excitement as I switched off the light and closed the door behind me. I was still trembling slightly when I found Shirley, back in the sitting room, refilling *Cava* glasses.

I handed her the purse. 'That's some picture you've got up there,' I said, quietly. 'Had it long?'

She beamed. 'Isn't it just! My lovely son gave it to me. He fancies himself as a bit of a collector. He came in with it one day when he was out here at Easter, and gave it to me, as an early birthday present.'

'Do you know where he found it?' I asked, all innocence. 'That's a gallery I wouldn't mind visiting.'

She shook her head. 'It wasn't from a gallery. John said that he bought it off Trevor Eames. He never told me how much he paid for it. Bet it was a right few hundred, though.'

I smiled, involuntarily, and nodded. 'I'll bet. Had you ever heard of the artist before?'

Shirley laughed, heartily. 'I couldn't tell you even now who painted it, and it's been hanging above my bed for six months. A picture's a picture as far as I'm concerned, love. You can ask John when he gets here on Monday. Or you can ask Trevor . . . if you can ever find the bugger!'

39

'Her son bought it for her?' Primavera gasped.

'That's what she told me. And he said that he bought it from Trevor Eames.'

We were outside in Shirley's garden, the two of us, with Davidoff. When I appeared, he had seemed put out, for an instant, but it passed and he welcomed me as if I was a brother in arms.

'He said that, but is it true?'

'It has to be,' said Davidoff, growling with what I took to be his distaste for Shirley's son. 'You have found two links with Ronald Starr; the auction, which you have just told me was a fake, and now the picture above Senora Shirley's bed. In each, the name of Trevor Eames comes up. Yes, I have to believe that he sold John the picture of Cadaques.'

Prim took his arm. I saw the muscles of his wrist and hand tense under her touch. 'Is it possible that John was the man at the auction?' she asked. 'Could he, or he and Eames together, have killed the real Ronnie Starr and stolen his pictures?'

Davidoff's eye narrowed, for several seconds as if he was considering her question. Then he shook his head, vigorously. 'I don't think so. John is not the man to be involved in something like this. Not that he is a paragon, you understand; he just lacks imagination and guts.

'Oz,' he said suddenly, 'this impostor at the auction, how was he described to you?'

'About forty, clean-shaven, dark hair beginning to go grey, ordinary looking, average height.'

'It was not John, then, for sure. John is fair, like his mother, and almost two metres tall. Trevor's partner was someone else.'

Something in his voice made me ask him, 'Do you know Eames?'

Davidoff shrugged. 'I see him around, I know who he is, I know where he lives, but I would not say I know him. I would not want to know him; he's an asshole.' He paused. 'I tell you this, though. He approached John to sell him the picture, not the other way around. John, he is a fucking philistine. He talks big but he wouldn't know a Picasso from a bull-fight poster, and he wouldn't know where to go to buy a picture like that. Yes,' he nodded, 'if you find Eames and you make him talk, you know all the answers.'

Our friend paused, and he looked at me, hard. 'But there is one thing, Oz. You never tell me why you believe Ronnie Starr is dead.'

So I told him the whole story, from the beginning to my meeting with Miguel's wife's nephew. Davidoff's face grew darker by the minute.

'These people,' he snarled. 'So fucking selfish. Nothing matters to them but the tourists. To treat a poor boy's body like that. I am ashamed that they are Catalan. And you, Oz, that you were involved in it. I am ashamed of you, too.'

Right then, the last of the sybarite Oz Blackstone vanished, and Mac the Dentist's son was finally back, imperfect as before, but with his old standards of decency. For right then, for the first time, I was ashamed of myself too.

Davidoff stood up, bent over Prim and kissed her, on both cheeks, and lightly on the lips. 'Good night, my dear one,' he said. 'I think I better go now. I hope I have not soured your enjoyment of the night with my lecture.'

He looked at me, over his shoulder. 'Don't take it to heart, my boy. I suppose you felt that you owed this Miguel a favour. If you feel that you are in someone's debt it's difficult to say no, sometimes. Come to think of it, to recognise a debt which you owe is a virtue. Take that from me.'

We sat in silence for a while, after he had gone back to the summer-house. Then we left too.

'He's right, Oz,' said Prim as she drove us home. 'It would have been difficult to say no.'

I shook my head. 'It would have been easy. No. There you are, that's how easy it is.'

'Well, it's done now. There's no point in belated guilt. Look back on how the rest of the evening went. We've got proof of a connection between Trevor Eames and the real Ronald Starr. That can't be bad, can it?'

'No, that was a surprise. It should help us persuade Eames to talk, when we find him. Hell, we may even force him to go to the police. It'd be as well if Starr's body turns up before then, though.'

I glanced across at her. 'How about your evening? Has he proposed yet?'

'Don't be childish,' she said, grinning. 'We had another long talk, about life and the meaning of the universe. In some ways I'm getting to know a lot about Davidoff, in others I still know nothing.'

'What do you mean?'

Primavera paused, reflecting. 'Well, for example, I know that he has two homes. I asked him where he lives when he's not at Shirley's. He said that he has somewhere on the coast, and somewhere else, a very little place, in the country. But he didn't tell me where either one was.

'I asked him what he did for a living, and if he still did it. He told me that he had been involved with his family business, and still is occasionally, on an advisory basis. He told me that the family had money, more than he needed. Yet he didn't tell me what that business was. I tried, but he changed the subject.

'Instead he began to tell me that I was wasted on a young guy like you. He held my hand, looked at me with that eye and said that I should drink deep from the well of experience, rather than sip from the pool of youth.'

I whistled, loudly, over the sound of the engine. 'Wow! I'm

going to write that line down, because when I'm his age I won't be able to trust myself to remember it. He didn't tell you how old he is, did he?'

She laughed, softly. 'No. He didn't throw out any more hints, either. He did tell me, though, that every day he sleeps for at least ten hours, swims for two kilometres or walks five, drinks two litres of water and eats three bananas. He also does forty press-ups and fifty sit-ups before he showers, shaves and dresses.'

'Is he regular as well?'

'He didn't say, but I'd guess he is. I am a nurse, you know. I can spot the signs of constipation.'

'How about the pecker department?' I asked her, flippantly. 'Did he raise that, so to speak?'

She frowned at me. 'No he did not. I told you, he's a gentleman.'

'He's a fucking old rogue, that's what he is.'

'He's a remarkable man; seriously. We know he's over seventy-five, at least. Physically he doesn't look more than mid-sixties, and he has a mind like a razor.'

I grunted. 'Old bastard. He'd better watch he doesn't cut himself.'

Primavera laughed like a peal of bells. 'I love it. You try to laugh it off, but you're jealous!'

'That'll be the day.' I didn't want to get into a discussion about jealousy, so, like Davidoff, I retreated from the subject.

'Listen,' I said, changing my tone, 'something occurred to me tonight, after I saw that picture. There may be a way we can find out more about Ronnie Starr; get a clue to what he did while he was here.'

'How?'

'Tomorrow I'll make another phone call. It'll mean I'm overdrawn in the favour department, but I'll do it nonetheless.'

40

I gave Eddie half an hour to settle in and have his first coffee of the day, then made the call, at around ten-thirty our time.

'Christ, Oz,' he barked by way of greeting. 'What the f . . . is it this time? I thought we were even.'

'We were. After this, I'll owe you one. The other day, you said there had been no action on the guy Starr's cards for about a year. I'd like to know what the last action was; where the cards were used and when.'

'You wh . . .' There was a long silence. I was relieved when it turned out to have been pregnant. 'You are sure that this guy is kaput, aren't you, China?'

'Dead certain, you might say. It is important, Eddie, honest.'

'Okay.' There was another pause, shorter this time. 'When are you due home again?' my source asked.

'Inside a month. But I need this before then.'

'Relax, I'll call you back tonight. But when you come home, I want a case of beer. Good stuff, mind, none of your weak French crap.'

I laughed. At Spanish prices, if Eddie's information paid off, I would be getting off lightly.

Prim and I put in a conscientious day's work, gathering information from the Consulate, and from the Barcelona Chamber of Commerce. I even attempted a conversation in Spanish, and was astonished to find that I could make sense of what I was told.

It was just after seven when the phone rang. 'Forget the beer,' said Eddie. 'I want a case of Rioja. Yes?'

I sighed. My pal wasn't a quick thinker, but he always got

there eventually. 'Okay, you're on. It'd better be worth it, though.'

'You can tell me,' he said. 'Your man's Visa was last used in Spain on the twelfth of September last year. He bought petrol with it, in a place called Verges. He seems to have taken his car over there.'

I took a deep breath. 'You don't know . . .'

Eddie laughed. 'He bought it on finance three years ago. The last payment was made in July last year. A Renault Five, L 213 NQZ. Who's a clever boy, then?'

'You are mate, you are. What else?'

'The Mastercard was used last on the twenty-fifth of September, last year again. He paid a restaurant bill with it in a place called Pubol. That's P, U, B, O, L. He signed for a debit of seven thousand pesetas. How much is that in real money?'

I barely heard the question. 'Oh,' I replied at last, 'about thirty-five quid. What was the restaurant called?'

'It doesn't say, just Ristorante.'

'How about other debits?'

'The three before that were in a bar stroke café in a place called La Pera. Need any more?'

I beamed across the table at Prim, who was watching me intently. 'No, Eddie. That's great. You've earned that Rioja, China. In fact we might even throw in the beer as well!'

41

'Eddie may have turned up trumps,' said Primavera, looking across the breakfast table as I crunched my way through half a *xapata* filled with boiled eggs, 'but we'd better think what use we can make of his information.'

Our successes of the day before had dulled the memory of our confrontation on Tuesday. Breakfast was a fun time once more, and play had resumed as well in other areas. The weather seemed to have responded to our change in mood. It was warmer than it had been; well into autumn, we could still feel the heat in the morning air.

'I've already done some thinking along those lines,' I said, when I could. I wiped the flour from the *xapata* from the corners of my mouth. 'In fact, when you were out getting the bread, and the eggs were boiling, I made a couple of phone calls.

'Ronnie Starr bought his petrol in Verges. He picked up the tab for at least one guest, maybe two, in Pubol on September twenty-five, and he seems to have been a regular at that bar in La Pera.

'All of that indicates that he was based somewhere in that area. Agreed?'

'Yes.' Prim nodded.

'In that case, if we can find out where he lived, we might find other people who knew him, and who can tell us more about him. Maybe someone will give us a lead to the phoney Starr.'

'Unless one of them is the phoney Starr.'

I grimaced. 'That had occurred to me. We'll just have to be

careful about the questions we ask.'

'Why don't we say that I'm his cousin and that we're out here trying to find him?' she suggested.

'Good idea. People are more likely to talk to us on that basis. Well done.'

She nodded. 'Don't mention it. Now, how are we going to find out where he lived?'

'We can ask around the hostels. But he was out here from the end of the academic year to the autumn. That's three months, at least. Isn't it more likely that he would have rented an apartment?'

'At summer prices?'

'It's cheaper inland. A small place in the area in which we're interested wouldn't cost you very much. I thought we might ask around the rental agencies in Verges, Flaça and La Bisbal, so I phoned Maggie and got some numbers from her.'

Prim looked at me doubtfully. 'That's fair enough; it's logical. But you've got an orderly mind. Couldn't Starr have done what we did? Stopped off somewhere and found a place to stay by accident? If you looked at our Visa slips what name would you find most often?'

I smiled at her. 'Casa Miñana.'

'Right,' she said, patiently. 'Which is next door to our apartment. So . . .'

'So the first place we should look for Starr is La Pera. Christ, Prim, I think I'll give up the detecting game. You're far better at it than I am.'

Primavera laughed. 'You've always said you're an enquiry agent, not a detective. Maybe you should stick to that and leave the detecting to me.'

'Okay,' I said. 'In that case, get out of those very fetching shorts and into your raincoat, trilby and gumshoes.'

She grinned across the table. 'Okay. But only if you'll help me.'

42

It was lunchtime when finally we arrived at the café-bar in what passes for the main street in La Pera. It wasn't difficult to find, being the only one in town. Prim had stopped short of the detective kit, settling instead for a cotton skirt and the style of white blouse in which, on occasion, she could stop heavy traffic.

The owner was fifty-something, a short, round-shouldered man, with a bad shave and greased hair. The sleeves of his creased, blue-and-white striped shirt were rolled up and he smelled of stale tobacco. When we walked in he had been deep in conversation with his only customer.

He leered at Prim as we took two seats at the bar. I could sense her displeasure, but she kept a smile set on her face.

I ordered a *café con leche para mi*, and a *copa de vino blanco para la senora*, in perfectly acceptable Spanish. The man gave an approving nod, and set a dish of small sweet olives before us as he prepared the drinks. I glanced around his café. There were bench seats along the wall between the two doors, and at the far end, beyond the bar, a dozen tables waited in vain for diners. The place was badly in need of a paint job, but it was clean and tidy. It reminded me a lot of *Al Forn*, in Tarragona. I wondered how long it had been in the same family, and whether there was another generation ready to take over.

The man came back with the coffee and wine. I thanked him and plundered my Spanish once more. Slowly and carefully I told him that we were from *Escocia*, and that we were looking for someone who had been in La Pera a year before, a cousin of *la senora aqui*. He frowned at me and replied in Catalan, a long rambling sentence.

I couldn't understand a word, but I knew what he was saying all right because I had encountered the same attitude many times before. He was telling me, 'I'll respond to your pidgin Spanish to sell you food and drink, but if you want information from me, boy, you'd better be able to talk to me in my own language.' It can be put much less subtly than that. In Port Lligat, there is a notice painted on the wall beside the jetty which reads: 'Only Catalan spoken here.'

Before I could even glare at the guy, Prim saved the day. She smiled at him and asked him the same question in perfect French, her eyes wide and beguiling. The man looked at her for a second or two, and was duly beguiled. He replied, in French as good as hers, even if his accent was a bit guttural.

They spoke quickly, so I couldn't follow all of it. When they were done, and when the man had retired to resume his conversation with his crony, she filled in the blanks. 'He remembers my cousin Ronnie,' she said. 'I was right. My friend says that Starr arrived here last summer. He remembers him very well because he spoke Catalan. Not many foreigners do. He had a meal here, and he took a room above the bar for one night.

'Next day he told him that he liked the place and wanted to find an apartment so that he could stay longer, somewhere with a little space for him to paint. At the end of this street there's a tabac and liquor store run by a Senora Sonas. There's an apartment above it which she used to rent out. It was empty at the time and so my friend sent him there.

'He took it, and he was here all summer. In the autumn, he said, he just went away; back to Wales, he assumed. He says that Senora Sonas will be able to tell us everything about my cousin Ronald.'

I squeezed her hand. 'Bullseye,' I said. 'Did you ask him if Starr ever came here with friends?'

'Of course I did. He says that he remembers him being here a couple of times with *deux Anglais*. One of them was a bald man, smallish, heavily tanned. He can't remember anything about the other one. Not young, not old, well dressed; that's all.'

I looked at my watch. It was almost two o'clock. 'Sod it,' I said. 'I suppose we'll have to wait to see Senora Sonas. She'll be shut for the afternoon.'

Prim shook her head. 'No. He says she doesn't close. The people here smoke a lot, it seems. They like the tabac to be open all day long.' She finished her drink and the last of the olives. 'Come on,' she said, waving goodbye to her new pal, 'let's go and see her.'

As far as I can see there's never quite enough room inside Spanish village liquor stores, for some of the stock is always lying out in the street; big carafes of dodgy wine, plastic blocks of spring water, much of it drawn free from the village well and sold to the unwary, and cases of beer, all set out on the ground, well below the height of the average dog's cocked leg. A tip: if you choose to drink straight from the bottle in Spain, always give the top a really good wipe first.

The sign above the door read 'Bodegas Sonas', not that there was much chance of us getting it wrong. La Pera is not a shopper's paradise. I suppose I was expecting the female equivalent of the man in the café-bar, and I guess Prim was too. The reality took us by surprise.

Inside the store was a tall woman, in her mid thirties, with jet black hair and skin which looked rich and creamy even in the dim light of her shop. It's my observation that there is a time in the lives of members of the human species, in their early fifties, when everything seems to head south at once. Senora Sonas was a long way short of that. She was in her prime. As I looked at her, tall and dark-haired, I thought at once of Jan, and felt a momentary pain.

Prim took the lead this time. Speaking French, as she had in the bar, she explained, untruthfully of course, who she was, and what she and I were looking for.

'That's funny,' said Senora Sonas, in almost flawless English.

'Ronnie told me that he had no relatives alive. You're not going to tell me now that he has a wife, are you?'

There was something in her tone that set the hair prickling at the back of my neck. Prim's too, I discovered later. A faint sound made me look into the corner of the room. There, on a metal stand, I saw a carry-cot. I'm no expert, but I guessed that the sleeping child was around four months old. I glanced quickly at the woman's left hand. There was no wedding ring; not even the mark of one.

'No, Senora,' I said. 'He doesn't have one of those. The truth is he doesn't have a cousin either. I'm Oz Blackstone, and this is Primavera Phillips. We're investigators, trying to discover why he disappeared a year ago. He hasn't been seen since.'

Her head dropped. 'I was afraid that something had happened. I could never believe that he would just go off and leave me like that.'

For the sake of it, I had to ask. 'The baby is . . . ?'

She nodded.

'Did he know, before he disappeared?'

'No, but neither did I at that time.'

'What happened?'

She held up a hand. 'Wait.' She stepped to the door and locked it, then turned the '*Obert*' sign round to show '*Tancat*'. 'Come through here,' she said, and led the way through to a comfortable sitting room behind the shop. She sat in a chair by the stone fireplace and offered us seats opposite. 'I used to live here,' she said. 'There is a bedroom, a bathroom and a kitchen. Since I had my little boy, I've moved upstairs to the apartment. It's lighter and there's more room.'

'Have you always been here, Senora?' Prim asked her.

She laughed. 'Call me Reis, why don't you; it's my name. No, I'm really a furniture designer. I worked in agencies in Paris, Brussels, then Barcelona, until my father died a couple of years ago, and I came back here to sell the place. I realised soon that it was only worth anything as a going concern.

Anyway, I could hardly close it and leave the village without a *tabac* or a *bodega*, or worse still, having to rely on that greedy bastard Mendes in the bar. So I kept it open while I waited for a buyer, and rented out the apartment to make some extra money.'

'That's how you met Starr?' I asked.

'Yes. Mendes sent him along to me at the beginning of July last year. I showed him the apartment and he took it for three months, rent paid in advance. He is very honest, is Ronnie: at least I thought so then.'

'What does he look like?' asked Prim.

'He has fair hair, much the same colour as yours, and he is very good looking. When I saw him first, I thought he might be gay, but we became friends, then more than friends and I found out for sure that he is not. He is an artist, I am an artist too, of a sort. We had a lot in common.'

'Did he tell you things about himself?'

Reis Sonas shrugged. 'At the time I thought he did. Then, when he vanished and never wrote, I guessed that they had all been stories. He told me that he taught painting in a college in Wales, and sold some original work, not through the galleries, but to businesses, through interior design agencies, like the ones I worked for.

'He said that like mine his father had died, a few years after his mother. He had sold their house, and they had left him a little money too. He came to Spain with the thought that after another year in college, he might come over here to paint. "In the footsteps of Dalí," he told me.

'He is an expert on his work,' she said, with sudden pride. 'He knows everything about him. That was why he came here, to be near Gala's castle in Pubol. He painted it. He took a photo of the plain, as you can see it from her window, and painted that. He went to Port Lligat and to Cadaques, and painted them.'

'Did he ever paint like Dalí?' I asked her. 'Did he copy his style?'

She nodded. 'Sometimes he did. He is very good. The soft colours, the surreal subjects, he can do them all. Just like Dalí, only not like him. Gentler in the concepts, you know what I mean. Not crazy, like he was.'

'What did he do with this work? Did he show any of it?'

'No, only to me. Then he painted over it, or burned it.'

'What!'

'Don't look so surprised,' she laughed. 'Ronnie is a real artist, in his own way. Copying he would do for fun, or to teach a class, but he would never try to pass it off.'

'You sure?'

'Certain. He told me so, and he meant it. He meant that at least.'

I paused, choosing my words carefully. 'Do you remember him ever painting a picture of a toreador?' I asked her. 'A toreador with a red cape and a tear running down his cheek?'

She looked at me as if she had caught me peering through her bedroom window. 'How did you know about that?'

'I've seen it. It was bought by a man in Scotland.'

She sighed and shook her head, 'Ronnie did not paint that picture. I went up to the apartment one day, and it was there, in the room he used as his studio. I asked him if he had done it, but he said, "I know I'm good, but I'm not that good." He said that he had been given it, as a present. I asked him who gave it to him, but he didn't tell me. He just said that it was someone he had met. It was an incredible picture, a *tour de force*.'

'Do you think it could have been an unknown Dalí?'

Reis looked at me and made a face. 'I can't say that. I can't say it wasn't. But I got the feeling that Ronnie thought it might have been. Not from anything he said, but from the way he looked at it, like it was a holy relic.'

'Can you remember when you saw the picture?'

She nodded. 'Yes, it was the twenty-fifth of September, last year. That's my birthday, that's how I know. I came up to the apartment and saw the picture, we had a drink, and then we went to the restaurant in Pubol and had dinner.

'Over dinner, Ronnie said that he was thinking about leaving the college right then, rather than a year later. He asked me how I would feel about not going back to Barça, but about us setting up home together, in La Pera or somewhere else around here.

'I said that sounded like a damn fine idea.' A tear came to her eye but she kept control. 'There and then, he took off the gold chain from round his neck, and gave it to me. "Till I can buy a ring," he said.' She reached up to her throat, and held the chain out for us to see. 'I didn't get no ring,' she snorted. 'I got Felipé instead. Ronnie said that he would have to go back to Wales to sort things out with the college. That's why I wasn't surprised when the man came.'

I frowned at her. 'What man?'

'An Englishman named Trevor. I'd met him once in the bar with Ronnie.'

'Was there another man with him? Around forty, medium everything?'

'Yes there was, but he never told me his name. I never saw him again after that.'

'So when did Trevor come?' I asked.

'Two days after my birthday. The day after it, I went to Barça, to visit a girlfriend. I told Ronnie about it and said I'd be staying overnight. He said okay, and that he would look after the shop for me.

'When I got back, the shop was closed, and there was no sign of Ronnie. I opened up and a couple of hours later, Trevor came in. He said that he had a message from Ronnie. He told me that he had to drive back to Wales very suddenly, the evening before, and had asked Trevor to pick up his things and send them on.'

'What things?'

'That's what I asked. "All of them," Trevor said. "His clothes, and his pictures." He said that Ronnie needed those for the college.'

'Didn't it strike you as odd that he had left without them?'

'Sure it did, at first. But Trevor explained that they had been having a drink on the previous afternoon when Ronnie had gone off to make a call to the college. He had returned in a panic and had said that the college wanted him back before the end of the next working day. "Or else," were the words Trevor used. He had to leave then if he was going to make it back in time, in his little car. He had been worried about his clothes and pictures, but Trevor had told him that his friend, the other guy, whose name I didn't know, was going back to England next day, and that he would take them and drop them off in Cardiff.'

'So you gave Trevor Ronnie's clothes and all his pictures?'

'Not all,' she said. 'I kept the one of Gala's castle, and of the plain. Ronnie gave me those as my birthday presents. They're upstairs, still. But the others I gave to Trevor, with his clothes.'

'Including the Toreador?'

'Yes. That and the painting of Cadaques.'

'What about the Port Lligat painting?' I asked.

'Ronnie told me he had traded that. But he didn't say where. Artists do that all the time; trade pictures for materials, or meals in restaurants.'

'When he didn't contact you,' asked Prim, sympathetically, 'did you try to get in touch with him, after a while?'

Reis shook her head. 'No. I knew I was pregnant by then. I reckoned that if Ronnie had wanted to get in touch with me he would. So I decided that he had been lying to me; and because of that I decided also that I would bring up my baby on my own.'

Her jaw was set in a hard line. Suddenly she didn't look quite so pretty.

'When Ronnie was here, did he get to know anyone else that you were aware of?'

A crease appeared between her eyebrows as she considered my question. 'No,' she began, 'but there was one time. Once on a Sunday afternoon when I was closed, and Ronnie wasn't painting, we went along to the bar in Pubol. While we were there a man walked past the doorway, looked in and said hello to Ronnie, in English. Ronnie waved back, then the man walked on. When I asked who he was, he said only that it was someone that he had met there before.'

'Can you describe him, after all this time?'

'Oh yes,' said Reis Sonas. 'I could still draw you his picture. He was Catalan, obviously, with olive skin, and he was wiry. He moved like a little cat, except he was not all that small. He looked ancient, yet not old, if you can understand me. And he had a patch over one eye.'

Beside me, I heard Primavera's quiet gulp.

'Have you seen him since, this man?' I asked. She shook her head.

'Reis, I don't think Ronnie was lying to you.' I took Starr's watch from my pocket and showed it to her. She went chalk white. 'I believe that Ronnie's dead, and I expect that pretty soon there will be proof of that.' I could almost hear her heart hammering, though she was on the other side of the room. As I looked at her, her eyes filled with tears, and she shook her head slowly, as if in denial of the truth.

'If I can give you some advice,' I said, 'if I were you I would raise a court action in Wales to have Felipé recognised legally as Ronnie's son. He could be in line for quite a legacy. I reckon his father would want him to have it, rather than the government, don't you?'

She squeezed her eyes shut tight, briefly, then nodded. 'If we can help,' I said. For the first time I felt the need of a business card. Instead I picked up a pen and paper from the fireside and wrote down our names and our telephone number. I handed it to her. 'If you need to contact us.'

'Thank you,' she said, as she took it.

She stood up and showed us to the door, past Ronnie Starr's son, who was beginning to stir in his cot.

As soon as we were out in the street Prim's breath exploded

in a loud gasp. 'Davidoff,' she burst out. 'He knew Ronnie Starr. And he didn't tell us.'

I took her arm. 'Hold on. Don't get your knickers in a twist. They were on talking terms, yes, but there's no proof it was any more than that. Starr didn't mention his name to Reis; maybe he didn't know it. Maybe Davidoff didn't know Starr's name either.'

'What?' she said. 'The most nationalistically biased man in Spain forms a nodding acquaintance with a foreigner, without finding out his name.' Still, she had cooled down.

'We'll ask him, okay?'

She frowned at me. 'Too bloody right we will!'

43

Our opportunity to confront Davidoff arose next day just after noon. We didn't have to go in search of it. We were on the terrace completing responses to two instant enquiries from our third advertisement, which had appeared in the press that same morning, when the door buzzer rang.

Assuming that the caller would be Miguel or his son, I pressed the button to release the lock without lifting the handset, left the door ajar and went back to Prim on the terrace. A minute later a theatrical cough sounded in the doorway.

'Good afternoon, my friends. Pardon this disturbance, but I have come for two reasons. The first is simply to see you both again . . . especially you, my dear,' he added, beaming at Prim and advancing towards us. 'The second is to invite you to dine with Davidoff on Sunday evening, in Shirley's summer-house.

'My friend Adrian will be leaving on Saturday, and the unpleasant John will arrive on Monday. I never visit his mother when he is there. I always feel in the way, and also, I don't like the asshole. But on Sunday, Shirley will be free and I can cook my special paella for her as I do every year, to thank her for putting up with me. I hope that you will be able to join us.'

Davidoff's visit had set us both on the back foot. We hadn't discussed how we were going to confront him with the previous day's discovery.

I played it by ear. 'We'd love to come. About eight o'clock?' He nodded.

I drew up a chair for him, at the terrace table. There was

hot coffee in a jug on the floor, and so Prim automatically went to the kitchen to fetch him a mug.

As she poured, I came straight to the point. 'Davidoff, you devious old bugger, you might have told us you knew Ronnie Starr?'

His face was a study of pure bewilderment. His eye widened, his eyebrow rose, furrowing his brow, and his jaw dropped, slightly. 'I?' he said. 'I knew him? Whatever makes you think that?'

'Yesterday,' I said, 'we met his girlfriend, by accident, really. She owns the *bodega* in La Pera. She told us she was with him in Pubol once, and you said hello to him.'

'I did?' he said, archly. 'When was this?'

'Summer of last year. If it refreshes your memory he was tall, fair-haired, in his thirties and British.'

The astonishment left his face and was replaced by a sorrowful look. 'That was Ronnie Starr, was it? What a sad coincidence. Yes, I met the young man in the bar at Pubol a couple of times. He bought me a drink, I bought him a drink and that was it. He was a pleasant fellow, but I never did learn his name. He said he was a painter, and that turned me off. I had hoped he would be more interesting than that; a doctor, say, or a lawyer. Over in Pubol, everyone you meet thinks he is a painter.'

He paused. 'So they were his poor sad bones that you and Senor Miñana dragged across L'Escala. My God, and I knew him; that makes it even worse.'

I nodded. 'There's more. Starr left his mark on La Pera, and no mistake. The girl who saw you with him had his baby a few months ago. A fine wee boy called Felipé; fair-haired, from what we could see of him in his cot.'

'Tsshhh!' sighed Davidoff, shaking his head. 'Appalling. Poor woman; poor child. To be left so.'

Prim took him by the arm. If she had been doubtful of him the day before, there was no sign of it now. 'Don't worry too much about them,' she said. 'The mother seems a very resourceful woman, and the baby stands to inherit Ronnie Starr's estate.'

'Ah, my darling,' he said, mournfully. 'All the estate in the world cannot make up for the lack of a father. But enough.' It was as if he had willed himself to brighten up. 'This affair will not spoil our evening on Sunday.'

He looked around at me. 'You found Starr's woman and child. Have you yet found Trevor Eames?'

'No, with one thing and another, we haven't had a chance to look for him lately. We were going to do that this evening, then go to Ventallo tomorrow night to see what we could find out there. You said to us that you knew where Eames lives. Can you show us?'

He shook his head. 'Someone told me once that he has an apartment in one of the old blocks up in Riells de D'Alt, but I don't know where. You could find out from the town hall.'

'I don't think so,' I said. 'That might draw attention to us, and we don't want that. We'll try the boat again.'

Davidoff patted my hand. 'Yes. That is probably the most sensible thing to do.' He stood up. 'Until Sunday then.' Prim walked to the door with him, taking his arm again. In the doorway he kissed her goodbye. She was barefoot, and so he stood a few inches taller than she was. As I watched them, I thought of Reis Sonas. 'Ancient, yet not old,' she had said.

Yes, I understood exactly what she meant.

44

We stopped in for coffee in the Trattoria that evening, and booked a table for dinner, although it was quiet and at that time in the season a reservation was probably unnecessary.

On the off-chance I asked our host, who knows everyone in L'Escala, if he had seen Trevor Eames lately, but he said that he hadn't. 'I hear he was crewing a German boat,' he volunteered. 'That Trevor, he is always crewing,' he added, backing the whispered innuendo with a heavy wink, out of Prim's sight.

Leaving the Frontera parked across the road we went for a leisurely walk round the marina, in the direction of *La Sirena Two*'s mooring. From a distance, it looked just as we had seen it on our last visit, locked up secure for the winter. When we reached it, that impression was confirmed. The dinghies were still strapped to the side, the classic wheel was lashed and immobilised, the cabin curtains were drawn.

'Bugger's not home yet,' I growled, frustrated. 'It's just like it was last time we looked.'

'Yes,' said Prim, 'except . . .' Her eyes narrowed. 'Look at the wheel. Last time we were here, I'm sure that it wasn't tied like that.' She pointed to the cabin. 'And there, that curtain's open just a fraction. If he isn't here now, he's been back.'

'Okay,' I said. 'Let's go on board and give the door a knock.'

'Careful,' Prim advised.

'Don't worry, I'm not as daft as all that. If he's in, I'll try to get him out on the deck, so that we can be seen from the quay when we're talking to him.'

'Do we mention Ronnie Starr?' she asked. 'I mean the fact that he's dead.'

'Hell, no! We don't know that, remember. No, we tell the truth more or less. We're working for Gavin Scott, looking for more info on the Toreador. We want to trace the Ronald Starr who staged the auction.'

'Do we mention the Cadaques picture?'

'No. Let's just try to win the guy's confidence.'

She looked doubtful: not scared, you understand, just doubtful. 'Oz, are you sure about this?'

'No. That's why I want to talk to him out in the open. Mind you, the chances are he's buggered off again, back to sea. Come on.'

I led the way, jumping on to the deck of the yacht, Prim landing lightly behind me. I leaned across and knocked on the cabin roof. 'Mr Eames,' I called. 'Can we have a word?'

There was no reply, not any sound after the crack of my knuckles on the plastic roof panel. I walked on and stepped down into the well in front of the tied wheel.

The cabin door was ajar: very slightly, hardly enough to notice, but ajar nonetheless. I rapped on it, calling again. 'Mr Eames.' The door swung open, into the darkness below decks.

The gulls were crying, the water was lapping against the sides of *La Sirena Two*, and boats all around were creaking at their moorings, but all of those sounds seemed to be drowned out by the silence of the cabin. It seemed to rush out to meet me, that silence; and the smell, one that I'd encountered before.

Primavera stood at my shoulder. 'Wait here,' I said. For once she obeyed me without an argument.

A short, four-step stair, almost steep enough to be called a ladder, led down below decks. It was panelled on either side and at the foot there was a second door, without lock or handle, swinging gently with the movement of the boat. I jumped down the steps and crashed into the cabin, into the heart of the silence.

For a second as the door lay open there was light, then it swung shut on its hinges and the darkness returned. But in that second I had seen the chair, and the shape of someone in it.

I fumbled my way along the walls till I found a curtain, and ripped it open. The evening outside was grey, and the cabin was still gloomy, yet I could see at once that Trevor Eames was dead. From the way his arms hung by his sides; from the way his left leg stretched out before him, with the right twisted under the chair; from the way his head lolled back, eyes staring at the ceiling, jaw hanging slack; from the dark blood which soaked the front of his blue-and-white hooped T-shirt, the crotch of his jeans, and the Ship's Wilton floor-covering: from all these things I could tell that he was dead.

I'm not sure how long I spent staring at him with my heart thumping – it always does that when I find a body – before the cabin door opened, framing Prim's silhouette. 'Don't come in!' I said, quickly.

'Don't be silly,' she said. But she stayed in the doorway.

'How did he die?' she asked.

I stepped up to the body. The light was better with the door open. 'I'd say he was stabbed. There looks to be a single puncture wound in his shirt, and there don't seem to be any signs of a struggle. He looks to have been quite powerfully built, so whoever did this couldn't have given him a chance.'

'And who could have done it?' she asked.

'It has to be a very short list,' I answered. 'Right at the top has to be the guy who killed Ronnie Starr: but we're further away than ever from tracking him down.'

The chug of a diesel-engined fishing boat on its way out of the harbour gave me a sudden sense of urgency. 'Let's get out of here,' I said. She had no argument with that; I followed her up the stairway, and across the deck, so scared that for once I barely noticed how well her jeans fitted round her bum. We stood on the quay, looking back at the floating mortuary.

'What do we do?' Prim asked. 'Leave him for someone else to find?'

I ruled that one out in an instant. 'No. Someone's bound to have seen us going on board. Look at all those apartments on the shore. There could be people watching us right now, in any one of them. No, I'll wait here. You run round to the Trattoria and have them call the police.'

She nodded and hurried off. I called after her. 'Hey, honey. Make sure they call the Guardia Civil, not the Municipal Police. I don't think they could smuggle this one out of town, but you never know.'

45

The Guardia Civil live up to their name, and after spending four hours with them, in their big yellow brick office on the outskirts of L'Escala, we were thankful for it.

Their investigators, Captain Fortunato and Sergeant Mendes, were meticulous, but meticulously polite, as they went over our story time and time again. Fortunato told us that he had spent a year on secondment with the Met, yet to be on the safe side, he had an interpreter sitting in to make sure that everyone understood everything absolutely and that at the end, everything was written down as it should be.

We fell back on the cover story we had given in Gary's restaurant as our reason for boarding *La Sirena Two*, hugely relieved in retrospect that we had come up with the throwaway line about booking sailing lessons for ourselves and Steve Miller. With a roomful of witnesses to back it up, our account was never going to be questioned seriously.

While we had waited for the police to arrive, Prim and I had agreed privately that it would be hugely dangerous to mention the name Ronald Starr. Had we started that hare running, we reasoned, it could have led straight back to our client, to the Toreador of the Apocalypse, and to criminal charges for poor old Gavin Scott in Spain and in Britain.

So we lied. We sat, all evening and into the night, with one of the most serious-minded police forces in the whole of Europe. We looked them in the eye, and we told them bare-faced porky pies. When it was over, they thanked us profusely, they extended their sympathy over our ordeal, and they wished us goodnight.

It was after midnight when we emerged from the police station. We were both high as kites, so we headed for La Lluna and found a table in the games room. We were just beginning to relax when Paco came across, to ask whether we were still pleased with our purchase of the previous week, and probably to assess whether we might be in the market for another.

He was still at our table, when his wife came over with word of Trevor Eames' murder, newly arrived courtesy of an off-duty Guardia Civil private. We explained that we had first-hand knowledge, and how.

'Did you know the guy?' I asked Paco, casually.

'He come in here now and again, looking for people to teach to sail.'

'Do you know if he dealt in pictures?'

He looked at me as if I was daft.

'The reason I ask,' I said, quickly, 'is that Shirley Gash told me her son bought a painting from him this year.'

Paco scowled. 'Hah! That is what they were doing, was it. I remember now, in the spring, I see Trevor and John Gash talking in this very room. I think then they make an odd couple. If I know Trevor was selling a picture in here, maybe I kill him myself.' He smiled. 'Of course, I didn't know.'

It was almost three o'clock before we made it home. Even then we sat on the balcony for an hour before going to bed.

The sound of a rainstorm battering our bedroom windows woke us eventually. I looked at my watch. 'Jesus, it's two in the afternoon,' I mumbled.

'Good,' said Prim, giving one of her finest stretches beside me. 'I like a lie-in on a Saturday. And it means that the police haven't kicked our door in.'

It was still chucking it down half an hour later. Showered and dressed, we stood and watched the weather through the glazed balcony doors. The storm was coming in off the sea, in a great grey wave, but behind it we could see a line of clear blue sky, stretching to the horizon. 'It'll blow itself out soon,'

I said, as if I was an expert on the local weather after three months.

Prim wound an arm around my waist. 'Oz,' she said, slowly. 'I've been wondering. Why was Eames killed?'

I looked down at her. 'To close off the trail to the phoney Ronnie Starr, I suppose.'

'If that's so, apart from Davidoff – who couldn't be the mystery man, on account of being twice his age, being Spanish, and having one eye – who would know that anyone was looking for the phoney Starr?'

Every so often Prim would say something that would catch me really off balance. This was one of the times. I thought about her question for a while, as the rain began to slacken. 'Reis Sonas, for one,' I offered at last. 'She knew about the picture, for a start. We only have her word for it that she handed the things over to Trevor, and she was careful to say that she didn't know the name of his chum. She could have been in on it. She could have set Starr up for murder.'

'But got herself knocked up by him first?'

'Accidents will happen. Besides, maybe the kid isn't Starr's.'

'Ha,' she laughed. 'How many wee, fair-haired Spanish babies have you seen? Also, how long did the police say Eames had been dead?'

'Twenty-four hours, at least, maybe a bit more.'

'Exactly, so by the time she finished with us on Thursday, she'd have been struggling for time to get along to L'Escala and knife him. Even if you think a woman could have done that.'

She had me, on all counts. 'David Foy, then,' I proposed. 'He's already admitted setting up Scott. Maybe he was in it all the way. Maybe he did know who the phoney Starr was all along. Maybe the story about he and Trevor being done out of their shares was a lot of cock.'

Prim nodded. 'That's more like it. I didn't like Foy at all.'

'There is another option, though. Maybe the phoney Starr didn't know that anyone was looking for him. Maybe Trevor found him, and was pressing him for his cash. Or maybe he just decided that having Trevor around as a witness to murder was too risky, and put him out of the way.'

'Mmm,' she said. 'But if he does know about us, let's hope he doesn't decide that we're too big a risk as well.'

She may have been joking, but I was still worrying about that one when we arrived in Ventallo at around eight. The rain and the wind were long gone, and the evening was calm, warm enough for a few tables to be set out in the garden of the farmhouse restaurant.

'Sure,' said the owner, in fractured English. 'I can give you table. But no food till nine o'clock. You can have drink in the bar, though.'

We agreed that we would go for a stroll around the quaint village for a while and come back around eight-thirty for an aperitif. I remembered their house red from our previous visit, and didn't want to be left alone with it for an hour on an empty stomach.

Idly, we headed back out into the unpaved street, as if making for the heart of the village, but as soon as we were out of sight we turned on our heels and headed back up the dirt track which led from the highway to the restaurant, and by which Ramona and her partner had dropped the remains of Ronnie Starr.

We had gone barely any distance before we realised that it was useless. It was too dark, the ditches were deep and full of water from the afternoon's storm, and the fields were rutted. It would have been dangerous to venture off the track, and very messy. 'Christ,' said Prim, 'we'd need a sniffer dog. Let's take that walk round the village after all.'

We wrote off any further reconnoitring and explored Ventallo, discovering that it had a second restaurant, a town hall, a small, bizarre zoo and sod all else. Our table was ready when we returned to the farmhouse, and the kitchen had been cranked into action, even though it was only eight forty-five.

We had almost finished our pork, with apples and Calvados sauce, and our first bottle of house red when I noticed the animal in the far corner of the garden. Even as Spanish dogs go, it was quite big: mostly Alsatian, it seemed. I recognised it from our earlier visit and guessed that it belonged to the place.

I thought no more of it, nor would I have to this day, had it not come into Prim's line of vision as it moved across the spotlit wall.

She stiffened and sat bolt upright in her chair. Her eyes, big at the best of times, became huge and completely round. She stared at the hound, and pointed, speechless. The owner was standing beside us, serving the next table. He laughed, in an apologetic sort of way. 'I sorry for my dog. Is bad manners to carry a bone into a restaurant.'

'It sure is,' Prim gasped at last, revealing the benefit of her years of nursing and her six months in an African war-zone. 'Especially when it's a human thigh-bone!'

The young proprietor looked at her, bewildered. She dropped her bombshell again, in French this time. He shrieked, and dropped his tray.

The rest of it was like a movie farce: the dog leashed, the bone taken from him, then given him again to scent, the five of us – the owner, the couple at the next table, Prim and I – following the straining animal, three of us with flashlights. We were barely out of the village before the mostly Alsatian veered off the track, and across the ditch that had become a small river. His master, the bloke from the next table, Prim and I all leapt over into the field beyond, leaving the second lady teetering on the edge, afraid of the jump.

I tripped twice over ploughed ruts, and was lagging behind when the short hue and cry came to a silent halt. When I caught up, covered in mud and waving my torch, the other three were standing in a semi-circle, with the mostly Alsatian held on a very tight leash. Two beams shone on the ground, on something white.

I flashed my light in the same direction, and fought off the urge to say, 'Hello again!' as the gleaming skull of Ronnie Starr grinned up at me. The rest of him was there too, apart from the major bones of one leg. Most of the scraps of clothing had been lost in transit, but he still wore his leather belt.

We all stared at him in silence for a while. Once the young restaurateur tugged at his curly hair, as if reaching for a hat to remove. At last he said, in English, to me, for some reason. 'We should call the police.'

'I think we should,' I agreed. 'You should call Captain Fortunato, of the Guardia Civil, in L'Escala. He's the head man for this whole area. If you fetch your local people, there's no saying where the poor bastard will end up.'

He nodded sagely, as if he understood me, then tugging at the dog's leash, turned back towards the village, with Prim and the second man at his heels. I followed hard behind, but only after, with no one looking, I had bent over the skeleton, and slipped Ronnie Starr's shiny Giorgio watch, wiped clean of fingerprints with the napkin which I had stuffed in my pocket as we left the restaurant, back on his shiny, bony wrist.

46

Captain Fortunato gave me the strangest look I've ever had from another human being. 'What are you, my friend?' he asked, in his slow English. 'Some kind of a fucking magnet?'

'Hold on a minute,' I said, staring back at him defensively across the restaurant bar, and pointing at the owner. 'It was his bloody dog found the thing. We only came here to eat!'

The Guardia Civil detective laughed. 'I don't care whose fucking dog it was, when someone is as close as you to two bodies in two days, then I start to think he must be a very special person.' But in almost the same moment, he made a shooing gesture with both hands. 'Go on,' he said. 'Get outta here, you and your girlfriend. I see enough of you last night.'

'Thank you, Captain,' I said, pushing my luck. 'But if it's all right with you, we'd like to finish our meal. Maybe, while we're doing that, you could interrogate the dog. He's probably the best witness you'll find.'

So while the captain and his assistant went back to the field, Prim and I went back to our table. The owner brought us some more pork, apples and sauce as a reward for our efforts. We had polished off that and two portions of seasonal fruits, when Fortunato returned alone.

He came over to our table and sat down, a tall, wide-shouldered man with black hair, dressed in the same lightweight tan suit that he had been wearing the night before. I asked for a third glass and poured him some wine. He sipped it and nodded appreciatively. 'It's good here, the wine. If you want to buy some, it comes from a place in San Pedro Pescador.' However, a sour look soon returned to his face.

'How are you doing?' Prim asked.

'I can tell you one thing for sure about the man in the field,' said the detective.

'What's that?'

'He's dead!' he snorted. 'The rest, we'll find out if we're lucky.' He reached into the left-hand pocket of his jacket, and tossed the Giorgio watch on to the table. 'That's his.' He reached into the right-hand pocket and produced the belt, rolled up. 'So's that. On the inside it says Marks & Spencer, so he could be British.'

'Or French, or Spanish, for M&S have stores there too,' I said, just to cheer him up. 'Or he could have been a foreign visitor to Britain.'

'Sure, but that is where we'll start nonetheless. There is a number on the watch: that may help us. Then, of course, there are his teeth.' He gritted his own, and muttered. 'Bastards!' under his breath.

'Who?'

Fortunato shot me a look. 'Whoever it was dumped those bones in that field. The guy's been dead for at least a year, but he can only have been there for a day or two, otherwise the dogs would have spread him all over town.' He scowled. 'These bastards in the local police. Either in L'Escala or Ampuriabrava; it was them, I know it. You would not believe it, but it happens all the time. They find a body like this one, with a big hole in the back of his skull. Do they call us in? Oh no, they move it on, out of their hair, to a place like this. Nothing gets in the way of the tourist business.

'Mind you, it's not usually bodies. Mostly it's cars. A couple of years ago, we found a Porsche which had ben stolen in Paris a week before. It was dumped inland, around twenty kilometres from where anyone who stole a Porsche in Paris would want to go. When he saw it, one of my guys recognised it as a car he had seen on the beach in Ampuriabrava. The local cops, they had moved it on. It's the same with this guy.'

Prim shook her head in sympathy. 'How are you getting on

with the Trevor Eames investigation?'

'About as well as we will get on with this one. The truth is Eames was a smuggler. Last week he was away crewing a boat which was moving drugs from Corsica to the Balearics. He mixed with some very bad people; any one of them could have been mad with him.'

He paused. 'Maybe you're lucky you didn't walk in on them when they caught up with him. Sleep on that thought. Now good night, and I hope that the next time I see you, there are no bodies around. There had better not be!'

47

I wakened that morning with what the psychologists would call a feeling of closure. We had gone as far as we could with Gavin Scott's commission. We had found the real Ronnie Starr, linked him to the picture, and established . . . for we both believed Reis Sonas . . . that he had not painted it. What we couldn't tell our client for sure was whether the picture was a fake or not.

Since that was why he had hired us in the first place, all we had to report were our suspicions and our failure.

So the only thing on the agenda for the first part of the day was a call to Gavin Scott, to tell him that we had found Ronnie Starr, that Trevor was dead and that his pal Foy, who had after all, set him up to buy the Toreador of the Apocalypse, was on our list of candidates for the post of killer, and might wind up on the list of the Guardia as well.

And with that thought, it came to me suddenly, half way through my morning run in fact, that I was knee-deep in ordure.

All of a sudden the next sequence of events fell into place. If Prim and I had been able to identify Ronnie Starr, trace him back to La Pera and Reis Sonas, then so, beyond doubt, would the very capable Captain Fortunato. From that he would make the connection to Trevor Eames, and from that he would discover that we had beaten him to it, asking questions about Ronnie Starr, and about a certain picture.

Fortunato might have come across as a nice guy, but not as a softy. I had no doubt what he would do after that. There are certain circumstances in which I would be prepared to go to jail to protect a client; but they don't extend to include a situation where said client has broken the law, still less to one in which Prim might end up in the next cell.

As soon as I was back in St Marti, rather than cooling out in front of the church as usual, I pounded up the stairs to the apartment. Prim looked at me from the balcony with a degree of disapproval as I sweated my way out to join her.

'Jan called,' she said. 'She's doing our invoices today. She wants a note of hours and expenses for Gavin Scott.'

'Does she indeed. How did she sound?'

'All right, as far as I could tell. Mind you, she didn't say much. I asked her how Noosh is doing, she just mumbled, "Fine," and hung up.'

'Okay. Look I'll call her back later. Meantime there's something I have to talk to you about. We've been so stupid I can hardly believe it. All this playing boy and girl detective could land us in jail. We have to go to see Fortunato, and tell him everything.'

'Why? What's brought this on all of a sudden?'

'My idiocy in telling the guy at the farmhouse to call him, rather than the local plods. I've engineered it so that he's investigating the murder of Trevor Eames, *and* he's trying to identify Ronnie Starr. He'll do that within a couple of days, just like we found him, by tracing the watch. Then he'll follow the same trail we did. As soon as he speaks to Reis, we're in the shit.'

Primavera's eyes were like saucers. 'Oh,' she said, theatrically. 'I rather think we are. What are we going to do?'

'I've just told you; we're going to the Guardia Civil.'

'But what about Scott? Don't we have some sort of an obligation to him?'

She had a point. If the problems over VAT and import duties hadn't occurred to me when Scott offered us the task, then they should have. Even if they had, I couldn't put my hand on my heart and say that I'd have turned down the job because of them.

'Tell you what,' I said. 'Fortunato can't make progress until tomorrow, until the shops open in the UK. We'll call Scott first, tell him the score and give him twenty-four hours to sort himself out with the Customs and Excise. If he pays them some duty, he should be in the clear.'

'Give him forty-eight hours,' she said.

'Yes, okay. There's no problem until our man the captain actually traces Starr's movements in Spain, and it could be a few days before he does that.'

We called Scott all day, without success. I rang his home, his office and his mobile, but none of them answered. I even called Jan and asked her to drive out to see him.

'What's the sudden panic, Oz?' she asked. 'Are you in trouble?' She sounded concerned. I felt a pang of pleasure.

'Potentially. Look, love, I'll tell you all about it when we come over for the wedding. For now, please, if you can, do us this favour.'

'Okay,' she said, with a faint chuckle. 'It'll cost you, mind.'

'Name your price. How are you doing, by the way?'

She was terse once more. 'Fine, thank you.' The line went dead.

She called back ninety minutes later. 'The house is locked up, Oz,' she said. 'Tight as a fish's ring. I met one of the neighbours, though. The Scotts are away for a long weekend at some bloody horse show down in England. The daughter's competing, apparently. Either Gavin's forgotten his mobile or he has to switch it off around the horses.'

'Bugger, bugger, bugger!' I cursed. 'He would pick this weekend. But thanks, love. At least we know now.'

'My pleasure. Incidentally, when I spoke to Prim this morning, I gathered that you haven't told her about Noosh and me.'

'True,' I said, with a glance at Prim, who was sitting on the other side of the terrace.

'Well, you bloody should have. I was taken aback this morning when she asked about her. The longer you delay,

Oz, the stranger she'll think it is.'

'I'll attend to it. See you, and thanks again.'

'Attend to what?' Primavera asked, casually.

'That list of time and costs for the Scott invoice.'

I tried the mobile number once more, just before it was time to leave for dinner with Davidoff, but it still came up with a smug, irritating voice telling me that it might respond if I tried later. 'I've been trying all effing day,' I growled back, leaving our client to his fate, until next morning at least.

48

Shirley was waiting for us at the foot of the stairway up to her front door as I parked the Frontera in her driveway, dead on time for dinner with Davidoff.

'We'll go straight round,' she said, leading us along the path to the rear of the house. 'Himself is a stickler for punctuality. He's been all hustle and bustle today, getting ready for tonight. He swam for bloody miles this afternoon, then he disappeared off to the fruit market and the fish shop. He's been cooking ever since he got back.

'Davidoff does his paella for me once a year. When Clive was alive he used to do it for us both, and he's kept the tradition going. There's never a set day, but he never forgets. Until now he's only ever done it for me. You two are the first guests he's ever invited.'

'We're honoured,' I said. 'But how are you getting on? It's a day or two since we've seen you.'

'I'm fine,' said Shirley. 'Apart from that bloody brother of mine.'

'Adrian?' Prim was surprised. 'I thought you and he got on so well.'

'We do. That's why I'm pissed off. He left yesterday without saying goodbye. I was down at Maggie's till around nine, and I know I was a bit late, but he might have waited. His flight wasn't due out until two a.m. All I got was a bloody note saying that he had to have a quick drink with a chum at the golf club, thanks for everything and goodbye.'

'Did you call him today to tell him off?'

'Wouldn't waste the call, Prim. Let him stew in it for a

couple of days. I'll wait until I know he's really busy in the office, then I'll phone him.'

As she finished, we reached the summer-house, and right on cue, Davidoff stepped out. As always he was dressed from head to foot in black, but this time it was satin; a shirt with long loose sleeves buttoned at the wrist, tight trousers, and of course, a matching eye patch. His skin was oiled, and his cropped dark hair was sleek. The garden lights were on against the gathering darkness. They shone on his clothes, making them seem to shimmer as he gave a courtly bow towards the ladies.

We had brought the best bottle of *Cava* that I could find in the *bodega*. It had been chilling all day, and was encased in an insulating sleeve. The dark eye shone as I handed it over. 'Thank you, my friend,' he said. 'I will open it first. It will make an acceptable aperitif.' I didn't quite know how to take that, until I saw the Krug chilling in an ice bucket, inside the guest bungalow's open-plan kitchen.

I felt that I should do something to help, but Davidoff shooed me away, to switch off the floodlights, then to join the girls, seated now at a white table beside the pool. I had barely joined them before he was fluttering around us, holding a tray with the *Cava* in four flutes, finely made, with gold leaf round their long stems.

'My dear friend Clive gave these to me, in the year before he died,' he said to Primavera, leaning towards her as he sat down. 'I have always kept them here. This is the first time since he died, is it not, Shirley, that all four have been filled together. That's good, because this is a special night. Look,' he said, pointing up to the darkening sky, 'I have even arranged the moonlight.'

I grinned. '*Never,*' I thought, '*have I heard bullshit of such a high order.*' But I kept the thought to myself, for our host was clearly firing on all cylinders and it would have been churlish to interrupt his flow.

I felt slightly huffed when he rushed us through the very

fine *Cava*. 'Come, come.' He stood up. 'To the table. Davidoff's paella does not suffer being kept waiting.'

A bowl of toasted bread was on the table, with halved beef tomatoes ready to rub into it, with olive oil and garlic and a dish of anchovies. 'The L'Escala starter,' the chef announced, 'is one of the world's simplest. It is also one of the best.'

He's right. Tomato-soaked toast, rubbed with garlic, with oil and anchovies doesn't sound like much: till you try it.

If Davidoff had a fault that night, it seemed to be a tendency to rush his guests, but we accepted it as being in the interests of arriving at the paella at exactly the right moment. There are regional variations of Spain's national dish; along the Costa Brava, as I had come to know, they favour seafood. But I never in my life tasted one like Davidoff served up that night, with the Krug.

How he persuaded the fish to remain in such substantial chunks, and yet be so moist, I'll never know. How he coaxed every mussel and clam to open its shell is quite beyond me. How he managed to keep the rice at such a consistency, while the cooking of every other ingredient should have militated against it, I have no idea.

He shared one secret with us, but only one. He bent towards Prim once again, and picked up a tiny crustacean. 'You must have these, my darling,' he said. 'You don't find them in the fish shops but on the quayside. The fishermen who catch the prawns throw these away. I gather them and cook them in my paella, for the extra flavour. Look.' He put the crab between his teeth and bit it, hard enough to crush the shell, then he sucked. 'Like that. Don't eat them. Just crack them for the juices and the taste.'

He had made enough for six at least. We finished it, disregarding even the Krug until we had whacked our way through the lot.

Davidoff grinned, as he looked at us, one by one. Then, lightning fast, he slapped his stomach. 'That's it,' he shouted. 'The best I can do.' He jumped to his feet and fetched a fruit bowl. 'This is to finish. God makes a better dessert than I do, but when it comes to paella, I can whip his ass.' He paused. 'As for coffee, well, we'll just have another bottle of Krug.'

I watched him as he leaned back in the moonlight, savouring his champagne and making small talk with Prim and Shirley. There was a grace about him, an economy of everything, as though his whole metabolism had been set up with an eye to longevity. When night came he seemed to be at the height of his powers, fascinating, charming and somehow provocative, and on that night in particular, I thought him the most amazing man that I had ever met. Nothing has happened since to change that view.

Shirley had gone to the bathroom, walking with a degree of concentration, when the phone rang in the villa.

Davidoff gestured to me. 'You better answer it. It could be Adrian, full of contrition, or better still, the awful John calling to say that he is not coming after all.'

I nodded and ran round the edge of the pool towards the house. The kitchen was dark, but I found the light switch in a second. The phone was on one of the work surfaces, and it was still ringing insistently. I strode across and picked it up.

'*Hola, este residencia* Senora Gash,' I said, in the best Spanish I could manage.

There was a long silence at the other end of the phone line. I waited for it to go dead, but instead, after a while, I heard a low rumbling sigh. 'Tell me, Mr Blackstone,' said Captain Fortunato, evenly, 'that I am having a bad dream, and that I have not just heard you trying to speak Spanish with an appalling Scottish accent. Tell me, please, that isn't you.'

I knew at once that the evening had taken a very unpleasant turn. 'I have a terrible feeling,' I muttered into the phone, 'that I should be saying much the same to you. But the trouble is, I don't think either of us is dreaming.'

'In that case, Senor, this is what I want you to do. I want you to wait at the villa of Senora Gash, until one of my cars gets there. Then I want you and she to get in, and let it bring you here to join me. Don't ask any questions of me, but between now and your getting to where I am, you should be thinking very carefully of what it is you were going to tell me two days ago, but which slipped your mind.'

'I'll wait for your car,' I croaked, and replaced the phone. I leaned against the surface, heart pounding, legs shaking, and looked out of the window, at Shirley, leading Prim and Davidoff towards the group of sofa loungers beneath the moonlit palms, he with his arm wound round my partner's waist, laughing softly in her ear.

I don't know why, but just then, my eye was caught by a photograph, one of a number pinned to the window-frame. I stared at it, and as I did, I saw Ronnie Starr's murderer: more than that, I knew instinctively in my gut, who, in turn, had killed him.

49

From the moment the car pulled away, Shirley asked the same question, over and over again.

'Where are we going?' she snapped at the driver, in Spanish, until she realised that his silence meant that he had been ordered not to speak to us at all.

'Where are we going?' she asked me, in my turn.

I told her, as I had in the villa, 'We're going to meet the regional commander of the Guardia Civil. But I don't know why, and I don't know where.'

I was pretty certain that I had told her one lie. As the car reached Verges, and turned left towards La Bisbal, I had a feeling that it might be two. When it turned right on to the road for Flaca, La Pera and Pubol, that suspicion hardened.

The driver raced recklessly along the twisting road to La Pera, then swung right. I expected him to stop in the Pubol car park, but he didn't. Instead, he drove right up to the entrance to Gala's castle, and screeched to a halt, giving a blast on the horn as he did so.

A green-uniformed officer at the top of the steps which led to the house beckoned to us as we stepped out. The approach was lit, but the building was still in darkness. 'Round there,' he said, in Spanish as we reached him, pointing not into the house, but to the garden.

We turned the corner, and saw a blaze of light coming from the garage doorway. Another uniformed policeman stood outside, waving to us to approach.

'What the 'ell's going on?' said Shirley. It was the first time she had spoken in fifteen minutes and she was ready to explode. We stepped inside the garage.

The Cadillac was still there, as it had been on my earlier visits to the castle, only this time the great lid of its cavernous trunk was raised. Captain Fortunato stood beside it. He smiled at me and called out something in Catalan. I stared blankly back at him.

'Eh?'

'I said three in a row can be bad luck, Senor. Come here.'

I moved towards him. Shirley followed me, but the detective held up his hand. 'Not you, Senora,' he said.

She glared back and kept walking. 'Don't try to stop me,' she spat. 'It could be embarrassing. Now what the bloody hell . . .'

Fortunato shook his head and stepped back, allowing Shirley and me to look into the boot of the Cadillac. I knew it would be him. The man in the photo in the kitchen, the man who had staged the auction, the man who had killed Ronnie Starr to lay his hand on a quarter of a million pounds' worth of Dalí.

I was expecting him. Shirley wasn't. She looked into the boot and she screamed. Then she turned and went for the Captain, snarling and spitting. She was as tall as he was, and powerful. She flailed at him with both arms, heaving big, sledging blows at him, until he was able to grab her hands and use his man's strength to restrain her.

I was barely interested in their struggle. I couldn't drag my attention away from the body in the car. I recognised him by the colour of his eyes and the line of his nose rather than anything else, just as I had in Shirley's kitchen. Even dead, with three bullet holes in the front of his polo shirt, one right in the centre of the golf club crest, he managed to look ordinary. Fortyish, dark hair greying, medium build, medium everything. The odd thing was that the last time I had seen him, and on every other occasion that we had met, Adrian Ford had been wearing a beard.

'When did he grow it, Shirley? The beard, I mean.' My

question was almost a shout, as I looked at her, over my shoulders, her shocked eyes swam back into focus, and looked at me, trying to comprehend what she had just seen.

'Last summer,' she moaned, at last. 'Why?'

'Was it unusual for him to wear one?'

'Yes, he'd never had one before. Why? What the bloody hell's this about? Oz, who killed my brother?' Exploding suddenly into tears, she tore her hands from Fortunato's grasp, turned to me and threw her arms around my neck, weeping on my shoulder.

I looked past her at the captain. 'Let's get out of here.' He nodded and led the way, out of the garage, through the castle's small courtyard and into the souvenir shop. He found a chair in the corner and brought it into the centre of the floor, for Shirley.

'Just before eight this evening,' said Fortunato, 'one of my men received an anonymous telephone call. The caller spoke in Catalan. That was why I addressed you in Catalan when you came in, Senor Blackstone. If you had understood me, you would have been in big trouble, but clearly you did not.

'The man on the phone said that we should come here, and look in the boot of the Cadillac. My guy had the sense to make him repeat the message, so that we kept him on the line long enough to trace the call. It was made somewhere in this area, on a Cellnet mobile telephone, sold in England and listed under the name of a company called CSG Products, Limited.' He stopped and looked at us.

'That's my company,' said Shirley. 'The caller must have used Adrian's phone. I was always telling him to programme a security code into it.'

'How long has he been dead?' I asked the captain.

'About a day, we think. As you can see, he was shot, at point-blank range.'

'How did you know to call Mrs Gash?'

'There was a business card left on the body. The name on it was Adrian Ford, and the Senora's number was written on the back. It was as if the murderer had left us instructions.'

Fortunato paused again, and his eyes narrowed. 'Why did you ask the lady about a beard?'

'Because until yesterday, her brother wore one.'

The policeman looked at me in astonishment. 'That's amazing. We found this in the Cadillac, with the body.' He reached into his jacket, produced a Phillips rechargeable shaver, and handed it to me. I examined it until I found a button beneath the blade assembly. I pressed it and the shaving surface, with its triple foiled cutters, swung up on a hinge. The chamber beneath was full of dark bristle. I showed it to Fortunato.

'This is fucking crazy,' he whispered, stepping away from Shirley. 'The killer brings his victim here, but before he shoots him, he makes him shave off his beard. Why, in god's name, would he do that?'

When I answered, it took him by surprise. 'So that I would know who he really was, and what he had done.'

'Pardon?'

'I'll tell you the whole story, but Shirley has to hear it too.'

There were still one or two curious locals in the bar of the restaurant across the street when we walked in. Fortunato cleared them out and ordered the owner to bring three coffees and three large brandies, before sitting down with Shirley and me at a table by the fireplace.

'Okay,' he said.

As quickly as I could, I explained how Gavin Scott had been set up at the auction, how he had paid four hundred thousand dollars for the purported lost masterpiece, and that my commission from him had been to prove the picture genuine or fake, one way or another.

'Pretty soon,' I said, 'but don't ask how, or we'll be here for a year, I discovered that the man calling himself Ronnie Starr at the auction in Peretellada had been an impostor. I learned that the real Ronnie had been murdered, and buried, about a year ago, and also that his body had been discovered but moved to Ventallo. Like you said last night, those local coppers had been at it.

'I found Ronnie's girlfriend, in La Pera. She told me that she had seen Ronnie with Trevor Eames and a third man, whose name she didn't know. She told me also that Ronnie had been in possession of the work which Scott bought, the alleged Dalí. He didn't paint it, though. He seems to have been given it.

'Shortly after that, he disappeared. Nine months later, the picture was sold by the impostor, at the auction set up by Trevor Eames and David Foy. A few weeks before that, Eames sold a picture which Ronnie Starr certainly did paint, to Shirley's son, John. Work it out for yourself. Eames, or Adrian, or both of them killed Starr, for the picture bearing the signature of Dalí, and for what they could get for it.'

'Was this man Foy in on the murder?' asked Fortunato, sharply.

'I doubt it very much, but if you want my advice, you should squeeze the bastard till he bleeds anyway.'

He nodded. 'I will, don't worry. So let's carry on. You go looking for Eames, but you find him dead. Then Starr's body turns up. Did you know that Senor Ford was the third man?'

'Honest to god, it never entered my head, not until tonight. I didn't think we'd ever find the phoney Starr. Prim and I were coming to you tomorrow' – I tweaked the truth a wee bit there, okay – 'with the story as we knew it. But someone beat us to it.'

I looked across at the big, handsome, tear-streaked woman in the chair. 'Shirley, I'm really sorry,' I said. 'This must all be a terrible shock.'

'Yes,' she said, 'and no. Though I loved my brother dearly, I always knew he was a rogue. But I can't believe that he could . . .

'Adrian was always just a bit . . . a bit chancy, if you know what I mean. Although we gave him a job with the company, we were always wary of him. We never let him become a shareholder, and when Clive died, I never thought for a moment of letting him take over. Maybe if we had given him a share of the business, and some wealth of his own, he wouldn't have been so greedy for it that he'd decide to get mixed up in something like this.' She wrung her hands. 'I loved my brother, and he was good to me. But both of us knew, without it having to be said, that I didn't trust him.

'Years back, Clive banned him from playing cards at any of my parties, after we found that he had cheated one of our friends out of two grand in a game at his bridge club. Adrian always had an eye out for a mug that he could take money off, at snooker or at golf. But the odds had to be weighed in his favour. He used to kid us on he couldn't play, but we'd heard all about him.

'When John bought that picture from Trevor, I had a nagging suspicion that Adrian was behind it. I'd known that the two of them knew each other. I never thought he'd go as far as this, though. And I still can't believe he'd kill anyone. That must have been Trevor Eames.'

I took her hand. 'Almost certainly,' I said, not really believing it.

'So who killed Ford and Eames?' Fortunato asked me.

'You're the detective, mate. I'm only a private enquiry agent.'

'What about the girlfriend? Maybe she did know who the third man was? Maybe she decided that the other two had to go?'

'In revenge for Ronnie,' I said. 'Hardly, she has his kid to look after now.'

'No, no. Not in revenge. For protection. You civilians, you see a pretty face and you think, "Poor girl, what a tragedy." You never ask yourself, "Could she have been behind the whole thing?" Maybe Ford and Eames were her partners, and she killed them before you could get too close. Maybe you and your girl are next on her list. You never think of that?'

I sucked in my breath. I never had, but there was a chilling ring to it.

50

Shirley spent the journey back to L'Escala with her head on my shoulder, sobbing occasionally, and tugging at her fingernails. She went straight indoors when we reached the villa. I had offered that we would stay with her for the night, but she preferred to be alone.

I went round to the garden, after she had gone inside. All the lights were out, but the night was still bright enough for me to find my way round to the sofa loungers by the palm trees. They were deserted. I looked around, puzzled, until I heard a smooth lapping sound from the pool.

Prim was swimming, slowly and rhythmically. I leaned against a palm tree, half-hidden by it, and watched her as she swam, length after length. Eventually I stepped out of the shadows, but still she didn't see me, not until I knelt by the edge of the pool.

She looked up, startled, her mouth slightly open, until she found her feet. 'Oz, I thought . . . I . . . Oh, you gave me a fright, that's all.' She stood and I saw that she had been swimming naked. I lent her my hand as she climbed up the tiled steps in one corner of the pool, and watched her as she dried herself on her skirt, struck all the time by her strange silence.

'What was the phone call about?' she asked, at last. 'Why did Fortunato want to see you?'

As I told her, her face grew more and more shocked. 'Oh,' she cried. 'Poor Shirley. We should stay with her.'

'She doesn't want that. Besides, the old chap's here.'

'No he isn't. He's gone. And stop calling him the old chap.'

'When did he go? And why?'

She began to dress. 'A while back. Before I had my swim. I think John's coming early tomorrow, and Davidoff won't stay here at the same time as him.'

'He must be a real charmer, this John,' I said. 'He'd better be on his best behaviour tomorrow.'

We were half-way home before she asked me, 'Who does Fortunato think killed Eames and Adrian? David Foy?'

I shook my head in the dark. 'No, he's not quoted. He's too rich, for a start. This thing was about money, and for now the captain is putting his cash on Reis. He thinks she could have been in it from the start. And he could be right. We only have her word about the visit from Trevor.'

'No,' she said, violently. 'No way. That poor girl. And her baby. She loved the man, Oz. I know that.'

And in the dark, she began to cry. She was still crying when we got home, and later as I kissed her face after she had made unexpected, furious love to me, I could still taste the salt of her tears, where they flowed soft, hot and wet.

51

I didn't believe it was Reis either, not for an instant. I knew who did it from the moment I saw the photograph in Shirley's kitchen. When I looked into the trunk of that Caddy, I knew I would see Adrian there, and in my blood, I knew who had executed him.

Fortunato held the girl for a couple of days, then let her go, as convinced finally of her innocence as I was.

He came to see us on the following Thursday, the day after we had seen Shirley and John off from Girona Airport, with Adrian's body in their chartered aircraft. We met him for lunch at one of the few tables which was still set up outside Casa Miñana, with the dying of the season.

'There's nothing you're holding out on me?' he asked. Behind him, in the doorway, Miguel watched us, nervously.

'No. What we know for certain, you know for certain,' I replied, truthfully. 'Have you developed a theory yet?'

Fortunato shook his head. 'It wasn't the girl; I accept that now. And like you said, I squeezed that man Foy until he sweated blood. He's a fool, and a bad friend to have, but no more than that.

'I did think that it might have been your Mr Scott, getting even for being conned. The Scottish police interviewed him yesterday, and reported that he can prove that he was nowhere near Spain at the time of either murder. Then of course there was you two. You were in the thick of it, but I realised pretty quickly that you couldn't have killed Adrian Ford.'

'Thanks for that,' said Primavera. 'What made you see that?'

'Simple. At the time he was being shot, you were in Ventallo, helping to discover Starr's remains.'

'I suppose you could have killed Trevor Eames, though. You didn't, did you?'

'Afraid not,' I said.

'That's all right, then.'

'So where do you go from here?' Prim asked.

'Back to my office, to sit and wait for something to turn up that I haven't thought of. Only, Senor Oz and Senora Prim, I don't think that it will. Of all the people who knew Starr well, only his girlfriend is left alive. I have spoken to everyone in La Pera, and in Pubol.

'Some of them remember him, but none well. Most never even knew his name. I know that the picture which your Mr Scott bought is the key. If I could discover who painted that, or who gave it to Starr, the mystery might be solved. But I don't see how I ever will find that out.'

'What about Scott,' I asked him, 'and the way he bought the picture? Will there be any comeback on that?'

Fortunato laughed. 'I'm no fucking tax man,' he said. 'I don't give a shit about Scott, or the goddamn picture. Spain is not so cruel, Senor, that if a man is stupid enough to pay four hundred thousand dollars for a phoney Dalí, she would expect him to pay tax on it as well. If he has a problem, it is in Britain.'

He finished his Cortado and stood up. 'Thanks for lunch, and thanks for your help, when you finally got round to giving it. I got to go now.'

'What'll happen to Starr's body?' asked Prim.

'Senora Sonas has claimed it. She is having him buried next Monday; properly, with respect, in La Pera.'

52

Of course, Prim and I went to Ronnie Starr's funeral. We had expected to be the only people there, other than Reis, but we were wrong. Mrs Adams, the principal of the Cardiff Art College, had flown over to pay her respects. She took me by surprise; from her voice, I had expected her to be an Amazon, but in fact she was a small, fat woman with bad hair, the kind you would always walk past in a crowd.

The discovery of Starr's body had made news in Britain, and as a result, the media outnumbered the mourners by two to one. They stood back silently as the coffin was slid into its hole in the white wall of the mausoleum, and as we filed out of the cemetery, but as soon as they were through the gates, they pounced on Reis.

Only one reporter approached us, a spotty wee girl in her mid-twenties. She had a Welsh accent, and she grinned all the time, as if she was enjoying her unexpected swan in Spain, regardless of the circumstances.

'What's your connection with the deceased?' she asked, without an 'excuse me', or a 'please', just the arrogant assumption that she had a right to an answer.

I told her that her mother was a hand-maiden of the whore of Babylon and that her father was a wild boar, and then I invited her to fuck off. Since I told her all this in Spanish, she simply grinned some more and walked away, to find someone who would understand her stupid questions. I watched her go with a feeling of accomplishment: my Spanish was improving all the time.

As I watched her, I took a long look around for someone

else, someone whom I thought just might have shown up, but I saw no one, save Reis, the principal, the TV cameraman, the reporters and the undertakers.

'Come on,' I said to Prim, 'Let's go along to Pubol.'

We drove the half-kilometre or so, and had a snack in the bar where I had sat last with Fortunato and with a stunned Shirley Gash. We were the only people there for a while, then an English family arrived, dad, mum and two loud, over-indulged kids, over for half-term at the villa, as they announced to the owner.

I waited for a little longer, in case I caught sight of someone else, but eventually, we headed back to L'Escala, to devote more time to our expanding business.

The growing work-list was done on time, good and full reports were submitted to our clients, and invoices were prepared. It was good, healthy, stimulating activity, and as it proceeded, Prim seemed to recover from her shock over Adrian's death, and possibly from delayed reaction to our encounters with the remains of Eames and Starr.

But for my part, I went through life as if I was in a bubble of unreality. Captain Fortunato had gone back to his office to wait for nothing to happen. Prim, even if she might be a little strange and distant, seemed to be putting the bizarre events behind us. Shirley Gash, who returned from England on the Friday after Starr's funeral, came to us for dinner next day with her grief under control.

Looking at them across the table, making their small talk, I saw them suddenly as someone had once noticed some people on a famous football pitch. They thought it was all over. I knew it wasn't.

I went back to Pubol three times in the week after Ronnie Starr's funeral. Once, I told Prim that I was going to make sure that Reis was all right. On the other occasions I simply went, unannounced. Each time, I sat in the bar, looking at the street outside. Each time I paid my money and I went into Gala's castle, into her garden, with its weird animals, into the garage, where the Cadillac stood on view to the tourists, roped off again as if it still had contained only one body in its lifetime, and into the Delma, where the stuffed giraffe and the statuary still stood guard over her lonely tomb, and over the redundant slab beside it.

I was looking for someone, but I never really expected to find him. Rather, I hoped that he would find me, but that didn't happen either. Eventually, leaving an empty feeling, my certainty began to slip away.

There were only three days left before Prim and I were due to fly back to Scotland for my dad's wedding, when at last I found the key. It was Tuesday morning, and Shirley had taken Prim to Girona to buy a dress for Saturday. I was sitting at the table on the balcony working alone on a report, when the thought fired itself like a bullet into my brain.

My wallet was in my jacket in the wardrobe. I rushed into the bedroom, and searched through it until I found the business card that Adrian Ford had given me, just after he had finished cleaning my clock at the snooker table.

Sure enough, it carried a mobile number. I picked up the phone and dialled it. At first, it was unobtainable, but I tried once more, using the UK code to link into the system. It rang three times before it was answered.

'It's taken you this long to figure it out,' said a familiar voice on the other end of the line. 'Oz, my boy, I'm disappointed in you. I was afraid I'd have to come and get you.'

'Where are you?'

'You don't need to know where I am right now. Come to the castle tonight at eleven o'clock. There's a side door beyond the garage. It will be unlocked and the alarm will be switched off. Come to the Delma: you'll find me there. Got that?'

'I've got it.'

'But listen to me. It is very important that you come alone. You must not bring Captain Fortunato and his gang, and most of all you must not bring the lovely Primavera. I could not bear that. You promise me this?'

'I promise.'

'Good. I see you. Before you come, one thing you can do. Take a look in the book about Dalí, the one I told you not to buy when I took you to the castle, but which I know you bought anyway. Take a look in there and see if you can find the answer.'

The line went dead. I sat at the table, gasping, realising that for the last thirty seconds I had been holding my breath.

I had looked at the book before, of course; at all of the colour plates and some of the text. However, I had found the translation patchy and confusing, altogether too heavy going for my taste, and I had chucked it before the end.

I fetched it from the coffee table and attacked it again, opening it more or less where I had given up before, around page 150. I scanned the pages for two hours, stopping occasionally to ponder a particularly obscure reference, then going on when I had satisfied myself that it signified bad translation rather than hidden meaning.

I finished the text proper, then the fine-printed notes. Finally, I turned to the section headed 'Appendices'. And there, from page 320, the answer jumped out at me, as clear as the bright day which lit the autumn snow on the tips of the high Pyrenees.

53

I left the apartment before Prim returned from Girona. I didn't want to have to spin her a story about why I was going out, and I didn't want any problems over her insisting on coming with me.

So I headed out of St Marti in mid-afternoon and drove up to Figueras. Parking near the Dalí museum is never a problem because of the concrete multi-storey hidden behind it. I stuck a long-term ticket on my windscreen and went for a wander round the lanes which surround it.

After almost an hour poring over the books, prints, T-shirts and other memorabilia, I paid my admission fee and went into the museum itself. I had been there before, of course, and essentially the Dalí is a pretty static exhibition. There's the car in the courtyard, which fills up with water whenever someone's daft enough to put 100 pesetas in the slot, there's the Mae West room, there's the ceiling with the sole of god's foot descending from it, and there's the stereoscopic painting which somehow turns, when seen through a viewer, into the head of Abraham Lincoln. All these plus dubious sketches from the early days, mad sculptures and other oddities, but very few of the recognisable great works. They are scattered in public galleries around the world, and in private collections . . . just like the Toreador of the Apocalypse.

I began to wonder if their absence was an accident of fate, or something else. Finally, just as the place was about to close for the day, I made my way down to the cellar. It's much bigger than the one at Pubol, and Dalí's tomb is much grander than Gala's, with a greater show of memorials.

I stood before it and I tried to recapture the feeling of loneliness that had come over both Prim and me as we stood before the grave in Pubol. Somehow, it wouldn't come. I had read all about the crazy artist and his equally crazy wife, and I had heard the tales of them in St Marti and L'Escala. It seemed natural that they should be buried side by side, yet here was Dalí in his emperor's tomb, and somehow that seemed right also.

There was another puzzle there, but I didn't have time right then to work it out, for a bell was ringing to chase the last of the visitors from the building.

I hung around in Figueras for most of the evening, reading the Dalí book and dining in a bar off one of the narrow streets. At last, with ten o'clock approaching, I went back to the multi-storey park, picked up the Frontera and headed south for Pubol.

The road from Figueras was almost straight. I drove slowly, taking my time, preparing myself for my meeting. More than once, the thought came into my mind that I had set myself up to be killed, but every time I put it aside. There was no possible reason to kill me. Well, maybe there was one, but I couldn't take that seriously; not even then.

I reached Pubol twenty minutes early, and parked in the big, flat, red-ash area which was as far as cars could venture, tucking the Frontera out of sight as best I could. The night was moonless and the stars stood out more vividly than they normally did in the southern sky, as I walked quietly into the hamlet.

The bar and restaurant were closed and shuttered. Nothing stirred as I slipped across the narrow street, and up the steps which led to Gala's castle. The gate was locked, but I climbed it, quickly and noiselessly. As I had been told, I hurried round the corner, my left hand on the wall in the darkness, and cursing myself for my stupidity in not bringing a torch.

I had never noticed the side door in all my earlier visits, but it wasn't difficult to find. Three metres along from the locked garage doors, behind a bush which deepened the darkness, my searching hand found a sudden break in the wall, and felt the touch of wood. There was a handle on the right. I turned it, opened the door and stepped inside. At first the blackness was complete. I stretched my hands out on both sides and realised that I was in a short corridor. Slowly, I inched along it, until my foot encountered something solid: another door. It opened easily too. Suddenly, the night was less dark, as the starlight shone down into the castle's open courtyard. I stood there, like a nervous burglar, listening for a footfall upstairs, until my eyes could make out the cellar door, and the light which shone under it.

I crossed to it in four long steps and slipped inside, opening and closing it as quickly as I could. Blinking at the sudden brightness, I tiptoed down the curving stone way, my heart thumping.

I knew he would be waiting for me in the Delma, beneath the castle. He was, but not where I had expected.

The second great stone slab, on the left of Gala's tomb, had been slewed round, through an angle of around sixty degrees. The area of surrounding stone over which it had passed was white with French chalk, used, I guessed, as a lubricant to ease its movement. As I stared at it, I saw that the stone was, in fact, a gateway. The stairway which it concealed was narrow, and very steep, as steep in fact as that on Trevor Eames' boat. But it went down much further, around eighteen feet, I guessed, as I looked into it. Light spilled up from a chamber, a catacomb, a hidden apartment below the Delma.

I guess I should have been scared shitless as I made my way down, bracing my hands against the stone on either side of the steps. But I wasn't. It never occurred to me that I should be scared of a friend.

The main chamber was big; thirty feet square, I guessed, and it had been cut out of rock. The air should have been stale, but it wasn't. A ventilator shaft had been cut in the far wall, leading, I guessed, to an outlet way beyond the garden.

Beside the stair, to my left, there was a wooden door, leading perhaps to other rooms.

The secret apartment was as brightly lit as the cellar above. At first my mind was blown. I had to force myself, but eventually I regained some kind of self-control and looked around. The stairway had opened out not quite into the centre of the room. It was furnished with a dining table without chairs, an old red leather chaise longue with mahogany legs, and an ornate, hand-carved bed, set away in the corner to my left. Around the walls, pictures were hanging. Magnificent, explosive paintings, full of life, full of colour, full of warmth; full, I could tell, of love. At another time, I would have stared at them for hours, but I couldn't because right there and then, my attention was drawn to the other things in the room.

There was a large television set, with a video recorder below, both plugged into a socket in the wall, and both switched on. The pause button on the video had been hit, and a face was frozen on the screen: a terrified face, that of Adrian Ford.

Beyond the appliances there were three easels, each supporting a picture covered by a sheet. They were all around three feet by four; the one in the centre was landscape format, while those on the outside were portrait.

Finally, on trestles, beside the far wall, there was an open coffin, a fine affair, a work of art, carved in dark wood, and highly polished. Beside it, on the floor, a dining chair lay, on its side. As I looked at it, I saw in its shadow a small brown plastic bottle, without a lid.

My eyes were on the floor as I stepped towards the bier. I knew what it was I would find, but I didn't want to see it. But finally I stood beside it, put my hand on its edge and lifted my gaze.

Davidoff didn't look old at all now. All of the lines had gone from his face, and from the hands which lay crossed over his chest. He was wearing his black satin outfit, his hair was sleek, and his skin was oiled, still with that olive tinge, only a little waxy.

I knew, all right, but I put my hand on his forehead just to make sure. It was the first time I had ever touched a dead person. He was still warm, but it was leaving him, as his life had ebbed away an hour or so earlier, on a tide of sleeping pills from the empty bottle on the floor, taken after he had used the chair to climb into his own coffin.

I looked at him, lying there. He'd won all the way, and I'll swear he was smiling.

I knew what he wanted me to do next. I picked up the chair, set it down in front of the television, then, when I had made myself as comfortable as the hard seat would allow, reached down and pressed the play button of the VCR.

'All right, all right,' said Adrian Ford, fear making his voice harsh and shrill. As the picture began to move, I could see that he was standing with his back to the gaping mouth of the Cadillac's open trunk. 'I'll do it, but come on, what for? What's all this about?'

'In good time.' Davidoff's voice came from off camera. 'First oblige me, and shave off that unspeakable fucking beard.'

'Dav, this is crazy. If I'd known you'd flipped at last I'd never have agreed to meet you.'

'Of course you would. You couldn't say no to your friend Davidoff, the guy who made you all that money. Now shave!'

On screen, Ford began to do as he was told. His beard was tough and tangled, but he hacked away at it with the trimmer of the Philishave, and smoothed it with the triple foil head. It took him ten minutes, but at last his chin and jaw were clean and white, and he had become the man in Shirley's photo.

'Satisfied?' he said eventually looking not at the camera, but behind it.

'Sure.' I heard Davidoff reply. 'Now you look like you did when you killed my young friend Ronnie.'

'What!' It was a shriek.

'You heard me. I know about it. You killed Ronnie Starr, up at St Marti, and you buried his body. Then a few months later, you sold his pictures. The picture of Cadaques, you had

Trevor Eames sell to your nephew to give to your sister. The other one, the one which Ronnie did not paint, the one with the authentic signature of Dalí, you sold in June, at a phoney auction for four hundred thousand US dollars; a quarter of a million sterling; fifty million pesetas. That's a good enough reason to kill someone; a good enough reason for you anyway. You going to admit it for my camera, or will I just shoot you like a dog?' Ford threw up his hands, as if to ward someone off. 'Okay, okay, I sold the pictures, but I didn't kill Starr. Trevor did that. We arranged to meet him up at St Marti, one night. After we'd eaten, and everyone was gone, we walked round to the headland. I suggested the auction idea to Ronnie. I said that Trevor and I would fix up the sale of the Dalí, and that we'd split the profits. He'd get half andTrevor and I would split the rest. Ronnie said no, no way. I'd have left it at that. But Trevor picked up a rock behind his back and smashed his head in. He's a violent man, is Trevor.'

'Was,' said Davidoff's voice.

Confusion mingled with the fear on Ford's face.

'Ah, you hadn't heard about Trevor, then. It's too bad. Somebody went on board his boat and killed him. Tragic.' Ford's right eye began to twitch, uncontrollably. 'Don't tell me such shit, Adrian,' said the off-screen voice, sighing contemptuously. 'Trevor Eames was no leader. He was a deckhand, not a captain. If he killed Ronnie, it was because you told him to. But I don't think that. I think you did. You have to be real greedy to kill someone. Trevor wasn't that greedy. You are.'

Ford began to beg with his eyes. 'No. Trevor killed him, honest. Afterwards, well we had to clear traces of him away. So Trev went and got his pictures from the woman in La Pera, and told her that Ronnie had done a runner. Since we were left with the pictures anyway, Trev said we should go ahead with the auction. He knew a chap up at Pals, who suggested that we set up some silly, picture-crazy chum of his. That's how it happened. It was all Trevor.'

I heard Davidoff snort. 'That is unspeakable bullshit. You made the booking at Peretellada. I checked. You paid for the dinner. And you paid for the dinner later, when Trevor and Foy came along to collect their cut . . . at least that's what Senor Foy thought he was there to do. You paid Trevor seventy five thousand dollars from the four hundred. John Gash even paid for the dinner at the auction, with the money he gave you for the Cadaques picture.'

'How can you know that?' Ford squealed.

'Simple. I asked. The manager at Peretellada, he's Catalan. My people will tell you anything, if you ask them in their own language. That's the key to them. As for Trevor; well, most people will tell you the truth if you hold a gun to their head. Only the really tough ones, like you, will try to lie their way out of danger, right to the end. I learned that in the Civil War, my friend. I wish I'd been able to blow Trevor's brains all over his boat. But I couldn't make so much noise. So I had to use a knife. I learned that in the war also. There's no one around here. I can make as much noise as I like.'

On screen, I could see Adrian Ford begin to shake. 'Wait a minute Dav,' he screamed, as if a gun had been raised. 'It's your fault too. If you hadn't introduced us to Starr in the bar across the road, none of this would have happened. He'd never have shown me the Dalí. He'd be alive today but for you.' A last flicker of defiance showed in his face. 'You evil old bastard!'

'I know that,' said the voice. 'And for that I must die too. But evil, no. Davidoff is good, and at the end, good usually wins.'

Pure astonishment spread across Ford's face, as the first bullet hit him, and as the first red flower bloomed on his chest, all of it simultaneous with the sound of the pistol as the shot cracked from the speaker of the television set. I think he died then, but Davidoff shot him twice more, just in case, hurling him backwards into the trunk of the Caddy.

His feet hung out over the body panel, until a slim figure, wearing a black T-shirt and trousers, stepped into the frame, swung them into the car, and slammed the lid shut. Then Davidoff turned, revolver held in his left hand, and reached for the camera.

The screen went blank, but only for a few seconds. When it cleared, Davidoff was sitting calmly, facing the camera. He held up a newspaper. 'This is to show you the date, Oz. It's today's, Tuesday's. They always do this in the movies, so I thought I would too. Not that I want you ever to let anyone else see this tape.

'That's how he died,' he said, 'that bastard Adrian, who betrayed my friendship and trust and who killed Ronnie Starr. For either, I'd have shot him.'

He smiled, then reached down and picked up a book. The Dalí volume. 'But enough of Adrian and Trevor,' he drawled, in that strange Hispanic American accent. 'Have you found the answer, on page three hundred and twenty? I know you; you're a smart boy. I reckon you have.' He grinned at me from the screen.

'There were two of you,' I said, as if he could hear me. 'You're his brother.'

'That's right,' Davidoff said, as if in answer, as he waved the heavy volume at the camera. 'The book says that Salvador Galo Anselmo Dalí i Domènech was born at Number 20 Carrer Monturiol, in the town of Figueras on the twelfth of October, 1901, and that he died in August, 1903. It says that Salvador Felipé Jacinto Dalí i Domènech was born in the same house on May 11, 1904.'

He beamed, like a magician about to pull a rabbit from his hat. 'I am Salvador Felipé Jacinto Dalí i Domènech. Yes Oz, what the book says is true. My father had two sons named Salvador. But it is not correct when it says that my elder brother died as an infant. That was a story which my father put about to cover the real truth. For my father was a very private man, with a misplaced sense of shame, and there were some things which he simply could not have borne had they become public knowledge and matters for discussion.

'From his earliest days, my brother Salvador behaved oddly. As a very small baby he did not smile, or laugh. Our mother used to say, when she could speak of it, that his eyes were always fierce.' He frowned. 'As he grew he seemed to have a hostile spirit within him. When he cut his teeth, he would bite the nipple at which he sucked, he would bite our father, he would bite himself. His fingernails had to be cut short, for he would scratch anything he could touch.

'Salvador was a strong, healthy child, yet he would not walk. He had a loud voice, yet he would not learn to speak. Instead, as he grew bigger he spat and snarled with fury in his eyes at anyone who would come near him. Everything that came into his hands he tore or threw about. He had to be force fed. If mother and father did not watch him he would eat his own shit, and they had to be careful he did not smear it on them.

'You have to understand, Oz, that my father was a very religious man. He believed in the embodiment of good and of evil. And he came to believe that his son was possessed by a devil.' He paused, to let his words have effect. 'I tell you something. Even today, so do I.

'When my brother was only eighteen months old, a priest was brought into the house, to perform the rite of exorcism. When he said the Latin words, Salvador, for the first time in his life, shrieked with a mad laughter. Afterwards, his behaviour continued unchanged.'

Davidoff glanced at the floor, looking away from the camera for the first time. 'No one from outside the family had ever been allowed to see my brother,' he said at last. 'When he was nine months old, my father dismissed his two servants, for fear that they would spread stories.

'As I said, he was ashamed, Oz, of this, this thing, that had been visited on him and on my mother. I think that if he had been a less strong-willed man, he might have killed Salvador for the child's own sake. Instead, he chose a more difficult road.

'When his mad son was about two years old he let it be known that he had died. He determined that he and my mother would look after him in secret, in the sound-proofed attic of the house in Carrer Monturiol, that they would be his nurses and his jailers, until he was full grown and could be put away in an asylum. They could simply have sent him away at that time too, of course, but my father believed in duty, and he loved Salvador, crazy or not.' Davidoff smiled. 'My father was a great man, Oz. He made Dalí, but as you could never have imagined.'

He paused, picked up a glass of red wine from the floor and took a sip. 'I was born in the year after my father made his choice. He named me Salvador also, hoping that he had not cursed me with the name. But he had not. I was the opposite of my brother in every way, a loving, thoughtful, intelligent, happy little boy.

'I was born into comfort. My father was a merchant, and rich. Many people worked for him in his warehouses. One of my earliest memories is of the sea, and of my mother. I remember visiting Cadaques by boat. I would have been three years old at the time. We took many excursions, my mother and I, when I was too young to wonder, far less ask, why my father never came with us.' He smiled for a second, his eye blank, looking into the past.

'I suppose I must have known from an early age that there was something strange about our house. I was never allowed to bring playmates home with me. In fact no one ever came there, other than my grandparents. As I met other children too, I noticed that their parents had servants, and I began to wonder why I had none. Yet I never asked. To complain about these things would have been rude, and as I have said, I was a polite little boy.'

Davidoff took another sip of wine, then topped up his glass, as I watched, fascinated. 'My parents felt that I was too young to understand, so they kept their secret from me for almost seven years. Maybe if they could, they would have held on to it for ever, but that would have been impossible. I suppose it was only because I was such a submissive little bastard that it lasted so long.

'Our house had three floors, and the attic. We lived during the day on the ground floor, mostly. My bedroom, the music room and the nursery were on the first floor, and my father's study and my parents' bedroom was on the second. I was allowed up there only rarely, and never at all was I allowed to go up to the attic.

'Of course I could not contain my curiosity for ever. My father used to spend long hours in his study, or so I was told. I wondered more and more what he did there. I had my toys, and eventually my crayons, pens, brushes and paints, for my talent began to emerge at an early age, but what did he have? Did he draw and paint too?

'I wanted to know, yet I had always been told that it was not polite to ask questions. So one day, just before my seventh birthday, I went up to his study, when I had been told by my mother that he was there, I opened the door just a fraction and I looked inside. The room was empty. I closed the door and turned to go. My father was standing on the stair to the attic, looking at me, very sadly. I got such a fright I almost pissed my pants.' As Davidoff grinned at the memory, I realised that my mouth was hanging open. I snapped it shut.

'I thought that he might beat me,' he went on, 'though he never had before. Instead, he took my hand and he led me up to the attic. At the top of the stair there was a big, heavy door. He unlocked it, and opened it, for me to see inside.

'Everything in the room was soft. The walls, the back of the door, even the floor coverings. They were all padded so that my brother could not damage himself. There was no bed as such, only a big cushion against one wall. There were toys on the floor, stuffed animals, all shapeless and battered.' He paused. 'I remember an elephant. It had no ears, because he had torn them off.

'Yet also there was the giraffe. It was stuffed like all the rest, but it was undamaged. My father told me that it was the one thing that he did not destroy, the only thing in his life, up to that point, for which he had shown any affection.'

Davidoff's face twisted with the sudden pain of his memories. 'Salvador was sat strapped into a harness, attached to a big padded chair,' he said. 'He was nine years old when first I saw him, yet he wore a diaper. There was a commode in the corner of the room, but when he was tied in his chair, as he usually was when my mother or father were not with him, he wore that diaper.

'You must understand, Oz, that they loved him as much as they loved me. All those years were an ordeal for them. They spent hours alone with him, feeding him, bathing him, touching him, although he was like a wild beast and would not respond to them. When I saw him first he was dressed in fresh white clothes, unusual only in that they had no buttons. My mother made them herself, as she made some of mine.

'I stared and stared at him from the doorway. Then I looked up at my father, and saw that he was weeping. That made me afraid. The boy in the chair stared at me. I asked my father, "Who is he?" He told me, "This is your poor brother. He is possessed."'

As he paused, I saw that his eye was glistened with tears, as, I realised too, were mine. 'I slipped free of his hand and I ran into the room, up to the boy in the chair. My father tried to stop me; he was afraid for me. But Salvador just looked at me, and he smiled. I said "Hello, brother." He made a strange baby sound. He was nine years old, yet he had not learned to speak properly. I unfastened the straps of his harness. I hugged him, and he hugged me. Behind me, I heard our father say, "It is a miracle."

'If Salvador was possessed, as I believe, maybe I drove some of the demons from him. I know that my father truly believed that. Certainly, from that day on, he was never violent again; at least never when I was about. When my parents were convinced that it was safe, he was brought down from the attic. He slept with me in my room. He watched me in the playroom. He copied me and he learned from me. There were no doctors for Salvador, only me. He learned to speak by listening to me. He learned to read and write by copying what I had done at school.

'Yet still he was a secret from the world. My parents were afraid for him, afraid to let people see him because of how they would react. I was forbidden to speak of him, and I withdrew from all my childhood friends. My poor mad brother became my life; we grew up together in our own little world.

'When Salvador was twelve, and I was ten, my father made a decision about our future. He bought a villa in Port Lligat, a tiny place near Cadaques. Salvador, my mother and I moved there, where no one knew our family, and where we could live a more normal life. There was a garden in which Salvador and I played, and a big room at the top of the house in which I was able to paint, and where my brother would draw. A tutor was hired, a nurse for us, and a maid for my mother. Father would visit at weekends, and for holidays. My parents' ordeal was over, and for the first time in our lives, we were a happy family, if not a normal one.'

Davidoff stopped again, and took a deep draught of his wine, then put the glass down again, out of camera shot. 'We stayed in the villa for seven years, in our contented isolation, until it was time to contemplate life as adults. Salvador had come a long way since first I met him in the attic. He had learned proper behaviour, and he could look after himself physically like anyone else. To a stranger he would have looked normal.

'But behind his eyes –' he reached up and tapped his head '– in here, he was still as crazy as a bedbug. Also, emotionally, he was completely reliant on me. I was only seventeen, but one thing was clear to me. I was, and I would always be, my brother's keeper.'

He paused. 'My talent as an artist was developing, until

finally I told my father that I wanted to study painting at college. He found a place in Madrid, with a good reputation but where the only entry requirement was money. Of course, Salvador had to go also. He had developed a limited talent for pen and ink drawing, and so he was enroled too.

'At that point, our shared name became a problem. I suppose I could have become Felipé, or Jacinto, but I hated them both. However I had just read a book in which the principal character, a young man like me, was called Davidoff. I persuaded my father to enrol me simply as Senor Davidoff, Salvador's cousin. That is who I have been from that day on.' He smiled again at the camera and gave a brief nod. I couldn't help it; as he resumed his story, I nodded back.

'College was a problem, for several reasons. First, having lived in virtual seclusion for most of my life, I found myself overwhelmed by the mass of humanity amongst whom I had thrust myself. I was shy, and reserved. My brother, on the other hand, in my company . . . and meeting outsiders for the first time, behaved as bizarrely as always. His flamboyance made him a celebrity. It was very difficult to control him at times. I never let him out of my sight, although by now he was not afraid to be without me. You will find references to that period in the book. You will also, if you look carefully, see a young Davidoff beside Salvador in a class photo which is reproduced there.

'Our studies were a drama also. Because we had to be in the same classes, Salvador had to take painting with me. The trouble was, while he could draw well enough, he could not paint worth a damn. His work was awful. Mine on the other hand, was technically far and away the best in the college. However, my subjects and my compositions were as shy and reserved as I was. There was no soul to them.

'That landed us in trouble. Once, my tutor said to me, in front of the class, "Senor Davidoff, you have a great talent: for painting biscuit tins. You should stick to that." Salvador roared and threw his paints at the man. He was almost expelled, but our father's fees were more important than the tutor's suiting.'

Davidoff laughed and shook his head. 'We left eventually, but for another reason. As my brother came to realise, if not to understand, his sexuality, he developed a fondness for girls, for very young girls. He touched no one, you understand, but he used to stare at them in the street, sometimes to the annoyance of their parents. It came to a head when he made some filthy, obscene drawings, and sold them for publication in a magazine for people who liked to indulge in that way. Someone gave the Principal a copy . . . or maybe he was a paedophile himself . . . and that was the end.

'Salvador passed it off by announcing that there was no one in the college fit to judge his work, and with that he and I returned to Port Lligat. We were hermits again, for a while, and it was in that period that we found our destiny.' His face lit up, with pride. As he paused, for more wine, I fidgeted in my seat, impatient for him to go on.

'As I have told you, Oz,' he resumed at last 'my brother Salvador was quite mad. Also, he could not paint. Yet he could draw; and he could see things, my friend, visions that were not accessible to a sane eye. One day at Port Lligat, while I was painting the same old hillside, he made a drawing of the scene. It was bizarre, but as he explained it to me, I could see what he meant, and I realised that I could paint it as he saw it.

'When I was finished, I signed it "Dalí" and we showed it to my mother. She didn't understand it; in fact it disturbed her. But next day, we took our art round to Cadaques, where many artists lived, and we put it in a gallery. My brother did the talking, for I was still a shy boy. Next day it was sold, and the gallery owner said, "Gimme more." So Salvador did more sketches, Davidoff painted them, and the gallery sold them. Gradually the reputation of Dalí spread, until one day, we were invited to exhibit in Figueras.

'We worked all winter in Port Lligat. The show opened in the spring, and it was a sensation. The newspaper critics came and declared Dalí a genius, the inventor of surrealism. Salvador spoke to them, and agreed with them all. I sat by his side, and said nothing.

'Surrealism is a good word, and appropriate. It means "surpassing reality"; some would say that means madness. The work of Dalí sprang from the visions of my possessed brother's mad eye, and for that reason, I was happy that he should take all the credit for our joint creations.

'The fame of the work spread beyond Spain. In 1929 we went to Paris to exhibit, and it was there that Dalí met and fell in love with Gala, the wife of a poet, Paul Eluard.'

He leaned forward and looked at the camera, hugely intense. 'I say "Dalí", Oz, deliberately, for Dalí is the artistic identity of the brothers Salvador and Davidoff, and it was both of them who fell in love with Gala. Yet it was Salvador she saw first. Before I could do anything about it, they had run off together. I was left to organise the exhibition in Paris, and to console Paul, while they fucked each other's brains out in Spain. It was the first time that Salvador and I had been apart in almost twenty years.'

He paused again, and even on the screen, I could see his eye mist over again. 'It didn't last long between them. Pretty soon, he became dysfunctional without me. Pretty soon, we were back at work in our studio in Port Lligat. Gala was there too, only now she was sleeping with me. Her influence began to pervade Dalí's work, because she was almost as crazy as Salvador, and she contributed to and featured in his visions.

'Our fame and our reputation grew through the thirties. So did Salvador's notoriety, for his public behaviour and his appearance were always bizarre. But then the Civil War came along, and with it the curse of Franco. I hated the fascists, although I was no communist. I was, as I still am, a liberal. Yet I left Salvador with Gala, and I went to fight against the dictator. Like I told you once, I learned many things in the war. How to kill, and how to avoid being killed. Most of all, I learned how to look after my body. Seeing so many torn to pieces made me realise what a precious gift a healthy body is.

'I never forgot that. Today, Oz, I am more than ninety, though no one would think me older than my seventies. I have looked after my body for all my life. I have treated it like a temple. I have always done what it permitted me to do, no more, no less. Ten years ago, I had a heart by-pass in New York. Seven years ago, my prostate gland was removed because of cancer. I survived both crises. I had intended to live until I was one hundred and ten. Sadly, because of what has happened, that cannot be.' He snapped his fingers suddenly and sharply, making me jump. 'But more of that later.

'My luck in the war ran out eventually, when I was wounded, and so, for a while, did our time in Spain. Dalí, the public face and the unknown brother, childhood roles reversed, went to America, taking Gala with them. Eventually, the dictator begged us to return. Like everyone else he thought it was all Salvador. He didn't know about me, or my part in the war against him.' He chuckled. 'In the end, I said we should go back just to spite the bastard!

'Through the decades Salvador's visions continued, and our riches grew to unbelievable proportions. As my crazy brother grew older, his madness deepened into true genius. Happily my art was able to grow with it. We saw the strangest things together in our joint life, and together we gave them to the world. The thread of Gala runs through it all, for we both loved her ceaselessly. Over the years, she moved from one of us to the other, then back again, time upon time. She was Dalí's woman, in the truest sense.'

Davidoff shook his head. 'It was Salvador who promised her the castle, but of course, he forgot, so it was I who kept his promise. I found it, I bought it, I restored it. It was I whom she invited to see her here, never Salvador. It was Davidoff who prepared the Delma as her tomb and who placed the second slab beside hers. Salvador never even thought of being buried here. He knew nothing of it.

'When she died, a very old lady, at Port Lligat, it was

Davidoff who put her in the Cadillac and drove her back here. Salvador's madness was edged with senility by then. I brought him to the funeral, though. He stood beside me, nodding and dribbling slightly, until it was over, then I took him back home.'

Davidoff reached up and wiped his eye. 'I have loved five people in my life, Oz. My parents, Salvador, Gala, and one other. When Gala went, I told Salvador that Dalí the artist had died also, and he agreed. She had been so much part of the visions, you see. It was her influence and her involvement that made the work truly great.

'My dear brother lived on, in my care as always, for a few more years, until 1989 when he died. It is quite fitting that he is buried in the museum, in the town where he was born, and where he spent his first strange and unhappy years. For most of the design of the place was his alone, his vision executed by others, not me . . .' He paused. '. . . apart from the great foot in the ceiling, of course. We did that in secret, by night.'

On the tape, he sighed audibly, looking incredibly sad. 'With Salvador's death, Davidoff was free. I was lonely, and bereft, but I was free. I handed over control of the Dalí Foundation, which I had exercised for many years, ostensibly as Salvador's Trustee. Then I came back here, to live in the secret apartments below the Delma, which I had discovered when I bought the place, and had made ready years earlier during the restoration, to become eventually my own tomb, beside that of Gala.

'You see, Oz, it was always my intention that in the end, I would have her to myself. What's wrong with that, I ask you? Everything else of my life, I gave to my brother: even my identity.'

All of a sudden, the shock and enormity of it all caught up with me. I hit the 'Pause' button. Davidoff's face froze, his eye staring at me, his mouth turned up in a smile. I shook my head, thinking back over everything he had told me, taking it all in, realising how perfectly the pieces of the puzzle fitted together. I looked around the room again, and my eye was caught by a bottle on the floor, not far from where I sat. It was red wine, a 1979 Rioja, I saw from the label, and it was half full. A glass stood beside it; clean, waiting for me. I walked across and poured myself some of Davidoff's fine vintage, then, taking the bottle with me, returned to my seat and set the video to play once more.

'There was a fire once,' Davidoff went on, 'while I was in Port Lligat with Salvador. I left the work of repair to the Foundation. Had I known they were going to open the castle to visitors, I would have forbidden it, but I did not find out their intention until too late. Still, I have come and gone by night for years, before and since the tourists. Occasionally I have lived at Port Lligat, and at Shirley's of course, but mostly here. No one knows of this apartment, and the secret entrance, not even the people in the Foundation. Gala never knew, nor Salvador; only me.

'I saw the years that were left to me as a kind of retirement. I painted a little, and found that even without Salvador's vision, I was still some sort of a genius. Some of my work is hanging on the walls of this room, to be with me for ever, as a sort of memorial. Though I say so myself, it is all quite brilliant.

'But my masterpiece, beyond a doubt, was the Toreador of the Apocalypse. You have seen it, my boy. You know what I mean. It is my tribute to my crazy brother, to our Gala, and to the unsurpassable artistic force which the three of us became. She is in it, the ghostly figure. So is he, in the skeleton of the giraffe, the only thing he loved in his early possessed years. And so am I. It is brilliant, and the crowning jewel within it, is the tear on the face of the toreador, on my face. It is glistening and as you look at it, you can feel its softness on your cheek.

'Nobody, Oz, nobody but Davidoff can paint the softness of a tear.' His slim chest puffed out with pride as he said it. I raised my glass and drank a toast to the truth of what he had said.

'I signed it Dalí, of course, although the vision was all mine.

For now, at the end, I realise that in my own way I am just as crazy as my brother.'

I shook my head at that. 'Not you, pal,' I whispered. 'Sanest man I ever met.'

Davidoff shifted in his chair, the one in which I now sat, making himself more comfortable, more relaxed. 'As I said, I treated my years down here as a kind of retirement. I had money, my secret home, and my little car. I hung around Pubol, La Bisbal, Girona. I walked a lot, and I swam in the sea. I was Davidoff, gentleman of means, man of mystery, who kept himself to himself.

'Then some things happened. First and best of all, in 1990 I met Clive Gash, in the bar in Pubol. I liked him at once. He was no artist, just an ordinary man who happened to have made himself a billion pesetas or so. When he invited me to his home, it was the first time in my life, would you believe, that I had ever been invited anywhere in my own right, not as my brother's appendage.

'I loved it there in L'Escala, with Clive and Shirley. I told them nothing about myself, and they never asked. We just got on. Clive said that their summer-house was mine whenever I wanted it, and I took him at his word.

'Shirley was devastated when he died, but she insisted that I should still come to L'Escala, to her little house in the garden. I decorated it for her, you know.' He laughed. 'Before, it had plain white walls; now they are covered with murals that are absolutely priceless, yet she hasn't a fucking clue what they are!'

His laughter subsided. 'Last year something else happened. A young man named Ronnie Starr came to Pubol. I met him in the bar, where I had met Clive, and I spoke to him. He was different, this young fellow, and he had talent, great talent as an artist. He could paint the sunlight, you see. Very few Northerners can do that, but Ronnie could. A great painter: not a genius, but still great.

'He had something else too; a huge knowledge of the work

of Dalí. He would talk to me about him for hours. He knew that two sons named Salvador had been born to my mother. And he told me something very interesting. He had a theory that some of the early work in the catalogues was wrongly attributed. He showed me illustrations of some early works, which he said were quite different in style and quality from what came after.

'Ronnie didn't realise what he was saying, of course, but he was right. When Salvador and I were back in Port Lligat after college, he sold some of his own work, through another gallery in Cadaques. Real crap it was. I put a stop to it as soon as I found out, but years later, it found its way into the listed works.

'My young friend from Wales had actually stumbled upon our secret. I couldn't tell him that, of course, but I felt I had to reward him. More than that, he was a disciple, a true apostle of Dalí, and I felt that he deserved recognition. So I gave him my masterpiece. I gave it to him, because in the end I could not bear the thought of it being buried in the dark for ever.

'You understand that Oz, don't you. You've seen it after all.' I nodded, as if he could see me. 'I told him that it was a Dalí, but that it could never be authenticated, or shown as such. I gave him it to keep for ever, and to show to his friends as his proudest possession, on condition that he never sold it, or told anyone how he had come by it.

'He agreed to all that, and he took it. In exchange, he gave me one of his paintings, of Port Lligat. It is very fine. You will find it hanging in this room.' He waved a hand, vaguely, over his shoulder.

'Then,' said Davidoff, 'soon after, I did the thing which cost him his life. I introduced him to Adrian Ford, Shirley's no-good, greedy, jealous, envious, grasping, murderous bastard of a brother. He befriended Ronnie, and Ronnie must have shown him the picture, of which he was so proud. You know the rest, and you have just seen how it finished.

'I almost died when you showed me the copy in your

apartment, Oz, and told me how you had come by it. I guessed at once what had happened. Tonight you know that I made amends. That is why I had to bring you here, and to make you the only man who knows all about Davidoff.

'I place this story in your hands, my boy. I make you the keeper of the truth, of the legend of Dalí. For it is time for me to die now. But one thing. I want to stay here for ever, beside Gala, and I don't want my tomb to be disturbed. I trust you with this, because I see the honour in you, like I saw it in my poor friend Ronnie.

'Some things you can do for me. First, finish the wine, for it's the best you'll drink this year. Share a last bottle with a friend.

'Second, take the pictures on the easels and put them where they're meant to be. They are what I've been doing since I shot that bastard Adrian.

'Third, put the lid on my coffin, and say a prayer for my soul, if you have one in you. I carved the box myself. Yes, my friend, Davidoff was a sculptor too.

'Fourth, switch out the light and seal my tomb on your way out. The mechanism which slides the slab is another work of genius. I designed it myself, and burned the plan, after I had it installed by a non-Spanish speaking engineer from America. He died in a car crash ten years ago . . . nothing to do with me, honest!

'It only works when you insert a steel bolt into a slot in the stone. It's in there now. The slab will slide back into place at a touch. When it's perfectly positioned, you'll be able to withdraw the shaft and it'll be locked for ever. Next time you cross a river, toss my key away.

'As a bonus for all these favours, you can keep the video camera. It's a good one, I promise, and it's only been used twice.'

He paused, and he looked at me. 'Oz, my true friend, for any wrong you may think subsequently that I have done you, I apologise most sincerely. Now go with God, and have a good life, one at least as long as mine. Remember, treat the body as a temple.' Then he winked his one eye, and gave me a long slow smile. 'Now, goodbye.'

There was a click, and the screen went dark.

I stood there staring at it, as I shared the last of his wine, savouring every drop. When it was done, I walked over to the three pictures, and took the sheet from the one on the left. It was a portrait of Shirley Gash, and a man I recognised from photos in her house as Clive, painted exquisitely, as if both were alive on the canvas.

Moving on after a while, I unveiled the one in the centre, and gasped, not for the first time that night. It was Primavera. She was lying on a couch in silver moonlight, and she was naked. It was so real, I wanted to touch her.

I was afraid, almost, to lift the third sheet, but I did.

It was me, of course. In the background, I picked out the ghostly figure of a woman, the skeleton of a giraffe, and the very faint shadow of a man, with a patch over his right eye. In the foreground, I was wearing a toreador's colourful uniform, with a red cape over my arm. My expression was solemn, and down my right cheek, a single tear ran, so bright that it seemed to glisten, so gently done that you could feel its softness. Like the other two, it was signed, 'Davidoff'.

When I could, I bent over the coffin and kissed my friend on his forehead. Then I lifted the heavy lid and laid it over him, settling it into the grooves which he had carved to receive it. As I straightened up, and as I said my prayer for Davidoff's soul, I looked into the eyes of Gala. Carved into the lid, she smiled up at me, with the same look that had bewitched the brothers Dalí.

54

There is a bridge across the Riu Ter, near Verges. I stopped the Frontera half way across, got out, and threw a two-inch thick, two-foot long stainless steel bolt into its rushing water.

As always, Davidoff's word had been his bond. The slab had moved at a touch. It looked like a good video camera too.

It was just after 2 a.m. when I slipped the Frontera silently into St Marti, and stepped silently up the stairs to the apartment. I didn't think that there were any more surprises for the old bastard to throw at me, but as always with him, I was wrong.

I had expected to find Prim asleep, but the balcony doors were ajar and she was sitting outside, looking at the sea with a white shawl around her shoulders. She looked round as the front door opened. As I stepped out of the darkness, all the shocks and horrors of the evening must have shown in my face, for a frown swept across hers. 'Oz . . .' she whispered.

Then she saw what I was carrying. I switched on the terrace light and showed her the portraits. The third, I had left in the boot of the car, to be delivered in the morning, once I had come up with a story to explain it.

Prim glanced at my likeness, and then she looked at herself, recumbent, nude. I had never seen her really blush before. The pinkness just exploded, from the swell of her breasts, into her neck, and to her face.

'The old bastard had quite an imagination,' I said, with a half-smile.

'Had?' she murmured, fearfully.

'Yes love. It's over.'

I sat down beside her and, because I know that he would have expected it, I told her the story of Davidoff, the second Dalí, of his secret life and of his secret love.

I told her, because I knew she wouldn't disturb the old man's rest, and because I knew that someone else had to share the burden. Davidoff believed in possession of the spirit. So do I now, because I'm certain that a part of his soul, a part too crazy to die, possesses me, and that in the final analysis he agrees with me that his story is just too magnificent to be lost forever.

So I related to Primavera the tale of Davidoff's gift to his friend, and of the revenge he had taken on the men who had betrayed him. My voice crackled several times during the tale, and at the end, as I described how I had positioned the beautiful carved lid of his coffin, and as I repeated my commendation of his soul, I broke down completely, crying like a baby for the first time as a man.

When I composed myself, she was looking at me, her hand on mine. Then she stood up, moved to the edge of the balcony, and turned back to face me. As I looked at her a disturbing feeling gripped my stomach.

'I have something to share with you now, Oz,' she murmured. 'Something about Davidoff. I have to tell you now, because every day I keep it secret, the more dangerous it will be to you and me.'

I looked at her, and realised at once why I was so disconcerted. She looked vulnerable, more so than I had ever seen her. 'Best tell me then,' I replied, as quietly as she.

'His portrait of me,' she said. 'It isn't painted from his imagination.' I looked at her, and I'm sure my jaw dropped, for the second time that night.

'When he and I were left alone together, at Shirley's,' she went on, 'after you and she had gone off to identify Adrian's body, Davidoff made love to me. And I let him; not as a gift to an old man, but because I wanted him.'

She stopped, and seemed to flinch, very slightly, as if she

was expecting me to roar at her, or worse. But such thoughts never crossed my mind; I just stood there staring at her, numb.

At last she went on. 'He touched me as we sat there in the garden. He held me with that black eye of his, and he touched me; he stroked my breast with the tips of his fingers. He just kissed my hand and reached across. And the strange thing is, I wasn't surprised, or shocked . . .' she hesitated '. . . or upset.

'His fingers were smooth, very soft, incredibly sensitive. As he stroked me, he just kept looking at me, until all I could see was that eye, and the depth there was to it. For a moment or two, I tried to break away by picturing you, but I couldn't. All that I was conscious of was him, his sandalwood smell, and his look. I knew that it was asking me a question.

'Neither of us said a word, but I answered him all the same. I took his hand from me, I stood up, and I undressed for him, slowly, completely. Then I lay back down with him on the lounger. He didn't seem old to me, not there in the dark. He was a man; and a unique, dynamic man at that, unlike anyone I've ever known. There and then I wanted him, very much, as much as I wanted you when we first met.

'I kissed him. I didn't feel anything but sincere when I asked him, "Would you like to make love?" He smiled at me and he said, "My darling, in the way you mean I could not do you justice, not any more." I rubbed my hand against those tight satin pants. "Let's try," I said. "Let's go into the summer-house, where it's warmer." But he shook his head. "Please," I asked him. "Let me drink from the well." The way he smiled at me, I thought I'd given him the keys to heaven. But when I reached down to unfasten him, still he stopped me.

'Instead, he laid me along the lounger, then he knelt beside me. And he showed me his way of making love. He began to massage me, with those soft, dark, velvet hands of his. They were strong too, stronger than you could imagine in anyone as old as him. He kneaded my body, slowly, turning me over on to my face, then back again: my arms, my back, my breasts, my legs, my belly, my thighs. I felt as if I was swimming, that light way you go. Until at last, he came to . . .' She stopped, and shivered slightly, as if in recollection.

'At the very end, there was a little trick he did with his fingers, the sort of thing that very few men learn in a whole lifetime. And I had an orgasm, as fine as any I've had with you. I really thought I might die.'

She looked down at me. 'There was nothing sordid about it, Oz. Davidoff made love to me, in his way, and in it he was an artist. I let him, because I wanted to. I sensed a huge longing in him, and it transferred itself to me.'

I stared at her wide-eyed, still numb, still stunned. And yet I realised, that there was no anger in me. I knew that I couldn't summon it up either, even if I'd tried. 'And afterwards?' I asked her, quietly.

'Afterwards,' she whispered, 'he cried. We lay there in the moonlight, on the lounger. I was gasping still, his hand was hot on my belly, and I could hear him sobbing, very gently.

'We looked at each other and I could see that there were tears running down his face, soft and glistening on his cheeks. "What's wrong?" I asked him. "You've given me pleasure. I wanted you."

'His face sort of crumpled. "That's it," he said, and I remember every word. "You wanted me, because you love Davidoff. The idea may be too ludicrous for you to admit, but tonight you love Davidoff. I know this, for my Primavera would not let a man touch her like that if she did not love him. Yet look at us. I glory in your body, so beautiful, and I think of mine, which just now I could not bear to let you see. You are so young, and I am so, so old. I have had my last moment, and that is what makes me sad. Now I must return you to my friend Oz. He is alive, and I am dead. But thank you for being the other love of my life. You will not see me again, after tonight."

'Then he stood up, and walked around the pool, back to the summer house. At first I thought he had gone inside. After a while, I stood up to follow him. I wanted to dry his tears; they had upset me. I wanted to ask him about his first love, who she was. I wanted . . .' Her voice faltered, for a moment.

'I was in the doorway of the summer house when I heard his car start, and he was gone. I listened until the engine sound had faded away. Then I dived into the pool, and swam and swam. I was still there, remember, when you got back and found me.'

Yes, maybe I should have been angry. I don't know. In the event, I was unspeakably moved. I gazed at her and saw her tears glistening, as had Davidoff's. I reached out and touched them on her cheeks. I felt their softness.

'I really won't see him again, Oz, will I?' She was only just beginning to believe that he was dead.

I shook my head. 'No.'

'And Davidoff killed Eames and Adrian? That's what he said?'

'Oh yes. You can believe it, too.'

'But why?'

'For what he saw as the best of motives, I suppose. For honour. They killed his friend. He killed them.'

'And the picture, the Toreador?'

'Davidoff painted it.'

'So it really isn't a fake, after all.'

I shrugged. 'Maybe it isn't, maybe it is. I don't know the answer to that. I've already told Gavin Scott that it is, though. I called him last week. He accepted it pretty well. He said he'd hang it on the wall of his boardroom anyway and let it be judged on its merit. The artist would have been okay with that. He'll have to tell the shareholders, of course, but he's made three million profit this year, so he reckons he'll survive.'

I looked at her again. 'But tell me, love. Just suppose Davidoff's Noddy car hadn't started first time. Would you have gone with him?'

She smiled through her tears. 'You mean would I have left

you and gone off with a man as old as Methuselah? Probably not.'

'But you did feel for him?'

She looked at me for a long time. 'I was drawn to him,' she said, at last. 'He was a fantasy, I suppose.'

'The coming together in the garden. Could that have been a fantasy too?'

She shook her head, vigorously. 'Oh no, Oz. That was for real. That's what's got me so shaken up.'

A large part of me wanted to hug her; but the ruling majority in my mind told me not to, that a moment of decision was approaching.

Instead I said, 'And has it affected the way you feel about us?'

Her face twisted into an expression that was half smile, half despair. 'You mean don't I love you any more?' she blurted out. 'Oh, I love you. That hasn't changed. But what Davidoff said about why I let him touch me . . . yes, let him make love to me . . . well, that was true. That night in Shirley's garden, I loved him too, and I will every time I remember it.

'I guess you can love two people at the same time.'

She paused. 'I have to ask you now; now that I've told you. Can you bear to touch me again?' She twisted her fingers together. 'The thing is, I can't say that I'm sorry for what happened, and I can't ask you to forgive me; because that would mean that I regretted it, and I don't. All I can say is that I love you just as much as I ever did, and that when you and I have made love since my night with Davidoff, there's been no one else in our bed.' She shivered in the cool of the night.

'Call me a selfish wee cow if you like, but I have to know that there's still a solid foundation to my life. I need you to ask me again like you did a couple of weeks ago, to know you still love me, even if it's only so I can tell you again to wait for a year.'

Her voice rose slightly. 'Whatever, I need some sort of

reaction. Christ, I confess my infidelity to you and you just stand there. Show me you care, can't you, even if it's by getting mad. Imagine I fucked Steve Miller, if that helps!'

I felt as if the floor was moving under my feet, but I just stood there. Inside my head, something swam to the surface. I opened my mouth to tell her, to spill the beans about Jan leaving Noosh, about our weekend together, about my infidelity to her, not with a demi-ghost like Davidoff, but with a strong, lasting spirit that I had loved since our childhood. I opened my mouth to tell her all that, and to throw her own question back at her. Could she still bear to touch *me*? But she cut me off.

'And anyway, Oz,' she burst out. 'I have to say this, I sense something else. Something in you. I don't know what it is, but I have a feeling that it's been there for a while now, waiting to come out. I think it's time that it did, don't you?'

I looked at Primavera, and as I did, the truth broke the surface at last. The fundamental reason for a life-time commitment for which I had been rummaging through my cluttered, untidy mind. Ellie, as always, had given it to me, only I had mislaid it for a while. I think that putting the lid on Davidoff's coffin must have helped me to recover it.

Like my sister said, 'If I died tomorrow, who would grieve for me the most?'

It isn't just about who you want to live with for the present, and to have with you. It's about who you'll want beside you to hold your hand at the very end of the last day, when it's all over. Or, if that can't be, it's about whose face you'll see with your mind's eye at the dying of the light.

I wondered how Prim would answer that one. I wondered how Gala would have answered it.

I looked at her some more, then smiled at her. 'Okay,' I said. 'But before it does emerge, if you don't mind I'm going for a walk. Down on the beach, to consult some of my own ghosts in the moonlight.'

So I left her in our apartment, and strode down the path to

the acres of sand below St Marti. And there I walked through the night, almost as far as L'Escala, and back again. I thought of Davidoff, of his honour, and of the softness of his tears. I thought of Jan. And I thought of Primavera.

She was right. You can love two people; but you can only be with one.

55

I felt as if I had been away for a long time. I suppose I had.

She was awake when finally I made it home. She stood in the open doorway, looking out across the balcony at the rosy autumn dawn.

She could have seen me approach from where she was standing. She might have heard my key as I stabbed at the lock with my trembling hand. But she must have heard the front door as it closed with a bang. She must have heard me climb the stairs, two at a time. Yet as I crossed the room she stayed there with her back towards me, gazing eastwards, until the moment when I put my hands on her hips, on the silk of her dressing gown. Gently, I turned her round to face me.

She wasn't startled, not at all. She just looked at me solemnly, almost eye to eye, as it all came tumbling out.

'I love you more than I have words to say,' I blurted breathlessly. 'I can't conceive of a world without you, and I sure wouldn't want to live in it. Please, please marry me and be with me until it's time to place the lid on my coffin.'

My declaration made, I waited, aware of the heavy thump of my heart. She gazed at me for an unmeasured time, inscrutable, offering me nothing in her expression. Until, finally . . .

'Since you put it that way . . .' she said, with her deep, raunchy chuckle. 'Okay.'

As I looked at her, a lock of her hair fell across her forehead, over one eye. And at last she smiled, and kissed me. 'I hoped that's how it would be,' she said, 'but I couldn't be sure.'

'How could you not?' I rebuked her, as I drew her to me in

a rustle of silk, and as the first rays of morning sun shone on us both. 'I'm Oz, and I haven't changed either.'